T0021442

Seeking Approval

Rachel Spangler

To Susie, who sees and loves me completely.
This is all your fault.

Chapter One

Arden Gilderson scooted a little further into the church pew and tried not to crane her neck too conspicuously. She appeared as if she were merely stretching, but of course, Luz saw through her. Her best friend noticed everything, but unlike Arden, she never minded being noticed in return.

"Who you looking for?" Luz adjusted the popped collar of her black tuxedo shirt and raised her chin as if someone might be about to photograph her. "Is the paparazzi here?"

"Inside the church? No, and we've been through this. There's no tabloid fodder in Amherst."

"I don't know." Luz glanced pointedly at their governor sitting next to the president of the university a few rows in front of them. "Seems like there's enough rich people to make the trip from Boston worthwhile."

"Wealth and celebrity don't always go hand in hand." Arden turned as someone else passed them in the aisle, but she didn't recognize the two men in black suits, or maybe she would have if she'd inspected their faces, but the boxy cut of their clothes and shuffling gait told her they weren't who she wanted most to see.

"So you keep telling me, but maybe sometime you could draw me a Venn diagram, because from the cheap seats, money and fame seem pretty closely related."

"Don't get me wrong, there are a lot of important people here. Mr. Pembroke meant so much to so many as a boss, as a neighbor, as a philanthropist. He really was what everyone always wants to believe they will be if they ever get rich, but so few people are."

1

Luz feigned a yawn. "Sounds boring. I hope his eulogies are better than that, or this is going to be the longest funeral ever."

"You're horrible," Arden squeaked. "A great man is dead. His poor family. Can you even imagine if they heard you say something so terrible?"

"What? I didn't rip on the guy. I'm sure he was nice enough. I just meant that I'm here for the drama. I wanna see people fight over family heirlooms or reveal themselves to be his illegitimate children. Oh, or mistresses throwing themselves over his coffin."

"Shh." Arden slapped her arm, then whispered, "You watch too many telenovelas. First of all, this is just a public memorial service. They buried him at a private family funeral last week."

"Well, that's disappointing."

"Second, you're at the wrong memorial service if you want scandal. Mr. Pembroke was a pillar of the community. He made his money in clean energy instead of the dirty businesses that usually garner his kind of wealth. He was open and gregarious and generous. There's never been a whiff of scandal around his company, and he totally adored his wife and daughter."

"Oh yes." Luz's grin widened. "The daughter. That's why we're here, right?"

"I'm here to pay my respects. I don't know why you're here."

"I already told you, I'm here for celebrities and gossip. Also because you invited me. I never get to go to fancy society things with you."

"You make it sound like I take someone else. I don't go to them either."

"But you're here now, which leads me right back to the daughter. Emma, right?"

2

"Emery." The name came out sounding a little dreamy, and Arden silently cursed herself.

"Ah, Emery, yes, I remember now. You were rich little debutante besties. Wasn't she like voted most likely to be successfully sexy as hell at your prep school for powerful people?"

"We didn't call it that, but yes, and also she wasn't a debutante, and we weren't besties."

A murmur rippled through the crowd as conversations all around them died. Arden turned instinctively, as if feeling the intangible tug of another presence, or perhaps merely the subtle hint of some type of drama, like Luz craved. But the moment her eyes found Emery Pembroke walking up the center aisle of the church, there was no denying the craving was all hers.

The woman was imposing. She wasn't much taller than average, maybe five nine, but the way she carried herself, upright, confident, with an easy yet purposeful gait, made her seem to take up more space. Her eyes managed to be both dark and bright at the same time, and her broad nose and proud chin had an almost royal bearing. Even if she'd been dressed in rags, she would've commanded attention, but of course she wasn't. Emery always had a knack for fashion that made her stand out, and over the years she'd apparently refined the skill. Today she wore a suit, all black, with the jacket tailored at the waist, left open to reveal a black silk vest over a gray tie, perfectly knotted, but loose enough not to constrict her elegant neck.

"Oh … my … Lord." Luz sounded like she might be having a hard time breathing, but Arden couldn't tear her eyes off Emery long enough to check. "She's flawless."

She wasn't alone in her assessment. Everyone in the room stared at Emery, but her own intense gaze was reserved only for her mother. Also wearing black, but in a more understated dress, Mrs. Pembroke's hand wrapped tightly around her daughter's arm. Her wedding ring stood out against the backdrop of the suit coat she clung to.

3

"Her style, her build, her bearing. Oh, and the androgyny. She could be the handsomest woman or the prettiest boi."

Arden merely nodded as they made their way forward.

"I would murder several people right now for the chance to dress her. Hell, I might even kill you for the chance to sleep with her."

That finally got Arden's attention enough for her to shoot daggers at Luz.

"What? I'd make it quick and painless." She didn't seem to have the decency to look chagrined. "But come on. Seriously, you've known that human for the entire time we've been friends, and you've never once introduced me?"

"I don't really know her," Arden whispered as Emery and her mother made their way slowly to the front of the church. "She was two years ahead of me in school, and we never hung out, for obvious reasons."

"Wait, why? What's obvious?"

She rolled her eyes. "In high school, Emery was everything you can imagine from looking at her now. She managed to be athletic and charismatic and quick-witted and fantastically good looking, while I ... well, you know, I was basically the same as I am now, too."

"What?" Luz's voice rose with her indignation. "Classically pretty? Understatedly funny? Rich as fuck? What kind of messed-up school did you go to where that wasn't enough to ensure popularity?"

"Shh." Arden dropped her own voice to demonstrate the tone she found acceptable. "Probably much the same as your school, but, you know, with higher test scores and more Maseratis in the parking lot."

"One Maserati would cost more than my entire high school," Luz laughed. "I guess the grass isn't always greener and whatnot, but if people like you weren't the coolest kids in the school, I don't know who could be."

4

Arden leaned forward slightly, unable to keep herself from sneaking another peek at Emery as she eased into the first pew, her beauty no less compelling in profile than head-on. "People like her."

"Did I mention I'd love to dress her? Though I have to admit, she does seem to have the task well in hand."

"Along with everything else, so take a good look now, because we're not likely to ever see her again." She tried not to let the thought depress her, but even the longing deep enough to make her teeth ache couldn't overcome the harsh realities at play.

"Why not? You have connections, you get invites, you could probably have a lot more access to her social circle if you wanted."

Arden shook her head. "I don't want to, and even if I did, her family is different. They're visible, they're present, they work meaningful jobs and effect meaningful change instead of attending endless garden parties."

"You could do those things, too," Luz said hurriedly as a series of altar boys and acolytes began their processional through the sanctuary to signify the start of the service. "You aren't required to turn into your parents."

Arden sighed. She didn't want to have this conversation now. Just being this close to Emery reminded her of all the reasons she wasn't cut out to break the mold. The comparison was too much for even Luz to deny. "I'll never be able to do what she's capable of. Mark my words, Emery will take over her father's business, she'll do it with grace and charisma, and she'll make the things people like us can't even imagine doing seem small."

"I don't know." Luz stole one more peek at Emery before settling back and facing forward. "I can imagine an awful lot."

Chapter Two

The helicopter hovered mere inches above the ground, grass blowing and bowing down from the full force of the rotors whirring overhead. Emery hopped out, her Italian loafers hitting the ground lightly and barely long enough to leave their imprint before she jogged toward the looming office headquarters of Pembroke and Sun. Once clear of the whirlwind, she turned back to offer a quick two-finger salute to the pilot, who nodded and took to the sky again.

Straightening her shoulders and shaking her short hair from her forehead, she blew out a heavy breath and slowed her gait. She could do this. She would do this. She had to. The mantra had played on repeat the entire flight from the city.

She passed between two long rows of solar panels and nearly bumped into her mother. "Oh, hello Eleanor."

"Don't call me that. I don't care how old you get, or who else dies. I'm your mother."

"Got it. Is that why you waited for me before going in?" She leaned in and gave her a little kiss on the cheek.

Instead of returning the gesture, she raised her eyes toward the retreating chopper. "That was a bit much, don't you think?"

"What?"

"You were in Boston, not Saigon. Did you really need to hop out of a helicopter onto the company lawn?"

"It's faster than a car. Besides, it's basically my first day at work. I'm young. I'm new. I have to exude confidence and mystique to make a good impression."

6

"Oh, you made an impression all right." She glanced up at the large wall of windows in the building looming over them. "We'll see what kind soon enough."

Emery looped an arm through hers. "I only make the good kind. Come on, let me show you."

The building was both its own landmark and an homage to the land it occupied, all glass and wood and stone managing to be modern and soothing at once. She tried not to focus on any one detail for fear she'd notice her father's touch or dwell on the foundations her grandfather had laid. She couldn't compare herself to them for a myriad of reasons, so instead she merely soaked up the sense of familiar. It had been too long since she'd been here. Then again, that was undoubtedly about to change.

As they strode across the lobby, the receptionist rose from her desk, a mask of sympathy crossing her features. "Mrs. Pembroke, Ms. Pembroke, I'm so sorry about Artie. He was just the best person anyone could have ever worked for."

"Thank you, Janet," Eleanor said in the way she had so many times over the last few weeks, sad and appreciative, but mostly weary.

"Yes, thank you." Emery echoed her mother. "And please, call me Emery. I'm about formality only when it comes to clothes, and well, food, and also—actually, a lot of things, but never relationships. You've known me since I was born. A new title attached to my name won't change that."

Janet's smile shifted from one of grief to something tighter. "Of course. Should I take you in now?"

"No need. We know the way." Emery sidestepped the reception counter and strode down the hall before stopping in front of the large, wooden doors carved with the image of a sun. She turned to her mother once more. "Thanks for coming to support me today. I'm sure it's hard."

She nodded. "It'll always be hard to come here and not see him, but I hope that's the worst of it for today."

"Well, it means a lot to have you here, and I'm glad the board invited both of us. It's a nice touch." She pulled open the door and held it for her mother to walk through before stepping into the conference room to find it occupied by only one other person.

She'd expected the entire board of trustees, but its president rose from the table and offered the same pitiful expression Janet had, only stiffer, like maybe he was aggrieved on their behalf, but also a little constipated.

"Eleanor."

"Brian," her mother said warmly as he took both her hands in his and kissed her on each cheek.

He offered his hand to Emery. "And you, it's been too long since you've popped in. You made quite an entrance, as usual."

She shook his hand and grinned. "I know it's a little different from my dad's style."

"Well, apparently you share his gift for understatement, at least conversationally. Please, have a seat. I won't drag this out. I'm sure you've both been through too many of these kinds of meetings over the last few weeks."

Her mother sagged into the chair. "Entirely too many. I'm sure you can imagine. Everyone wants to make statements or share opinions or have some sort of business to help us settle."

"Your husband was a cherished member of the community. He left quite a legacy, and it means so much to so many people in the area, but I'm sorry you've had to fill those shoes, which is why I don't relish this next part."

Emery took the seat next to her mother. "It's okay. We understand someone has to stay at the helm of Pembroke and Sun. I appreciate your holding off as long as you have to let us grieve." She steeled herself and lifted her shoulders, as if preparing to bear a great weight. "I'm ready to do my part now."

He perched uneasily on the chair across from them. "I hope so, and if I may be so bold, I know your father hoped so,

8

too, but he was also smart and forward thinking, and given his own father's early passing, he made provisions for a situation like this where the two of you might not have been afforded the chance to transition leadership of the company on your own terms."

Emery intertwined her fingers and rested her hands atop the table. "What do you mean?"

"Well." He opened a leather portfolio and slid two papers across to them. "His instructions in the case of his untimely death were very clear. The business must stay in the family. Under no circumstances should it go public or be sold unless agreed upon by both of you. However, if he passed before Emery was ready to assume the mantle of overseeing top-level decisions, he believed those responsibilities should fall to you, Eleanor."

Her mother sat back slowly with a wobbly little groan.

Emery leaned forward, the instinct to shield her strong. "It's fine. I'll do it."

"Emery," her mother whispered.

"No. I know you would if you had to, but you don't. This is my inheritance, my responsibility. It's what I've always known." She impressed herself a little by not choking on the words or the subtle twist of fear creeping up through her chest. "It's soon, but it's settled. I'll step into Dad's shoes. I'll run the company."

Brian cleared his throat, refusing to meet her eyes, and instead focused all the pity and pleading in his expression toward her mother.

"I hope you understand, this wasn't my doing. Artie was very clear. It's all written out and signed. He crossed every *t* and dotted every *i*."

Emery glanced down at the papers, but the words swam as her brain whirred. Nothing made sense, which threatened to confirm insecurities she'd never voiced to anyone. "Why are you talking to her? I just told you I'll do it. His will says the job is mine as soon as I'm ready, right? Well, I'm ready."

Her mother placed a hand on her leg under the table. "It seems some people disagree with you, dear."

She scoffed, anger at being challenged overtaking her own unease at what she'd come here resolved to do. "I don't care about their opinions. Mine is the one that matters. This company has been handed down in my family for generations, and it's mine now. Anyone who doesn't like it can go fu—"

Her mother squeezed her leg so tightly she felt the fingernails through her slacks. "I think what my daughter's questioning, with her ample vocabulary, is how the board reached its decision."

Brian nodded solemnly. "Of course, as per Artie's instructions, they discussed the matter at length, then held a closed vote."

Eleanor made a rolling motion with her hand. "And?"

"Six to one in favor of you."

This time her mother's vise grip wasn't strong enough to stem the profanity. "Sons of bitches."

They both ignored her.

"It's very kind of you to keep it from being unanimous, Brian. I appreciate the show of loyalty, and I'm sure Emery will as well when she settles down. How long?"

"How long?" she sputtered. "You can't seriously be considering taking the company from me?"

"Holding it for you," her mother corrected, even as she continued to focus on Brian. "Surely there must be provisions for reviewing the decision, right?"

"Six months, rolling terms. There's no reason to rush."

Her mother gave a strangled laugh. "Only my sanity."

"You know I'll be here to help, as long as it takes."

Emery hammered her fist on the table once to get their attention. "Takes for what? Am I even allowed to know on what grounds my birthright is being withheld from me? And more

10

importantly, what's the penance I need to satisfy in order to have it returned? A thousand Hail Marys? A hundred hours of community service? An advanced degree in economics from an Ivy League school? Oh wait, I already have one of those."

"And that's been well noted, Emery," Brian said with only a hint of patronizing. "Not a single board member doubts your intellect or innate skills with the type of interactions that made your father so successful in the job. You have his gift of gab and an undeniable likability."

"But?"

"Artie was steady and stable in his vision. He was confident, yes, but also community-oriented. The job of CEO is both visionary and trust building, a leader within and without," he explained calmly. "Your father had deep roots and strong bonds with the people around him. He was a real family man, a rock. What's more, he and your mother always presented a unified front and served to complement each other. He had his dreamer qualities, sure, but no one ever had to worry that he'd fly away."

"By jumping into a helicopter and not coming back?" her mother asked drolly.

"Exactly." Brian seemed grateful to her for helping to make his point. "By the time he took over the company at roughly the same age you are now, he had a wife and a baby on the way. He was committed, dedicated to his family. He had plans for the company, for the entire region. I think the trustees need to get the same sense from you before voting again."

"Are you kidding me?"

"Sadly, I'm not. The decision is set," Brian said. "We'd like to make the formal announcement as soon as you're ready, Eleanor, but we'd rather it be sooner than later. Continuity, consistency, it's important for the health of the company. It'll do everyone good for the staff, our partners, the whole town to see you at the helm."

"As opposed to seeing me." Emery's stomach turned from tight to queasy at all the implications behind the statement and the ways they dovetailed with her darkest thoughts.

"Brian, we can discuss details tomorrow after I've had a chance to let the dust settle, but for now, would you be so kind as to give us a few minutes alone?"

"Of course." He packed up his things quickly before finally turning to face Emery. "I'm sure you don't want to hear this from me in the moment, Emery, but I didn't just vote for you out of pity. I believe you're going to make a great CEO someday. A lot of the others do, too."

She opened her mouth to argue, but her mother cut her off by rising from the chair. "Thank you. It does mean a lot, to both of us."

She gritted her teeth and shook her head as her mother walked him to the door of the conference room, then closed it firmly behind him. No sooner had the latch clicked into place than Emery sprang forward like a lion in ambush mode. "They can't do this!"

"They can, and they apparently have."

"This is so wildly unfair." She paced around her mother. "Unfair and … and … discriminatory."

Eleanor rolled her eyes.

"I'm serious. I've expected to step into this role my whole life, and yes, it's earlier than anyone ever wanted, but I'm thirty-one years old. I have the degree, the pedigree, and the people skills. There's no reason for me not to assume the role I was born to hold, unless …" She trailed off. "This is homophobia. It has to be. I will sue the living shit out of them."

Her mother snorted. "You're grasping. The company produces green energy in Massachusetts. There are no backwoods bigots anywhere on the premises, only aging hippies."

"Oh, come on. They act all liberal and open-minded, but caring about the environment doesn't mean they're comfortable

12

taking orders from a woman who wears a suit better than the entire old boys' club put together."

"There are three women on the board."

"And I don't dress or act like any one of them." She snapped her fingers. "Sexual orientation and gender identity discrimination. Get our best lawyer on the phone."

"Stop," her mother commanded with a new gravity in her voice.

"What? Why?"

"Because none of this is about the fact that you're gay, or gender nonconforming. It's because you're *extra*."

Emery's mouth was already open to argue, but she closed it and pursed her lips together.

"Don't pout." Her mother finally cracked a smile. "You know it's true."

"I don't."

"You arrived in a helicopter. You've been in four countries in the last two months. The last time most of the trustees were over, you showed up in tails and a top hat ... to brunch!"

"In my defense, I'd worn the tails out the night before, and the evening got away from me. I didn't have time to change."

"Which just proves their point. Please stop ranting and use your brain. I don't want this job. I'm not going to hold it forever. I'm a grieving widow at sixty-four. I was planning for our retirement. I was supposed to take up gardening and go on river cruises with my best friend." Her voice broke. "You want to talk about unfair? I never wanted to be a CEO. I never wanted any of this."

"Mom." She ground her teeth as the grief threatened to overtake them both again, then swallowed the emotions. "I'm going to call Brian back. I'll call all of them in. I'm going to slam my fist on that desk and demand—"

"No!" she snapped. "You can't act like a petulant child. Didn't you hear a word he said?"

She'd heard a few, but she suspected not all of them had sunk in. "Which part?"

"The one where he said you have to show them you can be steady and stable."

"I am."

"You're not. You're wild. Your father and I always loved that about you. We didn't want to clip your wings. We thought we'd all have so much more time for you to settle down on your own." She placed her palm on Emery's cheek. "We both wanted you to ease into the role in your own time, and you can still do that if you need to, or you can rise to the occasion."

She leaned into her mother's touch. "I'm still not even sure what that means. Do I need to get married and pop out a couple of kids in the next six months?"

She gave her cheek a little pat. "As much as I'd like to see you try, that's also very extra. Why don't you start a little smaller?"

"Like what?"

"Stop running. Sleep in the same bed for more than a week at a time. Drive a car less than eighty miles an hour. Use your office here on a regular basis. Make genuine connections with people in the company and around town."

"I could do that." She lifted a shoulder toward the door Brian had left through. "But he kept talking about Dad being a family man, and your marriage and—"

Her mother pinched her a little. "Would that be the worst thing in the world?"

"I don't know, maybe not, eventually. But in six months?"

"You don't have to say 'I do' in that time frame. It would take me longer than that to plan the wedding, but couldn't you at least look for a local girl, someone nice, someone to offer you balance?" She let her hand fall to Emery's shoulder and gave it a gentle squeeze. "Not for them. For you."

"I'm fine."

14

"You don't know that yet. Neither of us do. We've been through a lot these last three weeks, and this is only the beginning of our emotional rollercoaster. The next few months will challenge us both in so many ways. I want you to have someone to help you through it all, someone to offer company and comfort and good counsel."

"And you think I'll find some woman who can do all that in Amherst?"

Her mother's grey eyes danced. "Your father did."

The corners of her mouth twitched up.

"Besides, if I know you, you'll have plenty of fun along the way. Think of it as a new adventure. Anyone with your looks and charm can find women for a weekend. It takes something special to find one who will stay forever, but I believe in you."

"You have to believe in me. You're my mom."

"No, I have to believe in you because I need you to save me, Emery. And I know that's unfair, too. The world is unfair, and no one is going to feel sorry for either of us for long. We've been richly blessed, and to whom much is given, much is expected."

Her heart pressed painfully against her ribs. "Dad used to tell me that every time we'd take on some community service."

"He lived by it, just like your grandfather. We have been handed their legacy, and it's a precious one. So many people are counting on us."

"They're counting on you."

"Maybe, but I'm counting on *you*."

She sighed, the weight of the world settling on her shoulders. "Okay. I'll do it."

"Do what?"

She shook her head, not totally sure. "Whatever you need."

☀ ☀ ☀

15

Arden sank her fingers into the cool soil she'd just poured into the flower boxes along the back wall of her greenhouse. The warm air around her dripped with humidity, and the last of the summer sun beat down on the glass overhead, but the dirt soothed her senses. She breathed in the rich, loamy scent, as the fresh oxygen given off by her more mature plants saturated her brain and lungs. She could always think better out here, and while she'd grown self-aware enough over the years to realize her introverted nature likely thrived in the solitude of the only room where none of her family members ever visited, she still liked to credit the healing properties of photosynthesis and new air.

It didn't matter that the rest of her family found gardening boring or beneath her station or a waste of time. She didn't do it for them. She planted seeds for her, and maybe, in the more idealistic moments, for the larger world. It wasn't that she believed she could make a dent in anything so large as global climate change, but doing her part to help even her small circle to breathe a little deeper couldn't hurt.

"I knew I'd find you in here." Luz hopped down the stairs from the house into her sanctuary in a single bound. She leaned close enough to kiss her once on each cheek, a habit they'd picked up after watching their first French film together as teens.

"Great detective work." She went back to churning the soil with her bare hands.

"Yeah, when I asked your butler where you were and she said she didn't know, I knew you must be avoiding people."

"I don't have a butler."

"Butler, housekeeper, cook, same difference." Luz waved her off. "I have gossip. Well, I mean it's not exactly a secret, but I bet you haven't heard and it's drama."

"I haven't heard anything, and I'm not much for drama."

"Oh, you will be for this drama because it's about your secret stud-muffin school crush."

16

She finally glanced up at her best friend, who wore a black T-shirt and skintight, neon-pink pants. "Sorry, my what?"

"Emery Pembroke."

Her stomach gave a happy little drop, but she kept her expression neutral. The last thing she wanted was to feed into Luz's ability to make mountains out of mole hills.

"They just had a big press conference over at Pembroke and Sun," Luz continued.

"To announce her as CEO?"

"No!" she said dramatically. "They're giving the job to her mother."

"They named Eleanor CEO?"

"I knew you'd be shocked!"

She wasn't sure she'd go all the way to shocked, but certainly surprised. Emery seemed the obvious choice, and the last time she'd seen her, at the funeral service, she had certainly seemed to be holding up better than her mother.

"There was a big, formal thing at the company headquarters. Some women came into the shop talking about it. They were aghast, but I played it cool because you gave me the inside track at the funeral, so I was all like, "Emery was born to step into that role. I was sure it would go to her." Luz affected the same posh accent she always used in recounting conversations of wealthy people. "And they were all like, 'Oh we know, everyone assumed it would go to her. Eleanor's been talking about retirement for years now. Something's gone wrong.'"

"Something like her husband dying unexpectedly of a massive heart attack?" Arden offered.

"No." Luz dismissed the idea immediately. "They think it has to be something with Emery, or maybe the company."

Arden finally stepped back and wiped her dirty hands on the front of her summer dress.

"Ew, don't," Luz scolded. "You'll ruin it."

17

She rolled her eyes. "Why do you care? You don't need my hand-me-downs anymore. My clothes haven't fit you for years, and it's not as if you have any trouble sourcing fabric these days."

"It's not about needing. It's about tradition and artistry. You're my muse. Besides, that shade of blue makes your eyes look just like the ocean on a sunny day."

Arden softened. Luz always gave such lovely compliments.

"Hey, I have an idea." Her friend brightened. "You should wear something in that shade this weekend."

"What's this weekend?"

"There's a big charity event to kick off the polo tournament."

"I don't like polo."

"No shit. It's a stupid sport, basically pony hockey, but the charity ball, that's going to be a banger."

"I doubt it."

"Okay, so maybe not a raucous good time, but the room will be filled with rich and influential people, and after that memorial service, I've decided I need to expand my client base to exactly that market."

"You don't need my help to do so. You're a fashion genius."

"I really am, but I need more people to realize what you've known for years, which means I need to be in their line of sight, which means you need to take me to them."

She shook her head. "I'm sorry. I could send some emails or something, but I don't do the social scene."

"I know, and I didn't expect you to just agree to this request when you've refused so many others over the last ten years."

She laughed. "So why keep asking?"

"Because this time is different."

"How so?"

18

"Because I know for a fact that you'll like at least one person attending this event."

"Who? You?"

"Okay, two people, because Emery Pembroke is going."

She faltered, her hands sinking deeper into the soil than she'd intended. She pulled them out and started to wipe them on her dress again before Luz called her off.

"Stop." She grabbed a rag off a nearby bench and tossed it at her. "I'm glad to know I've got your attention about the girl, if not about the dress."

She shook her head even as her heart beat a little faster. "It doesn't really matter, you know?"

"Like hell it doesn't. I saw you drooling over her last week, and I approve."

"Nothing new there. I drooled over her for years in school."

"Good. Admitting it is the first step."

"No, it's not a step, it's a statement of fact. Hundreds of people have drooled over her and will continue to do so. She probably doesn't notice anymore."

"She might, if you got within ten feet of her."

"I have been, many times. We had two art classes together. We've been to several holiday parties. She's come to events in our gardens. She doesn't even see me, never has, and I can't see any reason why this weekend would be any different."

Luz seemed to consider this for a second, her brow furrowing. "What if I could think of some way it would be different, some significant change, would you go then?"

"In theory?" She shrugged. "I suppose so."

"Okay, I thought of one."

She laughed. "Already?"

"Yes." Luz hopped forward and took her hand, tugging her close and then giving her a little spin so her dress flared out as she twirled. "This time I'm going to dress you."

She started to shake her head, but Luz spun her again.

"And, I'm going to be your wingman, er, wingwoman. You know you're my favorite model and my very best friend. You'll look amazing, you'll feel more confident—"

"I never feel confident."

"You will this time, I promise, and even if you don't, I'll be right there with you. I have enough confidence for both of us. You can talk to me all night or let me talk to people for you. Just make introductions, and I'll take it from there."

She couldn't argue with that. Luz had never once failed to carry a conversation.

"Doesn't a tiny part of you want to try?"

She closed her eyes and searched her emotions, but she didn't have to look far. She did want to try. She always wanted to be someone else, someone brighter, more shiny, more compelling, only in her experience, wanting to do something and successfully doing so were wildly different things.

"Why are you pretending? I know you," Luz plowed on. "What have you got to lose other than one more quiet night at home?"

"You should not underestimate how much I enjoy quiet nights at home."

"And you will undoubtedly have twenty-nine more of them this month, but gimme one. You get to see your sexy crush, I get to meet clients, you get to spend time showing off your best friend, and I do, too. Maybe we both have a great time. Stranger things have happened."

She threw back her head in exasperation and stared up at the foggy glass of the greenhouse. It wasn't that she didn't have any more arguments so much as she'd forgotten why she always had to make the arguments in the first place. "Fine."

"Fine?" Luz jumped up and down. "*Fine*-fine?"

She grinned. "Let's go."

Luz threw her arms around her shoulders and squeezed her tightly. "We are going to have such a great time."

She wasn't ready to get her hopes up quite so high, but she felt at least a sliver of excitement. "Yeah, it might not be terrible."

✳ ✳ ✳

Emery pushed open the door to her office suite and held it long enough for her assistant to scuttle through behind her, then shut it firmly before sagging against the wall. "I have never wanted to pull a fire alarm so badly in my life."

Theo deposited a pile of file folders on his desk and turned to face her. "I'm sorry. I know it's been hard to stand around all day shaking hands and faking smiles like you're happy about your mother taking over."

"I feel like a child again, standing at some function my parents dragged me to, trying to act polite when really I want to run around screaming about how I don't want to be here."

"I'm not sure that would help your case. Also it would've made things harder on your mom, and she already looked exhausted."

"She's like some Stepford zombie. She's just nodding and inserting inane comments where needed, and she's good at it, but I'm not sure how much more she can shoulder right now." Emery fought back the stupid tears trying to spring forward, shoving them back, along with the realization she'd already lost one parent to a heart attack at a young age, and how, if she didn't do something soon, she might relive that trauma. "Like I didn't have enough fucking pressure on me at this moment in my life, now I'm responsible for piling more stress on my mother's plate."

"Whoa." Theo held up his hands. "You didn't make this choice, the board did."

"Because I didn't mesh with their standards."

"No one told you their standards until they'd already made the call."

21

She shed her gray suit coat roughly and tossed it atop the file folders. "No, apparently jumping through hoops like a show pony was only spelled out in the fine print of the job application. Maybe you should go over it again with a magnifying glass or something to make sure there's nothing in there about bamboo shoots and fingernails."

He shook his head. "Okay, there can be only one drama queen in the office at a time, and I'm giving you this one because you just had to sit through multiple hours of meetings and receptions celebrating something you very much didn't want to happen, but you do know you're not exactly a prisoner of war here, right?"

She frowned. "I might end up a prisoner of an arranged marriage if the trustees get their say."

"Only if you arrange it yourself."

"Can't you just arrange one for me?" she asked. "You're my administrative assistant and a gay guy. Shouldn't matchmaking and wedding planning be a thing you do?"

He held up a finger. "First of all, that is a terrible stereotype. I'm offended. Second of all, yes, yes I would love to, and I'm so glad you asked because I took the liberty of doing a little research on your behalf."

She raised her eyebrows.

"I'm not saying you have to marry any of these women, but you do like women, and you're good with them, much better than you are at sitting behind a desk or running meetings or grinning and bearing your fate silently."

She grimaced at his blunt statement of fact.

"I just thought that with the list of things you were given to work on, we should start with the easiest."

"And you thought finding a wife was the easiest one?"

He shrugged and pushed her jacket off the files. "Obviously I'm not an expert, but I've known you a long time, and finding women to hang on your arm has never seemed like a challenge for you."

"You know, my mother said something similar last week, but she added the caveat that it would be more of a challenge to find someone who would stay forever."

His eyes went wide, and he looked like he might feign a faint. "Lord, who said anything about forever? Not me. I only set out to find someone you could marry."

She laughed. "I take it you don't find the two concepts synonymous?"

"I mean, they don't have to be, right? How many people do you know who stay married for their whole lives?"

She immediately thought of her parents, but the accompanying shot of pain kept her from saying so.

"I know for a fact half of those trustees sitting in judgment of you have been married at least twice, one of them three times. Besides, you have to play the part for only six months, find a girl, give her a ring, bada bing, you don't even have to go through with it. You just have to make everyone think you will."

She shifted from one foot to the other. "I don't know."

"Don't get cold feet on me before you even start." He patted the chair in front of his desk. "I seem to remember you sleeping with multiple women you didn't stick around long enough to even have breakfast with. You can't say that's any more or less shady than actually dating a woman for six months to see where things go."

"In those cases, I didn't lie to anyone or lead them on."

"And you don't have to here, either. I mean, it's not like you're going to hold a ball and tell the whole town full of eligible women they should come so you can pick a wife based on her glass slip—" He stopped mid-sentence and held up his hand. "Actually, that's not a terrible idea."

"Glass slippers?"

"No, the ball ... the charity ball." He started flipping through folders and spreading them out on the desk. "Anyone who's anyone will be at the charity ball this Friday. You could

23

study up on your best options, maybe whittle them down to three or four."

She leaned forward and scanned the files he'd revealed. Each one had a color photo of a woman paperclipped to what looked like a resume of sorts. She picked one up and read the first section. Name, age, sexual orientation, occupation. What followed was a few more short paragraphs detailing known relationship history, family and social connections, hobbies, and known dislikes or warnings. "Holy shit, Theo, have you been carrying around binders full of women all afternoon?"

He grinned. "I needed something to study during that horrendous question and answer session with the local press and partners."

"If someone had seen you with the personal credentials of Amherst's most eligible bachelorettes—"

"They would have been very confused, because the whole town knows I'm gay as a field full of daisies, but they didn't, because I'm good at my job. This is what you pay me for. I make you look good, and I make it look easy."

When she didn't argue, he continued. "I've done all the hard work. I've collected data on the daughters of the local elite, only including families who have been in the area at least as long as yours in order to give the impression of community connection. I weeded out all the married women and straight women, which cut the pool significantly, but not as much as you might suspect. Then I cast out a few with a history of scandal or just batshit crazy behavior."

"How'd you do that?"

"Social media helps tremendously. My deep appreciation for the local rumor mill doesn't hurt either. Also, I removed a couple of women you've already dated since few of those ended well."

"Good call." She unbuttoned the cuffs on her sleeves and began to roll them up as if preparing to dive in physically and mentally. "What's the grand total here?"

"Fifteen amazing candidates ... well, maybe ten amazing candidates, and a few outside possibilities."

He slid one of the open folders over to her. "I like this one."

She glanced at the picture and didn't immediately see any issues with the dark-haired beauty. "Isabella Trenton?"

"Pediatrician at the hospital her parents founded, so she will definitely be at the charity event this weekend. Thirty-six. Graduated top of her class at Cornell. She's a skier and a golfer," Theo recited without looking at the sheet.

"Do you have them all memorized?"

"I've got a good memory and attention to detail. For instance, she's reportedly a terrible cook and a bit of a workaholic, but wouldn't the two of you look smashing together with your matching dark and sultry looks?"

She rolled her eyes. She didn't care about the cooking, but she wasn't sure she wanted anyone who worked too much or outdid her in the sultry department. "Okay, put her in the maybe pile. Who's next?"

He sat down in the chair next to her and passed another open folder. "This one's interesting. Amber May is your age but was educated at boarding school. She went to Dartmouth, where she led their fencing team."

"Fencing as in she's a swordswoman?"

"Yes." He held up a picture of a redhead with intense green eyes. "She's also apparently a good dancer, though there are some reports she's got a bit of a temper."

"Hard pass."

"Wait a second, her father is business partners with one of the trustees."

"Still a no. The last thing I need is a woman with a hot temper and combat skills."

"Fair dues."

25

"Besides, you never know if someone's going to like my dating their daughter, and if the partner gets pissed about the big ole queer swooping in—"

"Good point, and if you didn't make a real go with this one, there are multiple ways it could turn ugly." He closed the folder and snatched up another. "How about Renata Wembley? Classically trained musician, known for supporting children's programs in the arts, so you know for sure she'll be in attendance Friday."

She glanced at the picture of a brunette, her classic figure accentuated in a floor-length dress as she sat at a grand piano. "Potential there, for sure. What are the red flags?"

"No major ones. She's just gotten out of a relationship with a French woman. Before that she dated a bi guy I know, and he said she was great. I think he still had a little thing for her, honestly. She's not as wealthy as some on the list, but her family's all over the area, from the university to the Hamptons."

"Move her to the contenders column." This time Emery chose a folder and flipped it up. Her breath caught at the sight of the photo. It wasn't slick or posed or professionally shot, but the woman it showcased in profile had a slight lift in her chin, a little upturn in her nose, and the sweetest quirk at the corner of her lips. Everything about her seemed to look up, and something in Emery fluttered upward too.

"Oh, that's one of the outliers," Theo said almost dismissively.

She shook her head slowly, unable to imagine why he'd think so.

"Arden Gilderson, a couple of years younger than you, and a lot richer. You overlapped at prep school a bit. Then she went on to Smith."

She nodded appreciatively but couldn't figure how she didn't remember ever crossing paths with her. "Gilderson, as in, like, the estate in the Hamptons, and the gardens?"

26

"And the library, and the art gallery, and the music conservatory. Yeah, the family is old money, like Vanderbilt old, made their first fortune in railroads, then the next one in marble and granite, and most recently, pretty much every bit of concrete poured in any major city for fifty years." He pointed to the docket. "Pretty stuffy reading there, and mostly about the family rather than her."

"Why?" she asked without flipping to the information he referenced, mostly because she couldn't bring herself to look away from the picture.

"There's honestly not much about her out in the rumor mill. She's not a total recluse, but certainly socially averse. Some people say she's quiet or shy, but others say she's awkward and anxious."

She frowned. Nothing about the woman in the picture seemed awkward. She looked calm and centered. "Other red flags?"

He shook his head. "She doesn't work. Apparently she likes to garden, and she's good with animals. Not much of a relationship history that I could find. There was a girlfriend at Smith."

She rolled her eyes. "Everyone has a girlfriend while they're at Smith."

"Right?" He laughed. "But there's never been a boyfriend, and the best friend is very much a lesbian, so it does sort of add up. But no one seems to get close enough to confirm or deny, which seems like a lot of work if you ask me. Plus, she's kind of plain, right?"

She finally glanced up at him, a little chuckle building in her throat, but his expression held no hint of teasing. "Oh, you're serious?"

"I was," he admitted. "You like her?"

"What's not to like? She's pretty." She let the understatement stand even as her stomach tightened when she

27

inspected the photo once more. "She comes from a good family with stronger ties to the community than mine."

"But not great with people, and you're talking about a very public role, plus you're like the epitome of a social gadfly. This woman almost never goes out. She's like a modern-day Emily Dickinson without the weirdly punctuated poetry."

"Will she be out this weekend?"

"Seems unlikely." He shrugged. "I'm sure she's got an invite, but I get the sense she turns down a lot of invitations."

"Do you think she'd turn down one from me?"

He shook his head and snagged the folder from her hand. "How about we keep your options open? There's no need to pick one. We'll put her in the maybe pile, but I really think you've got some better candidates here, and there's no need to even narrow down the field too much before Friday. You're going to have most of them in one place. You can scan the crowd, converse, work your legendary charm, and see which woman trips your trigger."

She laughed, even though a part of her rebelled against having him take the file away. "Trips my trigger?"

"Floats your boat, sparks your fancy, catches your eye, but don't go overboard. The last thing we need is twenty-five women thinking you're leading them on, or people worrying you're playing the field too hard. Look, don't touch. Then we can do some pros and cons lists or something next week. You need to be sensible and smart."

"Okay, okay, I get it." She raised three fingers in a Scout's honor pose as some of her humor returned. "This whole thing's kind of absurd, but I'll go to the ball and play my part. 'I'll look to like, if looking liking move; but no more deep will I endart mine eye than your consent gives strength to make it fly.'"

He gave her a blank stare. "Did you just quote Shakespeare to me?"

"*Romeo and Juliet.* I'm supposed to be wooing women at a ball full of eligible marriage partners to please society at large.

28

What could go wrong other than, like, a murder-suicide pact between young lovers?"

"Slow down, Romeo. This is why everyone thinks you're extra. You need to keep your head in your skull and your libido in your pants. If anyone suggests knives or poison, get out fast. No job or woman is worth getting hurt for."

"Fair enough." She shrugged. "It's good to set healthy boundaries. I don't want to wreck my family legacy in the first six months, or ever, but I think I'd honestly rather sell the business before I lose my head for anyone you had to cyberstalk for me."

Chapter Three

"Holy shit," Luz said under her breath as they entered the grand hall dripping with silver and blue accents. The lights were low, but not dim enough that she couldn't see the teeming mass of glittering people dressed to the nines as they sipped their champagne and mingled with a type of familiarity that was more bought than earned.

"Yeah." Arden's simple response carried none of the glee her friend shivered with.

"They didn't even, like, check our tickets or anything," Luz said.

"They don't have to. They know who belongs here and who doesn't."

"So, if I'd just tried to crash on my own?"

Her jaw tightened at the thought of how her friend might've been received in such circles without Arden's mother's significant donation to the charity du jour. At least this time it was a pediatric hospital instead of something silly or banal, but with entry fees in the multi-thousand dollar range, attendance also made a statement about more than a person's generous nature. It wasn't the wealth Arden objected to so much as the exclusivity and sense of superiority that came with it.

"Come on." Luz gave her arm a tug. "Let's get a drink, and then you can introduce me around."

They started through the crowd, turning a few heads as they went, and even Arden had to admit they made a striking pair. Luz exuded style in a satiny black suit with rich, deep purple lapels and a matching silk tie, while Arden wore the asymmetrical cobalt blue dress she'd whipped up for her. As long as she'd known Luz, she'd never figured out how her friend could just produce fashion miracles on such short notice, but it probably served as a creative outlet for the excitement she'd buzzed with ever since Arden had agreed to this little charade. Luz must've texted thirty times in four days, and she'd even made her come in for a fitting, which she rarely did anymore.

Still, the results were worth it as the dress hung perfectly from one shoulder and completely off the other before wrapping snuggly around her waist, then flaring out almost playfully down to her ankles. Equal parts tasteful and daring, she'd captured the mood of the evening flawlessly, and Arden smiled as Luz strolled through the room like a proud parent debuting her newest creation. The experience would've been even more enjoyable if not for the fact that admiring the dress also required them to look at Arden when she preferred to fly under the radar. Still, if one had to be noticed, she supposed she'd prefer it be for something good instead of something awkward.

"Darling." Her mother materialized at her side. "Don't you look beautiful."

"Thank you." She kissed her cheek. "And you're sparkling as always."

Her mother gave a happy twirl, showing off her floor-length dress. "One must do their part, but you've gone above and beyond. To what do we owe this honor?"

"Luz had a new creation to show off, so I obliged."

Her mother's smile faltered only a smidge as she turned. "Ah Luz, of course. I should've seen your hand in such a divine piece, and the way it seemed particularly suited to my daughter's frame."

Luz grinned. "She's an easy model to suit."

Her mother's expression never changed, but a muscle in her jaw twitched. "Well, I wouldn't know. She's always been rather persnickety about joining me in such endeavors, but you've always had your ways of working past her barriers."

Luz just grinned broadly. "Must be my charm and particular set of skills."

Her mother's eyes narrowed dangerously, and Arden stepped between the two women under the guise of snagging two champagne flutes from a passing waiter. "Mother, do you mind if Luz and I mingle a bit before we join you for dinner?"

"Not at all." She sounded downright relieved at the prospect. "I'm always thrilled when you finally deign to interact with … well, anyone."

She waited until the backhanded compliment had fully landed, then turned and disappeared into the crowd while Arden downed the entirety of her champagne glass and reached for Luz's.

Luz laughed lightly and raised the glass in mock salute before pulling it back out of reach. "That went well."

She rolled her eyes. "Do you have to antagonize her?"

"I didn't set out to. It just sort of happens, and I can't help it if she insists on believing we're sleeping together. When you come into a conversation with that mindset, everything's going to sound sexual."

"I don't disagree." Her mother had been laboring under that particular misconception for a good ten years, and nothing either of them had ever said to the contrary had been able to allay her suspicions. "But your 'charm and particular set of skills' at working past my so-called barriers is a bit on the nose."

She giggled. "Perhaps, but now you've just survived your first challenge of the evening, and didn't I do a good job of drawing fire my way?"

She sighed. "I suppose."

"Aside from the dig at the end, she didn't get to nitpick you at all."

"Okay, but seriously, she says she wants me to get out and be more social, then when I do, all she does is criticize me for—"

"Let it go," Luz said quickly. "She's got her own agenda and baggage. I think you're doing great. You look amazing, and

32

you're a woman who knows her own mind. She's not your target audience."

"I'm not sure I have a target audience."

"You most certainly do." Luz leaned to the side, looking around Arden as her eyes lit up. "And she just walked in looking like sex in a suit."

She turned as the whole room seemed to move in slow motion. Music swelled, or maybe that was only the revving of her own heart when her eyes landed on Emery. She strode down a set of stairs, a little jig in her step as if she moved to her own drumbeat. With each step, her black hair swayed back in a curve along the sides of her neck, shimmering in the low light. Her suit tonight was navy with a paisley vest over a white dress shirt, and the pants tapered down to patent leather loafers.

"God, she makes the look work for her," Luz said in awe. "Oh, and those shades of blue will layer beautifully when the two of you dance together later."

She snorted, rather unladylike.

"What? You'd like to dance with her, right?"

"She'd have to hold me tightly because I'd probably faint if she asked."

"It could be arranged," Luz said as they both watched Emery greet several people on the way in. "Who's she talking to?"

"Isabella Trenton." A hint of wistfulness crept into her voice.

"Trenton as in the hospital is named after her? Do you like her?"

"After her family, yes. And no, I don't, but pretty much everyone else does. She's smart and successful and beautiful, and Emery's talking to her, so why would she want to talk to anyone else, much less me?"

"Because you're smart, beautiful, and what else?"

"Successful," she said. Certainly Luz hadn't forgotten that one by chance. "Isabella is a doctor and I'm … nothing."

33

"You're an international woman of mystery. Besides, Emery doesn't have a job either. There's something you two can bond over."

"We're not going to bond. She doesn't even know I exist."

Luz took her hand and tugged. "She's about to."

"What? Wait. How are you …" She couldn't even get the words out around the mounting fear as Luz pulled her through the crowd. She went along, not wanting to make a scene, but Luz clearly had no such qualms. Turning to grin at Arden with more than a hint of mischief, she lifted her glass up as if she planned to drink, then seemed to trip over nothing at all and sent the dregs of her champagne right down the arm of Isabella's little black dress.

Isabella recoiled, and Luz released Arden's hand. "Oh my God. I am so sorry. I have no idea what happened. Look what I did. Is that satin or viscose fabric?"

Isabella seemed more bowled over by the verbal assault than the drink dripping down her sleeve. "I don't know."

"Ugh, what a klutz. I am so sorry, but I can fix it."

"Fix it?"

"Yes, no worries. I'm a designer."

"Designer?" Isabella clearly struggled to keep up.

"A genius with textiles, right Arden?"

They all turned to her, even Emery.

"She is," she managed to squeak out. "She made my dress."

Isabella nodded appreciatively as Arden's cheeks flamed under the group inspection.

"Excuse us for just a moment," Luz said to Emery as she nudged Isabella toward the exit. "Keep this one company for me for a few seconds, and I'll have her cleaned up and back to you in a jiffy."

"Certainly." Emery smiled. "We'll be right here."

34

Isabella opened her mouth like she might argue, but Luz clutched her hand the same way she had Arden's and began talking a mile a minute. "We've only got a few minutes before that starts to set. Wouldn't want to ruin a dress that suits you so magnificently. Who designed it? Your bone structure's fantastic."

There wasn't even a chance to catch a breath, much less put up a fight, and Arden almost felt bad for Isabella. She understood how easy it was to be railroaded so completely, but when they disappeared into the crowd, she became increasingly aware of eyes on her. A tingle ran up her spine, the kind that came from being noticed. No, more than noticed. Seen.

Emery flashed her a broad, genuine smile. "Well, that was interesting ... Arden, right?"

Her head grew light, and her heart did a kick line across her ribs, but she managed to nod.

"I'm Emery."

"I know." She chided herself for not saying something more clever. "I mean, I remember you from school, not that we knew each other, but I've seen you, like I used to see you, and I still do, sometimes."

Emery slipped her hands in the pockets of her slacks and waited patiently while Arden kept digging herself deeper.

"Which isn't to say I see you often, because I don't. I don't get out much, and now you're probably starting to understand why, because I just keep talking when I clearly should stop."

Emery laughed. "Not at all."

"You don't have to babysit me because my friend threw champagne on Isabella's dress."

"You make it sound like she did it on purpose."

"Well, I mean, she's impulsive. I'm not sure she really thought it through. She would never harm expensive fabric deliberately."

35

Emery leaned a little closer. "That's not quite a denial, is it?"

"I could stand here quietly until Isabella returns," Arden offered, mostly so she wouldn't combust from the proximity and attention she'd so long wanted without actually preparing for.

"Please don't."

"Why?"

"Because this is the best conversation I've had in a month, and I'd hate for it to end any sooner than it has to."

Arden's head wasn't just light anymore, it was spinning. Either that or the room was. She grew a little dizzy and closed her eyes to steady herself, but it didn't help. She was going to pass out, right here in front of Emery and the whole town, and maybe if she was lucky, she would hit her head and not wake up for a hundred years until the embarrassment and legend of her social awkwardness had faded, or at least until anyone here to witness it had died.

Her breath grew shallow and her chest tight, and just as her knees started to give way, a strong hand on her waist pulled her back as much as it held her up.

Her eyes fluttered open to meet Emery's, dark and deep, sensual and sympathetic. "I'm sorry."

Emery's gaze never wavered. "You're all right."

It wasn't a question, rather a statement of fact, and as Arden stared up at her, she had neither the will nor the inclination to argue. "Yes. I am."

※ ※ ※

Emery loved few things as much as being amused, and Arden Gilderson had already done so in spades. The woman didn't seem to have an ounce of pretense about her, and the picture Theo had provided didn't even begin to do her looks justice. She was almost shockingly pretty in an earnest and genuine sort of way. Her eyes shimmered a beautifully faint blue-green blend, and the glittering light gave occasional peeks of strawberry undercurrents in her blonde hair. Everything about her seemed on the edge of something else, even the almost frantic rambling had an on-edge quality about it, without ever feeling completely edgy. The combination was delightfully refreshing, and the curve of her hip under Emery's fingertips carried something so sweetly sensual she had to fight the urge to pull her closer.

Instead, she held her intense gaze for just long enough to make sure the woman wasn't going to swoon again, then stepped back. "You mentioned you don't get out often."

"Obviously."

She ignored the self-deprecation. "And yet you're here tonight. Why?"

"I'm supposed to say it's for a good cause, and that's true."

"Lots of things can be true at the same time. What else?"

"Luz wanted to dress me and show off her handiwork in a room full of rich people."

"So you're a good friend and an even better model. What else?"

Arden's cheeks flushed. "That's all, really."

She didn't buy it, and she didn't for a second think this woman was capable of holding out on her, so she leaned a little closer. "Come on, you can tell me. I promise I'll keep your secret."

Arden bit her lower lip as if trying to hold something in.

"It'll be between you and me. What's the other reason you graced us with your presence tonight?"

Arden screwed up her face, closing her eyes tightly as she whispered, "You."

"Me?"

She nodded, then peeked one eye open.

Her smile spread as she waited for more, allowing the silence to stretch uncomfortably between them.

37

"We saw you recently." Arden finally caved. "And I told Luz we'd gone to school together. She thought that meant we'd been friends, but I had to explain you didn't even know I was alive."

Her chest constricted at the shame in Arden's tone and the hint of the same it sparked in her, but she worked to keep her tone light. "And Luz, being the amazing friend she is, took it upon herself to right a wrong, and to guarantee an introduction. Hence the champagne throwing."

Arden nodded. "I am so sorry."

"I'm not," Emery said quickly. "In fact, I think I owe Luz a debt of gratitude, and you as well, for bringing this oversight to my attention."

"You don't have to be so nice about it. I know it's weird."

"No, what's weird is that you and I have moved in such close proximity for as long as we have without ever interacting. Though in my defense, I did know you were alive before tonight, and what's more, I know you, Arden Gilderson, are quiet and kind. I know you love animals and gardening. I know you're too quick to apologize, and you might not get out often, but you really should because I would very much like to see you again. Still, if this is a once-in-a-blue-moon sort of evening, then I intend to spend it learning some of those things about you I missed for too long."

Arden's lips parted slightly as her chest rose and fell more dramatically, only drawing Emery's eyes to the creamy expanse of skin below her collarbones for a second.

"Shall we go grab a drink and find someplace a little quieter?"

Arden glanced over her shoulder in the direction where Luz and Isabella had retreated. "We promised to stay put until they came back."

Emery shook her head. "No, we were *instructed* to stay put, and I think you will find that while I'm very good at keeping promises, I am very bad at following directions."

"I usually just do whatever other people tell me to do."

Emery leaned a little closer again. "What do you say to letting me be a bad influence on you tonight?"

Arden's smile quirked up with just enough to hint at a dormant rebelliousness of her own. "I think I may actually like that quite a bit."

Emery extended her arm, and Arden took it without hesitation, another good quality in a woman as far as she was concerned. She honestly wasn't so sure what Theo had been worried about. Sure, Arden wasn't as practiced or poised as just about any other woman in the room tonight, but she was certainly a lot more entertaining, and she wouldn't take much work to woo either. She'd all but admitted she wanted to know Emery, and now the feeling was mutual.

She snagged another champagne flute from a waiter they passed and offered it to Arden.

"No, thank you. I've already had one. If I drink another before dinner, I'll get tipsy for sure."

"That sounds fun." Emery tried to hand her the glass again, and this time she accepted. "If you're this forthright while sober, imagine how much fun we'd have with you tipsy."

"Forthright? My mother says I blather."

"No, trust me, I have spent the last week in endless meetings with my mother and various stakeholders. Isn't that a ridiculous term, stakeholders? Makes it sound like they've got sirloins in their hands."

"Or stakes like you use to kill vampires," Arden suggested.

"That would be infinitely too badass for these people, but I'm going to try to at least picture it during the next never-ending think-session, because blathering is all they do. I fear it must be a requirement of the job to love the sound of one's own voice, and they never manage to say anything half as interesting as you have in the last ten minutes."

"Oh, I'm not usually interesting. At least you have a job. I don't."

"The whole job thing is new for me, honestly. I mean I've had one, in theory, since graduation, but in practice ..." Her voice trailed off as too many possible ends to that sentence overwhelmed her. "Actually, let's not talk about work. It's such a cliché to attach undue weight to a person's productivity, and we've both admitted it's not our strong suit anyway."

Arden made no argument as they wove their way past the farthest reaches of the crowd, and Emery steered her out onto a patio strung with lights and overlooking the polo grounds. "Why don't we ask each other more interesting questions?"

"I'm not sure I know any interesting questions."

"Try."

"Um ..." Arden glanced around as if searching for some clues or inspiration.

"Don't think too hard. Just blurt out the first one that comes to mind."

"If a tomato is a fruit, is ketchup a jelly?"

Emery stared at her for a moment, then burst out laughing.

"Oh, I did it wrong, didn't I?"

"Not at all." Emery nearly doubled over from the sheer silliness of it. "Most women do some Proust questionnaire, or worse, something based in astrological signs. Yours is much more fun. I actually have to consider my answer."

Arden's eyes danced, and Emery thought about drawing it out to keep her watching her, but she got the sense she wouldn't look away even after she got her answer.

"Okay, so I don't know much about cooking, but I think jelly is just like fruit and sugar, and you put it on things to make them taste better, so wow, okay, I think by those standards ketchup is actually jelly."

Arden nodded. "I agree, even if I find the idea of eating ketchup on scones mildly disturbing."

"Just because you *can* doesn't mean you *should*, right?" Emery said with mock seriousness. "Okay, my turn. If you could be anywhere else in the world right now, where would you be?"

"Probably at home, reading. I already told you I'm boring. If I weren't here, I'd either be in my greenhouse or my library."

"Fair, but you didn't really give me any new information, so I get to go again."

"Sure."

The woman seemingly had endless reserves of agreeability. "If you could be any animal, what would you be?"

"See, I'm just going to be a rich girl cliché here, because I love so many animals, but none quite so much as horses."

"Then we'll be stereotypes together because that's my answer too."

"Really?"

"Cross my heart. I mean, don't get me wrong, monkeys have their appeal, really, but I've already got opposable thumbs, and I'm quite good at climbing trees. If I get to be something really different, why not go all out?"

Arden nodded. "I like that you thought things through and picked based on the boldness of the choice."

"Why did you choose horses, other than wealth and social standing, of course?"

She grinned. "I just like to ride. I always have, and wouldn't it be wonderful just to be one with the horses, no directing or second guessing, just running free over fields without anything to encumber you?"

Emery sighed happily. "I ache for it in my very bones. And for what it's worth, I love to ride, too. Do you play polo as well?"

"No," Arden said quickly. "I don't do sports."

"'Do sports?' The fact that you phrased it that way really drives home your point."

"Sorry, I didn't mean to make them sound so horrifying. It's only my own athletic ability, or lack thereof, that made me recoil. I admire people who can play, well, anything. I always admire people who can do things I can't, which is pretty much everything."

"But not actually," Emery countered. "You're very good at making me laugh, and no one else here has been so far. And you're adept at self-deprecation. Also, you asked the best icebreaker question I've ever encountered. Plus, I can't verify this as truth, but someone told me you're quite an impressive botanist."

"Hardly," Arden said, but the upward quirk of her lips gave her away. "I do have a greenhouse, and I like to tinker, but wait, who were you talking to about my gardening?"

"I can't divulge sources, but trust me, I do have them, and they aren't about gardens."

"About me? Why?"

Emery paused, both for dramatic effect and to consider how much she wanted to say. Certainly she had no intention of explaining the corporate pressure to mate, but she could at least tell Arden she was interested. It would undoubtedly please the woman, and Emery infinitely enjoyed pleasing women. And yet, coming on strong didn't seem like the right approach here. Theo had wanted her to consider all her options and debrief on Monday, but she was having fun, and prudence or patience had never been her style. Did she have to change everything about the way she interacted with women, or hadn't they decided to take this route precisely because she'd stood the greatest chance of success in the romantic arena?

She was still debating the best approach, and Arden was waiting so beautifully before her, when a woman pushed open the door they'd recently come through.

"There you are!" Exasperation dripped from her voice. "I thought for sure you'd slunk off somewhere to hide."

"No, Mother, we were just talking."

Her eyes narrowed, then widened. "Emery Pembroke, I didn't expect you of all people to be out here talking to my daughter."

"I'm always up for surprising people," Emery said. "I didn't mean to keep her though."

"You didn't," Arden said quickly, with a light touch on her wrist.

She glanced down at the gentle press of elegant fingers to her pulse point, and Arden drew back her hand.

"You're fine," her mother answered for her, "but they're about to serve dinner, and she's expected at our table."

"Of course." Emery stepped back.

"I hate to go," Arden said to no one in particular. "I've had such a lovely time."

"I assure you the pleasure's all mine, and if it wouldn't be too much of an imposition, I promise this won't be the last you'll see of me this evening."

Arden's smile turned a little sad. "You don't have to. You've already been so nice. You probably have plenty of things you're expected to do at an event like this."

"Undoubtedly," Emery agreed. "Endless expectations."

"Very well." Arden's mother cut back in, taking her daughter by the arm. "You're free to go. We'll keep Arden entertained so you can work the room as you need to."

Emery got the subtle instruction couched as freedom. It wasn't the first time she'd been warned in the form of a release. She stood her ground, watching them go until they were almost back through the door before calling out. "Arden?"

She turned, her eyes hopeful if not quite expectant.

"Remember what I said earlier about my penchant for promises and directions respectively?"

Arden bit her lower lip as if trying not to smile. "Yes."

"Good."

☀ ☀ ☀

"Dude, where'd you go?" Luz said under her breath as Arden took the seat indicated by her mother.

"I was outside getting some air." She responded loudly enough to be heard by everyone around them, not that any of her mother's friends were listening. Then, leaning over slightly, she whispered, "With Emery."

Luz's eyes about bulged out of her head. "Seriously?"

She nodded and unfolded her napkin before spreading it neatly across her lap. She sort of wished she had another one to tuck in the neckline of her dress to protect Luz's beautiful creation. Not that her mother would've allowed anything so gauche, but she didn't trust her hands not to tremble when she picked up her wine glass or attempted to move any food from her plate to her mouth. She still wasn't sure yet what could explain Emery's notice of her, much less her sustained attention, but if by some chance her attire held part of the appeal, she intended to wear it every day for the rest of her life.

"Are you going to tell me what happened after I left, or am I going to have to guess? Because you know I have a very active imagination, and I will not hesitate to fill in the blanks," Luz offered.

Arden shot a look at her mother, who was engaged in flattering the woman next to her, someone from the hospital board. "She's every bit as amazing as I always thought."

"And?" Luz pushed.

"And nothing. We talked. Well, she talked. I had a sort of verbal vomit where I told her all kinds of embarrassing things and basically admitted I was only here tonight to see her."

Luz groaned.

"I know, I know. I have no chill, and I never pretended I did, but the thing is, she didn't seem to mind. Or maybe she's just got enough social grace not to let it show."

44

"I mean, it's possible." Luz tried to sound reassuring. "You're always harder on yourself than you should be. Maybe you did great."

"I did not," she said flatly. "I was a mess, but she was really kind, and she laughed and she actually knew who I was before I introduced myself."

"See!" Luz said loud enough that a couple of people at the table glanced up at them, and she lowered her voice again. "You thought she didn't know you were alive before tonight, so maybe you're underestimating your interaction now, too. How did you leave it?"

She smiled slightly at the memory of Emery calling her, backlit in the moonlight, and the hint of a challenge in her smile. *Promises and directions.* She was good with one and not the other. That's what she'd said, and in the moment, Arden could hardly doubt her.

Still, her lived experience surely suggested she couldn't dare hope for something more than those moments of magic when she'd been the focus of Emery's attention. She didn't want to allow even the slightest hint of disappointment to creep into those memories by wishing for more. She wanted to scoop up that memory and place it safely on the shelf of her heart, so she finally told Luz, "My mother came out and called me to dinner."

Luz rolled her eyes. "Of course she did. What a cock block, or whatever the straight mother version of that is, a parental dam?"

"It's okay. The moments together were amazing. Thank you so much for being wild and absurd and a very good friend. You made my teenage dreams come true."

"Seriously? You only dreamed of a few minutes of talking?"

"A few minutes of undivided attention from someone like her seems fantastical enough."

"Your teenage self was way more tame than mine."

45

"The same is true of our adult selves, clearly. How did you make out with Isabella?"

Luz's smile turned a little more suggestive. "Well, we haven't actually made out yet, but I think there may be some possibility there."

"Really?"

She shrugged. "No, but she didn't, like, threaten to have me thrown out. She actually said she liked your dress better."

"Did you offer to make one for her?"

"You know I did. She didn't commit, but she sort of seemed open to stopping by the shop sometime. Maybe you could put in a good word for me?"

She nodded. "If I run into her, I will."

"Are you just saying so because you know you'll never run into her?"

"You know it's impolite to sit over there whispering all night," Arden's mother scolded lightly. "Who's got the two of you all huddled up? Not Emery Pembroke, I hope."

That raised several heads around the table, and suddenly all eyes were on Arden, and she froze. She didn't want to tell any of them anything. She didn't even want Emery's name on her mother's lips with their faint press of displeasure.

Luz jumped into the line of fire with her usual quick wit and enjoyment of drawing her mother's ire. "I was telling Arden I bumped into Isabella Trenton quite literally, and spilled a drink on her, but all's well. She's going to come by my shop sometime to see my designs."

"Isabella is lovely." Her mother softened. "And her family has the most divine wine cellar as well. Arden, what do you mean telling Luz you won't run into her? I see her parents all the time."

"Do you?" She answered with a question, as it gave her mother a greater chance to monologue rather than expecting her to respond.

46

"Of course, they'll be at the match tomorrow, and they were at our garden party at the end of the summer only a week ago. Wouldn't it be nice for you to make Isabella feel welcome as well? Perhaps you should go along with Luz when she comes by the shop. I'm sure the two of you could be quite close. Perhaps Luz could help."

"I'd love to," Luz said enthusiastically. "If you approve of Isabella, she must be quite a nice young woman."

"Indeed." Her mother's eyes lit up in a way that suggested she might be plotting some sort of merger, a direct contrast to the way she'd looked at Emery, but Arden didn't dare draw attention by asking why.

"Perhaps you could help her with the interaction, Luz. Maybe give her a few pointers on making conversation, help her come out of her shell a bit."

"Arden's never had any trouble coming out around me," Luz said airily, but before Arden's mother had a chance to register the suggestiveness of the comment, a team of waiters interrupted by setting the first course between them.

Mercifully, everyone at the table had to do the requisite complimenting of the food, some sort of French cheese and mushrooms wrapped in pastry. Salads followed, then chicken on creamy polenta. It wasn't hard for Arden to eat, and if she kept chewing, she didn't feel any pressure to talk to anyone else, though she had a significantly more difficult time pretending to be interested in conversations taking place around the table. Something about polo, someone's recent trip to Amsterdam, someone's new home in Vail. They all floated in and out through her brain as she fought the urge to feel down about her mother's implication that she needed intervention or fixing of some sort.

"Isn't that lovely, Arden?" her mother prompted at one point.

She automatically responded with her practiced look of interest and only the slightest twinge that once again she was being led into interaction rather than being allowed to make the choice based on her own comfort or interest. "Very much so."

"Arden has such a deep interest for the arts," her mother continued.

She nodded, though the statement wasn't particularly true.

"Maybe we should drop by sometime and see the Claytons' collection."

"What a nice idea," she said without any intention of joining her mother on such a trip.

"I've been talking to Edwin about adding to our own, though our dealer hasn't been active lately. Who do you use?"

Sensing her part of acting pretty and engaged had ended, she allowed her mind to drift off again. By the time dessert arrived, even Luz had picked up a conversation about fall fashions with the woman on the other side of her, and instead of feeling left out, she only managed to summon a bit of peace. And, of course, her mind wandered back to her conversation with Emery.

The subject shouldn't have inspired calm. She hadn't exactly put in a stellar social performance, and a couple of times she'd dipped into embarrassingly true confessions spouted in moments of profound awkwardness. Maybe she did need some sort of social coaching, but Emery had never once seemed put off. On the contrary, while Arden had floundered, she'd actually smiled the smile she usually reserved for only the brightest, most interesting girls in school. Arden had seen the expression plenty of times before, radiant, easy, full of self-assuredness and genuine pleasure, all things Arden most lacked, and yet, this time, Emery had pointed all those qualities at her.

The whole interaction had been more than a little mystifying, and she couldn't make much sense of it. Perhaps a part of her didn't want to pick those moments apart. She wanted to protect the memory, to keep it for herself, to hold onto it for warmth on cold nights when she really did worry perhaps everyone else was right, that she didn't deserve such attention. She may have sighed a little at that thought, because Luz glanced over at her. No, not at her, past her.

She followed her friend's gaze until it landed on Emery as she walked through the crowd toward her. Her heart beat faster as she approached, then stopped right next to the table. She gave a slight nod of acknowledgement to the others, but her eyes returned immediately to Arden. "Ms. Gilderson, I believe I have a promise to keep, and I'm so eager to do so. I hoped you might do the honor of giving me the first dance of the evening."

Arden's lips parted, but she couldn't manage to actually speak. She was vaguely aware of everyone's eyes on her and the sound of people shifting in their seats, but she couldn't make sense of any detail other than the dark chocolate ring of Emery's irises.

"What a lovely, if premature, offer," her mother answered for her with a tight laugh. "The music hasn't even started yet."

Emery first raised her eyebrows, then her hand, and with a mere glance at the band, a violin struck a chord, followed by an acoustic guitar, then a piano. Of course this woman could summon a melody by simply wanting one. The sound also broke the haze clouding Arden's brain, and she turned toward the dance floor to find it empty. "No one is dancing."

"Only because you haven't accepted my invitation." Emery paused for a beat before adding, "Yet."

"We'd be the only ones out there."

"Someone has to be the first, and then the rest will join in."

She realized the truth of Emery's words with sudden clarity. Surely everything in this woman's experience gave credence to the idea that all one had to do was lead and others would follow. She couldn't imagine what it must feel like to walk through the world with such self-assuredness, and this might be her only chance to actually find out.

Emery must've read her apprehension giving way to interest, because she extended her hand, palm up, and Arden placed her own in it.

She only had to accept the invitation, and Emery took over. In what felt like an instant, they were at the center of the dance floor and the apex of everyone's attention. Normally, Arden would've fainted at the thought of having every eye in the room on her, but as Emery slipped her other arm around her waist and gently eased her close, no one else in the room had any space to exist in her awareness.

They swayed to the music together. Just as Emery had assured, she needed only to lead, and Arden followed without so much as a conscious thought.

"How you doing?" Emery asked after a few seconds.

She nodded and managed to squeak out, "Good. You?"

Emery smiled. "I'm enjoying myself immensely, but I have to admit I wasn't sure you were actually breathing."

That might explain her lightheadedness, but then again, it could've also been Emery's proximity. Did one even need air when such a beautifully compelling woman pulled you into her arms? Surely the brush of her body offered something at least as sustaining as oxygen. "I'm not sure I have to."

"Well, that's a rather impressive skill. Tell me, what other ones are you hiding?"

"None," she said quickly.

"I don't believe you."

"It's true."

"What about the fact that you're a lovely dancer?"

"I'm not. You're leading."

"And you're moving with grace and ease. I think I'm going to have to twirl you."

"No." She shook her head. "Everyone's watching."

"Then let's give them a show."

"I'm not really a show kind of woman."

"Maybe you just haven't been given the spotlight often enough." With that, she extended and lifted her arm, then gave her a gentle push. Arden spun, her vision blurring momentarily, but she never wavered or wobbled. How could she, with Emery's arms to fall back into?

As Emery pulled her close again, she smiled down at her. "See, now that wasn't so bad, was it?"

She shook her head. "How do you do it?"

"Spin you? It's quick and easy with a responsive partner."

Her cheeks flushed at both the words 'responsive' and 'partner,' though for different reasons. "I meant, how do you manage to be so confident and smooth with all these people looking at you?"

A quick flicker of a shadow passed over Emery's expression before she glanced around a bit. Then, returning her attention only to Arden, she leaned a little closer and whispered, "Because they're not looking at me right now. They're looking at *us*. And for what it's worth, I wasn't thinking of them at all because I'm looking at you."

Chapter Four

"What the fuck?" Theo shot up from his desk before Emery even made it through the door to her suite of offices on Monday morning.

"Good morning to you too."

"Do you know how much time I spent making the reports on every eligible and suitable lesbian in all of Massachusetts?"

She grinned. "It was undoubtedly an epic undertaking, and I'd say a rather unqualified success."

He extended a hand with a coffee mug, and for a second, she wondered if he intended to throw it on her, but he only shook his head. "Was it?"

She'd thought so. She'd been in a great mood all weekend and had even shown up to work on time, eager to offer her report, but his tone suggested he had a few things of his own to report on. "Why don't you tell me?"

"Because you're going to listen this time?"

She accepted the coffee and tilted her head away from his reception area toward her own personal office. "Come on in, and probably close the door."

She shed her sport coat and tossed it onto one of the chairs in front of her desk and motioned for him to take the other.

"You know you're the talk of the whole town, and have been for the last two days, right?"

"I hadn't known, actually, but you have to admit, it's not unusual."

"No, and that's the point. You've got a reputation you're trying to break, and then you went and made a scene by fixating on the one woman I told you was the least advantageous to pair yourself with."

She sat in her leather high-back chair and tried not to fidget, even though it always felt a little too big and stiff for her. "I wouldn't say you put it quite that bluntly, and I don't think I fixated."

"Really? Because the room read it that way, which is what matters."

"I think my read on the situation should matter a little bit." She remembered Arden staring up at her, blue eyes full of wonder and adoration. "And probably some other women should get a say about the churning rumor mill as well."

"How many women?" Theo asked pointedly.

"What do you mean?"

"If you're being magnanimous about the agency of all the many women you interacted with for more than a few minutes in public with this weekend, what would that number be?"

She got the point, but he crossed one knee over the other and stared at her until it became clear the question wasn't rhetorical. "Well, I spoke to Isabella, and my mother—"

"Mothers don't count here."

"Okay, then two. I interacted with two of the women on your list."

"And would you say you split your time evenly between them?"

She rolled her eyes. "Why are you asking me questions you clearly already know the answers to?"

"I'm hoping you've just been your normal, impulsive self, and once you're forced to stop and think, or actually say these things aloud, you'll realize what you've done."

She rolled her eyes. "Why don't you just tell me what I've done."

"From what I heard from people at the event, you spent a whole five minutes talking to the absolutely perfect doctor,

53

then disappeared with the mousy woman who has no social skills."

"That's a bit of an overstatement."

"Which part?"

"The part about having no social skills. Arden's lovely and sweet, and yes, she's shy, but she's got this awkwardly honest, blunt sense of humor."

"I want you to replay the last part of that sentence in your head and ask yourself if 'shy,' 'awkward,' and 'blunt' is the kind of profile this company needs in the wife of a CEO."

She pressed her lips together tightly against the urge to clap back that she didn't give a damn what the board thought, because of course she did. Instead, she took a deep breath and sat back in the chair. "We had a really good time. The best night I've had since ... well, you know."

He softened his own posture as well. "As your best friend, I'm happy to hear it. I know the last month has been complete shit. You deserve something nice and easy and enjoyable, but as your administrative assistant, I'm also obligated to point out that the whole 'good time, playboy impulsiveness' is standing between you and the thing you claim is most important to you right now."

"I wasn't a playboy. I was a model of respectability. We chatted. We danced. We said good night. I didn't even kiss her goodbye."

"I'm not even sure what to do with that," Theo admitted. "You chose the most boring woman in the room, made her the center of everyone's attention, and then didn't leave with her? Nothing about that adds up for you."

She lifted a shoulder. "This girl's different, and I don't know why you assume she's boring. She's not. The rest of the crowd was. Do you know what Isabella and I talked about?"

He shook his head.

"The weather and her work schedule."

He grimaced. "Maybe if you'd given her more time?"

54

"What? We could've moved on to stock options and shoes? She's beautiful, but she's so polished and practiced. Arden was such a breath of fresh air. She held my attention in a room full of shiny people. Even you have to admit that's got to count for something if I'm trying to make a go at real relationships."

He sighed. "Yeah, you have the attention span of a gay club boy."

"Thanks."

"It's the truth, and I'm sort of conceding your point. If you can't find a woman to hold your attention for the next six months, then you'll only fuck this up even worse."

She clenched her teeth at the implication that she'd already fucked something up in order for there to be the possibility of making it worse. Then again, apparently her life up to this point had to have been a failure of some sort, or she wouldn't be in this position.

"Okay," Theo finally said resignedly.

"Okay what?"

"In addition to someone rich, well-connected, and locally based, we will also add 'holds your attention' to the list of key criteria."

"Don't you think it's a little odd it wasn't on there to begin with?"

He shrugged. "I've never arranged a marriage before. I'm still not sure any of this is even a good idea, but it's what we're doing, so do you think Arden fits the bill?"

"Honestly, I don't know. I haven't exactly been in this position before either. I've never drawn a profile of the type of woman I'd want to be with long term."

"You've got your motive now, but time's still short. I don't think you have the luxury of pondering," he said matter-of-factly. "You need to figure out quickly whether or not she's a viable candidate, because the longer you drag the process out, the harder it will make things for everyone."

She shifted in her chair. The last thing she wanted to do was make the situation worse, but she didn't love the idea of rushing into her first serious relationship, or talking about her prospects like some sort of business proposition.

Theo seemed to sense her growing discomfort. "Look, you don't have to actually marry this girl, right? See if you can make a good show of things until you get what you want. Take her out, talk to her, check your chemistry one-on-one."

She nodded slowly.

"And do it soon," he pushed. "The clock's ticking, and if Arden's not the right one, it's better to jump ship in shallow water. Do you think you could find it in your busy schedule to do a date later this week?"

"You keep my schedule," she pointed out with a little smile, both at the comment and the idea of seeing Arden again this week.

Theo pulled out his phone and tapped the screen a few times. "Tonight's out, too short notice, and no one does anything fun on Tuesday night. Wednesday you have dinner with your mother and Brian."

She frowned at that news. She consistently checked in on her mom, but with Brian there, the conversation would undoubtedly be all business and manners and polite small talk, the exact opposite of what she'd had with Arden on Friday.

"Thursday." He pulled her back. "You're open after three, and you don't have anything until ten on Friday morning. Thursday's a little early to start the weekend, but still totally respectable."

She hadn't known days of the week had varying levels of respectability, but she didn't argue. "Works for me."

"Shall I call and check her availability?"

"Nope. Get me the number and I'll do it."

He scrunched up his face as if trying to decide if she could be trusted with such a task.

"It's a date, Theo, not a business meeting. I'm not going to delegate my dates."

"Fair," he said, but as he closed the door to her private office, he cleared his throat and added, "for what it's worth, it's actually business *and* a date, so maybe, you know, don't lose sight of that."

She clenched her jaw, wanting to say so many things and yet not having the words or the fire to summon any of them. Instead, she gave a curt nod and made sure to close the door behind her.

☀ ☀ ☀

Arden didn't recognize the number on her phone, but it was local, and anyone seeking money or an appointment would've called her parents or their assistants. Still, she was so loath to speak to strangers she probably would've let it go to voicemail if not for Luz's habit of ending up in strange places and losing her phone, or simply grabbing someone else's. Steeling herself for literally anyone other than her best friend, she pressed the 'accept' button.

"Hello."

"Hi, Arden, it's Emery Pembroke."

Her mouth went dry at just the sound of Emery's rich, deep voice saying her name with such casual familiarity.

"I had a great time hanging out with you Friday."

Her head went a little light, and she backed up slowly until she leaned against the wall of her living room, just so she'd have something solid to prop herself up.

"And I thought maybe you and I could get together again later this week ... just the two of us ... Arden, are you still there?"

"Yes," she whispered.

"Good. So ..."

"Yes," she managed again, this time with only slightly more conviction. "To all of it."

"Oh." Emery's laugh was low and smooth. "Well, that's good to hear. Does Thursday evening work for you? Around eight?"

"Yes." She closed her eyes as if maybe this were a dream and she'd forgotten to close them, but if that were the case, she certainly didn't want to wake up now.

"Perfect, I'll swing by and pick you up."

"Um, do I need to—I mean, are there plans, or like, a dress code?"

"I was just thinking we could get a drink or maybe something to eat, not sure yet, but I know a club. Just leave it with me."

She nodded, even though Emery couldn't see her, and she hadn't exactly cleared anything up at all, but Arden didn't want to admit she didn't really know what any of that meant for what to wear. She didn't want to admit she wasn't prepared for any of this at all, and thankfully Emery couldn't seem to tell, but she managed to squeak out, "Perfect."

"Great, I'm glad you're amenable. See you Thursday."

She hung up, and Arden felt both elated and bereft at the briefness of her high. She'd never even thought to long for the sound of Emery's voice in her ear, but now that she'd experienced it, she didn't know how she'd ever go on without it.

She shook her head. That was melodramatic even for her, but seriously, how could she not surrender to overblown emotion in such an absurd situation. Emery'd just asked her out on a real date. The dance had been quite wonderful enough, more than she could really process. She'd only let herself remember it in small doses, and she hadn't spoken about it at all, much to Luz's displeasure. She simply couldn't handle reliving the feel of Emery's hand on the curve of her hip, or the husky timbre of her laugh, or the easy way she spun her out and pulled her back in again.

58

Arden sighed and allowed herself to slide down the wall until she sat on the floor with her knees curled to her chest. If she had to ration out her remembrances of a few dances in a crowded room, how did she have any hope of surviving an entire evening of Emery's undivided attention without her brain short-circuiting from the sensory overload?

"What's wrong with you?"

She glanced up to see her mother staring down at her. She blinked a few times, trying to make sense of the interruption more than the question.

"Did you fall?"

She shook her head.

"Did you have one of your little anxiety episodes?"

"No."

"Then why are you sitting on the floor in the library? You don't even have a book."

"Sorry," she said automatically, though she wasn't sure why sitting on the floor should offend anyone. Still, she pushed herself awkwardly up to standing.

Her mother simply watched and waited for more explanation.

"I got an unexpected phone call, and I just needed a moment to think."

"And the furniture was insufficient for your purpose?"

"I didn't consider any of it," she said honestly. She bent to retrieve her phone from the floor.

"Who could've possibly been so important as to make you literally drop everything, including yourself?"

She thought briefly about lying, but deceit was just one of many social wiles she didn't have the skill for. "Emery."

Her mother's eyebrows arched. "Emery?"

"Emery Pembroke."

"I gathered." Her mother walked deeper into the library and pulled back the heavy drapes to let some light in before

59

turning back to her. "And what did she have on her mind this morning?"

"She wanted to get together sometime, well, Thursday. She invited me out this Thursday. For drinks, maybe dinner, or a club." She'd hoped to sound as casual and smooth as Emery had. Instead, she conveyed nervousness and guilt.

"Of course she did." Her mother pinched the bridge of her nose. "Why?"

"What?"

"She's clearly taken a sudden interest in you since her father's death. Have you stopped to wonder why?"

She had, at least fleetingly, but she hadn't possessed the clarity of thought to make sense of much.

"It's not a long list, Arden." Her mother's impatience grew.

"I don't know, she's grieving, and she's working at the—
"

"No." Her mother raised her hand. "Stop. There's only one thing a woman like Emery wants from a girl like you."

Arden's face flushed, and she grew a little dizzy, but her mother rolled her eyes.

"It's not sex. Anyone with her looks and swagger gets that whenever she wants, which only leaves money."

She almost laughed, but she knew better. "Emery's family has plenty of money."

"There's no such thing," her mother said in the tone she might use with a silly child, "and when money is as new as hers, it only goes so far. You have the old kind of money families like hers can only dream of. You have pedigree. You have prestige. And it gives me no pleasure to say so, but you're just naive enough to fall for whatever she's up to."

"I'm not." The defense sounded weak, but she meant it. She'd never had any illusions of holding Emery's attention for long. She'd never even dreamed of holding it for a few minutes.

60

"You're more fragile than other girls your age, and much less experienced. Someone like Emery could pull you in over your head before you have a chance to fully grasp what you stand to lose. And I know you haven't gotten much attention, but you're very pretty when you try to be, plus you're kind and openhearted."

The words were right, but somehow in this context none of them quite felt like compliments.

"I don't want to see you get embarrassed."

She understood that to be code for not wanting to see the family embarrassed. "I promise I won't do anything rash or silly. You know I'm careful, and I don't ever want to be the center of attention. We're going to have drinks and talk." She shrugged partially to feign nonchalance and partially because she still wasn't quite clear on their actual plans. "Maybe we're becoming friends. Maybe she's just bored. I'm certainly not planning our wedding. You're the one always encouraging me to go out more often. Maybe this is a first step."

Her mother pursed her lips together for a second before nodding. "Fine, but mark my words, do not fall for this woman. She cannot possibly see anything in it but another rung on her social ladder. You need to set firm boundaries."

She forced out a strangled laugh, both at the idea that Emery could possibly need the likes of her for anything and the idea that she'd be able to deny her, even if that were the case. "It's just one evening. You know me. I'll probably be home in an hour."

Her mother's posture softened. "For once, I do take a little solace in your limitations and your easy acceptance of them."

She nodded, content to end the conversation without admitting that while she was endlessly aware of those limitations, in this case she ached not to accept them. For once in her life, she did wish she could simply enjoy the kind of little thrills other people took for granted, because ultimately she didn't care why Emery had suddenly grown interested in her, she simply loved that she had.

☀ ☀ ☀

"All right." Theo pushed a few more contracts across Emery's desk. "These are the last of the Bergman deal."

Emery ran her hands through her hair until her fingers curved around to her neck where they broke free of the tangles just above her collar. She wished she could detangle her work as smoothly. "Bergman, Bergman, Bergman."

Theo opened his mouth, but she shook her head. "Don't tell me. The Bergmans own a farm … near the Berkshires?"

"Nope, but I can see what your brain did there. These are the easements we needed for their farm in Western Mass," he supplied. "Mr. Bergman's the one with the mower concerns."

She rolled her eyes. "Right. He's holding up a multimillion-dollar solar installation because they don't like lawn mowers. Seriously?"

He nodded. "He says they're bad for the environment."

"You know what's bad for the environment?"

"Dependency on fossil fuels?"

She slapped her hand on the desk. "Bingo."

"Still, he wants us to send someone over with a manual push mower just to try it out before he sells."

"Is that something we can do?"

Theo shrugged. "You're the boss."

"Except I'm not." She sat back in her chair. "If I were the boss, I wouldn't be sitting here all day dealing with piddly complaints and kinks in the supply chain. Mom and Brian are spoon feeding me minor fusses while my dad was a visionary."

"One of the best," Theo agreed, "and he was also incredibly good at bringing people on board. You get that from him."

She shook her head, not able to respond for the sudden swell of emotion clogging her windpipe.

"It's true, which is why your mom kicked this can down the hall to you. She needs your skill set, and you need people to like you, to trust you, to put their faith in you."

She started to shake her head, but the sentiment reminded her of one person in particular she needed to like her. "Shit, it's almost six. I need to get out of here so I can shower and change before my date tonight."

Theo grimaced. "Actually, I wanted to talk to you about that little project as well before you go."

"Again?" She pushed back from the desk and rose. "We've been over it multiple times. Don't be rash, don't lose my head, just feel out the possibilities, keep my options open."

"All good points, and I'm glad you remember them, but there's one more, and it's a big one. You and I have been friends for a long time, right?"

"Like ten years."

"More like fifteen. We're getting older, and I think over the years we've both had our fair share of good times comparing notes on various escapades."

The corner of her mouth curled up as a slew of memories assaulted her. "So many escapades."

"And that, along with your mischievous smile there compels me to make a rather blunt point here."

"Which is?"

"You can't fuck this woman."

"What?" She laughed.

"It's not funny, Emery. I know you, what you're capable of, and trust me, I'm not judging."

"Sounds kind of judgy at the moment, which is interesting because you are just as—"

"I know." He cut her off. "I've had as many one-night stands as I've had second dates. I get it. Hell, I admire your skill. I'm envious even, but you have chosen to test the waters with this one, and while I'm still not in love with your choice, it is your choice, and I want you to be successful, which means you cannot come on too strong."

"I'm not like a predator or something. I'd never do anything she didn't enthusiastically consent to."

"And that's usually a great bar to set, but it's too low for your current scenario. Arden isn't like the women you're used to running with. She's not very experienced, and she's got a reputation for being nervous. You can't pour it on thick or you'll scare her off."

She grabbed her suit coat off the back of her chair. "She does seem skittish, I'll give you that, but she's also clearly enamored of me. I mean, you didn't see her last weekend." She wanted to make her point, but she'd also made a promise not to tell anyone what Arden had admitted about coming to the party specifically to see her. "Just know, I got all the green flags. She's already completely into me."

He sat back. "And you love nothing quite so much as being adored. Is that what sealed the deal?"

"What's that supposed to mean?"

"You jumped into this setup awfully fast without testing the waters, and I can't help but wonder if you didn't settle for her because she made it clear she wouldn't be a challenge for you."

She clenched her jaw, but she hadn't given it enough thought to deny the charge, and considering the tightness in her chest, she wasn't sure the barb hadn't landed squarely.

"Look, it doesn't matter." He shook his head. "Maybe it's even a plus quality for her to seem all in if you're going to convince people this relationship is a viable option. I'm only saying that there are dangers in moving too fast and breaking this girl's heart. The last thing you want is to be seen as toying with someone or leading her on."

She nodded, wanting to say she cared about more than appearance. She didn't want to actually do either of those things, but she couldn't rule out the possibility.

"The optics of a nasty breakup would be hard to overcome, and a scenario where you end up shattering the daughter of one of the most well-respected families in the region could sink you."

"Yeah." She managed to get the word out.

"Hey." His voice dropped. "I'm looking out for your interests here."

"I understand."

"Maybe if you'd gone with one of the other candidates who was more your emotional and social equal, you could've played the hot and heavy card, but Arden has a reputation for being mousy."

"Okay," she said firmly. "I get it. I appreciate your concern and the way things may appear, but let's not talk about her like she's a child."

"Fair enough," he conceded. "You know more about women than I do, because, honestly, I don't see the appeal when you stick them up next to all those Wall Street daddies who are starting to gray around the temples."

She snorted. "You're such a twink."

"To each their own." He shrugged. "I didn't mean to get paternalistic. I just want to make sure you remember Arden's not your usual fare, and you aren't used to playing the long game. Whatever instincts you have to bed her just because you can need to come second to the endgame. Pace yourself and keep your eyes on the prize."

He meant the company, the title, the legacy. She knew that, and still, when he said 'prize' she couldn't help but picture Arden in glittery light, her eyes, her dress, the way their bodies molded together on the dance floor.

"You get what I'm talking about?"

65

"Eyes on the prize." She smiled politely and moved toward the door. "Got it."

※ ※ ※

"Stop fidgeting," Luz commanded. "You look amazing."

Arden glanced over her shoulder at the trifold mirror in the back of Luz's design studio. She hardly recognized herself in the maroon dress. The hemline was respectable enough, but the slit up to her mid-thigh left her feeling exposed, and the large fashion belt cinched tightly at the narrowest part of her waist drew attention to curves normally well-hidden under baggy pants. "Are you sure it's not too much?"

"Not entirely," Luz admitted with a frown. "The agenda for the evening is a little vague for my taste, dinner and drinks are different endeavors, and 'club' could be like a dance club or a social club, and while I have tons of experience with the former, I've got nothing with the latter."

"If you're in over your head, what chance do I possibly have?"

"You have the *only* chance," Luz said seriously. "You're the woman on Emery's arm tonight, not me, not Isabella, not any of the other very willing volunteers. She chose you, and looking at you in that dress, I can totally see why. You're a fox. If it wouldn't feel like kissing my sister, I would totally hit on you."

She laughed, and tugged on the gap in the dress.

"I'm not joking. You're smoking hot right now, and here ..." She snagged a black velvet jacket off a chair. "If it's a social club and not dance club, throw this on, but for now, put it over your arm because I want her first look at you to be in this full-on gloriousness, and for the love of all things holy, stop trying to close that slit. Your legs are killer. Show some skin."

She blew out a slow, steady breath. "I'm not a skin kind of girl."

66

"Yeah." Luz rubbed the back of her own neck as if some tension might be building there. "I actually wanted to talk to you about that."

Her stomach tightened. "Oh?"

"You know I think you're the greatest, and Emery is lucky to have a shot at spending time with you."

She rolled her eyes. "But?"

"No buts. That's a full sentence. You're the pinnacle of best friends. So many people with your kind of life would've never given me the time of day when we were teenagers, much less stuck with me for years of wild ideas and dragging down your social cachet."

"Those people would've missed out on so much."

Luz smiled. "They would have, those assholes, but you're not like them. You see people, you understand things, you're so much bigger and more expansive than the role people expect rich girls to play. But, I also know you really like this woman, and Emery might be used to a different sort of way of interacting."

Her stomach did a little flop as she started to see where Luz was headed. "Faster women."

Luz shrugged. "I'm not sure that's the term I would've used, but yeah, basically. Certainly women with more experience."

Arden glanced back at her reflection in the mirror to confirm that she was blushing from her scalp to her neck.

"I'm not saying you have to sleep with her tonight, obviously. You're a fucking catch and totally worth working for. Don't ever sleep with anyone you're not completely aching to jump, but if you find that Emery does fall into that category, maybe, you know, don't wait."

She nodded. She understood the unspoken. She might not get a second or third date, so she should make the most of this one.

"I want you to have a shot at everything you've ever dreamed of, and if that's knocking boots with this fucking

67

dreamboat of a sexy human, let me be the person who encourages you to do so, not the person who overthinks and second guesses or bows to social pressure."

"Oh, did my mother call you too?"

Her eyebrows shot up. "What? No? I'd totally shit my pants if I got a personal phone call from Evita as she lorded her power from on high over the peasants."

"She's not that bad," Arden defended weakly.

"I'll be the judge of that. What did she have to say about tonight?"

"Basically that Emery's gold-digging new money who's using me to up her social standing, and when she gets the access she wants, I'll end up with a broken heart."

"Wow, that's ice-cold, even for Eva Perón." Luz laughed. "I think it goes without saying I also think it's incredibly dumb."

"Right. You think Emery's out for a piece of ass."

"I didn't say that. I honestly have no idea who Emery is or what she's after. I just know you, and I want you to get what you want. If that's a date, then go enjoy every minute of this one. If that's some sexy-hot fun times, then take that, right away. If you want to fall in love, that's up to you to assess the risks. I'll support you, always."

Once again, she got the sense Luz found two out of three of those possible outcomes more likely than the latter, but Arden wasn't naive enough to disagree. "Okay."

"Okay?" Luz didn't seem to find the answer sufficient.

"I'll think about what I want."

"And?"

"And try to take it."

"Take all of it, friend. Grab it with both fists and—"

"I said 'okay,'" she snapped, then caught herself. "I'm sorry. I'm just nervous."

"Don't be nervous."

"Telling someone not to be nervous doesn't actually help with nervousness."

Luz sighed. "I just want you to have fun, all the fun you deserve. This is a big night."

As if she didn't know that. She hadn't had a real date in years, and she'd never had one with the likes of Emery. She put plenty of pressure on herself; she didn't need it from everyone else too, and yet here she was, having her second conversation this week about how everyone else thought she should handle a situation she couldn't have even imagined being in four days ago. Their concern wasn't unwarranted. She had plenty of her own, but the more they butted in, the more they affirmed her own fears.

And with that happy thought, headlights swept past the front of the store windows.

"She's here," Luz said unnecessarily, as if there could've been anyone else swinging by in a red Porsche at this hour in downtown Amherst. "You're going to have a great time."

Arden nodded.

"She's here because she had fun with you."

Her nod grew a little more frantic.

"There's no pressure to be anything but yourself."

"Except I'm supposed to be sexier and more confident and assertive and totally sleep with someone on the first date, and—"

"Hey." Luz caught hold of her shoulders and gave her a little shake. "Breathe."

She sucked in a raw, deep breath that raked against her throat.

"Take another," Luz commanded.

She did as told, as usual. This one stretched her lungs to the point they protested.

"One more." Luz's tone dropped back into a more casual register.

She managed to inhale without anything shaking or burning.

"Okay?"

"Okay."

"She's waiting for you, Arden. Not me. Not your mom. You. Meet her in whatever way feels right in your bones. That's all I want for you, and if she's worth a damn, she will too."

She leaned forward and touched her forehead to Luz's quickly. "Thank you."

Luz grinned and released her. "You're welcome."

Chapter Five

"You look fantastic." The words tumbled out of Emery as naturally as an exhale. She didn't know that she'd had any conscious expectations for Arden's attire, but the dress exceeded them anyway.

"Thank, too," Arden said, then shook her head. "Sorry. Thank you, and you too. I started to say them both at once."

"I do that sometimes too."

Arden raised her eyes with both skepticism and hope. "Really?"

"Sure, doesn't everyone?"

"I don't know."

"I guess I don't either. I just assumed everyone's mouth got ahead of their brain occasionally, but now that I think about it, maybe that says something revealing about me." Emery laughed and opened the passenger side door for Arden to slide in, then closed the door and jogged around to the driver's side. By the time she slipped into the leather seat, Arden had already buckled up and turned to face her. "What do you think it says about you?"

She revved the engine and shifted directly into second gear as she took off down the town's main thoroughfare. "Probably something about needing to slow down or think? I'm sure my mother or my assistant would have plenty of thoughts on the subject."

"Do theirs matter as much as yours?"

She glanced over at the woman beside her. "You're not one for small talk, are you?"

"Sorry." Arden sat back. "I'm not very good at it."

"Excellent. Small talk is tedious."

71

"Honestly?"

"Sure." She shifted into third gear and broke the speed limit. "Wasn't I just saying I'm not one for easing into things. Hey, have you eaten yet?"

"No."

"Do you like Afro-Caribbean?"

"I don't. I mean, I haven't had it. I like most foods."

"Great. I know a club that's a little off the beaten path, but it's not far, and it's, like, wildly slick for the local scene." She took a turn with the speed and skill of someone who didn't mind a little drift.

"I'm sure I haven't been there."

"Pretty much no one we went to school with has. If you don't like it, we don't have to stay. I just thought, I don't know, you didn't seem to love being at the center of the social scene, and we definitely won't run into anyone who was at the benefit last week. It's mostly college students and some of the international faculty, along with an eclectic group of immigrants."

"Very different crowd," Arden agreed.

"Good different or scary different?"

"I guess it depends on who you ask."

Emery grinned. "I'm asking you."

"Oh," Arden said as if the news surprised her. "I don't know, but I think I might like to find out."

"Then we shall." She turned down another street, this one filled with student housing that gave way to low-rent multifamily homes, then warehouses.

Emery finally pulled into the lot of what looked like an industrial building, but she knew from experience had been rehabbed into a multi-use arts space. She parked between two trucks and killed the engine. She'd worried she might have to sell a woman from Arden's background on going into a place that looked like this on the outside, but she simply opened the door and climbed out without flinching.

Emery went to join her, offering a belated, "I promise it's way nicer on the inside."

Arden's eyes ran over her, from the tip of her leather oxfords to her tight-fitting navy slacks and her paisley dress shirt. "I sort of expected that from you."

She warmed under the appraisal and the confirmation she hadn't been totally off base when she'd told Theo that Arden seemed to know her own mind, at least when it came to attraction.

They walked toward a magenta door, the only splash of color on the entire facade, and were almost there when Arden wobbled and nearly went down. Emery caught her quickly by the elbow, pulling her close. "You all right?"

Arden's cheeks went as bright as the door. "Yes, I mean physically. How embarrassing."

"Are you kidding? You just traversed a gravel parking lot on stilts. I'm impressed."

"I don't wear heels often."

"I don't wear them ever," Emery said with a slight shudder, "but I'm glad you did, because you gave me an excuse to walk in here with a beautiful woman literally hanging off my arm. Really, you did me a favor."

Arden's eyes narrowed as if she didn't quite buy what she was selling, but she still accepted the elbow Emery extended to her and looped her own arm through. They both stepped into the club and paused in unison to adjust to the flashing, colored lights. The space was downright cavernous, starting with a large bar running the length of the massive room to their right. Further ahead, a set of tables teeming with people eating and laughing, gave way to an expansive dance floor, all under a ceiling full of mirrors. Towering above it all stood a stage filled with a jazz band currently showing off quite the horn section.

She began to bob her head as she wove through a throng of people waiting for drinks until she caught the eye of a young man dressed head to toe in white.

73

"Emery!" he called warmly.

"Julio," she greeted, then turned to include Arden. "We have a reservation."

"Of course, of course. Only the best." She saw him cast a sideways glance at Arden and nod appreciatively.

He led them to a table set atop a small riser, providing views of both the crowd and the stage. She glanced at Arden to see if she was impressed, but couldn't quite read her expression. The woman who'd peppered her with questions in the car seemed to have retreated behind a polite mask, eyes and mouth neutral with only a small crease in her brow, which could've signified either concentration or consternation.

Emery pulled out the chair for her and offered what she hoped was a reassuring smile. "The band's good."

Arden's smile seemed tight. "Very much."

Emery sat opposite her and leaned forward to be heard. "I love any music that's alive and vibrant, doesn't matter the genre. I think it's because I'm not musical at all in my own right, so I appreciate anyone who is."

Arden nodded.

"What about you? Any musical talent?"

"I play—" Arden's mouth kept moving, but her voice had grown so soft Emery couldn't hear a word she said.

"Sorry, what do you play?"

Arden scooted forward as much as the table would allow. "Piano and violin, but I'm not good at either."

"I suppose it's all comparative," Emery offered, and gestured to the keyboardist going to town on a solo. "Maybe you're not as good as he is, but you'd play circles around me. I can peck out 'Heart and Soul' that's all."

"It's something," Arden practically shouted.

The reply didn't give her much to work with, and she wondered if the noise might be too much to facilitate conversation. She'd brought other women here in the past, and it had never seemed like a big deal, but she remembered Theo's warning about Arden being different. "Would you like to go someplace quieter?"

She shook her head almost frantically. "No, no, not if you like it here. I, well, could I see a menu?"

Emery smiled and passed one over. "A woman after my own heart. I'm glad you're not one of those girls who doesn't eat on dates."

Arden raised her eyes in surprise. "Is that a thing? Is it uncouth to eat on dates?"

Emery laughed. "Maybe, but I hate it. Honestly, that's why I offered drinks first, because I always worry I'm going to take someone out to this amazing place with such fantastic food, and then I'll sit there with a whole platter of jerk chicken and jasmine rice while she regards me coolly over the rim of a martini or a side salad with no dressing."

Arden grimaced.

"Oh no. Were you going to order a side salad with no dressing?"

"No, I was going to get dressing on mine."

Emery's heart sank, but then Arden cracked a genuine smile and sent it soaring. "You're joking, right?"

She bit her lower lip before nodding.

Emery burst out laughing. "Well played."

Arden's smile grew, and so did a hint of confidence that Emery found absolutely alluring. "The king crab curry looks good," Arden finally said.

"It does," Emery agreed. "I'm thinking jerk chicken and lentils."

"I don't think I've ever had lentils."

"Then you'll have to try some of mine."

As if reading their minds, Julio appeared beside the table and took their orders, promising to let the chef know who they were for.

"Do you come here a lot?" Arden asked when he left them.

"I haven't been in town for long stretches of time the last few years, but I try to stop in when I can. I want to support innovative, local businesses. What about you?"

"I like that idea."

Emery waited for more, but when Arden looked away, she tried a more direct approach. "What are your favorite places to hang out?"

"Mostly my greenhouse or my library," Arden offered, and Emery's face may have relayed her surprise because she quickly recovered. "Oh, you mean hang out like out-in-public-out, didn't you? Wow, I just handled that badly, but, honestly, even if I'd understood what you meant, I wouldn't have had a more interesting answer."

"I don't know. I actually found your answer kind of interesting, certainly different from what I'm used to hearing."

"Because most people say someplace like this?" Arden swept her eyes across the room, squinting slightly into the red strobe lights flashing from the stage.

"No, I'm the only one who says places like this. Most people say some country club or social club or members only kind of place."

"My mother would've said one of those places."

"Oh, the one shooting daggers at me every time I spoke to you last week? She's kind of terrifying."

"She has strong opinions."

"Not always a bad quality in a woman."

Arden slouched back slightly. "So she tells me."

Emery's chest constricted at the resignation in the comment. "I take it you disagree?"

"I don't know. I guess that's the problem. I don't know much for sure, and it makes me seem weak."

Emery shrugged. "It could also make you open-minded."

76

She seemed to consider the point. "You think so? Also do you see how I just asked you to confirm your own opinion rather than giving my own?"

Emery laughed. "I did see that, and here's a thing you should know about me. I love to confirm my own opinions, always, and at the same time I'd like you to confirm them too."

Arden's smile returned. "I'm really good at agreeing with people, so as not to challenge anything."

"Well, I've recently been informed that's something I tend to excel at, not being challenged."

"Really? Who has the authority to say something like that to *you?*"

She grinned. "Quite a few people, actually, and several others have suggested it, but the blunt force trauma came from my best friend and closest colleague, Theo."

"You still run around with Theo?"

She arched an eyebrow.

"I just remember you with him at school. He's funny, right?"

"Don't tell him I said so, but yes, sometimes. Not as fun as he used to be, mind you, but still pretty funny. I forget we overlapped at school."

"I was easy to forget."

"Sorry." Emery cut back in with an almost knee-jerk reaction. "I know we're just talking about confirming opinions, but this is where you find out I only enjoy doing so when they're my opinions. Otherwise, I'm known for being rather argumentative, especially when I have such strong supporting evidence."

Arden shook her head as if the comment didn't make sense.

"I know for a fact you're not easy to forget. You weren't last Friday, and from the sight of you in that dress, you won't be tonight either."

77

Arden's cheeks colored so delightfully Emery couldn't resist pushing for more.

"In fact, I couldn't stop thinking about you. Looking forward to this evening has kept me going through several long, tedious meetings at work."

"Really?" Arden said the word with such quiet skepticism Emery had to read her lips.

"I swear. You're the only fun thing on my agenda all week."

Arden's lips parted as if she had lost her breath, and Emery's heart gave her ribs a little kick at the sight of her across the table, so pretty, and so unassumingly easy to please. Theo hadn't been off base in pointing out her differences from Emery's usual fare, but she doubted even he grasped all the ways that may actually appeal to her right now.

☀ ☀ ☀

Arden carefully spooned a mix of seasoned crab and rice into her mouth. She couldn't imagine who would be more horrified if she spilled food down the front of the dress, her, Emery, or Luz. So far she hadn't had any major disasters, but her lived experience suggested she wasn't capable of holding such a streak indefinitely. And perhaps her focus on avoiding the big slip up could account for the way the conversation had started to lag. Then again, as she glanced across the table to see Emery chewing to the rhythm of the music reverberating through the space, she realized maybe this woman was simply comfortable enough in her own skin not to need to prattle on endlessly or expect the same of her. The thought made her smile, and Emery caught her.

"You like the food?"

"It's very good," she said with honest enthusiasm, "but I was smiling at you."

Emery flashed her a wide grin. "Then let me return the favor."

Arden's cheeks warmed, but she tried to hold her gaze, at least for a few seconds, before looking away under the guise of inspecting the band. She took another bite with her due diligence not to drip, but she was starting to feel warm and full, and she didn't want anything to dull her senses tonight.

"Would you like to try mine?" Emery offered. "It's a little spicy, but not too much."

She nodded, not really processing the words so much as the joy she felt at Emery wanting to share anything with her.

She accepted the spoonful of lentils, and no sooner had her lips closed around it than she realized she'd made a mistake. Their definitions of "a little spicy" clearly varied greatly, and if she'd been with anyone else, excluding her mother, she would've spit the bite right back out again. Only she didn't want to do anything quite so humiliating in front of Emery, so she swallowed almost without chewing.

Everything burned the whole way down, but she gritted her teeth against the inclination to say so, pulling on every bit of social training she'd ever received to hide her abundant discomfort.

"What do you think?" Emery asked hopefully.

"It's really ..." She closed her eyes as if searching for the right word instead of trying to draw enough breath to speak. "Unique."

"In a good way?"

"Yes." She managed around a small cough. "So complex."

"Right?" Emery ladled a little more into her own mouth as if she weren't eating molten lava.

Sweat beaded on the back of Arden's neck, and her hair began to stick to it, but she prayed Emery wouldn't notice she was slowly cooking from the inside out as she reached for her drink. Downing the remainder of her water all at once, she moved on to the bottle of white wine Emery'd selected for them to share.

"You like the chardonnay?" Emery seemed pleased. "Go ahead and polish it off. I'm driving home, but hopefully not for a while, right?"

She smiled and drained the bottle, then sighed as the cool liquid washed over her still-steaming mouth.

Emery sat back and watched her drink half the glass at once. "You know, you seem really shy and reserved at first, but I think you're bolder than people would suspect."

She shook her head. "No, I really am very reserved."

"Maybe, but you're also game for a lot more than most of the women we know. I mean, you dig the music, you're an adventurous eater, you're not putting on airs."

She sipped the wine again, as the inferno in her stomach cooled with the injection of something akin to shame. None of those things were actually true, and she didn't want to lead Emery on, nor did she want to disappoint her. "I don't know that I would've done any of this without you. In fact, I'm sure I wouldn't have. Maybe my enjoyment has less to do with the activities and more to do with the company."

"Wow." Emery nodded appreciatively. "And you're smooth, too."

"Me?" She shook her head. "I'm the least smooth person you'll ever meet. I'm only being honest. You could've taken me anywhere tonight, and I would've been happy."

Emery seemed to consider the comment for a second. "You really don't have much pretense about you."

The way she said it didn't give Arden many clues as to how she should respond. "I suppose you're used to women who are much better at—"

"No." Emery cut her off. "I mean, maybe some of them are better at playing the games. I can't blame them. There's always a little thrill in a chase, but it's nice not to have to guess if someone's having a good time or playing coy or hard to get."

"I'm not adept at playing hard to get. I'm not very good at playing most things, really, or probably even at reading social cues. Usually I just state the obvious or put my foot in my mouth, like I'm doing right now, instead of just saying thank you."

"You have a long list of things you think you're not very good at."

She rolled her eyes. "You haven't even heard the start of it."

"I'd rather hear the other one."

"What other one?"

"The list of all the things you're amazing at."

"It's a much shorter list."

"What's on it?"

Arden shrugged. "I can't really think of anything."

Emery waited as if maybe she were just being humble, but the longer the silence grew conspicuous with only the sound of a saxophone solo filling it, the more insecure Arden felt. She couldn't think of anything, at least not anything worth sharing with someone as accomplished as Emery. Surely she wouldn't want to hear about gardening or poetry or her ability to evade social situations. Why couldn't she think of a single thing worth praising about herself? No, that was a rhetorical question. She knew the answer. She wasn't good at anything of value.

"You don't have to be modest around me," Emery nudged. "It's a virtue I've never connected to in any meaningful way."

"I'm not," she said, then added in a rush, "I wish I was good at something so much I can hardly stand it. If I were, I'd probably make sure the whole world knew."

Emery's gaze softened. "I believe you, honest, I do. But I think maybe you don't see yourself clearly. Maybe none of us do, or maybe that's something I just say to make myself feel better, but I could tell you something you're good at, or better yet, I could show you."

Arden arched her eyebrows. "Show me?"

81

Emery pushed back her chair and tossed her napkin on the table before rising and extending her hand. "Let's dance."

She let herself be led. She didn't really know any other way, especially not with her hand in Emery's. Still, even as she put one foot in front of another, a part of her brain screamed that she didn't actually know how to dance. Sure, she'd been able to hold her own with Emery's guidance the other night, but with the exception of one small spin, she'd had only to sway. This was a widely different situation with a proper dance floor pulsing with people and light. The bass beat made her temples throb, and if the song had a cohesive melody, she couldn't follow it.

Emery had no such issue. She closed her eyes and rolled her head as her body went almost liquid. Her frame moved with a loose sort of fluidity, and her dark hair shimmered in the flashing lights. Everything about her dripped with perfection, from her build to her grace, and, most of all, the complete absence of self-consciousness. Arden stood in awe of her, stockstill and staring, eager to imprint every detail from the slight part of her deep maroon lips to the way the open collar of her shirt revealed the hollow of her throat, to the roll of her hips as a Spanish guitar lick soared around them.

Then Emery's eyes flashed open, dark and sultry, and Arden's face flushed hot once more. She shuffled her feet from side to side, hyperaware of her high heels against the glassy surface below them. She became painfully cognizant that simply tapping her toes didn't actually constitute dancing, and the stark contrast between her own cautious movements and the total abandon of several people around her only amplified her self-consciousness.

She tried to rock her hips the way Emery had, but not only did the move feel halting and uneven, it caused the slit on the side of her dress to flap open, showing more skin than she ever wanted to. Still, she fought the urge to clutch at the pieces and hold them together, instead opting to back up in the hopes it may close on its own.

Only it didn't, and she bumped into the person behind her, and then stepping forward too quickly to avoid further contact, she landed right on Emery's toes.

"Sorry," she mumbled.

"What?" Emery asked, leaning forward.

"I'm sorry," she shouted.

Emery smiled sweetly and shook her head in a way that looked like another smooth dance move. She did a little turn and dropped lower at the same time the bass guitar did. Then, when both she and the music swung back up again, she slipped her arm around Arden's waist. The contact was so unexpected and easy, she wasn't even sure what had happened until she pressed close to Emery's body. If she'd been warm before, she was downright sweaty now, and she couldn't separate all the reasons why. The hot food, the heat of exertion, the flush of attraction, the burn of insufficiency, did any of the why really matter when the end result all culminated in perspiration soaking the back of her neck and the palms of her hands?

No. No. No. She felt herself slipping, but she couldn't lose it now. Mind over matter, that's what people always told her, though she'd never been sure what that phrase actually meant.

She grew light-headed from the overstimulation and leaned harder into Emery, who must've mistaken her instability for interest, because she deftly slipped one of her legs between Arden's and continued the same hypnotic groove. The room went red, then white, as her senses started shutting down. Her mother called these occasions "little episodes," but nothing about them felt small, on the contrary, everything seemed bigger, louder, more consuming the harder she tried to fight it.

She could hardly breathe, but the exquisite pressure of Emery sliding against her made a lack of oxygen seem like an insignificant concern right up until her head rolled forward onto Emery's shoulder.

"Hey." Emery seemed to sense something wasn't right, as her body tightened. "You okay?"

"Uh huh." Words were a little hard without air, but, then again, she must've been breathing at least a little because the scent of Emery's cologne still carried an intoxicating effect, spicy like cardamom and something deeper like amber or musk, or ... the thought floated through her haze that perhaps the base note was actually just Emery herself.

Her knees went weaker, and Emery leaned back far enough to look into her unfocused eyes.

"Need a break?"

She did. There wasn't any doubt, but the fortitude it would've taken to say so escaped her. She didn't want to make a hard decision right now, or set boundaries. She didn't want to be in over her head. She wanted to stay in those strong arms, and, at the same time, she wished she could do so without feeling like she might fall apart completely. Moreover, she wanted some assurance that if she wimped out after one song, it wouldn't be the last she ever got with Emery.

What had Luz said? Something about not holding back, or maybe it'd been something about only getting one chance to grab what she wanted. She couldn't really remember, neither could she process her options for blending what she wanted and what she actually had the capacity to handle, because those things seemed to be in conflict.

As if to drive home the unwelcome point, someone bumped into her from behind, knocking her off her heels. If not for Emery already holding onto her, she would've gone sprawling. She managed only to lose her balance, followed by a wave of dizziness that suggested the fall might quickly become a faint.

Then suddenly she was moving. Not dancing, actually moving off the floor. She opened her eyes more fully. The whir of people and lights made her close them again, but she

84

succeeded in making her feet move in tandem with the ones on either side of them.

"Hang on." Emery said the words so close to her ear they blew across her neck like a cooling breeze.

"Julio, get the door."

The person on the other side of her stepped away, and then there actually was a cool breeze, and while it didn't feel as good as Emery's, this one hit her whole body at once. When her lids fluttered open once more, the bright lights were gone, and the bodies were too, save for Emery's.

They were outside, the cool dark of night around them.

"You okay?" Julio asked, and she turned to see him holding open the door to the club.

"I'm so sorry," Arden gushed, but he looked right past her to Emery.

"We're great." Emery laughed nervously. "We're just too hot for the dance floor to handle."

Surely he didn't believe such a silly explanation, but he apparently respected Emery enough to leave them alone, and once the door clicked closed behind him, Arden doubled over. "Oh, how embarrassing."

"Not at all."

"Yes," she argued forcefully, "you don't have to pretend I didn't just panic almost to the point of passing out. I've been horrified enough in my lifetime to recognize those situations when they arise. Remember earlier when you asked what I was good at?"

Emery nodded.

"Well, you just found it. I'm exceedingly well versed at making a fool of myself in social situations. God, everyone saw you drag me out of there. How did you not just leave me on the floor? Aren't you freaking out right now?"

"Arden, it's okay," Emery started, then shrugged. "I'm not the kind of person who shies away from a little bit of a scene."

She shook her head. "Then I'm sorry again, this time for misleading you into thinking I could handle any of this, because I am absolutely the kind of person who does shy away from making scenes."

She sighed heavily. "All right. Come on. Let's get you home."

She bit back a sob, because no matter how much of herself wished she could be someone else sometimes, she knew her boundaries enough to realize when they'd been crossed. "Yeah, we better."

Chapter Six

They rode through town at a much slower speed than they had earlier, as Emery replayed the night trying to figure out where it had gone off the rails. Dancing had clearly been a bad idea, though she wasn't sure why. Arden had tensed up as soon as they set foot on the floor, but she hadn't been as chatty before that. In hindsight, she'd grown a little halting and quiet over dinner, and she had downed the wine with unexpected fervor after only having sipped before dinner. She'd never complained though. Most of the women she knew tended to make their displeasure known at the slightest opportunity, and even the ones who tended to go with the flow wouldn't have done so to the point of losing consciousness.

What kind of person would drive themselves to the point of physical failure just to keep the peace?

"I'm sorry," Arden whispered for about the hundredth time.

"It's okay." Emery used her most soothing voice. "You don't need to apologize to me anymore, or ever really."

"I knew I probably wouldn't be able to keep up with you." She went on in a small voice. "I should've said so. I didn't want to let you down."

"You didn't," she said more emphatically. Arden kept staring out the window, so Emery reached over and took her hand, giving it a tight squeeze. "If anything, I let you down. I'll do better next time."

"That's not true."

Her chest tightened. "Which part?"

Arden finally glanced at her. "The first part, but it's very nice of you to pretend there will be a next time."

Emery turned down a state highway and headed out into the country before asking, "Do you want there to be a next time?"

Arden laughed humorlessly. "I think tonight's a good indicator of how what I want and what I can do don't always line up."

The comment struck Emery as profound, and she was still pondering it when Arden went on.

"What's the use in doing this? This is not my first failed date."

"And here I was thinking the whole too-hot-to-handle thing made me special."

"I appreciate your trying to inject some levity into the situation. If I didn't already think you were special, I certainly would now, but that's all the more reason to ghost me."

"Ghost you?"

"I think we've had enough awkwardness without adding a conversation about all the reasons this isn't going to work."

"Arden." Emery didn't even know what to say. It wasn't as if she hadn't done it before, but hearing the expectation spoken so clearly, without any emotion other than exhaustion, didn't feel right. "I'm not going to ghost you."

"Why? Do you make a habit of hanging around women who have panic attacks after a single dance and one spoonful of spicy lentils."

Again, she had a hard time answering, not because she didn't know, but because she did. She'd walked away from women for much less, only this time, she wasn't sure she wanted to, and even if she did, what would that mean for her life, her business? Theo would tell her to get out now. She wasn't in too deep. They'd had one rough date, and Arden seemed fully invested in letting her off the hook. It would be so easy to back out, but as she pulled between two ornate gates onto Arden's family estate, she found herself finding reasons not to.

"It was just a little too much," she said slowly. "I had a really nice time with you over dinner. I like talking with you, and whatever you think about my type, I don't know, maybe I do have one, but I think you're very pretty."

Arden eyed her suspiciously, and why wouldn't she with such a weak defense. *Very pretty?* Not exactly the cleverest of compliments, but she didn't know what else to say. Nothing that had happened tonight had made much sense. Maybe Arden wasn't the only one who'd ended up in over her head. She wasn't sure what she should do, but as she pulled up in front of the sprawling mansion, she didn't want to do nothing.

"Can you go around back?" Arden asked.

"Sure. You don't use the big entrance with the castle doors?"

"The rest of the family does."

"Why not you? Too formal?"

"Partially, but mostly I don't use it because if I went in through the front of the house, I'd have to walk past too many rooms. This early, someone's bound to pounce and badger me with questions, and right now, I'd rather go wallow in my own embarrassment."

Emery tightened her grip on the steering wheel as she pulled to a stop near a back door with a single gas lamp alight overhead. Turning off the car, she unbuckled her seat belt and turned to face Arden with all the earnestness she could muster. "Can I walk you to the door?"

"Why?"

"Because I want to? Because I'm trying to figure something out? Because, I don't know, maybe I want another couple minutes together?"

Arden started to shake her head, but she said, "Okay."

They didn't have far to go, but Emery extended her arm, and Arden took it as they strolled a few steps toward the house in silence. As they stepped into the soft cone of yellow light, Arden turned to face her but didn't meet Emery's eyes. "I know

I'm not supposed to apologize anymore, but I very much wanted tonight to end differently, or maybe I wanted to be someone different for a while."

Emery understood the sentiment even if she still didn't understand where they'd gone wrong.

"I guess the flip side of 'I'm sorry' is 'thank you,'" Arden finished.

"Is it?"

"A therapist told me that once. Instead of saying 'I'm sorry for almost fainting on you,' I can say, 'Thank you for getting me home safely.'"

Emery nodded. "I kind of like that."

"I'm glad I can leave you with something to like."

She gritted her teeth against the emotions pushing up in her. She needed time to think. She'd promised Theo she'd be smart and careful, but she didn't have it in her to leave this woman on that note. "I'm not going to ghost you."

Arden closed her eyes and tilted back her head, and she was so damned beautiful, even in all her anguish Emery wanted to take hold of her, to pull her in, to kiss away the cloud of confusion that had enveloped them.

"You don't have to go out with me again because you feel bad," Arden whispered.

"I won't. I mean, I don't know when I'm going to see you again, or under what circumstances. My life is kind of chaotic right now, and I've got a lot of pressure and people— I'm not making excuses. I just want you to know that if I get busy at work or some time passes—"

"It's okay," Arden offered again and all too quickly for Emery to even figure out how she intended to end her previous thought. "If you ever do want to get ahold of me again, you'll know where to find me."

"Where?"

Arden pointed to a window on the second floor, with the outside curved like a little turret surrounded with windows. "I'll

90

be there, in my tower, with my books and my plants to keep me company, like Rapunzel."

Emery smiled at the image of Arden sitting at a window seat with a book, waiting for someone to come along and convince her to lower her guard. She reached out her hand and gently trailed her fingers through strawberry blonde strands all the way past her shoulders, and then held up just the end. "It is beautiful hair, but it's not long enough for me to climb, Rapunzel. You're going to have to meet me halfway so we can have a second date."

"Why would you want a second date?" Arden asked, then shook her head before Emery had a chance to answer. "No, never mind. Don't tell me. I don't think I want to know the real answer, and I don't want you to lie to me."

"What do you want?" Emery whispered.

Arden closed her eyes as if considering the question, before allowing them to flutter open again. "If this is really the last time I'm going to see you, could you kiss me goodbye?"

Emery started forward, but just before their lips met, she took a step back, startling them both. "That's the first time I have felt so much as a prick of disappointment in you, because I do think I would have liked to kiss you good night, but since you added that caveat, I cannot."

Arden's pupils went dark, and she wobbled slightly as if her knees might be giving out on her again, but Emery slipped an arm around her waist, pulling her close and relishing the way her body went all supple against her own. She felt Arden's breath catch as Emery lowered her head to her ear and whispered, "Good night, Arden. Not goodbye."

Then, going slowly to make sure neither of them would teeter or fall off the edge they seemed to be standing on, she stepped back and turned to go. She didn't need to glance over her shoulder at the woman leaning against the stone wall, small in the shadow of the big home. She'd seen everything she needed to   when   she'd   looked   into   her   eyes.

☀ ☀ ☀

"Arden, is that you?" her mother called from down the hall, but she didn't say a word. Slipping out of the torture heels that had damn near been her undoing several times over the evening, she padded barefoot up the stairs, and slunk past her father's personal den before easing open the door to her own room with great care and patience. She didn't have it in her to see anyone now, or ever again for that matter. She slipped out of the dress and dropped it on the floor, not even caring what Luz would say if she knew. She didn't care what Luz would say about anything ever again. She'd encouraged her on this fool's errand.

You should totally sleep with her tonight.

What an idiotic assertion. They both knew she couldn't pull that off. She couldn't even make it through dinner and a single dance, and now Emery knew it. She'd seen the concern in her dark eyes and heard the strain in her voice, and it would be ages before she could keep herself from physically cringing at those memories.

She climbed right into bed and pulled the down comforter all the way up over her head. A part of her was glad a person couldn't die from shame, but another part of her might've welcomed it. How would she ever show her face in public again? Even when Emery had tried to be polite, and she had made a valiant effort, Arden could clearly read the hesitation in her usually confident mannerisms. It might've been easier if she'd just registered her disgust plainly, then, at least, the break would be clean. But no, they'd both stood there, twisting in emotion, and tying themselves in knots trying to let the other down gently.

Why did Emery have to be so perfect and kind and considerate even in the most heart-wrenching moments? It only served to remind Arden how entirely out of her league she was.

Emery had more social grace in a single moment than she'd been able to summon all night, which only made Arden admire her more while respecting herself less.

"Ugh." She tossed onto her side and caught a mouthful of her own hair. She exhaled in frustration but only managed to make it flutter in her face. Reaching up, she pushed the strands roughly back, tangling her fingers, and ... she sighed. Emery had run her hand through her hair. Her heart seized, this time with something other than shame. Why had she done that? Why pull her close when she'd had every excuse to push her away?

Her body had ached for her, positively hummed with longing, and those full, maroon lips brushed so close to her ear. She groaned at the memories that would make this so much harder. To have her so close, to hear whispered promises she couldn't possibly mean to keep, and even if she did, how could Arden survive any more of what had almost broken her? Emery couldn't come back, she just couldn't, and she didn't even want her to. Not if it would only be more of the same. No, she couldn't keep fantasizing about a woman who lived up to every schoolgirl daydream when Arden had managed to turn every minute together into her actual lived nightmare.

No. Emery wouldn't come back. She would think less of her if she did.

She grabbed the pillow and pulled it tightly to her face before screaming.

Chapter Seven

"So?" Theo arched his eyebrows as Emery pushed through the door to their office suite.

Emery shook her head and went straight to her own space.

"Uh-oh." Theo hopped up and followed, closing the door behind them. "What happened?"

"I don't even know."

"Why?"

"I just, I have been over and over it all night, but ..." She flopped into her chair and twirled in a circle twice before grabbing hold of her desk. "That's what the whole night felt like, dizzying."

"I don't get it."

"Me either. I'm charming, right?"

He snorted.

"And kind, and thoughtful, and—"

"Yeah, yeah, a real prince among men. What happened?"

She sighed and launched into a painfully detailed account, from the way Arden looked in that dress, to the way she'd teetered in the heels, and how the conversation had never faltered right up until the point where it stopped, and she'd watched the woman she'd been with disappear into the girl who'd nearly fainted rather than admit what sort of disaster had silently caught hold of the evening.

She may've skimmed over a few parts right at the end, though. It didn't seem right to tell Theo about the pleading or the resignation in Arden's voice as she'd asked her to kiss her goodbye, and her own inability to grant that wish because of what it would have meant, and how she wasn't ready, though she still couldn't say why.

"Holy fuck, this so much worse than I feared. How'd you leave it?"

"I said I had a lot going on at work and I'd be busy for a while."

"Good. Good. Well done."

"I also told her I'd see her again."

"Right. Like a noncommittal, someday, somewhere, maybe at a party, who knows kind of see her again. Nice."

She shifted in her chair to the point where it squeaked, and he eyed her with more suspicion. "You're going to ghost her."

"Well, I mean, she seemed to expect it, but—"

"No buts," he said forcefully. "You tried. You kept an open mind, but you cannot date a woman who's going to keel over in public. That's not fiancé-to-the-CEO kind of material. Time to cut your losses."

"Cut my losses? She's a person, not a business proposition."

"She is absolutely a business proposition. You only went after her because you got an ultimatum from the board of directors. You've known this woman since like eighth grade, and you never once gave her so much as a glance until I put together a dating resume to mesh with your public image ... which she doesn't."

She didn't argue with any of his points. She couldn't. Theo was usually right, and any shred of levelheadedness she still possessed screamed at her to take his advice. She had no logical reason to chase Arden anymore, period, but especially now, with everything else going on. And yet, when she'd pulled her close last night, logic hadn't registered in her at all. Emotion had.

Arden had felt small and vulnerable, but also beautiful, frail but not broken, weak but also profoundly good. What's more, she'd looked up at Emery like she might be able to walk on water, and while she was self-aware enough to realize that sort of adoration might be problematic, she also craved it. Was it so horrible to have a beautiful woman who believed you were better than you actually felt?

"You're going to ghost her," Theo repeated. "You said she basically expects it."

"Yeah. She does."

"And it's not like you haven't done it to plenty of other women over the years."

"I have." She didn't add that it had never felt quite so shitty, or that she'd never even given those women enough thought for it to register much at all. "I just feel scuzzy with this one."

He rolled his eyes. "She's used to it. You're used to it. I don't see why you need to grow a sense of chivalry now with so much more at stake, unless you're trying to sabotage your chances of taking over your father's company."

She shook her head even as her chest tightened. She didn't want to give that question any credence, so she leaned forward. "What's on the docket for today?"

"The Bergman contract, but I didn't exactly hear a resolution to the whole Arden debacle. I need to know you're still in this to win it."

"Yeah, of course." She tried not to grit her teeth as she spoke. "I want to be CEO. I want to be good at it."

"And Arden won't help your chances."

"Probably not."

He narrowed his eyes. "And you're not broken up about this, right? I mean, after one bad date, you're not into that hot mess scene."

"Nah." She sat back. "You know me. I get wild ideas, but I've never had trouble abandoning them before."

"Like the time you were going to build your own sailboat, or when you thought you might backpack across Europe?"

She forced a little smile. "Probably. I guess I just enjoyed the idea of being liked right now."

His expression softened. "You are liked. Is this about the board not trusting you? Jeez, did that hurt your feelings?"

She laughed. "No. It pissed me off. And it hurt my mom, and that's all the more reason for me to get back to work, like actual work. We'll review the Bergman files and try to figure out what's behind this dude's fear of lawn mowers."

"Yeah, I mean, maybe the whole wife life plan isn't actually the path of least resistance. If you glad-hand your way out of a major land deal debacle, maybe the trustees won't care as much about who you're dating anyway. Then we can look back at the female files after lunch, too."

"Ew, don't call them that, but also, sure, there's nothing wrong with covering all our bases." She said the words easily enough, and she must've sounded more resolved than resigned, because Theo finally nodded as if he couldn't tell a movie of Arden was still flickering through the back of her brain. She could pretend with the best of them. She'd grown adept at faking confidence, or when that failed, apathy. It's what everyone wanted from her, and she could give them what they needed to put their minds at ease without any of them knowing what she'd already promised Arden. She wouldn't do exactly what everyone expected of her.

※ ※ ※

"I can't believe you kept all of this from me for almost a full week," Luz said, and she must've really been taken aback because she actually leaned against a window box filled with damp soil. She would've never risked getting her leather pants wet if she were in her right mind. "I mean, if I hadn't barged in here looking for the dress I lent you, would you have ever volunteered the story?"

97

"I didn't volunteer it today. You said yourself, you barged in, and then you badgered it out of me." Arden pressed a dahlia bulb into the patch of ground she'd tilled earlier in the day and covered it, envious of its ability to hide underground for an entire winter before anyone expected anything of it again.

"I don't even know what to make of any of this. You started strong, then turned into a full-on disaster-gay stereotype, and yet, she still finished like some sex dream that ends just before you, well, finish, which is good. But now she's left you all hot and bothered for six days?"

"Seven," Arden corrected. "Today's day seven."

"And she hasn't called or texted, or, I don't know, sent any sort of word?"

"Unless I missed a message via carrier pigeon."

Luz folded her arms across her chest. "It doesn't make a whole lot of sense."

"No, I've moved past the point of trying to find logic in any part of the experience. Not my behavior, or hers, or the aftermath. I mean, other than the part where she ghosted me. That makes a ton of sense."

"But she swore she wouldn't."

She rolled her eyes. "What else was she supposed to say? 'Sorry crazy-town, I am totally never calling you again.'"

"But, the whole kiss thing?"

"She clearly didn't want to kiss me. And seriously, why would she? What a stupid thing to even ask for. I think I'm more embarrassed about that than her having to carry me out of the club. I asked a woman to pity-kiss me." She covered her face with her dirty hand. "Who does that?"

"I kind of like the boldness. I mean, you'd crashed and burned, so you didn't have anything to lose."

"Just the remaining shreds of my dignity." She pushed herself up off the dirt and wiped her hands on her jeans. "The thing is, I gave her at least ten chances to get out, and I wouldn't have thought any less of her if she'd bolted. Honestly, if I

98

could've run away from myself, I would've done so way earlier in the evening. I guess she's too nice or polite or uncomfortable in the face of awkwardness, but I am disappointed she pretended she'd be back. I always admired that she didn't seem to play the same games the rest of our crowd does, with saying one thing and then doing another."

"I don't really know her, but something about the way she carried herself suggested a straight-shooter mentality. Maybe something honestly came up."

She turned on the hose and misted the quadrant of the massive flower bed she'd been planting for the last few hours. The repetitiveness of the task had helped settle her mind, until Luz had arrived and made her relive the thing she'd been trying so hard to avoid. "Please don't make excuses or try to get my hopes up again. I want to go back to knowing I'm not good enough for her."

"That's bullshit. You're too good for her. Especially if she's running lines and playing games."

"She's only done what any reasonable person would have done." Arden turned to collect the hose and the blanket she'd knelt on before picking up the book she'd brought out with her but hadn't been able to focus on. She set both on the low, stone wall around the flower bed before turning back to Luz. "You know, in some ways it's pretty kind of her not to tell me in person that I'm too weird to be around."

"You're only weird in the most wonderful ways, and besides, you were fucking hot in that dress. If she didn't want to tap that bad enough to deal with your subpar dance skills, maybe she's weird."

She actually laughed. "I love you so much for twisting the situation so wildly that my greatest fault was my dance skills or lack thereof, but, honestly, it's okay. I didn't have Emery in my life two weeks ago, and now I don't again. I deeply and profoundly wish I hadn't humiliated myself in the interim, but anyone with a brain could've seen it coming, and no one's surprised I couldn't hold her attention. If you'd told me last Thursday this was how it'd all end, I would've called that revelation the least shocking spoiler in history."

Luz opened her mouth as if she intended to argue, but eventually she sighed. "I'm still really proud of you for trying."

Arden couldn't agree. She wasn't proud of anything about her actions, not her absurd hope or the way she'd floundered, or the way she'd practically begged to be kissed even after she'd already been idiotic enough for two lifetimes, and certainly not the way she'd lain in bed for days replaying the feel of Emery's fingers through her hair.

"I mean it." Luz clasped a hand on her shoulder. "Going out with her was a huge step, and I know it didn't end how either of us hoped, but you actually dated the hottest lesbian in Massachusetts for a hot minute. How many women could say that?"

"Um, probably a lot of them."

Luz smirked. "Okay, maybe, but I'm not one of them. And I've never been to that club or ridden in a Porsche or had someone even offer to climb a tower using my hair, even if they didn't actually get around to trying. A week ago, you wouldn't have thought any of that within the realm of possibility for yourself."

"Probably not."

"You might not be a baller, but you're capable of more than you give yourself credit for. No matter how this ended, I'm in awe of you for going all in, and anyone with half a brain would be too."

Arden smiled weakly. "You're my best friend. You have to say that."

"What if I said it?"

Both of them jumped at the sound of the low, rich voice, and whirled around to see Emery leaning against the short garden wall next to Arden's blanket and book.

Arden gasped. "What are you doing here?"

100

Emery grinned. "It's nice to see you, too."

"I didn't mean it that way ... well, actually, I did."

"Fair enough. I was driving by on my way back from a site visit for work. You know, the job I mentioned being very busy with this week."

"Right." She nodded. "How'd it go?"

"Absolutely terrible. I may've single-handedly endangered a multimillion-dollar project, thanks for asking."

"I'm so sorry."

She waved her off. "Everyone sort of expects it, but as I drove up the road feeling mildly pouty and overall sorry for myself, I thought, you know what? The day doesn't have to be a total loss. I bet Arden would be happy to see me."

"I am," she practically gushed. "Always."

"I don't know. I think I might've misread the situation because I caught fragments of your conversation, and it sounded a bit like you didn't believe me when I said I'd be back." She turned to Luz. "Am I wrong?"

Luz shook her head. "Pretty much nailed it."

"Traitor," Arden whispered.

Emery laughed lightly and picked up the book, turning it over to look at the cover for a second before meeting her eyes again, all dark and intent. "You underestimate me, Arden ... and yourself."

"Me, yes. You? Never."

"No, I think you do." Emery's tone took on a hint of teasing. "And you know what? It's fine. I'm actually getting that a lot right now. Most people don't have much faith in me, and I suppose I understand."

"Why?" She couldn't imagine anyone not believing in Emery, especially as she stood there all casual and close, the late afternoon sun glistening off her dark hair.

"Between the three of us, and pretty much everyone else at work, I'm not exactly crushing the whole CEO-in-training thing. Then there's the fact that I haven't made a habit of

101

sticking around town much, combined with all the expectations that come with being the hottest lesbian in all of Massachusetts."

Luz practically choked on her own laughter. "You've been standing there a long time, haven't you?"

"Can you blame me for eavesdropping on such an engaging conversation?" Emery didn't look the least bit chagrined, and Arden couldn't keep herself from being drawn to her confidence even in the face of her own resurgent embarrassment. A part of her wanted to crawl into one of the holes she'd recently dug in the ground, but a bigger part of her wanted to beg Emery for one more chance. Instead, she stayed rooted right where she was.

"Maybe I should go and let you two chat," Luz finally said.

"No," Emery said lightly. "I can't stay this time, but maybe now you'll believe me when I say I'll be back?"

Arden pressed her lips together and nodded. So much for not getting her hopes up.

Emery flashed one more big grin her way before turning to go. "See you, Luz. See you sooner, Arden."

They both watched her stroll across the grounds as if she owned the place, easy, calm, self-assured. It took a full minute after her departure for Arden to draw an even breath, and when she blew it out, she worried she might sink all the way to the ground. It was only the residual horror of almost fainting last time that kept her upright as she turned to Luz, who wore a mystified expression.

"What was that?" Arden finally asked.

Luz laughed and spun in a giddy circle before saying, "Everything."

※ ※ ※

Emery pulled up the driveway of her parents' house, or rather now, her mother's house. She supposed it was also hers, as she currently resided there, but she didn't feel any ownership over it, especially tonight as she walked through the front door like a guest. She couldn't help noting the contrast between this and her arrival at Arden's. The Gilderson place was much more formal with its grandiose grounds and nearly gothic architecture, whereas her grandfather had built his sprawling mansion with an eye toward the natural world that had granted him his fortune. Warm light radiated out from lofty timber rafters and stone pillars. She greatly preferred his style, and yet Arden's presence had made her arrival there feel much more welcome than the team waiting for her as they entered the large living room she'd grown up playing in.

Her mother, Brian, and Theo all glanced up at her expectantly, but with none of the light in their eyes Arden had directed at her. While they all waited with guarded expressions, none of their breath had caught in anticipation or pleasure at the sight of her. And while she certainly had their attention, none of them regarded her with hope or amusement.

She walked to the bar cart in the back of the room and poured herself a glass of bourbon. She didn't relish what would come next, and yet the corner of her lips curled up as she slipped a book from under the arm of her coat. A collection of nature poems from New England. What a perfect companion to a woman up to her elbows in soil, a wildflower in her own right, spindly and blown by the wind.

"Does that little smile come with happy news?" Brian finally asked.

She turned to see them all watching her, and shook her head, both to convey the negative response and to clear her brain of the images of Arden in her element. "No, the meeting went exceedingly worse than anticipated."

They all sagged, and their disappointment filled the room like an oppressive heat. She shed her coat and loosened her tie in the hopes of bearing it better, but the sense of restraint persisted. "I admit, I didn't read the situation well."

"What happened?" her mother asked softly.

"I didn't honestly believe a farmer, someone who professes a deep attachment to the land, would really turn down both money of this magnitude and the chance to see his legacy protected with a long-term commitment to green energy. I didn't think he would really sacrifice a sustainable future over a fear of lawn care equipment. I thought for sure his hesitance had to be about something else, so I said so."

Her mother groaned, and Brian rose off the couch so he could pace. "It's okay."

"No, it might not be." She took a healthy swig of her drink. "When I suggested he might be angling for something else, Mr. Bergman took quite a bit of offense."

"How so?" Theo asked.

She recalled in great detail how the man's face had gone red and the veins in his neck had stood out as he explained rather forcefully that he wouldn't be called a liar on the land his family had worked for four generations, and if she didn't honor that tradition enough to treat him with respect, he'd rather donate his property than take all the money in the world from some hotshot city kid in a suit who'd never worked a day in her life. "Let's just say I made some considerable miscalculations and put the entire project in jeopardy."

Her mother gasped.

"I'm going to fix it." She didn't know how, but she didn't want to say so with all eyes on her.

"I can help," Brian offered. "I haven't met Mr. Bergman yet. Your dad was handling his account personally, but we had spoken about him."

"Dad was working this account himself?" No one had told her.

"He specialized in tough customers," her mother said with a hint of wistfulness. "That's why we thought you might be well suited to take over the contract."

Her stomach churned. She'd been given her first chance to step into his shoes personally, and she'd failed. "Great."

"Hey." Brian clasped his hand on her shoulder. "We didn't want to pressure you."

She shook her head. If that were the goal, they were apparently as bad at their jobs as she'd proven herself to be at hers.

"It's going to take time," he continued, then glanced at her mother. "Maybe we'll give it a couple of days, then the two of us can reach out to him, perhaps take a trip out in a week or so. That'll give us all time to brainstorm and him a chance to cool down."

"I don't know what there is to brainstorm. He wants a thirty-year commitment not to use any gas-powered mowers on the land, and there's not enough battery-powered mowers in the entire state to push-mow three hundred acres every five days through a Massachusetts summer."

"Not yet," Brian agreed, "but we're in the green energy business. It's our job to find new solutions to old problems. We'll put our heads together and figure this out."

"I'll clear the calendar for Monday," Theo offered, pulling out his phone. "Emery, come with me, and we'll knock out a few calls before dinner."

She turned to her mother, who'd once had a hard-and-fast rule about no cell phones anywhere near her dining room table.

Eleanor nodded. "You'd better go. Come join us when you finish. Supper will keep awhile."

The response tightened her shoulders more than if she'd yelled or expressed outright disappointment. Her mother wasn't even her mom right now. She was her boss, the CEO Emery should've been, putting work before family time, a situation she must have hated every bit as much as Emery did.

105

She followed Theo into the study, carrying Arden's book. They both waited patiently for her mother's and Brian's voices to fade before he whirled on her. "What the fuck, dude?"

"I don't know! I tried for this whole straight-shooter appeal, you know. I thought maybe a farmer would find a plain-spoken, let's-cut-the-bullshit approach refreshing. I didn't even think it a gamble, but he exploded on me like some angry hippy."

Theo shook his head. "Okay, that's bad. Seriously, kind of terrible, but Brian and your mom are going to step in there, and I honestly couldn't have advised you any differently, because I can't figure out the whole lawn mower bit either. It's very dumb."

"Thank you!" She sighed in relief.

"Oh, you're not off the hook. I tracked your phone on your way home."

"You what?"

"I do it all the time," he said nonchalantly. "I need to know where you are in order to make plans for your return. You don't think I just sit around all day waiting for you to arrive, do you?"

She'd never really given it any thought until now. "I suppose you're allowed to have a life."

"Damn right I am, but you're not."

"What?"

He clucked his tongue. "You have a job, at least for the moment, and you're trying to get a bigger one. Why did you stop at the Gilderson estate?"

"I wanted to see Arden."

"Fuck."

"What? I didn't propose to her. I just had a bad day, and I had to drive right past there anyway, and I thought it might be nice to say hello to someone who'd be happy to see me."

"You can't do this." He ran his hands through his short, sandy hair. "You can't string her along."

106

"I didn't string anyone anywhere. I only stayed, like, five minutes, and I left feeling better than I had in days." She hadn't actually realized that until she said it, but doing so freed her up to push on. "Do you think that might mean something?"

"It means you're messing around. You were supposed to be on a work trip."

"You're the one who told me I could attack my problem from both angles."

"I told you a bunch of things, and you're employing some super-selective hearing if you forget all the parts about how Arden isn't the right kind of woman for you to be angling for a promotion with. If you aren't careful, you'll have both work and relationship blowups simultaneously."

Emery heard what he was saying, she did, but she couldn't resist flipping open the book to a random page and letting her eyes drift to an underlined section. "I dwell in possibility."

"Are you reciting poetry?"

"Emily Dickinson's, apparently."

"Now? You've lived in Amherst your whole life and only right now show a hint of interest in her. I suppose that's something Emily and Arden have in common."

"Ouch." She closed the book.

"What? We went on a field trip to her house when we were in eighth grade, and you didn't even go inside."

"We took a field trip to Arden's house?"

"No, Emily Dickinson's. What's gotten into you?" He snatched the book from her and held it over the trash can.

"No." She lunged for it.

He pulled it out of reach surprisingly quickly for someone who regularly got benched in high school gym class. "Tell me what's going on, and no more games."

"I'm not playing games, but you have to give me the book back. It's Arden's. I took it without asking."

He dropped his guard and stared at it, incredulous. "You stole a book from her?"

She snatched it back. "Don't make it sound bad."

"It *is* bad, Emery. Everything's bad right now, and you're acting as unstable as she is."

"She's not unstable. Why are you being so unkind to her?"

"Because she's not my friend. You are, and you're in trouble. You're acting erratic and throwing your future down the drain for no apparent reason. You told me you had to be CEO for you, for your father, for your mom, and you'd do whatever it took to get it. Then literally everything you've done since has shown exactly the opposite impulse, from your shit-show date to fucking up meetings, and then stealing from the woman you swore you would ghost."

"I didn't promise. I agreed I probably should, but I didn't swear I would."

"What's wrong with you?" he asked with serious concern in his voice. "Why split hairs and cross your fingers behind your back? We've never been those people with each other. Why won't you level with me?"

"Because you don't want to hear what I have to say."

"Because you want to date Arden?"

She shrugged.

"You agreed she's not a great fit."

"She's a better fit than the business." Emery exploded. "You wanna talk about shit-shows? I jumped in so far over my head at the Bergman's, I couldn't even see the surface. I stood in a field and got screamed at by a seventy-year-old in overalls. Do you have any idea what that's like?"

He shook his head.

"It's horrible. I felt like a stupid, childish failure, and it didn't feel any better to come in here and tell my mommy what a disappointing little kid I've been with my chore list, or sit there and listen to the man who's reporting on my progress to the

108

board offer to teach me how not to fuck up the legacy of my dead father."

"Okay," he said placatingly.

"No. None of this is okay." Her voice cracked, and she turned away so he couldn't see her eyes shimmering. She took a deep breath and willed herself to pull it together. "I don't know what I'm doing. I don't even know what I should've done instead, or what I can possibly do next. The only time I felt like I had any semblance of a clue how to act was the five minutes I spent with Arden, and now you're telling me that's a mistake, too."

"I'm sorry."

"What does it matter?"

"I'm not sure, but it might. I didn't get the sense you had a great time with her or that she made you feel good, or in control."

"She doesn't always," Emery admitted, "but I do feel like I know what to do when I'm with her."

"Really?" He laughed, then seemed to catch himself. "'Cause you took the anxiety-ridden, reclusive daughter of a multimillionaire to a jazz club and danced until she passed out."

"*Almost* passed out."

"Again with the hairsplitting. It doesn't exactly scream 'competent.'"

"Ugh, maybe the concept's relative, but when I'm with her, I can't explain it. I feel like I might be able to crack the code. I feel like I can do better with her than I do at work." She shrugged and glanced at the book again. "I know she likes me, and I'm sorry if that sounds shallow, but it matters right now. And what's more, I'm figuring out what else she likes. She's mentioned books a couple times. She's got this huge library."

"So you thought she wouldn't mind if you just pilfered a few?"

"You make everything sound so heinous. This one was just laying out."

"Still not a reason to steal it, you big klepto."

"I only intended to borrow it. I thought it might give me some ideas in case I wanted to try again, and sue me, but after today, trying again with her is infinitely more appealing than going back to the Bergman's."

He extended his hand. "Let me see it."

She handed it over grudgingly.

Flipping through the pages quickly, he nodded. "They're all from around here."

"Who?"

"The authors. Dickinson, Alcott, Hawthorne, Thoreau. They all lived within like an hour of here. Several of them were notable naturalists and recluses, just like your girl. No wonder she's into them."

"Shit. You're right." Emery grabbed the book back. "I could plan a date or day out."

"Something for the two of you. Something quiet and not rushed," he offered. "You're going to have to go slower."

"Yeah, I know. You don't have to say I told you so."

"Can I think it?"

"If you also help me plan something better this time."

"Oh, now you want my advice." He pouted, but she could tell he was loving this, and some of the tension ebbed from her core. "I suppose if I got you out of town, we wouldn't run the risk of the two of you being spotted together, and if no one sees you dating, from the board's perspective, it never happened."

"But what if I wanted it to happen?"

He shrugged. "I guess you can decide that after your do-over, but for everyone's sake, I hope you do it a lot better this time."

Chapter Eight

Arden hadn't told anyone about the text message, certainly not her parents, but not even Luz. Thankfully, her life wasn't generally interesting enough for anyone to ask about her weekend plans. The few people she interacted with on a regular basis had long since grown used to her holing up in her room or garden or disappearing into the wooded areas of the estate for hours. Even if someone had seen her strolling down the long driveway in jeans and a light sweatshirt, no one would've thought anything of it. They certainly wouldn't have harbored any suspicion she'd headed out with the intention of running away for the day with Emery Pembroke, and she wanted to keep it that way.

She took her time, stopping to check a few flowering shrubs along the long path to the main road, but for the first time in ages, she had something more interesting to occupy her mind. Like last time, Emery's instructions hadn't contained any specifics about where they were going or what she'd planned, but they had contained several details that helped put her mind at ease.

She slipped her phone from her pocket and read them again the same way she had over and over in the week since they'd started coming in.

E: Are you free next Saturday?

A: I'm free every Saturday.

E: Would you like to spend the day with me?"

A: Always.

She'd second-guessed herself endlessly for that one, but ultimately decided Emery probably already knew the answer, and if she didn't, admitting it wasn't nearly as embarrassing as other things she'd revealed about herself in previous encounters.

E: Great. I'll pick you up at 8:00 … morning this time.

A: Dress code?

E: Casual. Like what you were wearing in the garden. It'll be just the two of us, so there's no one to impress.

A: Except for you.

The next answer took a long time to come in, long enough that she'd started to worry that maybe the conversation had ended, but she lacked the social graces to know. When her phone finally buzzed again, she'd had to read the message several times in order to start breathing again.

E: You've already impressed me, Arden, and I'm very much looking forward to spending a whole day with you, just the way you are.

She'd sighed every time she'd reread it or thought about it, or even felt her phone vibrate in her pocket. She'd lived in a dreamlike state ever since, and she hadn't wanted to shatter the illusion by inviting anyone else into the haze with her.

She didn't need her mother's warnings about gold diggers, or hierarchies, and she didn't need Luz's well-intentioned but overwhelming advice. She wanted, for once in her life, not to overthink something or worry it to death. In some ways, the worst had already happened. She'd had a terrible first date, she'd made an ass of herself, and she'd released Emery back into the wild. She didn't dare think she wasn't capable of messing up a second date as badly as she had the first, but the prospect felt less crippling knowing that, even after bringing her most awkward self to the table, Emery had still come back for more. She didn't understand it, not even a little, but she did feel lighter and more comfortable than she had in a long time as she stepped through the large, front gates just as a silver Bentley pulled to a stop.

Emery hopped out to greet her. "Your timing is impeccable."

"I think yours is."

"Then we'll make quite a pair today." Emery opened the passenger door.

"No Porsche?" she asked as she slid in.

"Nah, she's built for speed. The Bentley's built for comfort."

She pondered the choice as Emery eased them on the road again. The consideration mattered, not just because it signaled a shift in the tenor from their last outing, but also because it meant Emery had given more than a passing thought to what she might need.

"You're very considerate."

Emery chuckled. "No one's ever told me that before."

"Why?"

"Probably because I'm not. I tend to leap before I look. I never hurt anyone on purpose. I don't think any of my acquaintances or friends would call me antagonistic or mean, but I tend to do what I want when I want. Maybe I'm a bit self-centered, which isn't something I relish. Hey." Emery laughed. "You've induced me to self-reflection in under two minutes. How do you do that?"

She shook her head. "I only made an observation."

"Then you see me in wildly different ways than anyone else in my life."

The thought warmed Arden immensely. "Well, you've come back for a second date, which means you must see me differently, too."

"Yeah, I'm sorry about that."

"You're sorry?"

"I'm the one who planned the aforementioned bad date."

"You planned a lovely date. I'm the one who ruined it."

"Because you weren't given a fair opportunity to succeed," Emery shot back quickly.

"You don't have to do this, you know?"

"Do what?"

Arden gestured between them and then generally around them. "Anything. Everything."

Emery pulled onto the highway, then turned to face her as long as the road would allow. "Do you want to be with me today?"

"I do." The answer came clear and easy.

"Good, because I want to spend today with you, too. So maybe we can set aside the blame and apologies and attempts to offer forgiveness so we can enjoy date number two."

Arden drew a deep, slow breath. Could they just do that? Apparently Emery thought so, but she didn't have much frame of reference for extended amounts of time with others without making accommodations for her inadequacies, and since she didn't have much of a filter either, she said as much. "I'm not sure I've had much opportunity."

"To what?"

"To go on a second date without baggage. I honestly haven't had a second date at all for a very long time."

Emery's brow furrowed for a second. "Actually, I haven't either."

"Seriously?"

She nodded as she drove. "I'm in new territory. Everything with you has felt new and different."

"Not for me. The whole first date embarrassment was pretty standard in my experience. I've had so many bad ones, which is why I don't have practice with second ones."

"Huh." Emery seemed to find the concept amusing. "Mine almost always go great, which incidentally, may also be the reason I don't have much experience with second ones either. I mean, I've done, like, trips, certainly a few long weekends, but I generally let things play out until they run their course, and after a day or two ... wow, this is sounding worse by the minute for me, isn't it?"

"No."

"Why do you always make me see things differently? Saying the quiet part out loud is kind of horrible."

"I don't think so," Arden said, even though she understood the pattern Emery'd given voice to didn't bode well for the long term. "You know what you want, you go after it, you have a good time, and you don't cling to anything after it's finished just to conform."

"Oh my God, they were right."

"Who?"

"Everyone." Emery slapped her hand on the steering wheel.

"What about?" Arden asked excitedly.

"I can't believe we're talking about this. You probably can, though. You seem to get right to the heart of everything. We're not even halfway across the state yet, and you've got me revealing secrets, but, then again, maybe it's only news to me."

Arden did everything in her power to stay focused on the conversation and not the fact that Emery just suggested they were going more than halfway across the state. "What's news to you?"

Emery sighed. "I've recently been told I'm extra."

"Who thinks that?"

"Apparently everyone who even remotely knows me."

"Not me."

"You don't?"

Arden paused. She wasn't sure she knew Emery as well as others, but as she ran through the sum total of their interactions, she couldn't find anything egregious. "No, I think you have a real zest for life, a kind of vitality about you, a certain kind of *joie de vivre*."

Emery laughed. "I think if you have to resort to French to describe me, that just proves the point about being extra."

She smiled. "Okay, maybe I'm not the best person to ask about what constitutes 'extra,' but even if you are, who says it's

115

a bad thing? Aren't so many of the world's best people extraordinary?"

"You're not."

"Well, there you have it. I don't consider myself extraordinary. I'm barely regular ordinary."

"I disagree." Emery shifted lanes as the highway split. "You've got me in the deepest conversation I've had in ages. Most of the people I see daily would be shocked to hear this much introspection, and you've inspired it in record time. Normally I just listen to music in the car."

"Would you like to do that now?"

She laughed again. "I think it's a little late. No one's ever asked these kinds of things from me before. You're unlike anyone I've ever met."

"Because you usually hang out with shiny people," Arden said. "I only pry to keep the focus on you instead of me. I just don't want you to realize I'm plain and quiet and introverted."

"So was Henry David Thoreau. So was Emily Dickinson."

Arden paused at the weirdly specific examples, and Emery reached down next to her seat, pulling out a book and handing it to her.

"You found my book," Arden said, then rethought the assertion. "You *took* my book."

"Borrowed," Emery corrected with a little quirk of a smile. "I saw it with your stuff in the garden, and it piqued my curiosity. I thought it might provide some clues."

"Clues to what?"

"To you. Or at least a few insights into what type of outing might appeal to you more than a jazz club."

Her heart gave a little flutter. Emery had studied for her the way one might study for a big test. "And?"

"I learned a little bit about the poets and essayists of New England, and it turns out that they were also plain and quiet and introverted, but no one would dare call them ordinary."

116

Emotion caught in her throat at the perfection of such a statement.

"Or you know what?" Emery continued, "Maybe people did call them that in their own day, before they saw their real talent shine, but those people were wrong about them, just like they'd be wrong about you."

Arden reached over and took her hand. She hadn't thought about it, or she wouldn't have gone through with it, but in that moment, the only thing she could register was the need to cement this moment, this connection, this understanding shifting between them.

Emery accepted the gesture and slipped her fingers softly through hers, turning to face her for a second, their eyes locking and giving Arden the chance to whisper, "They're wrong about you, too."

☀ ☀ ☀

"Welcome to Walden Pond," Emery said as they stepped through a line of trees to a panoramic view of a glassy lake glimmering in the autumn sun.

Arden covered her mouth with her hands as if the excitement might be too much to bear. Her eyes scanned the scenery and reflected it back just like the water before them, more beautiful than the fall color just beginning to tinge the top of the maple trees. "You found this idea in my book?"

"Along with a few others, but I'm told we already went to Emily Dickinson's house in middle school, so I hoped this place was still on your bucket list."

"It is!"

"Really? You've never been here before?"

Arden shook her head. "No. I asked my parents to bring me when I was in high school, but they were pretty busy, and I don't think a literary vacation into isolationism is really their style."

117

The thought made Emery a little sad. She wouldn't have picked a visit to the remnants of an old writer's cabin as a top-tier travel destination either, but she couldn't imagine denying Arden such a little thing if it made her this happy. As she picked her way along a narrow path parallel to the water's edge, she seemed almost like a different woman than the one who'd worried and wobbled on the dance floor. Out here, her eyes shone, her complexion had more color, and she moved with a grace she'd never displayed indoors. As they walked, Emery wondered how many people had known Arden without ever seeing this side of her, which led her to wonder how many times she'd walked right past her without even looking.

"Do you like it?" Arden asked over her shoulder.

"It's beautiful," she said without looking anywhere but at her.

"I heard they found the remnants of Thoreau's writing cabin."

"It's just about a quarter mile up ahead," Emery said, then added almost sheepishly, "I read the guidebook online. There's also a replica of it back at the visitor center."

Arden paused her forward progress. "Really? Can we see that too?"

"Of course."

"It's not too much? I don't know what you have planned."

"I planned to spend the whole day with you, and that's the opposite of too much. It might not be enough." She hadn't meant for the words to spill out, but she was sort of getting used to that around Arden. There was something so open and unguarded about her that inspired the same in Emery.

"You're so smooth and kind, and a part of me keeps wondering why you'd waste all that on me, but I'm too excited to worry right now. I just want to enjoy this moment."

"I want you to as well. And as far as the plans go, I do have some other ideas, but ultimately we can spend our hours however you like."

"Then let's see the cabin site first, and the recreation after that." Arden set off again, leaving Emery torn between wondering why she kept assuming time and effort spent on her constituted a waste, and the thrill of finally making her happy enough to overcome that low opinion of herself.

She didn't have time to ponder either for long, though, before they stepped into a small clearing about a hundred feet from the pond's edge. Stone markers no more than a few feet high and linked by a chain mapped where the house would've stood, though the only remainder of its presence was a low hearthstone. A carving on one of the short pillars described the location simply as "Site of Thoreau's Cabin." There was little else in the area to offer many clues as to why that mattered or what it may have looked like, but Arden didn't seem to mind.

She stepped between the markers, up to the stone, closed her eyes, and held out her hands as if she could warm herself by some fire that had burned there nearly two hundred years earlier.

"He lived here for two years, two months, and two days," she finally said.

"Really? Was he super into numerology?"

Arden's lips curled up serenely. "Are you?"

She stepped inside the walls that no longer existed and stood beside her. "Not at all, but I'm open to learning if you are."

She finally opened her eyes and turned to face her. "That's a really wonderful sentiment."

"Is it?"

"So many people seem to know everything, or at least everything they care to. You could easily be one of them with everything you seem to have figured out."

"Not me." Emery edged closer. "I'm the first to admit I know very little of importance, and the last few weeks have made it achingly clear I didn't know even as much as I thought I did."

119

Arden arched her eyebrows.

"It's not worth going into here or now. Why don't you tell me what else you know about this place?"

"Henry David Thoreau came here as a sort of experiment. He thought maybe he'd be a better writer and maybe a better person if he escaped civilization and got back to the simplicity of nature."

"I suppose that's not really a hot take with so many people opting for tiny houses and living off the grid these days," Emery mused.

"No one we know, though," Arden said. "He actually used the term 'over civilization' and every time I read it, I think of our social circle."

"Wow, tell me how you really feel."

Arden's cheeks flushed, but this time, instead of backing away from her assertion, she dug deeper. "Thoreau wasn't a Puritan or anything, quite the contrary. He believed he might live life deeper and more richly if he cared less for other people's opinions. He didn't see nature as stark or bleak. He thought the trees, the lake, the earth were made up of real life, and things like social graces and materialism were the opposite. They actually got in the way of life."

"Hmm." Emery looked around, trying to take it in. She didn't spend much time in the woods, but after the last few weeks, she had a hard time arguing. Social pressure and materialism had certainly gotten in the way of her living life to the fullest. "And how did his experiment pan out?"

"He got a very famous book out of the experience and a lasting impact on American lit, but he ended up going back to society."

"So running from the world wasn't a long-term solution?"

"Probably not." Arden seemed a little too sad about that fact, but brightened a little as she added, "He did return as a

120

supposedly changed man, and I think he hoped to change the world with all he'd learned."

"Ah, now *that* I understand."

"The urge to change the world?"

She shrugged. "Maybe not on some profound level like Gandhi or Rosa Parks, but in my own little way, I think we all have a pull to want to do something good, or make some contribution, or at least to leave the world a little better than we found it."

"I don't know." Arden shook her head. "I do wish the world would change in so many ways, and I admire people who go out there and make things happen, but I've never felt any inclination to tackle anything on my own."

"Why?"

"Probably because I don't have the skills or the drive. Taking on the world has never seemed like a viable option for me. I'd much rather run away to the woods and hide from everyone and everything."

Emery stepped so close their bodies brushed together. "Would you hide from me?"

Arden looked up at her and seemed to give the question more thought than Emery would have liked. "Honestly, I did try to hide from you. Or at least I didn't expect to see you again, and I certainly wasn't going to try to do so on my own, but then you came and found me."

"And?" Emery pushed gently. "Are you glad I did?"

"I am," Arden said softly and simply, leaning into her the same way she had when she'd thought she might be kissed goodbye.

This time, when Emery lifted her hand, she didn't run it through her hair, but rather cupped Arden's cheek. She guided them together, hesitating only long enough to say, "Me too," before brushing their lips together.

Arden's kiss was every bit as soft as she may have expected, but not tentative. She melted into Emery, her whole

121

body softening as their mouths met. Emery wrapped her arm around Arden's slender waist on instinct, but she didn't need to. The woman wasn't pulling away, nor was she unsteady. On the contrary, she kissed her back, tender and satisfying. She ran her hands up Emery's arms and curled them along the back of Emery's neck. She parted her lips slightly. A small sound of pleasure escaped, and Emery wanted to draw another, to pull more from her, to explore and tease and play and sway with her, but for once, she didn't feel any rush to do all of those things immediately.

Instead she took her time, there under the trees, in a place meant for slowing down. She let go of everything else buzzing around her life and let herself simply live on the sustaining sweetness of Arden's lips.

Chapter Nine

"I could live in a place like this," Arden said as soon as she stepped into the tiny, one-room replica of Thoreau's cabin.

Emery ducked in behind her and extended her arms, as if attempting to touch both sides simultaneously, but she only grinned when she came up short. "I suppose it could be done, but it would be awfully snug."

Arden turned in a slow circle that brought her right back to Emery. "I like snug."

"Sure. At night, in bed, or cuddling, maybe even for a weekend, but ..." Emery wrapped her arms loosely around Arden's waist. "Do you think you could live in such close confines forever?"

"Yes," she said without hesitation, though perhaps her current state of mind held some responsibility for her agreeability, because right now, with this woman beside her, she might be able to live happily anywhere. If only Emery had kept kissing her, she could've lived back in the woods and slept under the stars.

She hadn't thought it possible to be any more taken with Emery than she had been the moment she'd stepped up to the side of Walden Pond. This amazing woman she'd admired from afar for half her life had put in the time and effort to really listen, to see, to understand her well enough to plan a trip that ended up in a place she'd always wanted to go. It was the kindest, most thoughtful thing any woman had ever done for her, and there on the shore with her, Arden thought they'd reached a sort of heaven, but when Emery's lips met hers, even that peak felt like a far-off valley.

Emery had been perfect in every way, slow, steady, confident, and oh so skilled. She hadn't pushed or pried, or even given the sense she wanted more, and yet she hadn't pulled away too soon either. She'd lingered softly, surely, until she filled all of Arden's senses with the certain press of her mouth, the brush of long lashes against her cheek, the scent of her cologne mixing with the crisp air, and the fluttering sound of leaves rustling in the trees broken only by a sweet, stolen breath. Arden came to life. Every part of her registered each detail simultaneously.

When Emery did finally step back with a smile, the colors around them seemed brighter, the air crisper, the beating of her own heart stronger. For her, everything had always been too much, or not enough, but right then, the whole world seemed just right.

"It's a little sparse, but I suppose there wouldn't be much to keep up with in the way of care or managing a household," Emery admitted. "Could I at least get a TV on that wall opposite the bed?"

Arden didn't care how out of place modern-day electronics would seem here. If Emery wanted to indulge any sort of fantasy with her, she could have whatever she liked. "Of course."

"Okay, I'm in." Emery smiled down at her. "Who knows? I haven't exactly been crushing it on my current trajectory. Maybe I shouldn't knock a more spartan lifestyle until I've tried it, but if this is all you really want in a home, you'll have to find a way to rent out all of those massive rooms I saw back at your house."

"My parents' house," Arden corrected, "but yes, I'd love to break it all up somehow. I kind of hate the place."

"You hate your palatial estate?" Emery laughed and released her only far enough to take a few steps around the single room before turning back. "I thought every little girl dreamed of a house like yours."

"Did you?"

124

Emery shook her head. "I mean, it's a bit formal for my tastes, but I'm not exactly living in a hovel."

"Right." Arden had never been inside Emery's home, but she'd seen it from the outside, much more natural and in harmony with the local hills and forests, but still mammoth in its own right. "I think the style of yours would suit me better, all the natural wood, but the scope and openness of it might overwhelm in the same way. I always feel so vulnerable in big spaces. When I was little, I knew every single nook and cranny I could squeeze my tiny body into around the house and the grounds."

"What do you mean?"

"Cupboards, closets, woodsheds, anywhere I could close myself up and feel protected. I even used to read under my big four-poster bed with a heavy blanket. The combination of being low to the ground and wrapped up tightly always made me feel safest."

Emery's expression turned pensive. "Who did you need to keep safe from?"

"I don't know," she admitted. "I'm not sure I had any cohesive fear, certainly never physical danger. I just never got over the vague sense of being too exposed."

"Never?" Emery pushed.

She considered the question as she looked around the room. "I like being in my greenhouse. It's small and warm and quiet. I also like the woods. They're bigger, of course, but the trees still feel like a sturdy sort of cover when I'm with them, and ..."

"What?" Emery pressed, stepping closer once more.

"I feel safe here with you." Arden grimaced. "Sorry, was that too much to admit, too soon?"

Emery slipped an arm around her once more, easing her in, and smiling down at her. "Well, normally I would hear something like that and probably make some cocky little quip like 'my work here is done.'"

125

"Usually?"

She nodded. "But not today."

"Why?"

"Because, while I'm not at all sure what comes next, I get the sense you and I are far from done."

Arden bit her lip to keep from releasing a happy sort of squeal and managed a shallow breath to try to compose herself. "In that case, I guess it's fair for me to admit that, under normal circumstances, that might've made me swoon again."

Emery tightened her hold on her, just in case, but still asked, "And today?"

"Today," Arden whispered as if the word might possess some kind of magic, "today I want to stay present so I can do more of this."

And then she kissed Emery.

Arden. Herself. She did the kissing. She didn't even know who she was becoming, or where this new version of her had found the sliver of boldness necessary to not only state what she wanted, but to actually initiate it, but as the kiss grew deeper and fuller and richer, she felt a little bit like she had, too.

※ ※ ※

"She wrote *Little Women* right there!" Arden clutched Emery's arm with one hand and pointed back to the house they'd just left with the other. "Do you know how many times I've read that book?"

Emery shook her head, enjoying the contact and Arden's unabashed joy. "How many?"

"I don't know," Arden laughed, "but it's a lot."

"I believe you, because even I think I've read it more than once, and I'm more of an action/adventure/travelogue kind of reader, but I remember being solidly 'team Jo' as a tweenager."

"Everyone's Team Jo," Arden said matter-of-factly. "Is there even another team to be on?"

126

"I don't know, but I think the scene where she broke Laurie's heart and refused to marry him made me gayer," Emery admitted, "and then I remember feeling kind of betrayed when she did marry someone else in the end."

"You, me, and Louisa May Alcott. She only ended the book that way because she had to in order to get it published. You know she was queer, right?"

Emery searched her memory. "Vaguely? I mean, it tracks."

"She never married, and later in her life, she said she'd never been in love with a man, but she'd been in love with women multiple times."

"I'll be damned."

"Oh, it gets better, or at least less straight, because some scholars have begun to consider the fact that she may actually have been trans, or at the very least genderqueer. She wore men's clothes, she adopted some kids and had them call her 'Papa' and there's an instance where her father, who was well-known in his own right, referred to 'Lou' as his son."

Emery's head spun, not just at the information, but at the excitement radiating off of Arden as she relayed it. She'd become a different woman here. She still had her quirky sense of humor, and she'd kept Emery amused all day, but now she radiated a sense of belonging, and knowledge she seemed eager to share. The nervous, retiring woman who'd wilted in a crowd bloomed here one-on-one.

They'd shared sandwiches on the shores of Walden Pond, then driven to Louisa May Alcott's Orchard House and taken a private tour of the house and grounds. Hours had passed, punctuated by kisses and conversation that had never lagged into anything other than pleasant breaks for reflection.

Emery stared at Arden as they walked arm in arm, and she continued talking about the progressive nature of the area and how it's always served as a hotbed for great thinkers and writers. She had so many examples, and Emery thought she

127

might have paid more attention to such lectures in school if she'd had such engaging or beautiful teachers as she did today.

Arden's eyes danced, and her voice carried a light lilt behind the studiousness of her topic. Even her cheeks held a natural sort of blush that for once didn't seem to stem from embarrassment or bashfulness.

Eventually Arden seemed to become aware of Emery's attention and came up short. "Oh wow, I have been rambling on and on. I must be boring you to death."

"Why would you assume boredom over rapt attention?"

"Because I've met myself, and your eyes have glazed over. I can't imagine what you must be thinking."

Emery stopped walking and turned to face her. "Do you honestly want to know?"

Arden hesitated as if afraid to ask, but she finally lifted her chin bravely and said, "Yes, I can handle the truth."

If it had been anyone else, Emery might have toyed with them or drawn out the moment for dramatic effect, but she couldn't meet Arden's earnestness with anything other than the same. "I was thinking about how pretty you are, and engaging, and how much I enjoy meeting this more relaxed side of you."

The breath she'd been holding flooded out in a rush that stirred the hair tucked behind Emery's ears. "Honestly, I'm enjoying meeting her, too."

They started strolling again. Without even talking about it, they headed toward the little apple orchard that gave the house its name.

"I'm not usually comfortable enough to talk to people so much. Even when I go out with Luz, she does all the talking, and it's fun to be with someone so confident in a crowd, but I've always felt a little like something might be off about me when I see how well other people do in those situations."

"Have you ever stopped to wonder how people like Luz or I would do in a cabin in the woods by ourselves?"

"Not once."

128

"Maybe we admire your ability to thrive in the silence without going mad when there's only yourself to keep you company."

"Do you really?"

"I don't know," Emery admitted. "I've never let myself be alone and quiet long enough to see how much I'd like it, but I doubt I'd be nearly as centered as you are."

"It never occurred to me that you weren't just good at everything."

Emery laughed outright. "Wow, that's the nicest, completely false thing anyone's ever said about me."

"I don't believe it."

"It's true. I'm terrible at so many things. You remember when I dropped by your house last week?"

"Of course."

"I'd just come from a truly disastrous meeting where I was epically bad at my job, or, well, the job I'm trying to hold but isn't really mine yet."

"What do you mean?"

She shook her head. "I don't want to dampen the remainder of our time here by telling sad or boring stories, and I certainly don't want to tarnish your brassy opinion of me by doing something embarrassing."

"What, like passing out on a dance floor and having to be carried out of a club?"

"Come on, I thought we moved past that. You weren't as bad as you think."

"And I'm sure your story won't be as bad as you think either." Arden frowned. "Or is that the point? You know mine was way worse and you're just saying all this to be nice?"

"No, no." Emery angled her head to duck under the low limb of an apple tree. "Mine's infinitely worse, both with much more at stake and because the shortcomings rest solely on my shoulders."

Arden kept walking, seeming to wait patiently but persistently for more.

As they reached the top of a small rise, Emery glanced back to see the small grove behind them and the house in the distance. It was such an idyllic little farm, and so well kept, which made her scoff slightly. "They don't mind lawn mowers here."

Arden raised her eyebrows.

"That's what I messed up." Emery sighed. "A multimillion-dollar, three-generation company all laid low in my first month of not even being in charge because I got into some weird pissing contest over lawn mowers."

"Lawn mowers?"

"Yeah, it's not a metaphor. We were close to closing a major deal to convert hundreds of acres of prime development land between a major highway and a river into a solar field, ensuring that, for generations to come, it would be protected from the prospect of strip malls or truck stops or worse, fracking. Instead of tearing up the environment, it would actually work to produce endless kilowatts of green, renewable energy while remaining safe for both wildlife and water sources."

"Sounds amazing."

"It would've been, except for the lawn mowers, because the old hippie guy who currently owns the land freaking hates them. It's like he sees them as a tool of Satan or something, and it didn't make any sense to me that he'd rather risk his beloved land turning into a parking lot than allow us to mow it enough so the grasses and shrubbery don't grow to the point where it could shade out the solar panels."

"What about using old-school rotating-blade push mowers?"

Emery rolled her eyes. "Not you, too. He asked the same thing, but the manpower it would take to use those things every week on hundreds of acres would be both cost- and labor-prohibitive, which I explained. Then I made things worse by

130

asking what his real deal was, because surely no smart, respectable, modern-day human could really care this much about mowers, and I said that if he was really being difficult to garner a more favorable financing deal—"

She didn't even finish before Arden grimaced.

"See, yeah, that's the first expression he made, and I should've read the room, or the field, better, but I didn't. I tried to play a hardball, straight-shooter deal, and guess what?"

"It really was about the lawn mowers?"

"Apparently."

"And you offended him?"

"Very much so."

"And now he's not working with you at all?"

"Threw me right off his land. I have never been kicked out of anywhere in my life. People like me. I am a likable person. I don't even know how it went this badly this fast, and the pieces still don't fit together even after a week of replaying and worrying and living in fear of sinking everything my father and grandfather built."

Arden cocked her head to the side and pressed her lips together.

"What?"

"I think that must have been really hard on your self-esteem."

"But?"

"No buts. I'm sorry you felt unwanted and insufficient. It's horrible, and I imagine it must be even worse with so many people counting on you. I can't imagine. I've never even had a job, much less a whole company. And you came into it so fast, so unexpectedly, I'm surprised you aren't getting more support from a team of people."

"Oh, well, I mean my mom's running the company officially. I think they've all rallied around her instead of me."

Arden curled her hand tighter around Emery's arm. "That probably feels pretty lonely too. I hate that they didn't set you up to succeed better. It's unfair to send you into a meeting like that without helping you understand all the variables at play."

"I suspect I'm the only real variable."

"How many people does the company employ?"

She shrugged. "All told, about a hundred."

Arden seemed to be treading carefully. "And I get that not all of them were in on the deal, or even have access to you, but in a company of one hundred people committed to green energy alternatives, it seems like someone should've told you lawn mowers, especially the big ones, are major sources of air and noise pollution to the point where it's pretty common for environmentalists to rail against them."

"What?"

"Someone should've helped prep you for this with facts and figures. For instance, running a lawn mower for one hour pollutes the air and burns enough fossil fuels to equate to eleven hours of driving a regular truck or car on standard gasoline."

Emery's head spun. "Fuck."

"You didn't know."

"I should have." Her vision turned a little hazy. "Do you mind if we sit down here?"

"Not at all."

They sank to the grass side by side. "So what you're saying is this conflict actually made perfect sense."

"I wouldn't go that far. It sounds like the guy you're dealing with didn't offer any alternatives of his own, and again, no one on your team did either. He got left alone with a young businesswoman who'd been on the job only a few weeks, and got thrown in unexpectedly at that, while you got stuck with an old hippie who's set in his ways and probably used to everyone in his line of work already being on the same page as him."

"But we both could've done more research and asked more questions, and I certainly could have listened better."

"It's not too late."

"I don't know. Nothing's changed other than now I know he's not the only unreasonable one. I don't have a viable solution, and I'm still not welcome on his farm, and the people in charge don't trust me to try again. Ugh." She rested her head on Arden's shoulder and stared out at the faint orange tint blending with blue on the horizon. "And now I've brought down the whole mood by talking about work and revealing myself to be an idiot all along."

"I don't think you're an idiot."

"No? You put the pieces together in minutes when I've failed to do so for weeks. I'm sorry I messed up yet another conversation I should've been better prepared for."

"Hey." Arden placed a kiss atop her head. "I don't think you ruined anything. I believe you can still save the work stuff, and I'm still having a great time with you."

Emery's lips quirked up a little. "Now who's saying things to make the other feel better?"

"Not me. I'm dead serious. I love this place. I've loved this whole day, even this moment, especially this one. I know it's getting late, and you probably have something to get back to, but if it were up to me, I would stay even longer."

She lifted her head to look at her. "Like, stay for dinner?"

"Yes," Arden said, holding her gaze, "and then, stay all night."

Emery's heart kicked her ribs, and the shock waves reverberated south from there. "All night?"

Arden worried her lower lip and nodded slowly. "If you wanted to."

Her brain screamed with echoes of Theo telling her not to sleep with this woman and all the reasons why they shouldn't move too fast. Hadn't she just mentioned how over her head she was at work, and, and, and … nothing.

As she leaned in to capture Arden's mouth once more, nothing else mattered.

133

Chapter Ten

The Hawthorne Inn was absolutely beautiful, the perfect mix of charm and elegance, and, with only a handful of guest rooms, it wasn't crowded or cavernous enough to be overwhelming. Which isn't to say Arden didn't feel in over her head as Emery checked them in. She tried not to fidget as she read a plaque about how the land the inn stood on had, at various times, belonged to Nathaniel Hawthorne, Bronson Alcott, and Ralph Waldo Emerson. She was aware enough to understand that under other circumstances she would've found such a thing thrilling, but in the moment where Emery Pembroke requested one bed and the clerk asked if they needed help with the luggage, entirely too many other things filled her brain to appropriately appreciate American literary history.

They didn't have any luggage. She was checking into a picturesque New England bed-and-breakfast with the hottest lesbian in Massachusetts without any luggage. Why was no one else's brain melting? And what would the others think if they'd known the idea had been hers? She had no idea who these 'others' were and why they would care, but she couldn't be the only person who'd felt the world tilt on its axis.

Emery turned around and held up a key. "Ready?"

She froze. Suddenly the question seemed too big to process, and also she'd forgotten how to speak.

Emery walked over to her with an amused sort of expression. "The clerk recommended some local restaurants we could check out, or order in, maybe veg out a bit, or we could check out the room and then go for a walk."

She nodded. "Okay."

Emery led the way up the stairs and to their room. She pushed open the door but waited for Arden to go first.

She stepped inside and glanced around without really seeing anything in focus. It wasn't that her eyes didn't work, they spun around various pieces of antique furniture and modern touches, but her brain refused to settle on anything other than the large bed draped with a lush comforter and ample pillows.

"Arden," Emery whispered, very close behind her.

"Um, hmm?"

She touched her elbow and urged her to turn around. "I've had such a wonderful time today."

The comment soothed something inside of her. "Me too."

"And nothing that happens this evening will change that," Emery continued.

She didn't believe that. She didn't see any way that tonight could end without changing everything, but she worked to keep Luz's voice from her head as she closed her eyes and took a few deep breaths. She didn't want anyone else's wishes or will to creep into this moment. She'd done a wonderful job of staying present all day, and it had led to such beautiful experiences, all of them culminating with the moment when she'd gotten out of her own way long enough to state clearly what she desired without shame or fear. It all felt so liberating, and she craved the ability to hold onto that version of herself almost as much as she ached to have Emery's arms around her again.

"We don't have to do anything you don't want," Emery said.

"Wanting isn't the problem." She reached up and cupped Emery's cheek in her hand. "For the first time in my life, the opposite is true. I want too much, and I'm worried I won't be able to handle it all. I've grown so used to being insufficient."

Emery closed her eyes and leaned into her touch. She was so beautiful it almost hurt to look at her in such an unguarded moment, but when heavy lids fluttered open once more, there was a deeper intensity to her gaze. "I want to make you feel good, and I want to help you see what I see when I look at you."

"What do you see?"

"That nothing about you has ever been insufficient for me."

Arden opened her mouth to argue, to list all the times she'd come up short or failed to be the person they both deserved, but she never had the chance, as Emery covered her mouth and smothered all her insecurities with a kiss.

And oh, what a kiss, so different than the others they'd stolen during the day. Emery moved with a lavish sort of purpose, consuming and exploring without rushing. She parted Arden's lips with her tongue, probing deeper without ever needing to push. She only needed to suggest a desire for more and Arden yielded, gratefully, gleefully.

Emery held her close with one hand on the small of her back and used the other to unbutton the front of her coat. Arden shrugged out of it, feeling lighter in every way, and the warmth of their proximity gave way to a heat building inside her. It had been so long since she'd given herself over to any impulse, and none of them had ever been as strong as the pull she felt toward Emery. She ran her tongue along her lush lower lip as her fingers twitched into action of their own accord. Taking hold of Emery's sweater, she pushed it up just enough to brush against the smooth skin below. The contact sent another surge of need through her. Pressing her palms flat to Emery's abs, she relished the unfettered sense of freedom.

Emery responded in kind, tugging at Arden's shirt as she pulled her lips along her cheek to her neck, sucking just enough to divide her attention between what she wanted to do and what was being done to her. Rolling her head back to expose her own vulnerability further, she scraped her way up over Emery's side and along the ridges of her ribs, failing to reach purchase until she reached the straps of her bra.

137

Emery seemed to sense her struggle and, lifting her arms, shimmied herself free from the sweater. That got Arden's attention, and she forced her eyes open to see the first full flash of the beautiful body before her, but Emery didn't stop there. She pulled the bra free, too, and stood unabashed in her own gloriousness.

It took several seconds for Arden to process the rush of emotions swirling through her at the sight of this amazing creature. Admiration and arousal certainly ranked high among them. Awe came in a healthy dose, too, but there was something else, something darker curling its tendrils through her body and brain.

Greed.

She felt greedy. The sensation was new. She'd never wanted to possess anything, much less anyone, but she couldn't deny the sensation now. She didn't even want to. She palmed one of Emery's breasts with one hand, and then curled her other hand up around the back of her neck to pull them together again. Kissing her deeply, Emery groaned, and her hips rolled forward. Arden had done that. She'd elicited that noise, that little thrust, and the desire she'd seen in her eyes.

She could have this woman any way she wanted tonight. The realization made her drunker than any liquor she'd ever consumed. Her head swam, but with the grip they had on each other, she had no fear of falling, at least not physically.

Shedding her own shirt and bra, the cool air of the room did nothing to lessen the fire spreading between them now. They moved together, skin on skin, hands exploring the planes and curves. When Emery's fingers circled Arden's nipples, the kiss faltered slightly as her mental resources drained along with all the blood rushing south. Still, as they teased and touched, they somehow found the coordination to wander toward the bed until Arden's legs hit the mattress. Reaching behind her, Emery yanked back the comforter, and then sank her fingers deep into

Arden's hair, tangling them together and cupping the back of her head as she lowered her to the bed.

She sighed dreamily as she surrendered to the fantasy made real.

Emery kicked her shoes off and settled lightly over her. "Are you okay?"

"Yes." For a second, it was the only word she knew.

"You're so beautiful." Emery buried her face in Arden's neck and kissed along her collarbone before running her open mouth down the center of her chest.

She bit her lip to keep from crying out as a warm tongue circled her nipple. Every ounce of her attention was so focused on that spot and the tantalizing pressure building there, she only managed to be distantly aware of Emery's hands unbuttoning her jeans and dragging the zipper down.

She must've lifted her hips off the bed at some point, because when Emery's mouth pulled away only long enough to switch sides, she also pulled her jeans free, and together they kicked them off completely. The denim of Emery's pants rubbed against her legs, wonderfully rough against raw nerves as she eased her thighs apart. Then she began her descent again.

Arden kept her eyes open and, with great effort, resisted the urge to sink into the pillow so she could watch what came next. She might not have even believed her eyes, but the sensations Emery sparked made it magnificently clear none of this was a dream.

Emery's hair fell from behind her ears and trailed along Arden's stomach as she sank lower, kissing her way to the now pulsing center of her need before glancing up. Dark eyes asked a silent question they both clearly knew the answer to. Thankfully she didn't make Arden say the words, instead accepting a single, enthusiastic nod. Then she lowered her mouth again, and Arden's world exploded into a thousand clichés. Stars, fireworks, white light, it all illuminated the back of her eyelids as she lost the battle to stay present enough to watch.

Her head hit the pillow with a muffled thump as Emery worked long, slow strokes through the liquid heat pooling between them. Then she began to rock in time to her rhythm. She didn't even know why or how she'd found the coordination when she felt like a puddle of need, but it must've been the same instinct that had allowed her to follow Emery's lead the first night as they'd danced. Her body knew, and more importantly, needed to see where this woman would take them. She arched and flexed and rolled forward again, her breath coming unevenly somewhere in between.

Emery's pace amplified as did her pressure, but never did either become frantic or too much to bear. She built steadily, skillfully, guiding Arden up to some unseen edge and holding her beautifully, almost painfully, until she wasn't sure she could withstand anymore. She tossed her head from side to side as her brain and body grew feverish from the desire. Clutching the sheets with one hand, her other found the back of Emery's head and sifted through those strands of dark hair in a simple sort of request she no longer had the words or the strength to force out.

Still keenly attuned and flawlessly timed, Emery granted her everything she couldn't quite plead for, and so much more. With steady pressure, she tipped the scales and sent Arden spinning, gasping, rising, and falling, only to crest again.

This time, even biting her lip couldn't stop her from crying out, and her hand slipped down, clutching Emery's shoulder to keep from falling to a place she might not return from. Emery eased but didn't stop, seeming to intuit exactly what Arden could manage and refusing to give her anything less. She sucked, lightly drawing out the shimmering remnants of her release, and then kissed her, slowly, lightly, with the same fluttering brushes she'd used on her lips earlier in the woods.

The perfection, the care, the sensuality of it all overwhelmed Arden, and hot tears stung the corners of her eyes as she sagged into the sheets.

Emery kissed her thighs, her stomach, her breasts, her neck, dragging her body up next to Arden's. As she reached her face, she settled beside her, one leg thrown across her body as she kissed her jaw, her cheeks, her eyelids, then stopped suddenly, and leaned back far enough to look at her. "Are you okay?"

She nodded.

"Really? Are you crying?"

"No, I mean yes, but it's just silly tears." She let out a shuddery breath. "I'm happy."

Emery's smile spread slowly. "Yeah? Good?"

"So good." Her whole body sang with satisfaction.

Emery relaxed beside her, resting her chin on her shoulder. "I'm glad to hear it met your expectations."

"More so," Arden said with a subtle edge of desperation budding in her to make her appreciation known. "Emery, that was the most amazing ... you are so ... I can hardly even ... I never let myself admit how much I always wanted to do that."

Emery's head lifted off the bed again quickly. "Always wanted, uh, but you have, right?"

"Have what?"

"Done that."

Arden's foggy brain took too long to process the question, but when she did, she laughed. "Oh yes, at least in theory. This wasn't my first time. I went to an all-girls college, but I do feel like this may've been my first time doing it quite so well."

Emery sighed and sagged against her. "Whew, okay, in that case, very good."

"Why? Would it have bothered you if this had been my first time ever."

"I don't know." Emery rolled onto her back and stared up at the ceiling. "I do think your first time should be special."

"I'm not sure it could've been any more special than that." Arden rolled onto her side and ran her hand across

141

Emery's bare torso. "At least for me. I'm sure you have a lot more experiences to compare—"

"No. Really great for me, too."

She trailed her hand lower until she could run one finger under the waistband of Emery's jeans. "I find that hard to believe."

"Arden, we've been through this. You are not insufficient, and just because I've been with more women doesn't mean you—"

She leaned over and silenced her with a kiss, slow and sultry, before easing back only long enough to say, "I didn't mean we'd come up short in anything we've done so far. I only meant I didn't think you could be fully satisfied yet, because you still have your pants on."

Emery smiled again. "Well, that's a much better line of reasoning, and one I think we could follow a little further."

Arden slipped her hand lower, and Emery helped by unfastening the button, revealing the waistband of navy-blue boxer briefs. Arden's exhaustion vanished, washed away by another surge of arousal. "I want you so much I can hardly stand it."

Emery kissed her deeply, rolling her onto her back so she hovered over her. Arden used the new position to push the jeans down, then slipped both hands into the briefs. She cupped Emery's amazing ass, urging her forward. The two of them rocked together, mound to mound, chest to chest, the erotic friction more than enough to send sparks flying once more. She started to think she might orgasm again when suddenly Emery hopped off her.

"Come back," she panted, almost blind with the desire to continue.

"I promise," Emery said as she pushed her jeans all the way to the floor and stepped out of them, then slowly peeled off the last barrier. She stood completely still, smiling down at her. "I love the way you look at me."

142

"I love the way you look."

It wasn't nearly long enough to admire her as much as she deserved, but neither of them had even a fraction of the patience they'd displayed at other points in the day. Still, what she lacked visually, they made up for in full body contact as Emery climbed atop her and against her. She covered Arden so completely, the weight of her magical, and the slide of their legs the sexiest thing she'd experienced yet. As she brought her own thigh up between Emery's, they both groaned.

"You feel how wet I am for you?" Emery whispered.

"Yes."

"I am so turned on by you."

She didn't even argue. She couldn't, not with the evidence slick between them.

They kissed again, novelty giving way to a growing familiarity and confidence. Emery placed one hand on either side of Arden's head and did a sexy sort of push-up, then angled back to increase the pressure of her own body on her thigh. Her hips moved in the most tantalizing circle. Arden ran both hands over her body, one across the muscles of her shoulder and down her back, the other over firm breasts and contracting abs. When Emery rolled forward again, Arden used the space to slide her fingers into slick folds.

"Yes." It was Emery's turn to say the magic word, and Arden thrilled to hear it directed at her.

The next time Emery rocked into Arden's palm, she curled around to cup her more fully. The pressure must have worked for them both, because now they were moaning in unison.

With each pull forward and push back, they ground a little harder into each other, until finally Arden's fingers slipped lower.

Emery's eyes flashed open and she nodded, slowing her momentum enough for Arden to slip inside. The sense of being surrounded by her was almost too exquisite to stand, and they both stilled to revel in the luxury of the new sensation. Then Emery began to move again, her hips rolling, circling, grinding into her.

Arden watched, rapt as Emery hovered over her, muscles flexing, sweat starting to bead along her neck. She lifted up enough to run her tongue along the curve of her throat, tasting the hint of salt before whispering, "What do you want?"

"This."

"I want to make you feel—"

"You are," Emery rasped as she ground into her. "You're perfect."

Arden shifted her fingers to curl deeper inside, and Emery bucked.

"Yeah. That's so good."

They kissed again, riding a frantic, panting edge as they moved together in a pattern only their bodies could anticipate until Emery's breath grew short and sharp. She pulled back, her arms trembling as she stared down at her. "Watch me, Arden."

She nodded. She couldn't have looked away even if the room caught fire now.

"Watch how much I want you." Then Emery threw her head back, her whole body pushing against her. Her muscles rippled in waves, and Arden marveled at the wonder of her perfect body reacting, pulsing, shaking for her. She didn't know how such a thing could be possible, and in the shining moment, awash in Emery's sweat and breath and radiance, she didn't need to.

Chapter Eleven

Emery hadn't even opened her eyes before she became aware of someone watching her. She didn't have to search the cobwebs of her memory to picture Arden's face or remember her name. Her dreams had been filled with images of her, sweet, smiling, surrendering. This wasn't the first night she'd spent ensconced with a woman in some charming little hotel, but it was certainly the first time in a long while she'd awoken looking forward to what would come next. "Good morning."

"Good morning," Arden said softly. "Did I wake you?"

"Yes." She stretched thoroughly, then allowed her eyes to open before adding, "But you are so much nicer than an alarm, so thank you."

Arden sighed happily. "Thank *you*, for everything."

"I'd say the pleasure was all mine, but I do hope some was yours, too."

"Very much so."

"Good. I wouldn't want the reality to fall short of that very high bar of being the hottest lesbian in Massachusetts."

Arden smiled. "I think Luz set that bar, not me, but either way you hurdled it easily."

She sort of thought she had, what with Arden's utter captivation with her throughout the evening and into the early hours of the morning, but she didn't hate hearing such an ego-boosting assessment. "How are you feeling this morning?"

"Amazing."

"Good." She kissed her quickly. "Because you *are* amazing."

"And how are you feeling?"

"Wonderful except for one thing."

145

Arden frowned.

Emery rushed to keep those creases in her forehead from taking hold. "I'm famished. It seems someone kept my mouth fully occupied all night, so we didn't get a chance to eat any actual food."

"Oh." Arden relaxed. "Well, sorry not sorry."

"Me too." Emery laughed. "But they serve breakfast downstairs, and seeing as how neither of us brought a change of clothes, it shouldn't take us long to get ready."

Arden didn't argue, nor did she seem too embarrassed to make do with a quick shower and some complimentary hotel mouthwash. Emery continued to marvel at her ability to lean into the opportunities before them.

She'd been a surprise almost every step of the way, and all of them pleasant this time around. It felt a little bit like she'd unlocked an entirely different woman from the shrinking violet she'd left on unsteady legs last time. And it had taken so very little affirmation and consideration to open up this side of Arden, which made her a little sad to think about what that meant for how she was used to being treated.

"What?" Arden asked as Emery pulled out a chair for her in the small breakfast area.

"Hmm?"

"You frowned."

"I was just thinking how many people walked right by you on a daily basis without ever getting to see this side of you."

Arden's cheeks flushed immediately.

"Don't get me wrong," Emery continued quickly, taking the seat opposite her. "I'm selfishly happy no one else beat me to the punch, but for your sake, I'm sorry so few other people have gotten to know the woman I'm seeing on this trip, because I think you'd be much more popular."

"I've never wanted to be popular," Arden said seriously. "I mean, I think everyone wants to be cared for, but staying atop a social ladder seems like a great deal of work."

She couldn't disagree, even though she'd never really given the topic much thought. She'd always been trendy and highly regarded in her own circles. Well, at least until the board of trustees had their say. "If you'd said that two months ago, I would've found the idea silly, but now, I don't know, winning people over seems to take a lot more effort than it used to."

"Because there's a lot more at stake for you in some of these new interactions, but, for what it's worth, I'm still very impressed with your interpersonal skills ... and several other skills, for that matter."

Emery grinned and began to fill the French press on their table with water. "You're very good for my confidence. Any chance you'd like to offer up a favorable reference on my behalf to a hippie farmer on our way home?"

"I doubt my word would carry much weight, given my frame of reference is wildly different from his, but I was thinking more about the problem last night."

"Last night?" She pretended to be wounded. "If you thought of lawn mowers while we were in bed, I did not hurdle that bar you mentioned earlier."

"No." She laughed, a light, bubbly sound Emery found a little too irresistible. "I only meant that in reflecting on how very good you are at seemingly everything, I'm sure you'll find a quick solution to your work problems, too, now that you have the missing information."

"I have *some* of the missing information," she corrected, and lifted the press. "Coffee?"

Arden nodded. "I'm not usually a caffeine drinker, but after last night, it seems warranted. What information are you still missing?"

She poured them both a mug. "I've figured out the 'why' of my communication breakdown with Mr. Bergman, but I still don't have any workable solutions."

"But surely you can think of one."

"I really do appreciate your faith in me."

"Come on," Arden pushed, then rose from the table. "Start thinking while I get us some of the amazing pastries from the sideboard over there. Then we can brainstorm and carbo-load simultaneously."

She started to walk away, but Emery caught her hand and pulled her back before placing a kiss on her palm.

"What was that for?"

"For you, for caring, for you snagging me one of those cinnamon rolls I noticed on the way in."

Arden laughed again as she walked away, and Emery watched her go. She knew she was supposed to return her focus to work. They'd had their fun, more fun than she could've imagined when they'd left yesterday, but she'd slept with plenty of women over the years without ever breaking her stride. She could see why last night might have felt like an incredibly big deal to Arden, but it shouldn't have to her, and Emery was surprised to find it did.

She tracked Arden's movements around the room, relishing little details from the curve of her waist to the way her hair spilled unencumbered over her shoulders. Whatever had happened between them over the last twenty-four hours hadn't been enough to give Emery her fill, or even enough of a quick fix to dull the edge of attraction. She probably would've found that disconcerting if left alone with her thoughts for too long, but as Arden turned to catch her watching, she couldn't fixate on anything other than her smile.

"So?" Arden asked as she returned to the table with enough baked goods to put them both into a carb coma. "What've you come up with?"

"Sorry, you were gone only two minutes. I wasn't able to broker world peace or negotiate new climate accords in your absence."

"Then I guess this is my cinnamon roll." Arden pulled the plate to her side of the table.

"What?" She laughed. "I agreed to no such terms."

"Look." She peeled off a piece and popped it into her mouth playfully. "We both had jobs to do, and I did mine. It's not my fault if you didn't."

"Wow, I see how it is. You got what you wanted last night, and now you're already domesticating me."

"I wouldn't dare. I like you wild, but a deal's a deal. You must have at least one idea worth workshopping before you get to inject sugar into the equation."

She rolled her eyes. "I didn't make that deal, but since I'm starving to death, I suppose necessity might be the mother of invention. I think electric lawn mowers might be a thing."

"There you go." Arden handed over the cinnamon roll. "What do you know about electric mowers?"

"A whole lot of nothing. I mean, we don't use them on our corporate campus, and we're a green energy supplier, which seems to imply the technology might still have a way to go."

"Well, you're in the business of adapting new technology, so maybe it would be worth looking into, or having your people see what they can do."

She nodded and took a bite, letting the doughy goodness melt in her mouth before going on. "It could help down the road, but I'm not sure a promise to develop solutions in the future would help my case much right now."

"And while the carbon emissions are probably the biggest issue with mowers, they aren't the only one. There are still the concerns about noise and the wear and tear on the ground over time, and the stress to local wildlife might still persist."

"So electric mowers are out?"

"Not at all, they're a possibility."

"What's a better one?"

"What do you think?" Arden asked.

"No. I've had enough of this game." Emery stuffed a larger bite of food into her mouth and made a show of not chewing quickly.

149

"Okay," Arden conceded. "Fair enough. I'll go, because as an avid gardener, I do have a couple ideas. One is a little labor-intensive, and one is going to sound super silly."

Emery made a rolling motion with her hand, hoping to skip the self-deprecation stage and get to the good stuff.

"There are a lot of native, low growth, shade or shade-adjacent plants you could cultivate in the field that wouldn't grow very tall. It would take a major investment up front, a lot of time and labor to clear out the grasses and natural brush in the area. Then you'd need to plant the new species and tend them carefully for the first few years, but after they were established, it would get easier, certainly easier than mowing once or twice a week. In the long run, it might end up even being cheaper than mowers."

"Do you know what species of plants could work for something like that?"

"I'd need to know more about the soil and irrigation and shade-to-sun ratios, but if I saw the land, I could probably figure it out easily enough, and, if not, I'd know who to ask."

"Wow." Emery probably had people on her staff who knew about plants and such, but none of them had made a similar offer or displayed nearly the same level of confidence, not that she'd put out a call for advice. "I'm impressed."

"Good, remember that when I tell you the next part."

"The silly part?"

"Yes."

"Lay it on me."

Arden paused to sip her coffee, then sat back and said one word, "Goats."

"Goats?" Emery grinned. "That's all I get?"

"Well, they're small, low-maintenance grazing animals. They are largely capable of wandering freely. They produce very little waste, and they'll eat nearly anything."

"Like grass?"

"Yeah, and weeds, poison ivy, shrubbery. I don't have the facts and figures memorized, but I think you'd be surprised how much a small herd of goats could consume, and the good news is they prefer to eat food that's around their height, so they'll likely start from the top-down on anything getting tall enough to cast shade on solar panels. That way they wouldn't have to completely clear everything in order to meet your basic needs."

"Seriously? They have a height preference for their meals?"

"Sure." Arden shrugged. "Don't you? I mean, we're using a table right now rather than bending over to pick our pastries off the floor."

"Huh, I've never thought of it that way before. Do you really think goats could work?"

"Maybe, or perhaps you could use them as a stopgap for a few years while you slowly change over whatever's growing there now into better-suited vegetation. That way you wouldn't have to do all the work or spend all the money up front."

"A one-two punch." Emery nodded. "I like it. We could do a small segment each summer, something manageable, and pair it with your super goats to patrol what we haven't gotten to yet." She paused. "Why are you better at my job than I am?"

"I'm not. I'm totally unemployable, and I hate that so much I might just apply to be your lowly goat herder if you find a way to make this work, but I do know some very capable people who could help you develop a purposeful five-year plan."

"You do? I thought you hated networking and social connecting."

"These people aren't social climbers. They're botanists."

"You have botanists on speed dial? Will the surprises never cease?"

"They're Luz's parents. That's how we met. We hired them to—"

"Arden? Emery?" A voice called from the doorway, and they both turned to see Marlo and Mitchell Clayton coming toward them.

"Oh shit. Incoming." Emery muttered, then rose to shake Mitchell's hand. "Good morning, Mr. and Mrs. Clayton. I would offer to introduce you to Arden, but it seems you already know each other."

"Marlo is one of my mother's friends," Arden said, her voice artificially light. "How do you two know each other?"

"Mr. Clayton is on the board at Pembroke and Sun."

"Wow, small world." Arden didn't stand, and Emery wondered if it were for fear of fainting again.

"I told you it was them," Marlo said triumphantly to her husband before addressing them again. "I was so sure I saw the two of you headed upstairs when we checked in last night, but Mitchell said I had an overactive imagination."

He shifted a little nervously. "I've been wrong so often over the years I should know better than to contradict her, but you have to admit, dear, you couldn't think of any logical reason for them to be here either."

Emery and Arden traded a little look as if asking the other to please have something to say other than explaining the real reason.

"True. We didn't know the two of you were friends, much less close enough to take girls' trips together."

Arden bit her lip so hard it went white, and Emery got the sense she shouldn't expect much help from her in this particular conversation, so she jumped in herself. "We went to school together, and we've recently reconnected since I've come back to town to stay."

"How wonderful," Marlo enthused. "I'm so glad to see you getting out there, Arden. You're always so quiet. I should've known Emery would be the one to broaden your horizons, though. She's so gregarious."

152

"Indeed." Mitchell glanced quickly from one of them to the other, clearly reading the situation differently than his wife. "We should let the two of you get back to your day."

"Oh, what's your rush? What sorts of activities have you girls done on your little excursion?"

Arden about choked on her own tongue, and Emery raised her voice to draw their attention back to her.

"So many things!" She injected excitement that verged on the edge of manic. "We've been on quite the literary tour. We spent the better part of yesterday at Walden Pond seeing the Thoreau sites, and then went to the Alcott house, because we're both such big fans of women, I mean *Little Women*, the book."

"That's such a favorite of mine." Marlo clearly approved of this itinerary, but her husband seemed more suspicious.

"I didn't know you were such a big reader, Emery," he said.

"You know, I haven't been for a few years, what with travel and my busy schedule, but since I'm settling back into Amherst and spending more time with Arden, I think she's done a nice job of rubbing off on me." *God why did everything sound so suggestive right now?* "Arden let me borrow a book about the poets and essayists of New England a couple weeks ago, and I realized she had a lot to teach me."

"It's always the quiet ones," Mitchell mused.

"That's just wonderful." Marlo plowed forward. "We've been doing the Revolutionary War sites. Mitchell's such a history nut, but maybe I'll sneak away this afternoon and go see the *Little Women* house myself."

"If you want time to do that, we'd better get going now," Mitchell said.

"Of course. Will we see you two here again this evening?"

"Nope," Emery said quickly. "I have a feeling we've already stayed a little longer than we should. Probably time to hit the road for us, too."

"Too bad. This was such a lovely surprise, wasn't it?" She turned to her husband.

"Quite the surprise," he said as he backed away. "You two enjoy whatever else you have planned for the weekend, and Emery, I'm sure I'll see you soon."

"I don't doubt it."

"And I'll see you, Arden." Marlo walked out the door adding, "I can't wait to tell your mother we ran into you."

Once they were out of sight, Emery sank slowly back into her seat and shoved the remainder of her breakfast into her mouth, but it didn't taste nearly as sweet as it had five minutes earlier.

Arden stared at her, eyes wide, hands folded neatly in her lap. She seemed small again all of a sudden, shocked, maybe a little stupefied, and most of all, silent.

Emery's own panic threatened to send her mind spinning with "what ifs" and "what nows," but she couldn't surrender to them. She couldn't even fully acknowledge the possible repercussions of a board member with a vote on her entire future running into the two of them after a spontaneous night of sex, not with Arden looking to her for answers, for confidence, for something she wasn't sure she possessed.

She forced a smile as she swallowed the remainder of what should've been a nice breakfast. "So, you know I'd love to linger here with you, and I don't want you to think even for a second that I'm rushing you out the door after what we did last night."

"No." Arden shook her head and pushed back from the table solemnly. "But we've got to get back to Amherst, right now."

🐐 🐐 🐐

154

They were less than half an hour outside Concord when Arden's phone buzzed the first time. Even though she'd been expecting it, she still jumped.

She glanced at the screen quickly in case she might not want to see what the message actually said, or who'd gotten to her first. Thankfully the initial salvo came from Luz, a simple but effective, "Where the fuck are you?"

Emery arched her eyebrow without looking away from the road.

"Luz." She offered in way of explanation.

"Could be worse."

"It will be," she said, then added, "Probably already is, because Luz doesn't exactly exist high up on the gossip chain."

Arden typed back. "In the car."

It wasn't the most descriptive answer, even if it were the truest. Luz took all of fifteen seconds to fire back. "With who?"

There was the crux of the matter, and if she knew enough to ask, there wasn't any use denying anything. "Emery."

"Holy fuck."

Leave it to Luz to sum up things so concisely.

"She knows?" Emery asked.

"She does now."

Emery nodded slowly. "I keep trying to think of something to say, something eloquent and thoughtful and poignant, but 'sorry' doesn't seem right since I don't regret anything we did. At the same time, I do not love the scrutiny we're about to face and the assumptions people will undoubtedly make."

"Totally agree," Arden said, finding what the statement lacked in poetry it made up for with heart. "Will being associated with me hurt you at work?"

"What? No." Emery took her hand. "I don't think so, but in a weird way, that's not worth going into now. It may put pressure on us, and certainly a lot of people will think they know what's going on, or make guesses."

155

Her phone buzzed again, but Arden didn't look this time. She'd deal with Luz later. Now she wanted to hold onto whatever solace she had left in Emery's touch. "And none of them will guess that I'm the one who propositioned you yesterday."

Emery laughed. "Is that what happened?"

"I asked you to stay all night."

"Yeah, I'm relatively certain no one will believe that."

"I won't let them think you corrupted me."

"I appreciate that, but you shouldn't worry about what other people think."

"And you? Have you mastered that skill?"

"A few months ago I would've said yes, but my life's gotten more complicated lately," Emery said. "Still, I had a really good time with you."

She didn't dare ask how many other women she'd had a really good time with in the past. She'd fully understood Emery's comments yesterday about second dates and how rarely they occurred for her after a first date had ended the way it had last night. She wasn't as naive as people seemed to think. She hadn't slept with Emery because she believed they were falling in love, or that she could somehow entice her to do so sexually. She'd slept with Emery because she wanted to, and she was glad she had, even if there would be some sort of hell to pay now.

As if on cue, Emery's phone began to ring and Theo's name popped up on the car's console screen.

"Probably a work thing," she said unconvincingly.

"A work thing like a member of the board of trustees called to report you sneaking away with one of his friend's daughters and shacking up for the night?"

"Yeah, possibly, but wait till he hears about the whole goat idea."

She smiled, glad one of them still had a sense of humor. "You can answer the call and tell him now if you want."

"Nah, it's a weekend. He can wait until I get home."

156

"It might not be a big deal," Arden said with false enthusiasm.

"It might not," Emery agreed. "I mean, I've done way more interesting things than visit Walden Pond in the past."

She knew it wasn't the idea of visiting literary sites that was burning up the gossip network, but Emery was doing the best she could to allude to other scandalous liaisons without mentioning them outright.

"Were you CEO when you did those things?"

"I'm not CEO now," she said flatly, and for the first time, Arden read more tension than awkwardness in her voice.

"If I need to step away—"

"No." Emery squeezed her hand tightly. "That would not help. People would think I threw you away like some cheap one-night stand, and it would hurt my reputation worse than …"

She waited for the end of the sentence, but Emery seemed to compose herself quickly and start over.

"I didn't take you out with the intention of scoring. I didn't have any grand plan other than having a nice day together, and I did, but I also didn't think about the prospect of locking either of us into anything."

She nodded as if she understood, but she wasn't sure she did. Was Emery trying to release her from the scrutiny they were facing now, or was she trying to find a way out for herself?

Arden's phone buzzed again, this time the low, steady pulse of a call rather than a text. She looked down once more and realized immediately that her mother's impeccable timing had struck again.

Emery must have sensed the shift in her too. "Who now?"

"My mom." She felt small even saying the words, and childish for how they made her feel.

"It's okay." Emery gave her hand a little squeeze. "You can answer if you want."

It wasn't a matter of wanting so much as she'd never ignored her mother, not once in her entire life. She had just enough awareness left to realize she should probably examine that fact at some point, but she didn't have the fortitude to do so here and now. With a shaky hand, she pressed "accept" and lifted the phone to her ear. "Hello."

"Arden, I am going to ask you this one time, very calmly." Her mother's voice was filled with steel. "Are you with Emery Pembroke?"

She closed her eyes. "Yes."

"And you have been since last night?"

"Yes."

"Very well," her mother said with an eerie sort of calm. "Come straight home. We'll discuss the consequences."

"Mother, I don't think—"

"Exactly," she interjected. "You don't think. You didn't think about any of us before you subjected the family to something like this. You didn't think of your future prospects, and you certainly don't think very highly of yourself in order to allow someone like her to use you, and then flaunt you around in front of our friends."

"That's not what—"

"I'm not having this conversation over the phone, and since you've shown yourself incapable of restraint or responsible decision-making, your father and I will begin damage control when you get home, which I suggest you do immediately."

"Mom," she started, but she was talking to dead air. The silence cut through her every bit as harshly as the words.

"Are you okay?" Emery whispered.

She nodded.

"I can go with you."

She snorted softly.

"No?"

"It would make everything worse, for both of us."

"Okay."

158

No, it wasn't. Nothing was okay. This morning should've been happy. She'd just had the best twenty-four hours of her life. She'd let herself believe she could actually be the kind of person who just enjoyed herself without fear or anxiety, and for those glorious hours with Emery, she had. But she should've known it couldn't be just the two of them forever. Emery had been wrong when she'd said Arden was like Thoreau. Introverted yes, but not nearly strong enough to withstand the pressure of society, of her family, of the chokehold of expectations. She wasn't ashamed of having slept with Emery, but she was deeply embarrassed about how she would surely wilt under the scrutiny from everyone around her.

She couldn't stand to have people talking about her. She didn't have the stomach for justifying her actions, or even existing fully in the public eye. What's more, now Emery would know all those things, too.

It hurt to breathe. Emery, who was so brave and strong and confident. She would handle everything so well. She would speak eloquently and refuse to lose sleep over anyone who dared to judge her. Emery would live her life with full authenticity that would crush Arden by comparison. They'd never be able to look each other in the eye again.

Her hands began to tremble, causing the phone to shake. She turned it over to see the messages she'd ignored from Luz. "Your mom is looking for you" followed quickly by "Let's get our stories straight."

She had no story, at least not one she wanted to share with anyone. She had no defense against the onslaught headed her way, and while Luz and Emery would both fight on her behalf, the best thing she could do now was to not ask them to. If she was going to face the music, she could at least do so alone. Maybe then they wouldn't see the worst of her.

Her teeth started to chatter as the tremors raced through her body.

"Hey?" Emery tried to get her attention. "Are you cold?"

159

She shook her head. She didn't think so. She didn't actually feel much as her system began to shut down. *Please no, please no, not here, not now, not in front of her.*

They were only twenty minutes away from home now. If she could just hold on, she could at least save some shred of her dignity, but the more she tightened up, the worse the shaking got.

"Arden." Emery's voice took on a nervous edge. "It's going to be okay. We're grown women. We aren't in trouble. No one is going to ground us or take away our phones for sneaking off together."

She would've very much liked to be sent to her room with no way for anyone to contact her, but she'd lost the ability to make jokes.

"We didn't do anything wrong. It's going to be awkward to have people in our business, but you don't owe anyone anything. Not an apology, not an explanation, nothing."

Her mother wouldn't see it that way. Neither would their friends, and while that clearly didn't matter to someone like Emery, the badgering, and underhanded comments, and knowing stares would be too much for Arden to bear. She could hardly stomach social events when people ignored her. The thoughts spun through her mind now, the same things over and over on a loop, and she grew completely helpless to stop the cycle or move it forward. Soon it wasn't just her mind spinning, but her vision too.

She was no longer trying to stop the panic attack. It had already overtaken her. The only option left was to try to limit the damage, but even that realization was hazy. Her parents had already likely begun their own version of damage control while she, on the other hand, didn't even have command over her body. She began to hyperventilate. Then the strangest sensation took over, a sudden, strong deceleration and a tightening across her chest. It took her entirely too long to process the sensation as external. Emery had stopped the car and pulled onto the wide, grassy shoulder of the road.

She ran around to Arden's door and helped her unbuckle before practically lifting her out and supporting her weight as they crossed quickly to the tree line. Emery led her between a tight cluster of tall pines and eased her down until they sat together on the ground, then wrapped an arm tightly around Arden's shoulder.

The move was so unexpected Arden's mind worked to process the swift change in scenery, and doing so caused a break in the shame spiral twisting through her brain.

"I'm right here," Emery whispered, clutching her tightly. "We're okay."

She shook her head as a new embarrassment took over. Emery was managing her anxiety. The one thing she'd still hoped to avoid had come to pass.

"Put your hands on the ground," Emery instructed gently.

Arden did as told and sank her fingers into the pine straw below them until her fingers touched hard-packed dirt.

"See, solid ground. You're safe with me."

She managed to take in a shallow, shuddering breath.

"God, doesn't the forest smell so good?" Emery asked.

She tried to breathe through her nose this time, catching hints of grass and soil.

"There you go," Emery encouraged, still hugging her close enough to her chest that, as Arden's own heart began to lessen its roar through her ears, she could make out the sound of Emery's beating rapidly as well. She tried to process the thought that Emery's pulse was racing too, no doubt elevated by fear of Arden crashing out on her, but she never gave any other outward sign. Her voice stayed calm and kind while the hold she had on her never wavered.

"I've got you. The ground has got you. The trees are watching over us. You're secure and you're safe."

161

The words washed over her, and she softened into Emery's chest as the tremors continued to work their way out of her system. As soon as she could string words together, she muttered, "You don't have to do this."

"I want to," Emery said. "I want to help."

"It's not your fault."

"It's not yours either."

She choked on a sound somewhere between a laugh and a sob.

Emery kissed her temple. "This is going to pass. All of it. It always blows over, and when it does, we're going to be okay. We will be stronger and wiser and more secure because we made it through."

Arden let herself go slack against Emery. She wasn't sure if she was talking about the panic attack or the scandal they'd sparked, or maybe even their time together, but she supposed she was right. They would all end eventually, and for the first time, she gave herself space to believe Emery might be right about the rest of it, too.

Chapter Twelve

"Fuck, fuck, fuck." Emery kicked the door shut behind her.

"Well, I'm glad you said it, or I was going to have to." Theo pounced. "No, actually, I still have to say it 'what the fuck?'"

"I don't know."

"So much for taking things slow and practicing discretion."

"I know." She fell into her desk chair and then hopped up again quickly. She had too much energy to collapse, even if part of her ached to do so. "For what it's worth, I didn't plan any of this."

"No. You never do, and that's what's so maddening." He'd been waiting for her at the office, and seeing it was a Sunday afternoon, they both made use of having the place to themselves by shouting out their frustration. They weren't really yelling at each other, or at least she wasn't yelling at him, but it felt good to vent.

"Believe it or not, she's the one who came on to me."

"I do not," he said frankly. "It doesn't track. She ended your last date in a free fall. I don't think the leap from Victorian fainting couch to ravenous sex kitten in two weeks is plausible. I mean, you're good with women, but not that good."

"It didn't work like that. I wasn't trying to be sexy at all. The day was decidedly bland in so many ways. No fast cars, no fancy meals, no wine, no dancing, there wasn't even any sexy banter."

"Maybe you didn't notice your own sexy banter. Sometimes it just rolls out of you."

She paused to check her memories. They'd been playful, and maybe even a bit teasing a time or two, but she hadn't played on innuendo or thinly veiled come-ons. "I think we just talked to each other."

"No, you and I talk to each other. With women, you flirt."

"I talked to her, Theo, really talked to her, about interests and books and snippets of our childhoods, and even our insecurities."

"You mean her insecurities since you don't have any, or at least not any you'd admit to."

She pursed her lips and looked away.

"Wait, what insecurities did you tell her about that you haven't told me about?"

"It doesn't matter." She started to pace. "The point is the date went really well, and it turned into a night that was unexpectedly amazing, all at her request."

"At her request? What, did she send you a monogrammed invitation to skip dinner and go right to eating her—"

"Hey," she snapped, surprising both of them.

He stared at her for a second as if waiting for some sort of explanation.

"It wasn't like that. We were having a good time. She said she wanted to stay. I asked if she wanted to grab dinner, and she said she'd rather stay all night."

He stared at her for a moment as if waiting for her to crack a joke or at least a smile, and when she didn't, he couldn't seem to figure out what to say. "I'm stuck. I'm trying to take what you're saying at face value, but you know no one else in town is going to believe that Arden jumped you and not the other way around."

"I know."

"They'll believe you corrupted her for the purpose of a one-night stand."

164

"Yeah." She'd already done all this math in her head.

"We're going to have to be proactive. I'd hoped we could talk pros and cons and get a full report on compatibility before we eased into the public eye, but that ship has sailed. There's no use talking about what could've been or what should've been. You're dating this woman now."

"Well, I mean, we did have a couple dates."

"One of them which ended with you sleeping with her in a way that the whole town knows about."

"Right, but—"

"No buts," Theo said quickly. "You cannot walk away from her now, not with everyone watching."

Emery shook her head. She didn't want to walk away from her, but it wasn't so clear-cut anymore.

"Emery," he said in a warning tone. "I know you don't like relationships or being tied down or limiting your options."

"It's not that."

"Bullshit. You're great at getting the girl who captures your attention, but we have to be honest about how short your attention span is. I've seen you pull off some lusty long weekends of pairing food, wine, and sex for three or four days, but when was the last time you actually dated someone, like left bed, went your separate ways for a few days, and then went out again?"

She didn't search her memory. She didn't want to know. "A long time."

"Right, but you have to now."

"I understand what you're saying. I do." She rubbed her forehead. "But I'm not sure going public with Arden is a good idea."

"Then, you should've thought about that before you bedded her down the hall from a board member and his wife, the aging socialite. I don't care how bored you are. You have to play this out now."

"I'm not bored with her," she snapped. "God, I understand the assumptions you're making right now aren't

165

unfair or unfounded, but Arden's different from any girl I've been with, and in every possible way. I'd love to spend more time with her. I'd love to see her again, talk to her again, sleep with her again."

"Really?" Theo couldn't seem to make it all make sense. "Like, to seal the CEO title?"

"No. I mean yes, but not just that, though she had some really great ideas I think I'm going to pitch to Bergman."

Theo eased into a chair. "I'm listening."

"We'll talk about business in a minute. Right now, I want to focus on Arden."

"The two are inseparable at the moment, but it sounds like that may actually be a good thing. If you can handle dating her, and she's good for work, why try to compartmentalize the two?"

"Because the work, the pressure, the title, the public eye, none of it's good for her."

Theo laughed lightly.

"I'm not kidding. She was a dream yesterday and last night, and if that woman could be on my arm through this whole thing, I'd absolutely find a way to make myself relationship material, or at least try, but as soon as people started calling this morning with their questions and accusations, she crumbled again."

"She fainted? Is that like a Victorian lady thing she does? Have you tried loosening her corset?"

"She didn't pass out this time, or the other time either, but I think she had a panic attack. I've never seen one in real life, but whatever it was, it hurt to watch. She turned on herself like she'd become a prisoner in her own body. She couldn't talk other than to repeat things over and over, and her eyes lost focus. She couldn't get a full breath."

"Shit." Theo's complexion went a little white. "What did you do?"

"I pulled over and led her into, like, this little grove of trees and held her real tight until the shaking stopped."

"Did it work?"

Not fast enough for her tastes. Every minute of watching Arden in distress had felt like an eternity. Her body had seemed so much smaller and frailer than when they'd been in each other's arms the night before. Still, she couldn't deny that she'd been able to talk her down, to soothe her, to offer much-needed comfort, and a part of her had warmed to the role in a way she didn't want to examine yet. "Yeah. It worked."

"How'd you know what to do? I mean the trees and, like, sitting on the ground?"

"The day before she said some things about hiding from the world when she was little. I guess I remembered?"

"That's not nothing. You don't normally have the ear for details, but you are really good with people. It sounds like you did well with her. I'm impressed, actually. Maybe this girl is different, or maybe you're different, too. I don't know, but you definitely have to see her again."

"I don't know if it's a good idea to drag her any further down this road."

"It's too late. She's standing in the middle of the road, and if you don't keep moving, you're both going to get hit by a truck."

Her stomach dropped, and it must've shown because Theo softened. "I know you don't want to hurt her. I don't understand where this new protective instinct is coming from, and under other circumstances, I might even enjoy watching the scene play out, but ghosting her at this point isn't going to save anyone from scandal or pain."

"But pushing forward won't either. It's not going to help my cause with the company. The wife of a CEO can't fall apart when they end up in the public eye. I'd be setting her up to fail and putting her through so much stress."

"If you walk away, she's still in the public eye, only now it's because she got duped into being a cheap trick, and you also earn the ire of the entire community."

"And prove myself unworthy of the company." She ran her hands through her hair roughly. "Either way, we end up losing both the company and her sanity. What if neither of us was ever really cut out for the things we're doing, not in any way?"

He shrugged. "It's possible, but what if you could both become better together?"

She raised her eyebrows.

"I know. It's weird for the pragmatist to play devil's advocate with some romantic notion, but if you care about Arden and you care about this company, I don't see how you have any other choice but to make the two work together."

She didn't even know what that would look like. A part of her wanted to be back in the woods, holding Arden close, whispering that everything would be okay. She wanted to believe herself. She wanted to be the strong one, the competent one, the one with the answers, but here in this office, she didn't feel like that person anymore. She had no idea how to be a good partner or daughter or CEO.

"Did you mention something about the Bergman deal?" Theo asked. "Something Arden helped with?"

"Yes!" She about jumped for joy. "I mean, it's crazy. Everything that's happened for a month is crazy, and I don't really know if it will work, but I do think it's worth trying … with Arden."

"You want Arden to go to see Bergman with you?"

She nodded slowly. She hadn't thought of that, but it made sense, especially in light of what he'd said about needing to get better on all fronts. "Yes. Call my mother and Brian. Set up a meeting, and um, get me some goats."

He stuck his finger in his ear as if trying to clear it. "Sorry, I must've misheard. I thought you said 'goats.'"

168

She laughed. "I did."

"What kind of goats? How many? Where does one even get goats?"

"I have no idea." A little bubble of hope rose up inside her. "But I know who does."

🐐 🐐 🐐

"What in God's name were you thinking?" Arden's mother pounced as soon as she joined her in the formal dining room.

"I didn't think about—"

"That's right. You didn't think. You couldn't have possibly." She and Arden's father were both seated at the long table that had been stripped bare so the glossy finish reflected distorted versions of their faces, or maybe those were just their expressions.

"Have a seat," her father said solemnly.

It wasn't an invitation, and she obeyed as always.

"We talked about it," her mother continued.

They hadn't really. Her mother had opined on the subject, but Arden hadn't talked about her thoughts or feelings at all. Still, she knew better than to point out the distinction.

"Honestly, Arden, I knew you had it in you to get a little silly over someone like Emery. You've always been prone to romantic notions, always stuck in a book or a garden like you fancy yourself some fairy-tale princess, but never in all my life would I have considered the possibility that you'd allow yourself to be lured into debauchery so easily."

"Patricia." Her father pushed up the rims of his glasses so he could pinch the bridge of his nose. "Is that really necessary?"

"What would you call it? Your daughter spent the weekend shacked up in an off-brand bed-and-breakfast with an infamous bon vivant and womanizer."

169

He sighed. "I think we should at least let her offer some sort of explanation."

"Explanation?" Her mother exploded in a way that made the single word sound like an incredulous question and painful exclamation simultaneously. "What's to explain? One of my dearest friends saw them with her own eyes, and don't for a second think that Emery didn't love that. If I had to place money on it, I wouldn't bet against the possibility she planned it that way."

"No one planned anything." Arden finally got a word in.

"You're so naive. It wouldn't at all be hard for her to lead you into a trap and then flaunt you around."

"I'm not exactly the flaunting type."

"See." She snapped her fingers. "That's exactly what I'm talking about. Just because people have left you well enough alone up to this point doesn't mean no one has anything to gain by sniffing around. In fact, I suspect it's precisely the fact that you haven't had many suitors that makes you so susceptible to people like Emery, who swoop in and offer the bare minimum in charm and flattery, then walk away with something you didn't even know you had to give."

"I'm not sure what you're talking about."

"Exactly my point. For you it was just a fun weekend doing God knows what, and please don't tell me."

Finally, something they could agree on.

"But Emery's no idiot. She understands that the more access she has to you, the more she can glean from your wealth, your reputation, your connections."

"She has plenty of all those things on her own. She doesn't need me—"

"Need? Maybe not. Want? Absolutely. Don't pretend you don't know several of the young women she's amused herself with over the years."

170

Arden clenched her jaw. She did know several people Emery had been seen around town with, going all the way back to high school.

"She does what suits her, anytime, all the time. And the minute she has what she wants, she's done, leaving everyone else a little worse off."

Arden didn't think that was true. She never had, but especially not after what they'd been through this morning. She couldn't imagine the woman in the tree grove who'd held her leaving anyone worse for having been close to her.

"Surely you can't think you're different than all the others, or that you'd fare better than any of them."

She shook her head. Surely she didn't even measure up to most of the people Emery knew. She'd buckled both times they'd been together. Emery had easier options, and probably better in every way. She harbored no visions of grandeur. She knew an infinite number of women who were prettier, flirtier, sexier, more fun, more social, more stable, and she didn't delude herself into thinking Emery couldn't have any one of them anytime she pleased.

"How do you think this is going to end?" her mother finally pushed. "Do you really believe there could ever be any kind of future with her?"

Her father cleared his throat. "I'm actually interested in the answer to that question as well."

She turned to him, reading the gentle concern in his eyes.

"I'm not as easily scandalized as your mother," he continued, "nor do I completely share her assessment of Emery's character. She always seemed like an engaging individual, and certainly her parents are both fine people, but I am left pondering what the two of you have in common."

She raised her eyebrows.

"Interests? Aspirations? Hobbies? Worldviews? I don't pretend to understand all the nuances, but I was a young person once and had some vague ideas about the kind of person I might like to spend my life with. Is Emery the kind of woman you see yourself marrying?"

She bit her lip. As much as she wanted to say yes, the idea felt rather far-fetched even after the way they'd spent the last twenty-four hours. The tender moments, the kisses, the chemistry, it had all been more than she'd ever dreamed, but when she considered what their respective lives might entail going forward, she couldn't see herself in Emery's world or at her level, and this morning had driven home the contrast rather cruelly. "I do like her very much, and she's been incredibly kind to me, but I don't know that either of us has thought of marriage compatibility."

"I don't know whether to be relieved or sad about that," he admitted. "I'm glad you weren't misled, because I do share your mother's sense that Emery isn't the kind of person to count on long-term. Mitchell shared those concerns when we spoke. He said the board over at Pembroke and Sun voted not to name her CEO of the company because she's too flighty."

Her heart gave an unpleasant thump, and she grimaced at the pain it caused to think of people showing so little faith in Emery. No wonder she doubted her capabilities at work. They hadn't just failed to support her in this recent deal, they'd withheld it at every level. How could they all miss the finer qualities Arden so clearly saw in her, the consideration she'd put into planning their date, the way she'd deferred to Arden and made her feel safe, the way she'd remembered all the details that really mattered, and her quiet, strong, emotional intelligence to navigate her anxiety.

"At the same time," he went on carefully, "if you didn't have some unifying commonality or plans for a bright future, I'm at a loss as to what you do hope for out of this association with her. You've always been so careful, so thoughtful. Your behavior seems so wildly out of character, which leaves me much more worried about my own daughter than I am for Emery, or anyone else for that matter."

She had no response to that level of fatherly concern. She couldn't possibly make him understand what she felt in that instant when she'd asked Emery to stay all night. She didn't even fully understand it herself, and by some sweet miracle, she didn't have to.

"Pardon me." Sonia, one of the house staff cracked open the door from the kitchen. "There's a caller for Miss Arden."

"Tell them she's not available at the moment," her mother said curtly.

"I tried, but it's Miss Luz."

"Of course it is."

"She says Miss Arden has a dress she needs for an event this evening, and she can't wait."

"It's true," Arden said, not because she knew what Luz was up to, but because she always had one of her dresses somewhere.

"Let her go, Patricia," her father said.

"We still have too much to discuss."

"And I'm sure we will, ad nauseam, but give us all a few minutes to reflect on round one. Then you can regroup before you fire the next salvo."

Her mother pursed her lips so tightly the expression tugged at the corner of her eyes.

Arden didn't wait long enough to see if she'd relent or self-detonate. She saw her window and ran.

Luz was waiting at the back door, but Arden didn't even offer so much as a hello before grabbing her hand and dragging her up the stairs to her room and slamming the door behind them.

She fell onto her own bed and screamed into a pillow.

"Wow," Luz finally said, "big day?"

She sat up and stared at her. She couldn't even fathom, and Arden didn't know where to start. No words could convey what she'd experienced over the last twenty-four hours, and there was no way of retelling what had happened in a way that

173

would make sense to anyone who knew her. She assumed the details would all pour out eventually in some disconnected and convoluted fashion, but if her parents were to be believed, everything would be over long before she found a way to convey any meaning.

"I don't care," she finally said.

"Good for you," Luz said enthusiastically. "About what?"

"Any of it."

"Can I get a little more of your internal dialogue for context?"

"My parents. They were just grilling me."

"Oh yeah, I saw that coming. When your mom called me, I knew she must be losing her mind because her favorite pastime is pretending I'm not alive."

"She called you?"

Luz nodded. "She said she was hoping I was with you."

"That's a first."

"No shit. I almost fell out of my chair. I didn't want to reveal anything if you were supposed to be with me, but if you were missing, I didn't know if I should worry, so I made up some shit about getting another call, and tracked your phone. When I saw you were on the interstate, I got worried maybe you'd been kidnapped because you never go anywhere alone."

"I wasn't alone."

"Yeah, I figured that out. Dude, you should have told me. I would've run interference for you. It would've been such an honor to lie to your mom while you ran off for sexy times with a smoking-hot dreamboat."

"Thanks. I didn't know I needed anyone to cover for me. It all sort of happened, and it was amazing and so much more than I could've imagined, even if I had considered the possibility."

Luz hopped onto the bed next to her. "That good?"

"Beyond good. I've never felt that way in my life, at least when it was just the two of us together, but then this morning it all went to hell. We ran into people we knew, everyone started calling, my mom lost her mind, I had a panic attack, and Emery had to pick up the pieces. Then I had the most awkward conversation ever with my parents."

"That's saying a lot."

"Right? All my conversations are awkward, especially with them, but this one shattered all the records. My mom's flipping out about my reputation, which isn't even the least bit surprising, but my dad's concerned about Emery's intentions and me getting my heart broken, and I don't know how to tell them that I just don't care."

"Okay, yeah, that's great context. Thank you," Luz said seriously.

"You're welcome, and does that make me a bad person?"

"To not care what anyone else thinks? No."

Arden sagged against her shoulder. "It's a new feeling for me, but I think it's even bigger than public opinion. I don't care about any of it, not Emery's intentions, not the long-term plan, not even about getting my heart broken."

"Well, I wouldn't go that far."

"I would." Arden's laugh sounded slightly manic. "I'd go so far with her, as far as she'll let me for as long as we can, and I have no illusions about being able to hold her attention, but for a few hours last night I did have it completely, and that was life-changing. Even if I can just feel that way in a series of moments, I want all of them. I want to live those experiences for everything they are without thinking about weddings or babies or any sort of a shared future."

Luz wrapped an arm around her waist. "I'm so proud of you. You're finally going after what you want. I mean, it's a lot. It's a big shift really fast, but if you're sure you can keep your heart intact ..."

"I'm not," Arden admitted as a slew of memories flashed through her mind. Emery kissing her sweetly in the woods. Emery staring down at her last night. Emery whispering soothing words in her ear. "I think there's a good chance I lose my heart, or at least a big part of it to her, but I don't mind. When the two of us are alone together, nothing else matters. I like her, and even more importantly, I like who I am when I'm with her."

Luz sighed.

"Yeah." Arden agreed with all the unspoken. "It might be a high price to pay, but I've never felt this way before, and I want as many of these feelings as I can get. I want to be the person she inspires me to be for every minute I can steal instead of fixating on all the ways things could go wrong, because of course they will. They always do. They already have."

"How did you leave things with her?"

"She offered to come in with me and face my parents."

"Seriously?"

"Yeah, but I didn't want her to see me fall apart again. She'd already defused one panic attack beautifully, and she kissed me goodbye, and she said she'd find a way to be in touch, but she's got some stuff blowing up at work." Arden stopped rambling for long enough to draw a deep breath. "I don't know, maybe it's over already. She said herself she doesn't make a habit of second dates, so I've already lasted longer than either of us expected."

"There's something to be said for beating the curve."

She smiled slightly. "Maybe. I don't know if I'll get another shot, but if today really was the end, I hope she doesn't tell me yet. For better or worse, whatever we have left or don't, I want to feel this way as long as possible, and for once in my life, I want to enjoy something for what it is, consequences be damned."

Chapter Thirteen

Emery tried not to fidget, but she couldn't help wondering if she'd bitten off a little more than she could chew. The last week hadn't exactly gone swimmingly at work. There'd been plenty of pushback to the research she'd asked people to assist her in, and the logistics had proved much harder than she'd anticipated. Then there was the work of getting Mr. Bergman to even consider seeing her again. She'd nearly suffocated in endless meetings and strategy sessions, each of them punctuated by doubt from everyone, including herself, which led to more questions she was never quite sure she'd answered fully or in a truly satisfactory fashion.

Then there were other questions she refused to answer or even acknowledge. Everyone she knew had heard about her getaway with Arden. They all seemed to be waiting for her to show her hand. Would she seriously try to make them believe she had good intentions or any hope of a serious relationship with an anxiety-ridden daughter of one of their contemporaries, or would she reveal herself to be the selfish cad they all saw her as? The defiant streak that usually sustained her bucked back hard against the idea that any of them had any right to her personal life, and it might've been enough this time, too, if not for her own internal war on the subject.

The personal struggle ultimately convinced her that inviting Arden today was a good idea, and when she'd first seen her standing in front of the office wearing jeans and a cozy cream sweater, it had taken everything Emery had not to pull her into a crushing hug.

However, as the drive out to Bergman's land wore on with Arden beside her and Brian in the back seat trying to make polite conversation, the worry began to plague Emery once more. Their interactions felt awkward and tense, like the two of them had a chaperone. Gone was the easy banter, gone were Arden's probing questions, gone were the casual touches. Emery thought it would be good for everyone's confidence to see her succeed, but the closer they got to the farm, the more she began to consider the possibility that she might fail. Mr. Bergman had made it abundantly clear he'd have a very short fuse today. Throw in the added pressure of crashing out in front of both her one supporter on the board and Arden, and her blood pressure started to rise.

"There's the turn." Brian pointed to an exit ramp off the highway, and Emery took the turn.

"When do I get to know where we're going?" Arden's voice held more than a hint of anxiety.

"I guess now would be fine," Emery admitted. She hadn't really had any reason to hide the details from her, other than she wasn't sure Arden would've come if she'd known she was accompanying Emery on a work trip with ridiculously high stakes. The last thing she wanted was to put more pressure on her.

The thought refocused her sense of purpose as she drove along the frontage road. "I spent all last week working on a new proposal for the deal I told you about, and I incorporated a lot of your ideas."

"Really?" Arden's voice rose, along with her eyebrows.

"In fact, almost the entire foundation of the plan came from our conversations last weekend, so I thought it only fitting for you to be there when I presented it."

"You're taking me to meet the old hippie?"

She laughed nervously. "I hope that's okay because we're almost there, but I promise you don't have to take part in the presentation or even talk. I'd like to have you there with me, and I hope I do your concepts justice and don't humiliate us all."

Arden reached over and took her hand. "I know you won't. I'm kind of nervous because someone who's never had a job probably shouldn't be pulled into the most important moment of yours, but I'm honored, truly."

"Good," Emery said in a rush of relief. She pulled the car over to where a man waited on the side of the road next to an open field and livestock truck. "Because we're here."

They all exited the car, and while Brian went straight to greet Mr. Bergman, Emery walked around to open the door for Arden.

"Sorry about all the company," she whispered, "and for not finding time for just the two of us before now. I thought maybe seeing all the work I've put in might be better than any excuse I could've offered via text or call."

"Absolutely," Arden said without hesitation. "You don't owe me any excuses, though. Go shine."

She nodded and turned back to the men. "Mr. Bergman, I see you've already met my board representative, but may I introduce my good friend Arden Gilderson."

"Pleasure." He shook Arden's hand.

"Ms. Gilderson is the one who sparked the proposal I'm here to make, but first I wanted to apologize for not taking the time to fully understand your position before we met last time. I'll admit I saw it as silly and surface level to care about lawn mowers in the grand scheme of a great green energy initiative, but Arden helped me understand I was the one being shortsighted. The type of commercial mowers it would take to care for a site this size would produce enough greenhouse gases to undercut our mission significantly, and it wouldn't align with either your personal values or the mission of Pembroke and Sun."

Mr. Bergman puffed out his chest. "I'm glad someone at that company of yours finally pulled their heads out of their backsides long enough to do the research."

"We did, and at Arden's urging, we also worked up a thirty-year, multistage plan to make sure we do better going forward." Emery produced a binder filled with pages of graphs and landscape blueprints. "In there you'll find a detailed schema and timeline, but the basic gist is that over the next five years, we'll slowly section off various parts of the property and recultivate the vegetation so the dominant species of grasses and ground cover will consist of native, low-growth plants."

He rubbed the stubble on his chin as he flipped through the book, ultimately stopping on the timeline. "This says here, they won't finish planting for five years, and it won't reach full growth for at least a few years after that. Am I supposed to accept mowing until then?"

"No," Emery said seriously, then flashed a smile at Arden. "We have a slightly unconventional, but adorable offer to make on that front as well. If you'll open the gate to the field, I'd be happy to demonstrate."

"Adorable?" he muttered, but he seemed curious enough to comply with her request, and as he worked on unfastening the metal gate, Emery walked over to the livestock truck and nodded for its driver to fold down the back. No sooner had the ramp hit the ground than three anxious and wary goats rattled their way down.

"Brian? Arden?" she called. "Care to give me a hand with the new lawn mowers?"

They jogged to her side, and while Brian quickly grabbed one of the goat's leashes, Arden's hands covered her mouth but failed to hold in a giddy little giggle.

"What?" Emery whispered as she took hold of the other two leashes and urged the reluctant goats forward. "You didn't think I'd actually do it?"

Arden shook her head. "I don't know. I didn't know what you thought or even if you remembered after everything that happened."

180

"It's a good idea, Arden. I believe in it. Now I just have to sell it to him." She lifted her head and smiled at Mr. Bergman as they herded the goats toward the gate. "I know this may look silly, and I don't want you to get the idea that I'm not taking this seriously, so I wanted to show you rather than tell you or draw a diagram."

Once the goats were through the gate, she unhooked the leads and closed them inside the fence. Upon being freed, they immediately put some distance between themselves and the onlookers, then began exploring their surroundings.

"We'll need to install a system of barriers and fences eventually, but we can start with movable pens, which are low cost and easy to shift based on need. Since goats tend to eat grass and shrubbery from the top-down, they'll deal with the shadiest bits of the plants first, and as you can see, we've currently got three sizes here—small, medium, and large—so they'll eat plants at different heights rather than competing for the same ones."

"Well I'll be darned," Mr. Bergman said. Sure enough, all three goats began sniffing around different areas.

"And again, none of this will be governed by whims," Emery reiterated. "We plan to study every aspect of the program to ensure we have the right breed, the right number, and the right plants. We envision this becoming a real opportunity to study the impact of grazing animals on solar sites if you choose to move forward."

"So your people will care for them?"

"Yes sir. We haven't worked out all the contacts yet, as we are awaiting your approval, but the general idea is that they'd live here late spring through fall, with regular visits from their caretakers. Then they'll winter in a pasture and walled enclosure of some sort we'd have built on our corporate grounds, or nearby.

"Goats are my granddaughter's favorite animal." He grinned, then nodded. "Okay, I'm not going to sign anything until my lawyers look at it, but I have to admit I like the concept,

181

and I appreciate your total turnaround. I'm a big fan of thinking outside the box."

"That's a quality I aspire to. I'm sorry it took so long for me to figure it out."

"You're still a little wet behind the ears." He clasped her on the shoulder. "But your dad was one of the best, and this makes me think you're growing in the right direction."

Emery's throat constricted so quickly she barely managed to squeak out, "Thank you."

"All right, I'm not going to drag this out." He stepped back. "I'll get the proposal to my lawyers, and if they don't see any contractual issues, we'll get this signed and finalized probably sometime next week."

"Thank you, sir." Brian stepped forward to shake his hand. "If you have any questions about the sustainability program, you can contact Emery's office, and if you need any more information about the contract itself, don't hesitate to call me. Both of our numbers are in the packet there."

"And the goats can stay in the meantime?" he asked a little sheepishly. "I'd like the grandkids to see them."

"Of course," Emery said seriously, then turned to grin back at Arden, who'd wandered over to the fence closest to the smallest goat. "We already checked the fencing in this section, and we'll send someone out in a day or two to see how they're acclimating."

"Very well." He held up the packet and headed toward his truck. "I'll get right on this."

They all stood and waved as he pulled out onto the road, then as he drove off, broke into celebration.

Brian gave a fist pump, and Emery let out a little whoop before almost doubling over. She might have sunk all the way to the ground in her relief if not for Arden's hand on her back. She straightened up to meet her eyes, dancing blue-green, and full of awe.

182

"I knew you could do it." Arden's cheeks colored with pleasure or pride.

"But I couldn't have without you." Emery wrapped her arms around her waist, then lifted her off the ground in a happy little twirl. "This idea was all yours."

"Maybe the theory, but you put it into practice," Arden said seriously. "That man was not happy to see you. I could read it in every inch of his body language when we pulled up, but you softened him. You disarmed him and made him listen, and you won him over with both logic and sentiment. I could never do that."

"You're both right." Brian cut back in. "Every part of this meeting from concept to plan to practice had to work together, and while we have to stop short of calling it a done deal, I don't see how we could consider this stage anything short of a triumph."

"Thank you for giving me another chance," Emery said to him, one arm still around Arden's waist.

"I meant what I said. I believe in you, and I'm rooting for you to succeed."

"Me too." Arden beamed.

"Come on." Brian started back toward the car. "Lunch is on me to celebrate."

"Deal." Emery started to follow, but Arden tugged her back.

"Wait, I have to say goodbye to the goats."

Emery laughed. "You really like them that much?"

"Oh, I do. They are so cute and curious, and look at them already doing their jobs like pros."

They turned to watch the goats already chomping away.

"They certainly warmed to their roles faster than I did."

"I wish I could stay here and watch them all day." Arden's voice took on a calm, almost dreamy quality.

"Well, about that ..." Emery started, then got hit with a wave of nervousness almost as strong as the one she'd suffered when they'd arrived. The last thing she wanted was to overstep her bounds or stress either of them out any more than the last week had, but she'd been quietly holding onto one last part of the plan, one she hadn't shared with anyone.

"What is it?" Arden touched her hand, and the little hint of connection gave her the spark she needed to go on.

"Well, it's already fall, so the goats won't be able to stay here long. We'll need to set up something for them closer to home, and I'm sure we could hire a local farmer to board them, but I was thinking that if we moved them onto some of my family's land, I could hire someone to care for them. I know it's a bit beneath your station, but you seemed kind of upset not to have a job, and you mentioned sort of offhandedly you'd like being a goat herder."

Arden launched herself at Emery, wrapping her arms around her neck and hugging her tightly.

"So, yes?" Emery laughed while holding her close.

"Yes," Arden whispered. "Yes, yes, yes."

The words sent a shiver down her spine as the echoes of their night together reverberated through her senses. She soaked up the feel of her, the warmth, the affection, the pull this woman had over both her body and her emotions.

Slowly, Arden eased back, and they stared at each other for a long moment before Brian cleared his throat and they stepped apart like little kids who'd been caught mooning over each other.

"Sorry," Arden finally said. "I'll say goodbye to my new friends. It'll be easier now since I know I'll see them again soon."

"Take all the time you need," Emery called as Arden went back to the fence once more. "And start thinking of names."

"I get to name them, too?" Arden sounded over the moon.

"Of course." Emery folded her arms across her chest and watched for a few minutes as Arden said her elaborate goodbyes

184

until she felt Brian's gaze on her. She didn't turn to face him, "What's wrong?"

"Nothing," he said. "I think we're both just enjoying the moment, though probably for different reasons."

"What's yours? The future of the company?"

"No. Though I did feel that earlier. Right now, I'm thinking more about your future."

She shook her head. "Don't read too much into anything, okay. I don't know if this, any of it, is going to become what you or the board wants. It's complicated, and for a lot of reasons."

"I can only imagine," he said softly, "but I've known you your whole life. We all saw your charisma from a young age, and then I remember when you came out and the women started to line up. You've always been so smooth and charming and engaging, and even a little full of yourself, but today, right there, was the first time I've ever seen you be genuinely *affectionate* with any of them."

Emery sighed, grateful for the word he'd chosen. It didn't feel off or dangerous. It fit in so many ways, but still, even in all its warmth and comfort, she couldn't help wondering if it might offer an on-ramp to something more.

🐐 🐐 🐐

"No, I totally understand," Arden said as Emery explained she couldn't see her again tonight.

"I'm not putting you off, I swear." Emery's voice filtered through the speakerphone of her car. "I would've invited you along on this trip if it weren't such short notice, and also, I didn't know if either of us wanted to tempt fate by sneaking away overnight again so soon after our last brush with all-out scandal."

"No, I suppose it's not wise to poke the bear, or rather bears, because there seem to be many of them," Arden said sadly. It hadn't even been a full two weeks since their night in Concord,

185

and her mother had yet to pass her in the hallway or let a family meal go by without verbally accosting her. Emery hadn't shared specifics, but a few offhanded comments about questions at work and from friends made it clear she'd faced her share of questions as well. Then there'd been all the pressure of Emery's job and the prospect of Arden taking on even the small role of goat herder. Everything had happened so fast. She understood the wisdom of laying low, and yet if Emery had swung by on her way to Boston, she would've hopped in the car with her anyway. "But you'll have fun in the big city, right?"

"Not as much fun as I used to. I might meet a couple of friends for drinks tonight, but I'm in meetings bright and early tomorrow, and while the optimist in me hopes I can wrap everything up around lunchtime tomorrow, I've learned not to expect quick or easy solutions anymore. I'll probably drive home well after dark to be back for a presentation with my mom Wednesday morning."

"I hate the idea of your driving into the night two nights in a row."

"Me too, but I've been told that hopping out of helicopters is frowned upon around here."

Arden laughed. "Were you really?"

"Yeah. Why?"

"Because that's a phrase I've never had an occasion to utter."

"Well, if you ever want to try jumping out of one, I'll show you, but not on company property." Emery's tone made it clear she was smiling, and Arden could picture her behind the wheel, eyes on the road, her profile perfectly illuminated in the setting sun.

She lay back on the bed and reveled both in the image and the sound of Emery's voice.

"I don't know. Everyone expects me to either be a perfect model of a modern major corporate leader, or an utter and abject failure. Sometimes people seem to expect both in different

186

moments, and I'm just over here trying to decide when I'm allowed to take which form of transportation."

"I'm sure any choice you make is the right one."

"I'm not sure I've managed to make very many choices the right one lately, except for the one you hand-fed to me last week."

"I just sparked the idea. You fleshed out the plan, made it work for you, then sold it to your client. You did all the hard work."

"No way." Emery laughed. "Finding the solution is the hard part. Once you have the answers, they're easy to spin."

"I was so in awe of you. Even if I'd had all those resources in my hands, I would've choked on my own tongue if I'd had to share them with someone else."

"You shared them with me."

"That's different," Arden said quickly. "You're different. You listened, and you cared. You didn't judge me or laugh at me for being silly."

"You aren't silly. You're smart, brilliant."

"I'm not sure goats qualify me as any sort of genius."

"Well, I could've sat there all day and not landed on goats." Emery sighed. "I actually had been racking my brain all week. Arden, I'm not sure you fully realize what this deal meant for me, and not just now that I've almost wrapped it up, but in the moment, when I thought I'd blown it for good. The weight of those expectations was crushing me."

Arden rolled onto her side and pulled her pillow closer, as if it might offer them both some comfort. "I think you're probably right. You come across as confident and competent all the time. It's hard to imagine you questioning your capabilities."

"It's not just me. Pretty much everyone is questioning something about my fitness right now, either mentally, emotionally, or commitment-wise."

"I know how that feels, all of it," Arden admitted, "and with me, it makes sense. I'd question me, too. I just can't figure

187

out why anyone would ever doubt you. You're everything my parents wish I could be."

"I seriously doubt that. I think your mom would straight up off me if given half the chance."

Arden didn't argue that point, as her mom was still livid even after a week and a half, but she also didn't see Emery for who she really was. "You're bold and bright and smooth and so good in social interactions. You're full of grace and charisma, and you look put together all the time. My mother would kill to have me display any of those qualities, but I've never managed to live up to the image she had in her mind of the kind of daughter she deserved."

"But the same qualities she ignores in you are the ones I fail to summon when needed," Emery said. "You're sweet and thoughtful and measured and mild-mannered. You're the perfect, dutiful daughter who never flies off the handle or shoots off your mouth or gets carried away with wild whims. Social graces can be taught with practice, really. It's not hard to make conversation. Most people want to talk about themselves anyway."

"Not from my experience. I fall apart regularly." It wasn't even hard for Arden to admit. She knew herself and her limitations so well by now. "I can't remember a single time I managed to live up to my family's expectations, but I can't imagine you not being good enough for anyone."

"Even after you saw me cleaning up the mess I made with Mr. Bergman last week?"

"You fixed that."

"It shouldn't have needed fixing in the first place. If my mom or Brian or, better yet, my dad ..." Emery's voice cracked slightly, and her thought drifted off. "It doesn't matter. I put the whole team in jeopardy, and it just drove home how little I meet—"

"Emery," Arden cut in softly. "You made a mistake. People make mistakes. I'm sure your parents have made them.

188

You learned from it, just like they did. You tried again. You did better the next time. You can't beat yourself up forever, and you can't let that shake your confidence so badly you're afraid to try again."

"Why do you make everything sound so easy?"

Arden laughed. "I don't know. I don't mean to. I'm the last one who should be giving this pep talk, honestly. I live in constant fear of coming up short or disappointing people."

"You've never disappointed me," Emery said, in her easy, even tone.

"I find that hard to believe. We've been out two times, and I melted down on both occasions."

"And I worried for you. I wanted to help. I thought maybe I should've been better, but I promise I never once felt disappointed in you."

She shook her head and sighed. "It's just so hard to believe you when you say things along those lines, but I'm starting to."

"Then I'll have to say them more, because they're true. I, on the other hand—"

"You're perfect."

"Hardly. We've been back from Concord for like ten days, and I haven't managed to take you out a single time."

"Not true," Arden said quickly. "You took me to see the goats, and then out to lunch."

"You went to a work meeting, and then Brian took us both out to eat. Hardly top-tier date material."

"And yet I greatly enjoyed both," she said, and not just to assuage the guilt in Emery's voice. She would've loved to see her alone, of course, but she loved it just as much that she'd taken the time to call, or stay in touch at all. It wasn't everything she wanted, but still much more than she expected. "Maybe I'm just an easy date."

189

"Well, I'm going to take time to be grateful for that, but we do need to work on setting the bar a little higher for you. What are your plans for the rest of the week?"

"Let me check my schedule and get back to you." She waited half a second, then laughed. "Just kidding, I have no schedule. I have nothing planned at all."

"Okay," Emery said seriously. "I'm coming into city traffic now, and I do have some stuff coming up, but before I let you go, I promise I'm going to find some time for us one way or another."

"I'll hold you to it," Arden said.

"No, you won't."

"No, I won't," she agreed, and with a smile added, "but you promised, so I know you will."

☀ ☀ ☀

"Emery!" The call went up from the back corner of the bar as soon as she walked in the door, and several of the worries she'd been shouldering through the streets of Boston fell away.

"Get this woman a Negroni," Lydia called to the barback, then grabbed her arm and made her spin around. "Let me get a good look at you, Boo."

Emery obliged and didn't even wave off the whistles and catcalls from their friends.

"Yes, yes," Lydia groaned. "Still a tall, sexy drink of water, even if you are a lousy louse of a friend who left us high and dry for nearly two months."

"You're often high, but I don't believe for a second you've been dry in my absence."

Lydia threw back her head and cackled. "Not in any sense of the word, but I have missed that wit and humor. None of the rest of this lot can keep up with me."

"Now *that* I believe," Emery said, "and also apologize."

Lydia reached around and cupped both of her ass cheeks to pull her into a crushing hug. "You're almost forgiven."

"Almost?" She slipped into the booth across from her friends, and Lydia edged in close enough for their sides to press together.

"Yes, come sit down and regale us with tales of your conquests on the western front. Do the young ladies of Amherst still swoon into your bed, or do you have to work a little harder now that you can't pass for a coed yourself?" Callum called from the other side of the table.

"Who says I can't?"

"And who says she's interested in coeds with a women's college so close by?" Jane added.

"Yes." Lydia hopped back in. "Which university's undergraduates have most benefited from your recent sojourn to the frontier?"

"No coeds."

"So you've moved up to grad students?"

"No." She didn't really want to tell tales about Arden, not after what they'd both been through in recent weeks. "I've been busy establishing myself in different circles."

"So back to socialites then?" Jane teased.

"Something like that. Honestly, I've been working a lot," she explained. "That's why I'm back in town. I've got an early meeting tomorrow with—"

"No." Lydia held a well-manicured finger to Emery's lips. "No one wants to hear about your board meeting, darling, and I refuse to believe a notorious cad like yourself can't do better in the drama department."

"Sorry. I've done little other than work since my father's memorial service."

They all glanced at one another, and Jane finally said, "I'm still sorry we couldn't make it out for that."

Her chest constricted at the memory, but she waved them off. "Tell me about all of you. How's newlywed life?"

"No complaints yet," Jane said. "Callum here still puts out regularly."

"As if there was any doubt." He kissed his bride.

"We're planning a ski trip for New Year's," Lydia said cheerfully. "I assume you're in?"

"Where?"

"Does it matter?" Lydia asked, passing Emery's Negroni over from the bar.

"I don't know."

"I'm pushing for France," Lydia said.

"Only so you can show off your native tongue." Jane shot back.

"I find plenty of ways to show off my tongue anywhere we go." She stuck it out at Emery for emphasis, and Jane snapped a picture while Emery nearly snorted gin up her nose.

"Be honest," Callum said to her. "You've missed this."

"I have," she admitted without arm-twisting. She'd been back for only a matter of minutes and already felt more comfortable than she had in weeks. Well, maybe not more comfortable than she had with Arden, but this kind of comfort was easy. Arden's comfort was deep and soothing, but complex. With this crowd, she never had to work hard or think outside the box. She'd known everyone around the table for at least ten years and never once had she needed to bend herself or plan ahead or take caution.

Honestly, if she had, they probably wouldn't be friends. The cadre had largely come together around their identities as trust fund babies, and none of them had ever displayed any guilt. They traveled rather than work summer jobs. They took on classes, then hobbies, that caught their interest. They lived carefree, and they adored her for doing the same. The conversations flowed naturally, and usually suggestively, and as the tension drained from her muscles, she sank deeper into the natural rhythm of the banter.

192

Two hours and at least as many drinks later, Lydia declared they should all head back to her place for a nightcap and perhaps a card game.

"I don't know," Emery said, suddenly aware the evening had slipped into night.

"You don't have to know anything." Lydia looped an arm through hers. "You're pretty, and witty, and gay."

"Guilty as charged." Emery threw a wad of cash on the bar. "And I also have a meeting in the morning."

"Then we'll be sure to release you back out into the corporate world by dawn."

She shook her head. "Let me rephrase. I have a meeting I must be in top mental and physical shape for in the morning."

Lydia's eyes ran over the length of her body. "You've managed to secure one of those two qualifications already."

"The other's necessary, too."

"Talk and walk at the same time," Callum shouted from the door, holding up his phone to get a picture of all of them.

"You can at least do that, can't you?" Lydia gave her a little tug.

Their apartments were in the same general direction, so she acquiesced, but for the first time, she got the sense that maybe she shouldn't.

"What's going on with you?" Lydia asked once they were on the street.

"Nothing. I told you. I'm boring."

"I know, which is why I think something must be wrong."

"I'm seriously just working a lot."

"I don't buy it."

"Why?"

"Because," Lydia said matter-of-factly, "you don't have to."

"I really do." She dropped her voice. "They didn't make me CEO. I have to prove myself to earn the title. I'm jumping through hoops, both in the company and in my personal life."

Lydia snorted. "Emery Pembroke, do I need to shake you silly?"

"Please don't."

"Then stop with all this 'have to' business, and well, the 'business' business, and certainly the personal life, pity-party business. You don't owe anyone anything. You're young and beautiful and filthy rich. Not obscenely rich, that's my job, but wealthy enough to drink, snort, and dance your way through life with abandon."

"My father's gone."

Lydia leaned over and kissed her cheek. "I know. And you were so fond of him, which is more than most of us can say, but it's also why you need time to relax. You should be here with your people. We love you. We miss you. Isn't it time to come home?"

She sighed.

Lydia rubbed her shoulders. "I can feel the knots here. It's not like you. You're better than this. Haven't you at least thought of chucking it all and running back to us?"

"I almost did a couple weeks ago. God, Lydie, I had the most awful meeting, ended up with some farmer screaming at me, and as I pulled back onto the road, every part of my body tried to turn east instead of west."

"You should have," Lydia said emphatically. "We would've scooped you up and reminded you who you are, then plied you with drinks and women, and we could've put all of this behind us, easy peasy."

"Yeah." They could have. She could have, too. And it would've been so simple.

"Other people can run companies," Lydia said breezily. "You could hire a proxy, or you could sell it. I hate the thought of your toiling away or getting yelled at or living like a nun,

194

though I can't even believe such a thing. They don't deserve you if they try to rein you in like some toy pony. You're a fucking stallion."

She laughed. "You're drunk."

"Just tipsy, and you should be, too. Think how much easier the last few weeks would've been if you'd made that turn back toward this life instead of the one that's giving you all those frowny wrinkles."

"Infinitely easier." She couldn't deny the truth of Lydia's reasoning. If she had thrown in the towel after that first awful meeting with Mr. Bergman, the worst would be over now. The board would've released her. Her mother would've made her own choices. She could've wrapped up everything in Amherst and returned to Boston by now. Her city, her friends, her life. She would be able to pick it all back up again effortlessly. A part of her still ached to accept the easy way out, but now she also had a competing narrative.

If she had chucked the whole company weeks ago, she would've lost out on so much she couldn't have even imagined then. She wouldn't have felt the satisfaction of constructing a successful solution to a real-world problem. She would've also missed out on seeing the respect in Brian's eyes, and the joy in Arden's.

One realization led to another. If she'd left Amherst when she'd had the chance, she wouldn't have only abandoned work, she would've missed out on the second date with Arden. The prospect wouldn't have meant much at the time, but now she could hardly imagine not knowing her. The night they'd spent together had been so unexpected and amazing that even what came after couldn't make her wish it had never happened. The week's worth of stress and strain on both of them was unlike anything she would've ever tolerated in the city, but she still wouldn't trade it away for nothingness.

Nothingness? Is that what her life here amounted to? She glanced around at the streets she'd called home and the people

195

who'd brought them to life for her. She loved them in a way, and they loved her as well as they could. Sure, none of them had come to visit, or even called in the weeks since she'd been gone, and the city had kept moving without her. She'd never considered herself important, but she'd never thought she could disappear with so little notice, and yet stopping in the middle of the sidewalk, she realized her presence or disappearance from this life had barely made a ripple.

"What's wrong?" Lydia asked, pulling her on once more.

"It would be easy to come back here."

"Good, then do it."

She nodded without actually agreeing. "I'm needed at home."

"Pshaw." Lydia started up the front steps to her grandiose townhouse. "You're not a medical courier. They'll survive without you."

She didn't deny the charge or inflate her value, nor could she share in the dismissiveness. "People are counting on me. I know it's weird and a bit hard to comprehend. Maybe it's a terrible choice for them to make, but they have. My mother, my colleagues, my friend."

"Friend? Singular?" Lydia laughed. "You have only the one?"

She sighed. "One in particular who's counting on me to keep my promises, and I want to. I want to try anyway."

Lydia sighed. "Fine, fine, you're vying for the role of corporate bigwig. I'll allow it if I must, but your meeting is tomorrow. Can't we have you for a few more hours?"

"I really should call it a night."

"No." Lydia threw open the door. "I can't. I simply cannot go on in the world while Emery Pembroke is a working stiff that goes to bed early."

She laughed. "I think you'll survive."

Lydia flew into full-on extra-drama mode, tossing back her head and pressing the back of her hand to her forehead like some 1940s Hollywood starlet. "I shan't. I will wither away like your social prospects."

Jane and Callum got into the act.

"Stay with us," Jane wailed from the sidewalk, causing several other people to turn and stare. "Don't go yet, corporate daddy. Don't leave us all alone because you love your job more than our family."

Callum circled them with his phone out, clearly encouraging the performance.

"If you desert us now, before we've had a chance to hold a proper wake, I will be too distraught to function," Lydia called loudly.

"Come on." She shifted uneasily. "Lay off."

"Nay." Lydia winked at her. "I will climb to the top of this building and hurl myself off the lavish terrace rather than live in a world where the best of us has fallen into servitude without a ceremonial send-off. We're your people, too. We deserve our due."

Emery hung her head. She could probably make a break for it if she were willing to sprint, but at least a smidge of her enjoyed being fawned and fussed over again. And what's more, Lydia wasn't wrong. Extra, certainly, but not off base in seeing this as a major shift in their lives. She wavered slightly, and it was enough for them to pounce.

Two sets of long, slender fingers curled around the lapels of her coat as Lydia shouted in triumph, "We've got her now."

Then she allowed herself to be pulled inside.

Chapter Fourteen

Arden sprinkled water over the hanging plants in her greenhouse, enjoying the wet heat as it steamed against the rapidly cooling glass. The temperature outside had begun to drop, but inside still dripped with warmth, and she wrapped herself in the comfort of her last remaining sanctuary.

This was the only room in the house her mother wouldn't enter. Even the library, which had never interested her in the past, had become fair game. Arden had hoped things would get easier over time and the novelty faded, but her mother wasn't easily deterred. Every time she left the house, she returned with some report of how the rumors continued to spread and a renewed passion for reminding Arden how much anguish her behavior had caused. Last night, she'd even come into Arden's room to relay a dire message about how even the women from the ladies' auxiliary had heard about her scandalous getaway and dared to ask if the two of them were dating.

When Arden asked how she'd responded, her mother had only stopped just short of pulling hair and gnashing teeth, as she admitted she hadn't known how to answer. The idea of Arden being a one-night stand was unthinkable, and yet the prospects of an actual relationship didn't seem any easier to swallow. Honestly, Arden was left wondering which bothered her mother more, being the subject of gossip or her own inability to contribute to it.

Still, when her mother had finally worked up the courage to ask what she should've said, Arden hadn't had any answer of her own. She and Emery hadn't gone on any more dates, so it felt disingenuous to say they were dating, and yet they'd stayed in close enough contact that it didn't quite feel like they weren't.

She had so few experiences to compare this to, she couldn't make much of a determination one way or the other. Still, she hadn't wanted to explain any nuance to her nearly apoplectic mother, so she'd summoned some strength from Emery by parroting her mantra, "My relationship, or lack thereof, isn't anyone's business."

That had gone over about as well as one would expect, and the house still vibrated from her mother's unique blend of rage and betrayal.

While she was no longer a child who hid under her bed, the greenhouse felt like the next best thing. Still, even while she enjoyed the hope and industry of gardening, she did find herself wishing for more. Ever since she'd seen Emery at work, a feeling had lingered in the back of her mind, the vague sense that she lacked purpose and direction. She couldn't begin to bring it into focus, much less figure out what she should do, nor could she shake the sensation completely.

The buzz of her phone saved her from having to ponder the question too much at the moment, and she picked up quickly, with a little smile when Emery's name flashed across the screen. "Hello?"

"That was fast. Were you expecting me?"

"Never," she said happily, "but I was just thinking about you. Could you sense it?"

"I must have, because I've been thinking about you too."

Her heart pressed against her ribs. "Really? Why?"

"Well, I didn't get out of my meetings nearly as quickly as I would have liked, but when I did, I had a message I've been waiting for."

"Oh? What?"

"I could tell you, but it would be so much more fun to show you. Are you free in about an hour?"

"Always." She wiped her hands on her gardening apron and headed for her room. "What's the plan?"

"Just come as you are."

199

"I'm in the greenhouse. My hair's a mess, and I'm covered in dirt."

"Okay, then wash your hands and come as you are. I like the disheveled look on you. It reminds me of the morning we woke up together."

Arden had to grab hold of the handrail on the stairway after the way the intimacy of the comment made her knees wobble. "Okay. What else?"

"That's all," Emery said, her voice tired but relaxed. "I admit I could've planned more, but I had a long night and an exhausting morning."

"Then I can wait." She didn't want to, but she didn't want to become one more person draining Emery's emotional or mental resources either.

"I appreciate that more than you can possibly know. You may be the only person in my life who gives me that kind of freedom and consideration. You're certainly the only one who isn't actively trying to make me into someone else, which is why I don't want to wait any longer to share what I've been working on."

"Another business plan?"

"In part, but this one's just for you. No clients, no colleagues, no rumor mills. Can I pick you up on my way back into town?"

"I'll be waiting eagerly."

And she was.

Once again, she'd walked down the driveway rather than risk the drama of having Emery come to the house. She didn't want to let apprehension or anxiety mar the joy of seeing her. Emery pulled up in yet another car, a sporty BMW crossover, and Arden practically vaulted inside.

Emery leaned across the center console and kissed her. The move was both comfortable and hot. Arden couldn't remember the last time someone had kissed her so thoroughly and casually at the same time. There was a familiarity that

200

stopped just short of possessiveness, and even though it didn't last nearly long enough, she had a hard time catching her breath as Emery pulled back onto the road and picked up speed.

"How was Boston?"

Emery shrugged. "Complicated, but I think I did what I needed to do in a couple different arenas."

"And what were those?"

"Actually," Emery said, "do you mind if we talk about something else? I've been so immersed in that world, I want to be back here now, with you."

"Of course." She didn't know exactly what that meant, and she couldn't ignore the slight smudge of shadow under those dark eyes, but she liked the sound of wanting to be together in this moment. "Do I get to know where we're going yet?"

"You can know the where, but not the why." Emery's lips curled up slightly. "My family owns a rather large tract of land that starts on the edge of town. That's where we've got our corporate campus for Pembroke and Sun, and on the far end, my grandfather built our family home."

Arden tried to picture the layout in her mind. "You own everything in between?"

"Yes, and most of it has been designated for natural preservation. My grandfather was a big conservationist, hence the family business, but he also wanted to protect wild spaces, so save for a few small roads between home and work, the area consists of largely untouched meadow and forest."

"That's amazing."

"I've never been quite the outdoor aficionado he and my father were," Emery admitted as she turned off the highway onto a street Arden had never taken, "but the land is stunning. I think you'll like it."

"I'm sure I will." She watched the terrain shift from residential streets to rolling hills. On either side of them, fields unfolded. They crossed over a small stream as they headed toward a tree line.

"We're on the southern edge now, about in the middle lengthwise, and close to your home," Emery explained, then pointed up ahead. "We're headed over that hill where the tree line springs up."

"Why?"

"That's the question you don't get answered just yet, but you won't have to wait long."

Her anticipation rose as she scanned the horizon, but all she could see for miles were fields and patches of forest, though the closer they got to one of those, the more she could make out a small structure. From a distance, it looked like a garden shed, set back just behind the first line of trees, but when they reached the shadows cast by the tall pines and maples, she realized it was more like a tiny house, or cabin.

She reached over and placed her hand on Emery's arm. "Is that … is it … Walden?"

Emery bit the inside of her cheek as if trying to hold in a smile. She pulled up between two trees, where a small path led to the little building. "Do you like it? No, wait, don't tell me. Let's see the whole thing first."

Arden climbed out of the car in a bit of a haze, and, taking Emery's arm, allowed herself to be led down the short walkway to the door. Emery grabbed a key from her pocket and fitted it into the lock, but turned to face her before opening it. "I haven't seen the finished product yet. I got the call only this morning that they'd completed it, but I thought it fitting for us to share this moment."

Arden leaned forward and kissed her quickly. She didn't even know what this moment was, but she loved sharing it with her.

Standing back with a smile, Emery turned the latch and swung open the door, and Arden gasped. The space itself was almost a complete replica of the model they'd visited of Thoreau's cabin, but this iteration wasn't nearly as sparse. The walls were rich wood, polished and gleaming, trimmed in white.

To the left stood a small table with two cozy-looking, upholstered wingback chairs. To their right, a simple yet charming wood-frame bed draped in a beautiful quilt. On the far wall, instead of an open fireplace there stood a gleaming wood-burning stove, and on one side of it, a knotty pine bookcase stretched from floor to ceiling.

"The back door leads to a small bathroom with a shower. There's no city plumbing or electricity out here, but I happen to know people who specialize in green energy solutions, so I assure you, nothing quite qualifies as roughing it."

"It's amazing." She stepped all the way inside and turned in a slow circle, letting her eyes linger on each sweet detail before she made it all the way back to Emery. "How did you make all this happen, and when?"

"I started as soon as we left the meeting with Mr. Bergman, and let me tell you, I have thrown a lot of money at things over the years, but I'm not sure any of them have been quite as satisfying as this. I put my best people on making it comfortable and yet consistent with the dream you articulated back on our date."

"What dream?"

"You said you could live like this. You said you could be happy with a little place in the woods, and you talked about feeling safe in the woods and small places. You also said you'd like to be a goat herder, though, mind you, we wouldn't call it that. We'll come up with a better title, one to suit the importance of the role, seeing as how a major deal hinges on the success of the project. I haven't thought of anything official yet, maybe something along the lines of 'Director of Animal Assets' or you could have a say in the verbiage if you like."

Arden shook her head slowly.

"No? You want a say in the position?"

"No. I don't know what position you're talking about."

"Oh." Emery pushed her hands through her hair, tucking the dark strands behind her ears and grinning. "I get a little ahead of myself sometimes. I guess I've been thinking about this for so long, I forget I'm surprising you."

"It's a beautiful surprise." Arden took her hands. "And whatever you're asking, I'm sure my answer will be yes."

Emery kissed her again quickly. "I enjoy that so much about you, but you should at least have the information needed to consent fully, or at least as much information as I have. I already told you we need someone to care for the goats, and you expressed interest. Turns out they need to be checked on in the winter to make sure their food supply is sufficient, and they need fresh straw and such a few times a week. It won't pay much."

"I don't need money at all."

"I know, but you earned certain benefits by conceiving the whole idea, and that's why your job will come with access to this little cottage to serve as your base of operations."

"This place is for me? Like my office? I'll work here?"

Emery nodded. "Plus all your coworkers who really matter will be animals, because we're going to build a little pen and stable right next door. You could come and go as you please here, no one to answer to other than the goats. Though if things go well with the first group, who knows, maybe we'll expand the project."

"Really?" Hope made her almost dizzy with lightness. "More goats?"

"More sites, more plans, I don't know. I hadn't even given it much thought until it popped out of my mouth, but it could happen, right?"

She shrugged. She didn't really know anything about Emery's job or the constraints that came with it, but she didn't care, not with her close enough to smell her cologne and see the lighter flecks of brown around carob-colored eyes. Emery seemed so happy, and here in this space, safe and snug and secure, Arden couldn't imagine ever feeling anything else. "Right now, I believe almost anything is possible."

"Yeah?" Emery stepped close enough to take hold of Arden's waist, her hands strong and confident as she drew her near.

"Yes." She bit her lip to keep from saying more, when what she really wanted more than anything was to show her.

☀ ☀ ☀

Arden kissed her. It wasn't unexpected. Emery had been the one to pull her in, but this time she hadn't had to close the final distance. All of Arden melded to her, lithe and supple in the places where their bodies met. Then she parted her lips, darting her tongue out to sweep against Emery's. Everything escalated so quickly from there, hands, mouths, heat. In the blur it took Emery several minutes to realize she wasn't driving the action.

Arden tugged the hem of her dress shirt from her slacks and slipped her hands underneath, causing Emery to gasp, both from the chill of her fingertips against hot skin and the shock of how fast they were moving. Arden didn't seem concerned, though, as she only continued to pick up steam. She scraped her nails over Emery's ribs, pushing the shirt up as she went until Emery had to pop open the top button in order for her to lift it all the way off. They had to break the kiss in order to clear it out of the way, but instead of returning to her mouth, Arden went for the jugular, quite literally running her tongue down the arc of Emery's throat. She rolled her head back, giving her access and relishing in the sensation of being desired.

She kept her hold loosely around Arden's waist, allowing enough room to move where she wanted without breaking the contact between their hips. Arden sucked on Emery's neck while she cupped her breasts through her bra, then worked one hand around her back and found the clasp.

Emery smiled as the restraint went slack. The woman before her now had come a long way from the tentativeness of

205

their first time, and while she hadn't brought her here tonight expecting any such thing, she'd stopped trying to anticipate anything from Arden. She'd surprised her at every turn and in every way, though none of them quite like this.

She sucked in a sharp breath as Arden's lips closed around one hard nipple and began to suck. Her hands tangled in her hair, soaking up the luxuriousness of the silky strands while encouraging her to continue working the magic of her mouth. She need not have worried, though, because Arden didn't seem inclined to pull back. On the contrary, she plowed forward, raking her fingernails down her abs before flattening her palm to Emery's stomach and slipping it beneath her waistband. Emery's hips bucked forward, and her eyes shot open as Arden skimmed over and then into the wetness between them.

"Whoa," she said, remembering who she was and where she was in a flash of arousal.

She grabbed the bottom of Emery's Aran sweater and pulled it over her head, barely registering the break in their full-body press before Arden bent forward once more and captured her other nipple. She gritted her teeth against the urge to surrender to this woman's skill, but she wanted more than a quick release. She needed to feel her, all of her. She needed to remember who they were and what they could do to each other. She had to cling to it, to the understanding that surrender didn't mean sacrifice, not the way Lydia had made it sound last night.

She unhooked Arden's bra and let it fall to the floor, then cupped both her hands over the firm breasts, causing her mouth to falter momentarily. Emery grinned to know she still had the power to break her concentration, but the sense of superiority faded in a flash as Arden's fingers sank deeper. Emery's hips rolled forward of their own accord, and then it was Arden's turn to smile against her skin.

"Oh, I see how it's going to be." She groaned.

Arden leaned back slightly, staring up at her with eyes such a magical shade of aurora borealis green. She was so beautiful, Emery almost forgot the very tactile power she held over her until she felt the button on her slacks give way, and Arden urged them to the floor. Then, peeling down her briefs, she placed her other hand flat against Emery's chest and pushed her back onto the bed so her legs draped over the side.

In a move she couldn't have possibly visualized until it happened, Arden sank gracefully to the floor between her knees and lowered her head.

"What is even happening?" Emery whispered in awe, but Arden's only answer came in the form of her mouth pressing against the center of her need.

Emery fought a battle between closing her eyes to let the waves of pleasure carry her away and the need to keep them open so she could imprint every second of this erotic display onto her memory forever.

Arden's head worked up and down slowly with each long stroke of her tongue, and Emery sifted her hands through the soft strands of her hair as the pressure coiled in her. This wasn't like the first time. It didn't overtake her in a fevered rush. She felt every single swirl of her tongue, the heat of her mouth, the rise and fall of each stroke. Soon her body anticipated the rhythm, clenching and flexing in a way that nearly lifted her off the edge of the bed to meet Arden more fully.

And she did want more. She wanted this woman all over her, to move with her, to meld with her. She noticed the hitch of her breath and the press of her shoulders between splayed knees. Every detail of Arden sent her soaring closer to a peak she ached to hurl herself over.

It occurred to her in a far-off sense that this might be the product of taking the time to get to know someone better, to see them again, to facilitate a repeat performance, but the reasoning felt as weak as her trembling core muscles. No other woman had made her want to do the things she'd done for this one, and that meant she'd never wanted to do this with anyone else in quite the same way.

Her vision swam as she stared down at her, trying to make sense of what those realizations may amount to, but as her breath grew ragged and her fingers twitched against Arden's scalp, the only thing that made any sense in the world was that mouth pulling on her need.

The release rocked through her, hard and fast, but not short. Arden drew her forward, dragging her tongue in the most enticingly slow stretch, holding her up and guiding everything out of her in wave after wave until she fell completely flat on her back, exhausted.

Only when she went limp, half of her still draped over the side of the mattress, did Arden relent and rise to stand over her, smiling down with both arousal and pride.

Emery squinted up under heavy lids. "What did you just do to me?"

Arden sat down next to her and cupped her cheek tenderly. "Only the things I've always wanted to do."

"Hmm." She wrapped an arm around her waist and pulled her down. "In that case, what took you so long?"

"No one's ever made me feel safe enough to try." Arden kissed her, still tasting of salt and sex, before adding, "Until now."

Chapter Fifteen

Emery had offered to start a fire in the wood-burning stove, but there was no need. The autumn night was mild, and the heat of their bodies under the heavy quilt provided all the warmth Arden required.

She lay with her head on Emery's shoulder listening to her breathe, taking comfort in the slow rise and fall of her chest, accentuated by the steady beat of her heart. She'd imagined this woman would bring excitement to her life, and she had, but she hadn't anticipated the level of comfort she'd found as well. She hadn't even dared to dream of a time when Emery wouldn't make her nervous or jittery, but now, cradled in her arms, ensconced in a literal manifestation of her fantasies, she suspected she would dream of nothing else for the rest of her life.

"What are you thinking about?" Emery asked.

She considered lying. Surely it was uncouth to admit everything she'd felt for her in this place, and yet subterfuge had never been her strength. "Just that this moment is everything I ever wanted to experience in my life."

"Wow," Emery whispered.

"Too much?"

"No. I'm honored, and envious."

She laughed lightly.

"What's funny?"

"Emery Pembroke envious of me."

"I am. I've never really gotten what I wanted, or I got what I thought I wanted, but only afterward realized I'd been wrong."

She pondered the statement for a moment, letting it settle and expand around them. She could imagine some of the things Emery had craved and found empty. She'd seen them all a hundred times in their circle, so there was no sense talking about cars and women and expensive thrills. Instead she asked, "What did you want when you were a kid? Before other people had a chance to infiltrate and influence your desires?"

"Hmm." Emery hummed low in her throat.

"Too hard to remember?"

"Not at all. I just haven't thought about it in a while. My earliest memories are following my dad around. He used to take me with him on Friday mornings to give my mom a break. We would stop by and see all the projects the company had going at any point in time. Solar fields, windmills, he even rehabbed an old, water-driven gristmill one summer. He would explain to me how things worked, and I tried to follow along, but I never really got into the mechanics. I just remember how happy people were to see him."

Arden's heart swelled. "What a lovely thing for a kid to notice about their parents."

"Yeah, and I did, all the time. No matter where we went, people's faces lit up when they saw him. It didn't matter if they were a colleague or a contractor, an employee or a neighbor. They would smile and shake his hand and tell him excitedly about work or family. I didn't understand until I was a lot older that there were different power dynamics at play because he talked to them all the same way, and they all responded with the same kind of affection."

"Affection," Arden repeated almost dreamily. "You inspire the same in people."

She scoffed, the sound harsh and cold, such a contrast to everything about their current position.

"You do." Arden stayed gentle but firm. "I saw the way your mom looked at you at the memorial service when you practically held her up, and the way Brian stood back and tried

210

to hide his smile when you won Mr. Bergman over. Even Theo is still working for you after all these years because of the affection you inspired in him all the way back in school."

Emery's posture relaxed again. "And you?"

"I think I've moved from affection to adoration," she admitted. "You don't have to validate it, mind you, but when someone builds you an actual version of paradise, I think it's warranted."

"You set the bar very low for yourself. Your version of paradise took only a week to build."

"For you. For me, it took all my life."

"And what now, then?" Emery kissed the top of her head. "You have your safe space in the woods. You have a new job. You can start overseeing the design and construction of the goat paddock next week if you want, but beyond those things, what are you freed up to desire now?"

Her chest constricted. She didn't know. She'd barely even been able to dream this, and she was so overwhelmed to have gotten it, even for a minute. She wasn't at all sure she had the strength or imagination to conceive of anything beyond the perfection of right now. The prospect of doing so overwhelmed her brain.

"Take your time." Emery seemed to pick up on her anxiety and moved to defuse it. "You don't have to make a five-year plan. Why don't you tell me what you wanted when you were a kid, too."

The question caused her mind to flood with a thousand memories, not all of them pleasant, but the one that rose to the surface caused her to melt fully back into her warm cocoon. "I wanted to be Luz."

"A designer?"

"No." She actually chuckled at the image her mind summoned of little Luz, no more than six or seven, standing behind her parents in a set of overalls, arms folded across her chest and a scowl etched across her defiant features. "I wanted to be the old Luz, little Luz, the one her parents dragged all over the northeast encouraging to run wild and dig in the dirt. They never put her in fancy clothes that couldn't be played in, and she never had to sit at a table listening to ladies talk on sunny days. She got to use wheelbarrows."

"Wheelbarrows?" Emery acted as if maybe she'd heard her incorrectly.

"I know it doesn't seem like much of a lark now, but as a kid, I thought they looked like the most fun contraption that ever existed. Once, I saw Luz's dad pushing her in one, her little body balanced atop a pile of mulch, and wheeled right past the window where I was suffering through tea with some tedious team of women my mother was entertaining. I almost burst into tears."

Emery held onto her tighter but didn't interrupt, giving her space to grieve for a second before going on.

"So, I screwed up my nerve one day, and when my parents weren't looking, I sneaked out to the garden and sort of semi-introduced myself, which is to say I stood there watching quietly until they noticed me. Luz's eyes absolutely lit up when they landed on my dress. She hopped up and ran over, asking me a million questions all at once. I barely got a word in before she seemed to decide I was her new best friend."

"So, she was the same person then, just smaller?"

"Exactly. Within half an hour, we had switched outfits, and she was teaching me about gardening, which was just an elaborate way to get me to do her chores for her, but I didn't care. I was in heaven, and her parents seemed happy to have someone take an interest in the things their own daughter turned up her nose at."

"How'd your own mother take it?" Emery's tone suggested she already knew the answer.

"Yeah, she threatened to burn the clothes off me, but my dad always thought highly of Luz's parents. They're educated and sought after, both as academics and landscape designers. I

212

adored them. I still do, and even my mother had to respect the fact that they'd made her gardens the envy of Amherst, so she didn't want to burn that bridge."

"How magnanimous of her."

"Yeah, she's actually pretty good at ignoring things she can't control, so after a while, she just started pretending Luz didn't exist, but my dad sort of looked at her like a practice friend for me, someone to help bring me out of my shell a bit, and occasionally she does."

"Like the night we met, or re-met officially?"

She smiled against the skin of Emery's bare chest. "That's her finest work to date."

"I agree, though the dress you wore on our first date wasn't too shabby."

"She's a genius," Arden said with a hint of pride. "She used to take all my hand-me-down dresses when she was smaller. Then, after she hit her growth spurt, she would still take all my second season stuff and redesign them to suit her tastes. I think it drove my mother nuts because even though she bought my clothes from the finest designers she had access to, everything Luz created even as a teenager managed to one-up them. When she grew bored with reworking a certain piece, she'd sell it. It didn't take long for other people to notice."

"Which is how she got her own shop," Emery finished. "I never ceased to be amazed by self-made success. I'd give anything to have that kind of drive and grit and talent."

The comment surprised Arden. "Don't you?"

"No," Emery replied flatly, all intimacy fading from her voice. "I've told you before."

"I know you worry about mistakes you made in the past few weeks and meeting expectations of your new job, but, overall, you're wildly successful."

"Arden." Emery started to shift away, but she caught hold of her and held her close until she relaxed back onto the bed, though the tension still remained through her shoulders. "I

213

don't know where you get your ideas about me, and I'll admit, I enjoyed them at first. Who doesn't want to be admired, but you have to know by now, you're the only one who sees me that way."

"But what does it matter what any of us sees? Don't you know how enviable your life, your charisma, your skills with people are?"

"Not when they don't hold up under scrutiny."

"Don't they?"

Emery sighed. "I don't know. I've never been low on self-esteem. I lived in Boston for years in between travel and other far-flung adventures. I know people like me, women especially. I made friends easily, and I can hold a conversation with anyone. I'm great at parties, and I never even stopped to wonder if that was enough until I got the call … the call that my dad …"

Arden kissed her shoulder, her jaw, her ear, until Emery could go on.

"Anyway, the last few months have made me wonder if any of it had any real meaning. Then going back to Boston last night, my friends wanted me to slip back into who I used to be, and I wanted that, too, but I also started looking for meaning where there just wasn't any. I sort of ended up feeling stuck between the life where I could feel confident that doesn't feel like as much as it used to, and the one where I might have the chance to do something meaningful, but I don't have any confidence that I can."

"I have enough confidence for you," Arden said softly. "I have so much more in you than I've ever had in myself. What if I just held onto it until you have time to settle into your new role?"

"God, that sounds so lovely, every part of it." Emery's jaw clenched, causing Arden to glance up at her long, dark lashes fluttering as if she were trying to blink away something covering her gaze. "But, I'm living under this ticking clock that sometimes feels more like a bomb. Months have slipped away, and I still can't find my footing at work."

Arden heard the echo of her father saying the board hadn't entrusted Emery with the company because they worried she was flighty.

"Like I just want the ease and comfort of my old life and the meaning I feel like I'm standing on the edge of here, but all I feel when I try to combine the two is pressure."

"Pressure to do what?"

"To become this leader who's above reproach. To become this squeaky-clean community member. To become someone people can count on, to lift up, to look to for guidance and assurance instead of just someone who's fun to party with. To become someone who's visible and available and infallible." She shook her head. "And they want me to ..."

Her voice trailed off. Arden lifted her head and looked up at her more fully. "They want you to what?"

Emery forced a weak smile. "It doesn't matter."

"It matters to me."

Emery lifted up enough to kiss her quickly. "Please don't let it. You're my only good thing right now, and I appreciate you so much. I don't even know how to explain all the things you make me feel, but I don't want any of them to mingle with the pressure trying to suffocate me."

She didn't love the idea of being left out of anything that could tie Emery in knots, but she also understood the power of safe places. Emery had built a sanctuary for her, and she wanted almost desperately to offer her some sliver of the same in return, so instead of pushing for more, she leaned in to kiss her again, stopping just short of the point where their lips would meet, to whisper, "I promise. I only want to make you feel as good as you make me feel."

Chapter Sixteen

Sunlight slanted low through the small, single window of the cabin, and Emery watched little flecks of dust dance through the golden rays. The peace she lay shrouded in was a strange sensation. She'd never been a morning person, but then again, she'd never woken to any of them quite like this.

She lay under a quilt and curled around Arden, chin on her shoulder, breathing the scent of her shampoo and the crisp fall air. The warmth that enveloped her now went so much deeper than the skin pressed against her. It settled in her core and curled all the way through her limbs.

"Good morning," Arden whispered.

"Good morning." Emery kissed her shoulder. "Did I wake you?"

"No," Arden said, then seemed to think about it. "You didn't move or anything. I could just sense you."

She smiled softly, wondering if anyone had ever been so attuned to her presence.

"Do you have to go?" Arden asked, a hint of apprehension in her voice.

She had a fleeting sort of awareness that with most other women she would've already been gone, and with the small remainder of those she'd managed to spend a couple of days ensconced with, she would've at least been calculating her eventual exit, but this morning, she found herself wanting to delay the inevitable. "I have to be at work in a couple hours, but I don't want to."

"It's okay. I understand."

"I'm not sure I do," she admitted.

"Why?"

"Because I don't have anything major to do today except rehash everything I did yesterday in an attempt to convince everyone I'm actually capable of attending meetings on my own. I'm sure they've all gotten a full report by now. They probably had it before I even made it halfway home last night. I'm living in a fishbowl, like they keep waiting for me to either perform some trick or hurl myself out of contention completely, but I just keep swimming in circles."

Arden rolled over and searched her eyes, which made Emery feel suddenly sheepish.

"Sorry, that's not a very good sentiment to wake up to. I'm just being pouty because I'd rather stay here with you all day than sit in my office pretending to know what I'm doing."

Arden smiled at her. "I know the feeling. I'd much rather stay here with you than go back to my house and wander around aimlessly while simultaneously hiding from my mother."

Emery kissed her. "We're like kids secretly playing hooky. Are we super immature?"

"Didn't feel like it last night," Arden said with a hint of coyness.

"No, last night was definitely adult-level activities, and you were very good. I mean, top-level achievement there. Actually, maybe you should come to work with me today and give me some pointers on ... hey." She propped herself up on her elbow. "That's not a terrible idea."

"I don't disagree with you often, but my going to work with you so we can replay last night is the very definition of a terrible idea."

She smiled down at her. "I wouldn't go all the way to 'terrible,' but yeah, hooking up in my office during business hours is probably something we should save until I'm more secure in my job. I actually meant you should come to a work function with me."

Arden's eyes went wide, and she shook her head. "Still in terrible idea territory."

"I know," she said in her most soothing tone. "I get that public events aren't your thing, but we've got a very small gathering on the grounds of corporate headquarters this Friday to celebrate the installation of our most modern solar panels yet. It's not exactly the highlight of the social calendar. We're basically going to cut a ribbon on a machine that doesn't do anything visible to the naked eye and then stand around drinking wine while we stare at it."

"Are you trying to make it sound boring because I'm boring?"

"Not at all. I'm just saying it'll be subdued, like less than fifty people, and half of them will be techs who don't like making small talk any more than you do. There's no band, no dance floor, and it will only last like an hour and a half, tops."

"Good, then maybe you can come visit me out here, because I've decided I'm actually not ever going back to my parents' house."

"Come on." Emery nudged her. "I've got to do some adulting, and I don't want to do it alone."

"You won't be alone. Fifty people will be there, and you'll know all of them. I won't know any of them."

"Not true. You'll know Theo."

"I don't know if I've ever spoken to him in my life."

"Then you could start. Just ask him about boys or theater, or well anything, really. He loves to talk about himself. Besides, he's pretty much my best friend." She frowned. "Or if the last few days were any indication, my only real one."

"I find that hard to believe."

"Sad but true." She didn't want to dwell on the fact that she wasn't sure when she'd see her Boston crew again, or the knowledge that when she did, things probably wouldn't feel the same, but the thought did make it seem even more important to have Arden with her tomorrow night. "Please come. It wouldn't have to be a big thing."

"If I go to your office function, it would absolutely be a big thing. It's so out of character for me. People will definitely notice."

"Would that be such a terrible thing? I mean, half the town knows we shared a weekend away together. They're already assuming plenty of tawdry details, most of which are true, but this could at least lay to rest the idea that I seduced you into a one-night stand."

"But no one would believe I seduced you into a second night."

Emery laughed at every part of that statement. "Not in a million years, and I don't want to pressure you into a big declaration, but would it be the worst thing in the world for people to know we enjoy spending time together?"

She shook her head. "Of course not. A month ago, I could've hardly conceived of a world where that was true, and even now I have to pinch myself to believe you're really here with me. Honestly, it just doesn't make a lot of sense."

"Really?" Emery rolled on top of her, grinding down seductively. "You can't think of any reason why I'd enjoy your company?"

Arden bit her lip and closed her eyes as if she found the increased contact a little distracting.

"Okay." Emery eased up. "I don't want to pressure you. I respect your introversion, at least in theory, but I want you to know I'd enjoy having you there. I'm not ashamed of whatever this is we're doing here. I like having you beside me, and you'd make the tedium of this event so much more bearable."

Arden gave a little whimper. "Okay, okay."

"Okay what? Okay stop talking, or okay you'll go?"

"Both." Arden opened her eyes, more blue than green this morning. "I can't tell you no, and I don't even want to. I'm just not used to all this."

"All what?"

Arden waved around vaguely before focusing on Emery. "All of everything. No one has ever wanted me around before. I don't know what to do with it. Who will I talk to? What will I do with my hands? What if I spill something?"

Emery kissed her forehead, her temple, her cheek, her jaw, until Arden lifted her chin, exposing her throat, and she kissed along there too until she felt her relax. "You will talk to me, you can wear something with pockets to put your hands in, and if you spill something, no one will care because we will be outside."

"But what if you have to talk to other people, and I don't know if I have something with pockets, and what if I spill something on me, or on you?"

Emery thought for a moment. She didn't want to dismiss Arden's fears even if they didn't quite resonate with her. She cared about her, and if Arden cared about pockets and stains, then she cared about them too. Still, she also very much wanted to make this work. She needed it both personally and professionally, so she racked her brain until she found an answer to all three questions, and it was the same answer for each. "Luz."

"My friend, Luz?"

"Yes. Bring her with you. I'd love to get to know her better. She's such a big part of your life, and I want her to be my friend, too."

"Oh my God, she would *love* that." Arden smiled brightly for the first time since the conversation began. "She always wants to be invited to things, but no one ever does."

"Then, I invite her right now. I'll call her personally if you need, but if she came too, you'd have someone to talk to while I work, and she'll undoubtedly be able to find you a fashionable ensemble with pockets. Plus, I know for a fact she's a genius with people spilling things. Her ability to handle stains brought us together."

Arden laughed. "Why do you have to be so perfect all the time?"

"It's my curse," Emery teased, then added, "and because it would make me really happy to have you both there with me."

Arden stared up at her with more adoration than anxiety once more. "It makes me happy to make you happy."

☀ ☀ ☀

"She said my outfit could have pockets," Arden explained to Luz, who stared at her in disbelief.

"Seriously?"

"Yes, that's all I have. It's a work event Friday at 4:00, outside her office, and I can have pockets. Why isn't that enough?" She let out a little whine. "I'm trying not to freak out, and your face is not helping. You have on your judgy face."

Luz rolled her eyes but then forced a smile. "Sorry, I'm excited, honest. I just want to make sure we do this right. It's my first corporate event, and I've never read any articles about dressing for a solar panel's baby christening. Let's say we go with business fashionable. I'm thinking maybe power suits, but not like the '80s shoulder pads and sneakers look, something sleek and stylish with a splash of color."

"And pockets," Arden reiterated as she tried to regulate her breathing and blood pressure.

"Right, I heard the importance of pockets." Luz started to rummage around in drawers full of sketch pads. "I can't start from scratch here, but I've actually got a couple jackets in the back I was working on for a professor. How do you feel about jewel tones?"

She shook her head. She had no feelings on the topic whatsoever, but she understood the question to be rhetorical. When Luz got into work mode, she talked way more to herself than to anyone else.

221

"I've got one in emerald, which is tempting because of your eyes, but it's dark and your eyes are light. I'm wondering about this." She held up a drawing of a model in a suit coat with thin, notched lapels and a close taper at the waist. "I've got it in a burgundy, and I'll have to take it in just a bit, but with the right lipstick, it could really pop against your creamy skin and the summer highlights in your hair."

"And the—"

"Pockets, yes." Luz laughed. "Black slacks, skinny cut, but with room at the waist for you to slip your hands in, then a taper down to the ankle with a bit of exposed skin, and black heels, nothing too high. All very sleek and dignified, office appropriate and yet warm enough for total autumn vibes."

"Okay." She nodded with enthusiasm that bordered on frantic. "I can do this."

"You can totally do this. I mean, you are doing it, and apparently doing it well, because this woman really likes you. And I'm not surprised she likes you, because you're fucking amazing, but I'm impressed she took the time to really notice. A couple people who come in my shop have been buzzing with all sorts of gossip."

Arden rolled her eyes as if she found the idea silly, when in reality, the thought of other people talking about her personal life made her stomach clench.

"I'm serious. Emery's a mover and a shaker, and I get the sense she doesn't make a habit of hanging around the same women for long."

"No. She's been honest about that. We even joked that we were both pretty inexperienced with second dates, though for wildly different reasons."

Luz snorted. "That's funny ... I mean, it's funny if you think it is."

She shrugged. "I'm not getting my hopes up for a happily-ever-after, if that's what you mean."

"I don't know what I mean. I kind of thought you were in this for a fun fling, and I really wanted you to get that. You deserve to have a good time and make some shady decisions, but then she seemed like maybe more than that. She took you on that amazing date, and I liked her a lot more because she took the time to really see you, but now this whole fuck-hut thing she built for you …"

Arden nearly choked on plain air and shock. "The what?"

"You know, the sex shed."

"My Henry David Thoreau replica cabin?"

"Doesn't really have the same ring to it, but yeah, that's like not even sweetly-trying-things-out, first-girlfriend material. That's like next-level shit. She literally made your dreams come true."

Her heart gave a flutter. "I don't know that I ever really let myself dream such a big thing. I honestly don't even know what to make of it all, but I do want to try to make something of it as long as I can, which is why I agreed to go to this event at her job."

"Which you're freaking out about," Luz said matter-of-factly.

"Of course. She's being so amazing to me, and I want to repay her kindness, but I'm not sure this is the best way to do it."

"Why not?"

"Because I think she wants me to be there for her."

"And?"

"I'm not an asset in social situations. She's way better off without my getting weird and awkward. She's actually great with people. I know now it's not all effortless, but she makes it look easy, and I don't. I'm much more likely to bring down her average than lift her up."

"Maybe she doesn't need you to do anything but show up," Luz offered. "She seems to like having you around."

"But it doesn't make any sense. She could get any number of women to be around. She mentioned friends from Boston almost wistfully. Maybe she misses them, and I'm sort of a placeholder."

"I don't think you build sex sheds for placeholders, and it's not like she couldn't find someone here to keep her company. I think she genuinely likes you."

"When we're together, I get that sense, too. She's sweet and attentive and oh so very amazing in all the ways you'd imagine just from looking at her."

"Oh, I imagine a lot of things when looking at her." Luz grinned wickedly.

"I'm sure, because that's who you are. That's who you've always been. I'm not sure I ever could be, and while I've made my peace with just enjoying whatever it is we're doing for as long as we can, I'm starting to worry maybe she expects more from me, and it would break my heart to let her down."

Luz's smile turned a little sad. "Well, now, that is ironic, don't you think?"

"What is?"

"Everyone who knows either of you probably heard about you two knocking boots and assumed she was using you for a good time, but not a long time, when in reality, you're the one enjoying a roll in the hay while she may be looking for more."

Arden sighed. She didn't enjoy the sound of any of that, and her chest tightened at all the complexities surrounding them, but it didn't matter which way you cut it, nothing made sense right now, least of all her own emotions.

Chapter Seventeen

"Wow, wow, wow." Emery stared at Arden as she came up the front walkway of Pembroke and Sun's campus. "You're more stunning every time I see you."

Arden's cheeks flushed at the compliment, and Emery kissed each one in greeting before stealing a quick peck on the lips as well. She needed to get back to the party, but she hadn't wanted Arden to have to walk in without her, so she'd come to meet them, and as she pulled back to take her in again, she was glad she had. She didn't want the others to witness the way this woman continued to catch her off guard.

"It's all Luz's handiwork," Arden finally said.

"It's all you," Emery whispered before turning to acknowledge the best friend, designer, wingman, and chaperone all rolled into one. "But Luz, I had no idea you did suits, as well as dresses, or I would've hunted you down sooner."

"If I'd known you were in the market for a designer, I would've thrown that drink on Arden the first night so I could talk to you instead of Isabella."

Emery laughed. "I like you already. Arden's told me so much about how the two of you met, and I'm looking forward to getting to know you better. Maybe the three of us could go grab drinks someplace quiet after I do my requisite song and dance here tonight?"

"Now you're talking," Luz agreed enthusiastically. "I want you to show me these hip hotspots you seem to have a line on, but first introduce me to all your rich investors' wives and daughters."

"You looking to design or date?"

Luz shrugged. "I don't see why I need to limit my options until I see the playing field."

She laughed again. "I think the two of us are going to be great friends."

Extending her arm to Arden, they walked through the building and out the other side to a wide, terraced patio overlooking a green space dotted with solar panels, one in particular with a big red bow around it.

"I take it that's the new baby?" Arden asked.

"Our latest bundle of joy," she confirmed, then glanced at the sun hanging low in the sky, "and I really should get this show on the road. It won't look good to have a ribbon cutting on a solar installation after dusk, but can I tell you a secret?"

"Always," Arden said so quickly and earnestly it made Emery's heart beat a little harder.

"It's been on all day."

"No, that's cheating."

"How's anyone going to know? It's not like they spin around or make noise. Those are actually two selling points of solar. It's unintrusive."

"Now, if only you could make them a little less unattractive," Luz said.

Arden shot her a look.

"What?" she asked without a hint of chagrin. "They aren't exactly landscape features, are they?"

Emery frowned. She'd never really looked at them from an aesthetic standpoint. She didn't exactly find them ugly. They were black and sleek. As they got more modern, each model grew more efficient, but she couldn't deny that they didn't exactly blend into the pastoral setting.

"Hey," Arden whispered. "I think it's lovely."

"Honestly?"

"Well." She seemed to weigh her answer thoughtfully, and Emery appreciated that she didn't just say the polite thing and move on. "I think they have a lot of potential."

"How so?"

"They provide shade, which is nice."

"Seeing as how they catch the sun, I suppose it makes sense."

Arden lifted her hand and traced a line through the air from the new set of panels to some of the older ones as if connecting them. "If you drew a path from one to the other, they'd make a nice wandering walk across the grounds and around the pond."

"Like a tour of the company product," Luz offered. "You could like put a name tag on each one, but it'd still be pretty boring reading material."

"No." Arden cut back in before Emery had a chance to feel deflated. "You could link them with trellises and grow wide-leaf plants, oh, like grapevines. You could also do archways, maybe some hedgerows, almost like labyrinths. A green space to support green energy. It would create a shady walk, but also remind people of the nature of your business."

"Nature," Emery said a little in awe. "That's great wordplay. We could call it something like that, 'The nature-of-our-business preserve.'"

Even Luz nodded appreciatively. "It'd be a lot nicer to have events here."

"And you could line the walkway with solar-powered fairy lights for nighttime functions."

"And holiday lights in the winter." Emery's excitement bubbled over. "It could become a real showpiece. People from the area could take tours. It would help us build community ties, it could aid in recruitment, and it would be a fun way to really boast about what we can do without making it feel like a dull corporate presentation."

Arden beamed at her. "I love the way you think."

"I'm only building on your ideas … again."

Arden opened her mouth as if she might argue, but stopped short as she seemed to notice something over Emery's shoulder.

Emery turned to see her mother and Brian approaching, both of them wearing smiles and looking right at Arden, who'd unfortunately frozen in a deer-in-the-headlights sort of expression. Wanting to help soothe her nerves, Emery reached down, intertwining their fingers as if it were the most natural thing in the world, but as her mother's eyebrows rose, she realized she didn't know when she'd last held a woman's hand in public.

"Darling, we've got to start the presentation, but before we do, please introduce me to your date, or perhaps reintroduce me, because if I'm not mistaken this is the same young Ms. Gilderson who gave me a tour of her hydrangea garden many years ago."

Arden blushed. "I can't believe you remember."

"How could I not? It's not every day a person gets such a lovely and detailed explanation of growing patterns from a thirteen-year-old. To this day, I still save all my coffee grounds to go into our garden so my flowers will stay a vibrant shade of blue."

Some of the tension left Arden's posture. "I like the blue better, too, but sometimes I use dishwater on one side of a root ball and coffee grounds on the other to create a full-spectrum effect."

"Brilliant," Eleanor said brightly.

"I have no idea what half of that meant," Emery admitted, "but I agree Arden is brilliant. She just came up with the most amazing idea to completely rework this outdoor area using the solar panels to create a sort of linked path, and possibly the basis for making us a holiday destination of sorts while showing off our evolution as a green energy provider."

"All that in the ten minutes since you all walked in?" Brian laughed. "I'm impressed, but not surprised, after your

228

ingenuity with the goats. How long before you have an office here as well?"

Arden shook her head a little too forcefully. "Not me. No. I could never. I only learned about landscaping from Luz's parents."

She used the hand not currently clutching Emery's to snag Luz and practically pull her in front of Brian.

Luz didn't seem surprised, and quickly jumped into the role of human buffer. "Hola, I'm Luz Rivas, child of a horticulturalist and a botanist, but in no way connected to the landscaping conversation."

"Not true," Emery cut back in. "You sparked the whole thing by pointing out the lack of visual value in our new technology, and you're right because you have a brilliant eye for aesthetics."

"Now, that's true," Luz agreed. "Flawless taste, really."

"Luz is a designer," Emery explained. "She created Arden's suit tonight, and also the dress she wore to the polo ball last month."

"How wonderful." Eleanor's interest surged again. "I'm at the office so much more than I used to be. I've been looking for some new business attire ..."

She and Luz took off like fire to paper, giving Emery a chance to lean a little closer to Arden and whisper, "You're doing great."

She managed to smile tightly.

"I'm serious." She brushed Arden's shoulder with her own. "Brian is already in awe of you, and I think my mother might be the next Pembroke to fall for your charms."

Arden turned to stare up at her, eyes shimmering blue to green. "I don't have any charms."

She lowered her lips to Arden's ears and whispered, "I think our last night together proves otherwise."

Arden squeezed her hand tightly, and Emery grinned. She liked having her here. She liked making her blush. She liked little secrets and easy touches. She wasn't sure why she'd foregone relationships as long as she had if they all had the power to feel like this rush of energy at having someone so close in so many ways. Then again, maybe not just any someone would spark such a reaction. Maybe only Arden had this kind of power over her.

A hand on the sleeve of her suit coat pulled her mind from the questions before they had a chance to fully form, and she turned to see Theo standing behind her.

"Hey Theo." She brightened even further to have him join their little circle, daring to think for just a second that all the people she cared most about might be close and happy all at the same time before she read the warning in his expression. "What is it?"

"Can I speak to you inside for just a moment?"

"Can it wait? I'm reintroducing everyone, and then we have to make a short presentation."

"It's urgent, and it'll only take a moment." He turned briefly to the others. "Please excuse us."

Emery set her jaw, not at all liking this turn of events, but she managed to squeeze Arden's hand reassuringly before forcing some levity into her tone for the sake of appearances. "Duty calls."

She followed Theo back inside the building and around a few corners before finally saying, "I'm sure we're far enough away for whatever's going on."

He stopped and glanced around as if checking to make sure they were actually alone before turning to face her with an expression of exasperation.

"What?"

He sighed and scanned her up and down as if searching for some flaw he was sure had to be there.

She chuckled nervously. "Come on, is my fly down or something?"

230

He snorted. "Only metaphorically. Why didn't you tell me?"

"Tell you what?"

He fished his phone from his pocket. "You've been back for two days. You came to work and talked about meetings and looked at spreadsheets, and you invited Arden here tonight? I know you're not cruel. You've never once been cruel in all the years I've known you, but this level of carelessness is like some epic self-sabotage bullshit."

She grabbed the phone from his hand, still not sure what he was alluding to, but it sounded very bad. It took her a second to make sense of what she saw on the screen. A photo, no, several photos, all from Callum's social media. The first shot showed them all at the bar together, then some artistic snaps of their hands on glasses, then Lydia's hand on her arm. "I told you we went out for drinks."

"Keep scrolling."

She thumbed through a pic of them leaving the bar and then walking arm in arm down the street, followed by the one of Lydia kissing her cheek. "Okay, that looks bad, but it's not indiscrete. She's touchy. We're all touchy."

Then she flipped to the last of the sequence, and her stomach dropped. It was an artistically stunning photograph, and if the average picture was worth a thousand words, this one certainly carried enough for an entire novel, albeit a purely fantastical one.

Emery stood on the doorstep, her back to the camera but perfectly framed over her shoulder. Lydia leered at her like a lioness might eye something she intended to devour. She was backlit in the open doorway, her fingers curled around Emery's lapels while the slight tug and the forward rock of Emery's feet made it clear she was in the earliest stages of being dragged inside. It looked as if the two of them were alone. There was no video or audio to give context to the conversation, and only darkness around them to hint at the hour.

231

She quickly swiped back up, hoping for some comment or title that might assert the social nature of the evening, but no, fucking Callum and his flare for drama had written only, "These two are back up to their old shenanigans."

She backed up until she braced herself on the wall, and Theo snatched his phone back.

"What the fuck?" he whispered harshly.

"Exactly," she said. "What the fuck? I didn't do anything wrong. We had drinks, we walked back to her place, we had more drinks and talked shit about people we knew from school."

"You didn't spend the night there?"

"I mean, kind of, I did, but only in the strictest sense that we were still awake at dawn, but we weren't alone, and we sure as hell didn't sleep together."

He pursed his lips and arched his eyebrows.

"Come on, this is bullshit, Theo." She pushed off the wall as anger overtook her. "It's bad enough to have to overcome the crap I've actually done wrong, but I can't be tried and convicted for something I never took part in. You know I'd never sleep with Lydia."

He cocked his head to the side and scrunched up his face as if trying to make the statement compute.

"Again," she added. "You know I would never sleep with Lydia again."

He shrugged. "Fine. If you say so, I believe you, but I'm not the one you need to convince."

"Callum? You want me to have him take the photos down?"

He shook his head. "Too late. He put this shit up last night. The comments are off the wall. If you delete it now, you'll look even more guilty."

"What comments? From who?" Her pulse began to throb at her temples.

"Everyone we went to high school or college with, and yes, it's as bad as you can imagine. The college crew is thrilled because they always knew you two belonged together, and the high school crew is pretending to be scandalized because they heard you were dating Arden, but, honestly, they're thrilled, too. Those vultures love to pick at dead meat, which you are now, because several of the people who mentioned Arden by name definitely know her family, and your family, and the families of several board members."

She closed her eyes and pinched the bridge of her nose.

"If you have any hope of saving this thing, you need to go into damage control mode right now."

She thought of Arden standing on the patio, nervous but still present, still showing up to support her, still believing in her ability to rise to any challenge. "I need to go find her."

"Her?" Theo asked, confused.

"Arden."

"No, she's going to have to wait. You need to get ahold of board members right now, unless maybe you could take her with you to meet board members. That would look good. You could present a united front. I could round up the various stakeholders—"

"Stop. She's not a prop. There are only two stakeholders right now, Arden and me. I need to talk to her before she sees this. I need to make sure she feels safe and supported."

"See, I think it's more important that you actually *are* safe and supported."

"She's going to struggle if public attention lands on her."

He rolled his eyes. "Yeah, and I told you that a month ago. You didn't listen then, and it's too late now. This is baptism by fire. You both need to be quick and nimble. You go back out there, do your presentation. Wow the crowd like you do, and for the love of God, drag that speech out long enough for me to get a read on the room. Then you can make the rounds with Arden on your arm and try to schmooze your way into convincing people you're a happy couple.

"We are a happy couple."

233

That gave him some pause. "Do you, like, love her?"

Her heart kicked her in the ribs so hard she had to raise her hand to her sternum and rub it gently. "I don't—we've only been together a few weeks, and I've never really—I mean, I've thought about ... I don't have anything to compare."

"For fuck's sake, can we focus on one crisis at a time? If you can't say for sure that you're head over heels for this woman, can you please stick to the script?"

She nodded numbly.

"Seriously, you need to go to work right now. No one needs you to be sincere, but you have got to be charming. It's all you have left."

She grimaced, wanting with everything in her to assert something else, anything else, but he was right. She didn't have clear answers, she didn't have any better options, she didn't have any more apparent choices, and everyone was outside waiting on her to be some version of herself they'd all agreed to.

She nodded again, this time more forcefully. "Okay. Yeah. Back to work."

☀ ☀ ☀

"God, she's magnificent," Arden whispered as Emery took to the small riser under the looming solar panel and clinked the champagne glass in her hand. Every eye in the area gravitated to her, and she held their attention simply by existing.

"She's a stellar specimen," Luz agreed. "I can't believe the first time you ever cut loose you manage to bag the holy grail of lesbian style and sex appeal. All this time I thought of myself as a mentor to you when it turns out you're a true master."

She shook her head, but she didn't argue. She lived in a constant state of disbelief that she'd ever sparked Emery's attention, much less managed to hold it for a month. Watching her here tonight, the easy way she made conversation, her steady charm, her affability, the way she could hold an entire crowd spellbound, even when talking about something as banal as solar tech, Emery was a wonder even without factoring in how utterly delectable she looked in her suit with a tailored shirt open at the collar.

"Are you undressing her with your eyes right now?" Luz asked.

"Totally."

"And you can do that with authority because you have actually undressed her."

"I have." She heard the hint of disbelief in her own voice.

"Okay, look, I've tried to be respectful because I know you're an introvert, but you know I'm dying for all the horny details, right?"

"Take a good look at her," Arden instructed. "Use your imagination as to what you'd picture sex with someone of her caliber to be like."

"Yeah?"

"It's way better than that."

Luz feigned a swoon, and Arden caught her by the arm as several people glanced in their direction.

"Shh, she's working. Don't make a scene."

"How could I not? My whole world is spinning. My shy, withdrawn, socially-averse best friend is talking sexy talk at a public function with her droolworthy Princess Charming working the crowd like a boss. I knew rich people lived more interesting lives, but this is a lot to take in. You didn't just nab a girlfriend, you nabbed the pinnacle of girlfriends."

"No, no, no," she whispered quickly. "We aren't using that word, remember? I'm doing casual."

"You may be." Luz shot a pointed look at Emery, who smiled over the crowd directly at them. "But she's got no chill around you. She brought you to work with her. She held your hand. She made sure you talked to her mother. She's showing you off."

235

Arden's throat tightened. She didn't want that, and not just because of the absurdity of the situation. She didn't want to be seen or noticed or held up for inspection. She couldn't stand the thought of people watching her or talking about her, or worse, talking *to* her.

"Hey, you two." She turned to see Isabella Trenton walking toward them in the perfect little black dress and holding a champagne flute between her fingers. "I thought I saw you when I walked in."

"What are you doing here?" Arden practically blurted.

"Yes." Luz laughed with contrived gusto. "What a wonderful surprise to run into you at a solar function."

"Ah, yes, not my usual fare, but my new friend, Mallory," she lifted a glass in the direction of a redhead who stood watching Emery's presentation with rapt attention, "is a tech investor, and when she heard I knew the Pembrokes, she wanted to see the new panels. What about you all? What brings you to this little soiree?"

Arden froze. She didn't know what to say. She didn't want to say anything that could be used as gossip fodder, and still she didn't want to be rude or awkward, which would only draw more attention to her.

Thankfully Luz had no such hang-ups. "We're both friends of Emery's. We're all going out tonight, so we decided to come celebrate her accomplishment before dinner."

"That's lovely, and I'm so glad to hear things haven't gotten awkward after all the hubbub."

"What hubbub?" Arden tried to sound airy, but the words just came out high-pitched.

"Oh, you know, all the talk about you and Emery maybe dating, and then that other woman from the pictures in Boston earlier in the week. I have to admit, I didn't really follow all the gossip, but I know so many people always trying to stick their noses into other people's business. Still, you two seemed so close at the polo grounds, I'm glad things haven't soured."

Arden's vision started to tunnel, dark around the edges as her brain diverted resources to try to make sense of all the pieces. Even though she didn't want to snap any of them into place, her mind spun around words like dating, gossip, other people, and other woman.

Luz placed a hand on her back as if holding her up as she spoke for them. "Isn't the rumor mill the worst? Can't believe a word of it. If I had a dollar for every time someone suggested the two of us were sleeping together, I'd be richer than she is."

Isabella laughed breezily. "I've been practically married off in people's minds at least four times this year. Like the only interesting thing about a woman is whose ring she's about to wear. I'm sure you hear worse than I do, Arden."

She managed to nod as Luz pushed a wine glass into her palm. She drank without tasting anything.

"Well, I really should be getting back to Mallory, but I just wanted to say hi to the only two people I knew here. Also, Arden, your suit is stunning."

"Luz," she forced out, "her work."

"I should've known."

Luz held up her phone and waved. "Call me and I'll make one for you."

"I will." Isabella smiled over her shoulder as she worked her way back into the crowd.

"Luz." Arden repeated, this time in more of a whimper.

"On it." She tapped her phone screen with her thumb. "Drink your wine and continue smiling."

She did as instructed but couldn't keep the tremble from her hand as she raised her glass. "What's she talking about?"

"I don't know. I mean, I heard people in my shop last weekend talking about you and Emery, but it was very much an 'are they, aren't they' kind of thing."

"Why didn't you tell me?"

"Nothing worth getting worked up about, nothing about another woman in—shit."

237

Her heart seized, and not in the good way it did every time Emery looked at her. "What?"

"I found it, or them, the pictures. Emery's not tagged, but someone mentioned her in the comments, and it, um, it's not like a smoking gun, but doesn't look great."

Arden closed her eyes and swayed.

"Hey now." Luz wrapped an arm around her waist and edged her back toward the building. She pulled open the door and pushed her inside. "There's a bathroom, go."

She listened, not knowing what else to do, but as she reached for the door to the ladies' room, Marlo Clayton nearly collided with her.

"Excuse me." She chuckled, then seemed to realize who she'd almost hit. "Arden, honey, I didn't expect to see you around here. I'm so sorry about all the drama with Emery. When we saw you two in Concord, I never even put it together, not that I would've known what to do. I mean, she's very charming. You're not the first to fall for those eyes and that swagger, and you won't be the last."

She started to hyperventilate.

"We're just here to support the environment," Luz said from behind her.

"Of course." Marlo took her hand and squeezed it. "And good for you. Hold your head up, sweetie. Everyone who matters already knows Emery only intended to marry you to satisfy the board."

"Marry?" Luz practically choked.

"Of course." Marlo acted as if she found the question silly. "That's why Emery can't take over the company. She has to find a suitable partner to stabilize her image before they name her CEO. She's been running quite a PR push with Arden here, but she never fooled Mitchell. He saw through everything right away, and he's going to start contacting board members Monday morning. We'll take care of everything."

238

"What?" Arden squeaked, but couldn't manage to clarify her confusion.

"Don't get worked up now," Marlo said, her sweet expression undercut with a healthy dose of patronizing. "No one really believed you knew what she was after. I doubt anyone was taken in for long. The idea of you being one half of some power couple, I honestly don't know what Emery was thinking."

"Okay." Luz stepped in. "We gotta go. Arden's headed for the ladies' room. Aunt Flow's come to visit."

Marlo's eyes widened. "Of course, go go. We'll catch up later."

Luz shoved her through the door, then locked them in the restroom.

Arden braced herself on the sink and squeezed her eyes shut. "I cannot fall apart here."

"I'd rather you didn't," Luz agreed, "but it wouldn't be totally unwarranted."

She shook her head so hard a few strands of her hair fell into her face, and she blew them up with each heavy breath.

"I take it that was new information to you? What with all your talk of keeping things light?"

She opened her eyes enough to give Luz a death stare via the mirror. "I'm having a panic attack in a bathroom at Emery's place of employment while half the town thinks she corrupted me, and the other half thinks she's trying to entrap me in a marriage of convenience. I think the keeping-it-light option is off the table."

"Yeah, well," Luz shrugged, "the marriage ultimatum is really messed up, and yet, so is her sleeping with some sidepiece in Boston."

The words hit her like a kick to her stomach, and she must've looked like she was about to vomit because Luz reached up like she intended to hold her hair out of the way. "Gimme the suit jacket."

Arden slapped her hand away. "Show me the pictures."

239

"I'm not sure that's a good idea."

She snatched the phone from her anyway and entered the passcode.

"Damn you and your powers of observation," Luz mumbled, but she glanced over Arden's shoulder while she flipped through the photo series.

Arden studied each one. From an objective standpoint, it wasn't hard to see why people had made assumptions, but they didn't bother her to see.

Yes, the woman's hands and even her lips were all over Emery, but none of the gestures were returned. Emery didn't touch her back. She didn't kiss her back. She didn't lean into her the way she did with Arden. Her smile was genuine, but her eyes didn't sparkle. In the last one, she was literally being tugged somewhere she was reluctant to go.

She glanced up at Luz again. "She didn't sleep with her."

"Yeah, maybe." She rubbed the back of her neck. "Stranger things have happened. I mean, I've had women who looked like her drag me into their apartment late at night, then totally walked away."

"Really?"

Luz shook her head. "Absolutely not, but physically it's not impossible if someone were inclined to be a prude. Emery's not known for, well, you know how people talk about her, so there's no need to read the comments."

Her stomach revolted again as she did just that. Every single person on there, and she knew more than half the names, had very much assumed the same thing Luz had. She began to shake again as her name popped up more and more frequently. She'd never seen it written so many times in her life, much less in a public forum. These people who'd passed her by for years without so much as deigning to speak to her suddenly spoke with indignance, as if they had some right to or inside knowledge of her personal life. "What the hell?"

"Yeah." Luz drew out the word uncomfortably. "I got nothing, and I'm so sorry."

"Why?"

"Clearly I misjudged how things were going to go. I know I encouraged you to get out there and have a little fun."

"And now?"

"Now, I don't know. She seemed to really get you for a bit, but she's running off with other people."

"She didn't sleep with her."

"Sure," Luz said without a hint of conviction. "But she didn't tell you about this. You got blindsided, and now you're here like some kind of arm candy while she smiles for the board of directors or something."

"And they thought she wanted to marry me."

"But only for appearances."

She groaned, wishing she could dismiss that charge as quickly as she'd written off some sort of affair. Emery had been under so much pressure both professionally and personally. It also made a lot of sense as to why she'd shown an interest in her so suddenly after years of sharing the same social circle. "Oh God."

"What? What?" Luz asked frantically.

"I think she did start dating me because she wanted wife material. It's the only explanation that's ever added up."

"Wow, this just keeps getting more and more messed up." Luz's expression dripped with disgust. "I know I said I wanted in on the rich-people drama, but I think I changed my mind."

"I think Emery might have, too," she said slowly as she mentally replayed the same sort of contrasting images she'd summoned when refuting the suspicions about the affair.

Emery had looked at Arden differently, held her differently, related to her differently than the women she'd slept with then left. She'd seen Arden through panic attacks and built dreams into reality. She'd trusted her, if not with all the details

241

about a marriage ultimatum, at least with significant parts of her fears and insecurities. If she were playing a game, there were much easier ways to win.

The realization came over her in a series of mental steps. Emery may've started out trying to fulfill some asinine requirement, but somewhere along the way, she'd wandered into the deep end, and that upset Arden infinitely more than the thought of all of this being some elaborate ruse. "I can't marry her."

Luz snorted. "No kidding. You're shy and a bit awkward, but you're not an idiot, and you're not some kind of inanimate trophy. I won't let my best friend serve as some sort of prop—"

"No." Arden cut her off. "It's not like that. She's not like that."

"She's not a great person either," Luz shot back. "Those photos, she's mugging for the camera in half of them, and she knew what people would think. She knew what the board members would think about you. Hell, she knew what the role of society wife would be like for you, and she pushed on anyway."

Arden hadn't thought of that. Had Emery known they were headed for a firestorm? Had she hidden it from her, or had she just not thought to tell her because it didn't matter to her? "I think maybe she has too much faith in me, in us, but this is going to shatter it all because I cannot be that person for her."

"For her? What about for you? Do you even want to be the kind of person who props her up when her bosses want to get into her personal business?"

"The business." Her stomach flopped. "Mr. Clayton's going to rile up the board. They'll take the company, her future, her legacy."

"Probably," Luz admitted. "I don't know that I care. She's been nice enough, and Lord knows you had some fun, which I encouraged, but whatever's happening here, it's clearly not the little romp you signed up for. And I'm afraid it's going to drag you under."

Every part of Arden hurt to hear it, especially coming from the person who always threw caution to the wind. If Luz didn't think something was a good idea, what hope did some anxiety-ridden worrier like Arden have of surviving the scandal, or scandals, because there seemed to be more than one brewing.

She couldn't take it. She wasn't strong enough. Her heartbeat whirred at the thought of going back out into that party with everyone looking at her and thinking they knew anything. How could they possibly, when she didn't even know herself?

She'd only ever wanted Emery, but not this way.

She wanted Emery kissing her softly in the woods. She wanted Emery in the car on the open road, holding her hand and sharing her plans. She wanted Emery ensconced in their tiny cabin, naked and dreamy and open.

She wanted Emery all to herself.

"No," she finally said aloud.

"No what?" Luz said. "I kind of forgot the question when you went into your trance."

"It doesn't matter. It can't work. Or if it could, the price would be too high for one of us. All I want to do is disappear, and Emery can't. I don't even want her to, but if I stay here or in places like it, I'll never have another moment's peace, not out there, and not in here." She tapped her own forehead to indicate all the torment spinning through her brain. "I have to go. I have to get away from all this ... now."

"Okay." Luz lifted her hands. "I'm not arguing anymore. I'm sorry I ever did."

"I'm not," she said with a sad sort of finality. "I'm not sorry about anything I've done. Only for what I'm about to do."

Chapter Eighteen

Emery saw Arden leave. There'd never been a moment all night when she hadn't been aware of her presence, not when she was talking to other people, not when she was on stage, and certainly not when she'd watched Arden and Luz's body language change as they chatted with Isabella. Now she felt her absence with the same acuteness.

At first she thought maybe Arden needed space or a moment to collect herself, but as she wrapped up her speech and cut the ceremonial ribbon, she had the sinking suspicion she wasn't coming back.

Several people came up to congratulate her, and Emery did her best to shake hands or smile for the camera, but she glanced over every shoulder even as her hope dissipated. Finally, she caught Theo's eye and jerked her head for him to rescue her.

"Thank you all for coming tonight," he cut in immediately. "I hope you don't mind if I steal the boss for a minute."

She didn't even wait to hear their reply before heading for the door, but at least she waited until they made it inside before spinning on him. "Where'd Arden go?"

"I don't know," he admitted, "but she and Luz didn't look happy."

"Fuck."

"I don't think anyone noticed. They were in the back, and everyone was focusing on you. Nicely done on that front by the way. Still, the optics of her not staying for the cocktail hour aren't great."

"Stop talking about optics for a second."

His eyes narrowed. "You pay me to think about how things look, so unless you're about to do something rash enough to get us both fired, I'm going to keep doing my job."

She set her jaw and ground her teeth together.

"Oh shit, are you serious?" A hint of panic crept into his voice. "Come on, don't throw everything away over one mistake. You've worked so hard. We can spin this. She was here, people saw her with you, that looks good."

She held up her hand. "I don't want it to *look* good. I actually want it to *be* good. *I* want to be good."

"For who? Her? Yourself? Your mom? Your company?"

"All of it!" She exploded. "I want to become the person I've been trying to convince everyone I am. I don't want to pretend or fake it. I want to actually be worthy. Is that so impossible?"

He seemed to think about the question just a little too long for her liking.

"You know what? Never mind. I don't need you to tell me what I already know, and I don't need you to spin anything either." She turned on her heel and headed for the exit.

"Where are you going?" he called after her. "The party's not over."

"It's all going to be over if I don't go after her."

"What am I supposed to tell people?"

"Don't tell them anything." She made it to the door, then turned around. "Or tell them my priorities are changing, and if they don't like that, they shouldn't have messed with my life in the first place."

It felt good to storm out. She loved the sound of the door closing behind her and the way the wind blew back her hair as she jogged to the parking lot in the fading autumn light. She loved the sense of moving, running, both away from and toward something, but as she hopped in her car and fired up the engine, she realized she had no idea where she was going.

Arden had left with Luz. Maybe they'd gone back to her shop or her apartment. Then again, maybe she'd run home to hide in her bedroom. She was upset, obviously, if she'd left without saying goodbye, and as much as she wanted to believe she'd gotten overwhelmed only by the public nature of the event, she suspected more at play. If Theo had seen the pictures online, plenty of others probably had too.

She wished she could believe no one would be that bold or cruel, but she knew better. People who would mandate her marriage for the sake of the family business wouldn't hesitate to comment directly to Arden about her fitness or intentions.

She slapped the steering wheel. Maybe she shouldn't even be chasing Arden. Maybe she should go to Boston and kill Callum, or go back to the party and demand someone tell her what they'd said to her so she could know who to murder there, too.

The anger felt good and justified, but it wasn't going to help her, or heal the damage she'd done. The almost desperate need to get to Arden overtook every other impulse, and she started driving without even fully realizing where she was headed until she turned off the highway onto a side road leading into the forest.

Arden had to be in the cabin. Emery needed to find her there almost as much as she needed to breathe. If she'd gone anywhere else, the hill between them might be too steep to climb, but if she'd gone back to their spot, it meant she still felt safe there. It meant they still had a sanctuary. It meant they were both still clinging to some peace they'd found together.

She crested the last rise to see a light on and smoke curling from the little chimney. She almost sobbed. Her heart pushed against her ribs, swelling with emotions too big and complex to be sorted out in the second it took her to speed down to the cabin and sprint up the path.

"Arden!" she called before she even reached the door. "Arden, please let me in."

She tried the lock and found it open, then swung the door wide to see Arden standing in the middle of the space, tears streaming down her face.

"Oh baby." Emery pulled her into a crushing hug, holding her tightly, fiercely, kissing the top of her head and whispering, "I'm sorry. I'm so, so sorry."

Arden sniffled against her chest. "Not your fault."

"Totally my fault. I shouldn't have made you come with me. I wanted you to see. I wanted to share it with you. I wanted ... shit, it doesn't matter what I wanted. I don't know what you heard or saw, but I swear to you," she held her back far enough to stare into her eyes, "nothing happened in Boston."

"I know," Arden said shakily.

"I didn't think about the photos. I didn't even hear Callum had posted them until right before I took the stage, but even if I had, it would've never occurred to me people might assume I slept with Lydia, because I didn't."

"I know," Arden repeated.

"She is just a friend, and—you know?"

Arden reached up and cupped her cheek. "I believe you. I believed you before you even told me."

"What? How? Why?"

"Because I know you." She said the words so clear and simple as if the explanation were self-evident. "I know you like to go out and have fun, but you've got a good heart. I know you have big dreams and good intentions. I know you're whimsical and fun, but you're not crass or careless. I know I can trust you. Emery, you are so easy to believe in."

She nearly choked on her relief. "You are the only one in my life who really does."

"Then none of them truly know you. If they did, they wouldn't have to rely on assumptions or innuendo. All anyone should have to do is look closely at those photos to see your expressions, your body language, the way you look at that

247

woman to know you weren't interested in her the way they suspected."

"But, why couldn't anyone else see what you saw?"

"Because I know what you look like when you care about someone."

"And I didn't look at her the way I do you?"

Arden bit her lip and shook her head.

Emery sighed. "I love you."

The words rolled off her tongue so easily, she hardly knew they were out until Arden stiffened in her arms. "Please don't."

"Don't what?"

"Love me." She barely managed to get the words out before dissolving into her again.

Emery's heart twisted. She'd never in her entire life told a woman she loved her, and maybe she hadn't even intended to do so now, but she'd always thought that if she did, she'd get a much happier response. "What's wrong? Why are you crying? And if you believed me even before I got here, why were you crying then too?"

"Because you're looking for a wife."

"Oh." She eased back. "Someone told you about the board's directive?"

Arden didn't respond, but her eyes spoke volumes of fear and confusion.

"Okay." She rubbed her face. "Yes, I'm sorry I didn't tell you. It's such a crazy thing to be told. Trust me, I know. I already sat through that conversation, and I wish I could make it make sense, because, honestly, I did pick you out of this pile of possible candidates."

"Why?"

"Well, Theo made a list of women and cross-references, and I'm not trying to make any of this sound normal because it's not, but the assumption was that I'd be better at finding someone to marry than actually becoming good at my job."

"Emery." Arden started to step closer again, but then seemed to catch herself. "I'm sorry, but I meant why pick me if you had piles of other candidates? Surely you had better choices."

"No," she said quickly. "Other people tried to convince me I did, but I chose you from day one. You were the only one with any appeal for me."

"But, I had a panic attack on our first date. Why not cut and run when you realized I wasn't the person you needed?"

"Because you were the person I wanted." Emery's voice cracked. "Everyone else was making all the decisions for me. Where I'd live, where I'd work, how I'd start a family. It just seemed that I should at least get to pick who I did those things with, and no matter what happened, I just kept wanting you."

"What about what I wanted?" Arden asked softly.

Emery's breath caught, and she had a hard time forcing air all the way into her lungs. "I, well, I thought … I guess I didn't give you that consideration. I just assumed maybe you wanted me, too."

"I did. I do. I think a part of me always will."

"Wow. Why doesn't that feel as great as it should?"

"Because it's not enough, and we both know it."

"I don't." She pushed back. "I think it's enough. We're enough."

Arden's tears spilled over again. "Maybe in here, maybe right now or on stolen nights, but you're talking about a marriage and a family and a full-fledged partner and I can't be that even if I wanted to, which I don't know I do, but I do know I can't, Emery."

"You could." Her voice sounded small and shaky in her own ears. "If you wanted to."

"That's not fair," Arden whispered. "Please don't be one more person who tries to change me or feeds me some mind-over-matter cliché about coming out of my shell or suggests you or love can fix me."

"I didn't mean that." Emery protested even while suspecting she might have. "I just meant you are good enough for me. You are everything I need."

"Let's not lie to each other. However we started this, we've both been incredibly vulnerable up until this point."

"I'm not lying to you, Arden. You're the most honest thing in my life."

"Then you're lying to yourself, because deep down, you have to know I'm not the kind of woman the board wants you to marry or the type of person you need by your side if you intend to make your dreams a reality. I'm not good enough for you."

"I think you said that backward. I'm the one who hasn't measured up to expectations. The whole town is talking right now about how I don't deserve you. I'm the flighty one, the constant screwup, the one voted most likely to accidentally burn the whole place down."

"They're wrong, so horribly wrong." Arden took hold of Emery's dress shirt as if she wanted to ball the whole thing up in her fists. "They're wrong and unfair and stupid, and I'd like to tell them all so, but I can't. I'm not strong enough to defend myself, let alone you, or us. I couldn't even stand by your side tonight, and you deserve better."

"I'm sorry I left you alone. I'm sorry I focused on work to the exclusion of you. I'm even more sorry people felt entitled to talk to you about—"

"Stop." Arden cut her off. "Do you hear yourself? You're apologizing for your life, for your job, for people you barely know. It's not fair. You shouldn't have to coddle me or make excuses or shield me. Emery, you're a star on the rise. People look up to you."

She snorted softly.

"They do, and they will even more as time goes on. You're a born leader, a bright light, a big target. You should have someone who can share the spotlight, good or bad, up or down, and I'm not strong enough. I'm always going to collapse under

250

the slightest hint of social pressure. I'm always going to let you down, because I'm always going to fall apart."

Emery sighed and pulled her gently toward the bed until they both sat on the edge of the mattress. Arden curled into the crook of her arm and pressed their heads together.

"Listen to me," Emery said gently but with conviction. "I know you've had other people who made you feel weak and small because you're sensitive, and clearly you've come to believe what they've told you about your worth as a friend or a partner or a daughter, but it's not true. At least not for me."

Arden shook her head.

Emery pulled back and looked her in the eyes, willing her to see the truth the way she'd seen through the photos earlier. "You told me everyone was wrong to write me off, and if you really believe they've failed to see the full me, you have to believe the same about yourself. You've never let me down by crying or caring enough to feel anxious. Isn't that what's at the heart of anxiety? Caring about something so much it hurts?"

"I don't know."

"I hate to see you suffer, but I've never once thought less of you for it any more than I'd think less of someone who pulled a muscle by running too fast or sprained their wrist while trying to carry something too heavy."

Deep creases crossed Arden's forehead. "It doesn't embarrass you to see me freak out?"

"I've felt a lot of things when you've had panic attacks, but embarrassment doesn't register among them."

"What does?"

Emery considered the question with the same seriousness Arden had offered her. "I worry about you. It hurts to see you hurting, but I also feel a strong, protective instinct. I want to help you feel safe. I want so badly to be the person you can cling to. I didn't understand it the first time, or maybe even the second, but I know now it's because I care about you, and because I do, it feels good to take care of you."

251

Emery paused as she remembered holding her by the side of the road on the way back from Concord. There'd been another feeling mixed in with all the others. She'd barely registered it then, but she felt it again now as Arden pressed into her, tears streaming down her neck and soaking their shirts as she allowed Emery to bear the weight of her body. "And I feel envious."

Arden's breathing slowed. "What did you say?"

"I feel envious." Her throat constricted, but she kept pushing the words out. "It feels dangerous to admit, but it's true. I envy your ability to fall apart."

She eased back, eyes curious. "Anyone can melt down. It's not a special skill."

"And yet, I don't know if I've ever really let myself. At least not as far or for as long as I've wanted to, and I've wanted to every day for as long as I can remember."

Arden gasped. "Emery, what do you mean?"

She shrugged. "What does it feel like to really let go, to let it all just overtake you and send everything crashing down?"

"It feels awful, unhinged, terrifying."

"So does holding it in. Isn't there at least some sort of catharsis in letting go?"

"Actually, there kind of is a release. For a second, there's an almost weightless quality when you've been hanging on by your fingernails and then you just relax and let yourself fall."

Emery smiled slightly.

"But it doesn't last," Arden went on quickly. "I always worry if it goes on too long it might end up becoming worse than fighting it, like if I fall too low, I might not be able to drag myself back out."

"I get that."

"You do?" Arden sounded more surprised than skeptical.

"Sure. I'm always pushing boundaries and sparking matches near bridges I'm not really sure I want to burn. I constantly toe the line between bending and breaking." She

252

smiled at the mix of wistfulness and worry inside her. "I used to push buttons in fun ways, with women, adventure, fast rides, or silly stunts, but lately, just going to the office feels like walking a tightrope. Every interaction has the potential to contain the mistake that reveals my unworthiness."

"You are so far from worthless."

"But, that's how I feel way too often now, and I'm always strung so tight, I worry the slightest misstep could trigger a gun I don't even want to be holding, which is why I know what you mean about being afraid to fall too far down. It's why I haven't let go or given in even though I've wanted to cry every single day since my dad died."

Arden reached for her hands. "You don't talk about him."

"I can't." The words rasped across her dry lips.

"You can to me."

"If I did, I would cry, and if I started, I'm not sure I'd ever stop."

She squeezed her hand. "You haven't let yourself grieve at all?"

"It wells up in me all the time, but I blink it away or swallow it."

"Always?"

"When I got the call from the hospital, I crumbled to the floor and sobbed all alone. I don't even know how long, but when the phone rang again, it was my mom. She needed me to be strong. Then the board needed me to be better, and then you came along, and—"

"And I needed you to shelter me," Arden finished.

"I liked it," Emery admitted, "maybe more than I should have at first. Theo accused me of wanting to be adored, but that's not true. I liked the way you looked at me, not because I enjoyed being fawned over like some egomaniac. I just preferred being seen as strong to feeling scared and sad and broken."

"You're not broken."

"But, I'm not whole either." Her voice cracked. "Not without him here. He was supposed to be with me, you know? He was supposed to show me how to do this. He was supposed to teach me, and no one seems to realize how bad it hurts that he's not."

She wasn't even sure how it happened, but somehow their positions reversed. Suddenly Arden was holding her. She ran her fingers through Emery's hair until she cradled the back of her head as something inside Emery started to crack.

"It's okay," Arden whispered.

She shook her head on instinct. It wasn't okay, nothing was okay, and she had to fight. She'd been fighting so long. "It's not okay."

Arden kissed the top of her head. "No, you're right. Nothing's okay right now."

Her eyes started to water at the affirmation. "But everyone expects me to soldier on."

"I don't. I don't expect you to be anything other than a loving daughter who just lost her adoring dad."

The first tear spilled over, and she wiped it away quickly, but before she could catch the next one, Arden took hold of her face and kissed it. "Let them fall."

Her breath caught, barely holding the dam in place.

"Emery." Arden stared into her eyes. "I won't think less of you. I never could. You're safe here. You're safe with me."

Every last piece of her resolve crumbled, and she pitched forward into Arden's embrace. She didn't just cry, she sobbed. Her whole body shook as grief ripped through her, but, this time, she wasn't alone on the floor. Arden's small frame absorbed the shock. Her strength and tenderness enveloped Emery.

She cried for her dad and his vibrant, generous heart that gave out too soon. She cried for the life she'd lost, the carefree youth and the hope of a future she'd expected to be so much kinder. She cried for her mourning mom and all the ways she'd let her down. She cried for the company that meant so much more than money, for the legacy, the lights she wanted so desperately to keep from going out. She cried for Arden, for everything she'd put her through and the way she still managed to believe in her so beautifully, even though neither of them could believe in themselves. She cried for all her deepest insecurities, the pain of a child inside her who died with her dad, for the fear she'd shouldered since then, for the loneliness she'd never slowed down long enough to let herself feel, and for the friends who lived the same, empty existence. She cried because she wanted so much more for everyone, but she had no idea how to do better for any of them.

She cried until her eyes burned and her chest ached. She cried until her mind stopped spinning and her extremities went numb. This was the point where she should start to worry. The current had welled up to carry her into total darkness, but the fear never came, or at least not in the way it had consumed her before. This time, the terror couldn't overtake Emery because deep in her soul she knew she couldn't possibly drift away now, not with something as beautiful as Arden to cling to.

Chapter Nineteen

For the second time in one week, Arden awoke to the most delicious kind of weight on her chest. Instead of anxiety or shame pinning her down, it was Emery's arm thrown across her with an almost reckless sort of possessiveness. They'd each shed their shoes and suit coats somewhere along the way, but everything else remained on, if entirely rumpled.

She didn't know what time they'd fallen asleep, but Emery had gone first, and without comment. She'd simply cried until she couldn't cry anymore, and even after the tears had ceased to flow, her breathing had come in short, ragged bursts that Arden knew well. It had been a wildly different experience to be on the other side of a breakdown, sad and solemn. She'd certainly felt a kind of helplessness in the face of Emery's pain, but she'd also experienced a kind of strength she hadn't known before. Even after Emery's limbs had relaxed and her breath had turned to the shallow rhythm of deep sleep, Arden had lain awake, marveling at the unique perspective of being the one to hold instead of being held. It had never occurred to her she'd be capable of such a thing.

She supposed that wasn't unexpected. She hadn't thought herself capable of a lot of things until Emery had come along. Honestly, some of them she now knew for sure she didn't have in her. She was even worse in public spaces and formal interactions than she'd feared, and no amount of desire or connection could save her there, but in these quiet, private moments, she had more beneath still waters than she'd imagined.

She opened her eyes, squinting against the low rays of morning sun to survey the single room she'd attached herself to so deeply, so quickly. She felt like she could solve any problem or face any fear if only she could do so here with this woman beside her. She laughed lightly, causing Emery to stir.

She stretched sleepily, then without opening her eyes asked, "What's funny?"

"A silly thought."

Emery stifled a yawn against her shoulder. "Tell me."

"Just that when I'm here with you, I feel like I can take on the world."

"Why's that silly?"

"Because the problems of the world don't touch us here. It's just us, and we're perfect. It's everything else outside that overwhelms me. You know, out in the world where all the world's problems actually exist?"

Emery's dark lashes fluttered open to reveal red-rimmed eyes. "What if we just stayed here forever?"

"I'd love that."

"Then it's settled."

"No." She eased back from the warmth and comfort that clouded her judgement. "What's good for the goose is not good for the gander in this case."

"I get confused in the morning." Emery yawned again. "Am I the goose or the gander here? Is 'gander' a boy goose? Am I the boy goose?"

Arden smiled in spite of the tension creeping back into her shoulders. She was used to Emery being alluring and sexy and commanding. She wasn't sure she could take her being all sleepy and adorable, too. "You're a silly goose, and you're making it very hard for me to be serious."

"Good." Emery wrapped her arms around her and tried to pull her close again.

"Wait." She summoned all her resolve not to melt back into her. "The original point stands, goose references aside. You can't stay here forever. You have a job to do."

"It's Saturday."

"Emery."

She sighed and sat up. "Do we really have to do this?"

"I'm afraid we do."

"But last night ..."

"Was a lot." She stroked Emery's cheek with the back of her hand, noting still-swollen skin around puffy eyes. "You were so beautifully vulnerable, and I can't tell you how honored I am that you let me see you in that moment."

Emery tried to look away, but Arden gently turned her face so their eyes met. "You asked me if there was a release associated with a breakdown, and there is, right?"

She nodded.

"You feel a little better this morning without all the pressure built up inside you?"

"Yes."

"I'm glad, because you have to go back."

"No," Emery almost whimpered.

"Yes. You ran out after me last night. You left people in the middle of an event, and there were questions to be answered even before then."

"I don't care."

"You do." Arden pushed back. "You care so much more than you let anyone see. You're scared to try too hard and still fail. Believe me, I understand how fear can freeze you until all you want to feel is nothing, but that's where the similarities between us end. You can do so much more. Your work is important. It has the meaning you crave deep inside. You can't cheat yourself out of that. You can't cheat the world out of everything you could contribute."

"What about you?"

"I have to figure that out. You helped me see last night that I have some strength and value I hadn't considered before, but we need different things."

Emery gestured around the tiny cabin. "Isn't this what you need?"

258

"It is." She kissed her quickly for emphasis. "It's everything for me, and I can never repay you, but I can't do the same for you."

"You did last night."

"I always want to be the person you run to when you need a safe place to fall apart, but I won't be the person who lets you hide away. You deserve someone who can help in the world where you belong. You deserve someone to hold your hand out in the open, someone to stand beside you when you make amazing presentations, someone who's not just hanging on your arm, but who can have your back when you face something hard or harsh."

Emery opened her mouth to argue, but Arden kept talking. She had to get through this. "You were right about your dad. He should be here, and he's not. You shouldn't have to face all those lessons and all the responsibility on your own. You deserve a partner who makes you better, who makes you feel out there the way you've made me feel in here."

"You are that person."

"I'm not." The sadness overtook her, and she fought to power through. "I know you want me to be, but I can't, and it's not fair of you to keep asking me to be someone I'm not, the same way it would be wrong of me to expect the same from you."

Emery covered her face with her hands as if she didn't want to see the truth of the statement.

Arden took her hands in her own and pulled them away. "We're both going to be okay. We're not the same people who stumbled into these roles."

"You don't think?"

She shook her head. "And neither do you."

"I can't do this alone. Everyone told me so, and they were right. You said so yourself."

"No, I said you *deserve* someone else, and you will find that by being yourself. You have everything you need inside of you already. Just give yourself space and time to grow."

259

"What if they won't allow me space or time?"

"Make them. Use your charm and wit and the smile that can melt stone." Arden grinned up at her, still every bit as taken with her as she'd always been. "You can convince anyone of anything. It's one of your many gifts. You even made me believe all my dreams could come true."

"They still can."

Arden cupped her face and pulled her almost close enough to kiss. "They have. I'll be grateful to you forever as I sit here all winter with my books and my goats and my cabin. Oh, and by the way, I still work for you. I'm not giving up my job."

Emery laughed. "Good."

"We're just never going to be a power couple or a corporate merger or a business asset."

"Then what are we going to be?"

"The very best of friends. Confidantes. The people who can laugh and cry and scream together."

"And sleep together?" Emery asked hopefully.

This time, the body part that reacted was decidedly lower than her heart. It ached for Emery in ways she couldn't have imagined a month ago, before she'd known her, before she'd kissed her, before she'd shaken and cried out for her. "Yes."

"Okay." Emery smiled brightly.

"No," Arden corrected. "I meant no. Ugh, I hate this, but no sleeping together, no kissing, no touching each other in ways we wouldn't touch Luz or Theo or our other friends."

"Why?"

"Because then we're not friends, we're secret girlfriends."

"Which sounds awesome. All the good parts, none of the drama or parents or board members in our business."

Arden laughed. "Don't be funny right now. I'm trying to break up with you."

Emery rested her head on Arden's shoulder. "You know you have spun me around and blown my expectations every minute I've ever spent with you. I wish the rest of the world could see you the way I do."

"It's enough that you do."

"It's too much for you, though, really."

She nodded as the sadness returned. "I'm sorry. I don't want to hurt you, but I don't want to marry you either, and it's ripping me apart."

"And I don't want to hurt you either." Emery squeezed her hands. "You know that, right?"

"I know, which is why we have to end this. If we don't, one of us will have to give up too much. One of us is going to lose too much of ourselves trying to make everyone else happy, and then neither of us will really have a shot at the happiness we both deserve."

"I hate that." Emery hung her head. "But I love you enough to let you go if that's what you need from me."

"And I love you the same way," Arden said. "I love you more than I want to keep you to myself, and that's a lot. It's more than I've ever loved anything in my life."

Emery kissed her shoulder, her cheek, her lips, parting them and sweeping inside as if savoring one more last taste of them together. Then she slid back and pushed off the bed. "I'm going to miss you."

Arden shook her head. "I'll be right here if you need a shoulder to cry on."

She smiled sadly as she slipped into the shoes she'd kicked off at some point last night, then stood. "Okay, I'm going to take you up on that, but in the meantime, I'm going to miss us."

Arden nodded, clenching her jaw and willing back the tears until Emery closed the door behind her. Then she fell to the bed once more and cried.

"Me too."

Chapter Twenty

Emery couldn't remember the last time she'd slept as hard as she had the last two days, which wasn't to say she slept well or awoke rested. Something about the crying jag on Friday night and the emotionally rending conversation Saturday morning had stripped her of her mental resources. She didn't even remember what she'd done after she'd left the cabin or all day on Sunday, but both nights she'd crashed into bed and practically passed out from the weight of her own sadness. She'd slept for hours that felt like minutes, deep and dark without relief or renewal. When the alarm on her phone sounded early Monday, she felt no more ready to face what came next than she'd been ready to face anything that had come before it.

She drove to the office in a fugue state with only a sliver of awareness that probably should have worried her, since she had no distinct memories of getting there. She didn't even manage to mumble a hello to anyone on the way to her office suite and practically headbutted the door open.

Theo jumped up from his desk. "Where the hell have you been?"

She tossed her keys on his desk. "Don't know."

"What's that mean?"

"Exactly what I said. I went to Arden's Friday. Poured my heart out. Got broken up with. Everything's kind of blank after that."

"Shit." He grabbed her arm and tugged her into her private office before shutting the door behind them. "Sit."

She did as instructed, then waited while he started brewing coffee. "So she didn't forgive you for Lydia?"

"There's nothing to forgive. I didn't sleep with Lydia."

262

"Sure, but everyone believes—"

"She believes *me*." Emery laughed bitterly. "She believes me, and she believes *in* me more than anyone, including you."

He turned slowly to face her. "I believe in you."

She rolled her eyes.

"I'm here, aren't I?" he said quietly. "I've been here every day since you were fifteen. I keep showing up even when you run out and run wild and change the rules and take off on whims, and even when you ditch everyone at a party to go chasing after someone who can't handle the slightest whiff of unpleasantness. So yeah, please tell me more about her vast belief in you."

"It's not like that."

"What's it like?" he asked as he poured some coffee into a mug.

"She let me cry."

"You don't cry," he said dismissively. When she didn't respond, Theo turned to face her again.

She stared up at him, her jaw twitching from the effort to hold in the tears.

"Fuck."

"Yeah." She buried her face in her hands and might've surrendered it all again if not for a knock on her door.

"Stay." Theo commanded. "I'll handle it."

He cracked open the door just a sliver, and she watched his shoulders tighten so much they nearly touched his ears. "Ms. Pembroke, to what do we owe this honor?"

"I'd like to speak to my daughter."

"She's on a call." He lied quickly and with enough conviction to remind her why she'd always loved him. "I'll have her find you after she wraps."

Her mother stuck her foot in front of the doorjamb before he had a chance to close it. "No, Theodore. You'll have her hang up right now."

He let out a low whistle. "Yes ma'am."

Emery sighed. She didn't blame him for caving. Few people could withstand their friend's parents using their full names. "Come in, Mother. Goodbye, Theo."

"Good luck," he called on his way out, "and when she's done with you, we're still not finished."

She hung her head, getting the sinking sense none of this would ever really be finished.

Her mother shut the door behind him and stared down at her. "Were you home all weekend?"

"Yes."

"And you didn't think to come speak to me?"

"No."

"It didn't occur to you that I deserved an explanation for your disappearance Friday night?"

"It did not."

She let out an exasperated sigh. "Have I failed you in some way I don't know about?"

"What?" She finally met her eyes. "No."

"Honestly? Have I not taken a job I never wanted in order to cover for you? Have I not given you multiple handcrafted opportunities to succeed? Have I not stressed that I want what's best for you and given you ample opportunity to weigh in on how and when you'd like to craft that future?"

"You have," she admitted, feeling worse than she had moments ago even though she hadn't really conceived that a possibility.

"Then please help me understand why you didn't think me worth the walk across an admittedly large house so I could hear about Arden Gilderson from you instead of one of my board members this morning?"

"Oh, for fuck's sake."

"My sentiments exactly." Eleanor sat down across from her and leaned forward. "What's going on?"

"I don't know. I mean, I know what's happened, but I'm not sure why, or what it all means, and I'm trying as hard as I

264

know how, but I made things worse somehow, and I miss dad so damn bad."

"Oh honey." She reached across the desk and took her hands. "I miss him, too. Every morning without him hurts so bad, it's all I can do to get out of bed and ask myself what he would do. I'm sorry I've used all my energy to stay upright without realizing you were doing the same."

"I didn't let you see. I didn't let anyone see, well, at least not at first. I wanted everyone to believe I was still carefree and confident. I wanted to be those things again so badly I tried to force it by faking it."

"Is that where Arden came in?"

She sucked in a painful breath. "I don't know."

Her mother shook her head. "I think you may need to figure it out, because the whole town is trying to do it for you, and it's not pretty."

"I can only imagine. They think I seduced her for a one-night stand, or maybe I strung her along under false pretenses, or maybe she's my girlfriend for appearances, but I also have a sidepiece in Boston, or maybe Arden is merely one of many. Does that cover it?"

Her mom sat back and eyed her. "Those seem to be the prevailing theories, but since we're finally talking honestly, I have to admit I have two others."

"What's a couple more logs on the fire? Lay them on me."

"I wonder if you actually are serious about her, more than you ever intended." She waited only a second before plowing on. "Or maybe you're trying to self-sabotage."

"Self-sabotage?"

"If so, I want you to know I'd understand if you don't want to run this company." She hung her head. "I understand it better than anyone else could. It's so much weight to carry. I have wanted to chuck it about fifty times in the last few months, and I didn't give up nearly as much as you did. I wouldn't blame

265

you for wanting to take a match to this whole place so you could go back to the life where you drive fast cars and jump out of helicopters."

She managed a weak smile. "I thought about it a time or two."

"It's okay to admit, but I wish you'd come and talked to me. I'm sorry you didn't feel I could handle those conversations, but honey, you didn't give me a chance. Instead, you went and dragged poor, innocent Arden into a scandal and broke her heart."

Her shoulders sagged. She didn't quite agree with the sentiment in total, but she couldn't argue the bare facts. She had pulled Arden in over her head, and she'd hurt her. She supposed that was all that really mattered in the end, at least as far as anyone else was concerned. Still, it felt horribly unfair, and it had for so long she wasn't sure how much more she could take.

She clenched her jaw, trying to hold in the tears once more, but frustration overtook sadness as the dominant emotion.

"What is it?" her mom asked.

"Nothing."

"Emery." Her voice carried a warning tone only a mother could use. "I just told you I wish you would talk to me instead of bottling everything up."

"Yeah, but then you accused me of using Arden somehow, when you're one of the people who told me I needed to find someone to marry in the first place."

"Marry?" Her mother laughed, then seemed to realize she wasn't joking. "Did you go out with Arden because you needed someone to marry?"

She shrugged. "At the beginning, yes, and please try not to sound so incredulous, because you were in that meeting, and even if you didn't make the rules, you certainly didn't argue against them."

"I said I wanted you to be happy. I wanted you to find peace and support."

"Yes, but you also shared the board's very strong opinions on exactly how I should do that. Everyone and their dog has a vote on how I should live my life except for me."

"I'm not sure that's totally accurate."

"Seriously?" Now she did laugh, but there was no humor to the sound. "You said you wanted me to talk to you about my feelings. Feel free to revoke consent at any time, but this is how I feel. My dad died. I'm devastated. I want to be good, to learn, to work, to give up a life where I felt safe and comfortable so I can honor him and ease the burden on you, but that's not good enough. Not the impulse, not the motivations, not the willingness to grow. No, all anyone talks about is my personal life, which is both self-esteem crushing and personally humiliating."

Her mother sat back. "I'm sorry I wasn't in a better place during that initial meeting. I should've seen that conversation from your point of view. I was a little selfish."

"No, you were exhausted and grieving and facing an impossibly daunting task, but so was I. And I wanted so desperately to be good at something, but no one seemed to think I had it in me to just excel at the actual job, so I let everyone, from the board to you to Theo, convince me my best shot for success was to find a woman who'd marry me. I mean, I'm reliable with the ladies, right? That's my one talent."

"No, no, no, you have so many talents. You're my bright, bold, engaging daughter."

"Except I'm apparently none of those things quite enough, because not only did people not trust me to function on my own, they also don't believe I'm capable of picking a person to share my life with. No one has believed for a minute that I genuinely enjoy being with Arden."

"You do?"

"Yes."

"Little Arden Gilderson?"

"What's that? What's the tone and the descriptor?" Emery's voice rose. "It's condescending, and everyone does it."

"I don't mean to belittle her. She seems almost painfully sweet, but honey, you have to admit, she's not your type."

"Right, because the type of women I date are not the type of women any of you would want me to marry, and points for you there, because they aren't the type of woman I'd want to marry either. So I looked for something different, and I found it. Only now she's too different, or I'm not different enough, and when is it going to stop? When do two grown women get to make their own decisions?"

"I suspect it's hard for people to wrap their minds around the two of you being a serious couple. Your personality is so strong, and she's so—"

"Strong," Emery finished for her. "She's incredibly strong. She fights anxiety every day. She gets pushed around by every person who should love her. She lives with judgment and people meddling and telling her she's not good enough, and she still has it in her to be kind and thoughtful and observant. She thinks outside the box, and she finds beauty in simple things, and she can stand being alone with herself. Do you know how appealing that is to me?"

Her mother shook her head.

"I'm in awe of her, and I can't for the life of me figure out why no one else can see her as clearly as I do. Everyone seems to think she's some poor girl who's being railroaded or misled here, and I honestly can't figure out who that offends more. On one hand, I think it's me, because I'm being painted as some reckless philanderer. On the other hand, it's Arden, who they seem to think is both weak-minded and kind of naive to fall for my tricks."

"I don't think anyone would have put it in quite those terms," her mother said. "I certainly wouldn't have. I suspect most of us are just trying to make sense of what's happening, because it's so out of character for both of you."

268

"Has it ever occurred to anyone to give either of us the benefit of the doubt? Or say, 'Hey, they're good people. Maybe they are figuring things out?" Or maybe consider the possibility we're real, dynamic humans? Yes, Arden's shy and suffers from social anxiety, but she's also talented and insightful with a quirky sense of humor that amuses me. And yes, I'm reactionary and prone to whims, but I care deeply about the people around me, and I like being valuable, and I want to be seen as much as anyone else."

"And she sees you? Really sees you, not just the devil-may-care, fun-time attitude you project to the world?"

"Yeah." She smiled thinking of how Arden looked at her, talked to her, held her. "If you're looking for something to make sense about us, that's what we have in common. We see in each other what no one else in our lives does."

Her mother's eyes watered. "That's a very big thing, bigger than probably anything else you could share."

"Yeah, well." Her throat constricted. "It's not big enough. Not for anyone else, not for her even, because she won't have me."

"What do you mean?"

"She broke up with me. Turns out it wasn't enough to find someone who gives me peace and comfort and a safe place to fall, because I can't give her the same in return. Not while living in the public eye, not while doing what it takes to keep this company in our family. She knows that matters to me, and I matter so much to her she won't let me throw it away, so we're stuck."

"Oh honey." She rose and walked over to Emery's chair, wrapping her in a hug and cradling her head to her chest the way she had as a child. "I can't apologize enough for not making myself clear before, but please hear me now. I never intended to pressure you into finding someone suitable for a job. I wanted you to find someone who made you happy. The relationship only matters to me to that end. I want my child to love and to be loved in return."

"But the company—"

"Fuck it."

"Mom!"

"I'm serious." She crouched down to look her in the eye. "I thought you could grow into this role with someone by your side, but if you have to choose between one or the other, choose to be happy."

"But Dad—"

"Would agree with me. And he'd hate you making yourself miserable to please him. He wrote that whole board-based approval caveat because he didn't want you saddled with anything you weren't ready for."

"I want to do good things, though. I want to carry on his legacy. I swear I do."

"Your dad had more than one legacy." She squeezed her shoulders. "And he would rather you burn this whole place to the ground than give up on a real chance at happiness. The only thing he cared about more than the legacy he built at this company was the one he built at home, with us, with his family, with the real loves of his life."

☀ ☀ ☀

"Where in God's name have you been?" Arden's mother pounced as soon as she came through the back door.

Everything about the situation knocked her off guard, from the low rasp of fury in her whisper to the frantic gleam in her eye, even the location of the ambush. Arden couldn't remember a single time she'd ever seen the lady of the house in their kitchen. How long had she even been waiting there? Or had she convinced some member of the house staff to watch for her approach and summon her on arrival? Neither option seemed great.

"Well, I spent the weekend in a cabin."

"A what?"

"A cabin, like a little house in the woods. It's a model of Thoreau's cabin on Walden Pond." Her mother's stony expression made it clear she didn't find the description helpful or appealing. "Is everything okay?"

"No. Nothing's okay, and unfortunately we don't have time to pull anything back together again."

She didn't have any idea what that meant, so she merely stood there hoping the less she argued, the quicker this could end, but her mother's eyes raked over her as if waiting for something more.

"Are those the clothes you wore Friday night?"

She glanced down at her black silk shell and tapered slacks. "Some of them."

"I'm going to pass out," her mother whined. "No. I will not allow you to make me behave like you, Arden, I swear. You will run upstairs as quickly as possible and throw on something suitable in under three minutes, then meet us in the parlor."

"Us?"

"Yes!" Her voice rose an octave before she caught herself. "The Claytons are here."

"Holy fuck."

"I share your sentiments, but I suggest for everyone's sake, and I do mean everyone, even people who aren't here, you pull yourself together enough to present a graceful front. If you don't, the consequences will be far-reaching."

She understood the threat. This wasn't just about gossip anymore. She'd known it last Friday when talking to Marlo, but she hadn't let herself dwell on the outer reaches of their actions, not with more personal pain so close and present. Now she didn't seem to have much choice.

She ran up the stairs and pulled on some jeans she'd worn in the greenhouse, but in a nod to her mother, she paired them with a cream-colored cashmere sweater and pinned her hair in a

271

casually elegant updo before adding some diamond stud earrings. She was merely slapping pieces of respectability to a fallen facade, but she didn't know what else to do. She lacked Luz's fashion sense or Emery's natural confidence. Still, her fear of what might happen if she didn't at least try drove her forward with a rapidly beating heart.

She jogged down the stairs and through the house until she skidded to a stop outside the parlor door, chest heaving as she tried to catch her breath. She couldn't remember the last time she'd run anywhere, much less toward a conflict. Still, Marlo's comment echoed through her brain. *"She never fooled Mitchell. He saw through everything right away, and he's going to start contacting board members Monday morning. We'll take care of everything."*

Her hand trembled a bit as it pushed open the French door to reveal both her parents and the Claytons sitting around a coffee table. Her father and the Claytons all stood as she entered, but her mother looked as if she might need to hide her eyes so she didn't see what came next.

"Good morning," she said as evenly as she could. "I'm sorry to keep you waiting. I didn't expect visitors this morning."

"It's no problem, dear. We only called ahead by a little bit. Honestly, we've spent the last few days agonizing over what to do."

"I hope not on my account."

Marlo and Mitchell exchanged an awkward glance, and Arden eased into a nearby wingback chair to keep her knees from buckling.

"Honey," her dad started, "the Claytons have come to us with some rather serious information, in confidence as friends. I honestly haven't had much time to decide what to make of everything, but we all agree it's in your best interest to hear from people who care about you."

She nodded slowly and folded her hands in her lap, trying not to tighten them to the point where her knuckles went

272

white. She wasn't sure she could handle any more bombshells or emotional wringers, but she needed to know what had them so worked up before she could decide if the charges warranted a panic attack. "I'm listening."

Mitchell cleared his throat and settled back into his chair, looking in her direction but not quite into her eyes. "The thing is, you know I'm on the board at Pembroke and Sun, and I had the utmost respect for the late Mr. Pembroke. He was unconventional but committed, and we were all deeply saddened by his passing."

Arden's jaw tightened as she waited for the "but" portion of the statement that would surely come as he finished his minimal obligation to not speak ill of the dead.

"When we met to appoint the new CEO of the company, a great deal of thought was given to what qualities Emery possessed and which ones she lacked. Keep in mind we don't think she's a bad person per se ..."

"I'm familiar with Emery's character." Arden found her voice even though it wavered slightly.

"I know you two are, well, friends, at the least, but I suspect she may not have told you that one of the recommendations the board made in order to help her cultivate the kind of stability befitting the head of a corporation was a suitably steady relationship, a partner, someone she could lean on."

Arden's jaw twitched at his attempt to make the absurd edict sound more reasonable. "You made getting married to the right kind of woman a job requirement."

"Exactly," Marlo said before her husband could spin the response.

"We thought, given her tendency to bounce around, a long-term relationship might show a capacity for commitment to something bigger than herself."

Arden frowned. "I don't really understand why she couldn't have demonstrated her commitment by upholding her family legacy."

"I'm sure she could have, and still can. Business is complicated, which is why we don't spell these things out in concrete terms," Mitchell said, with a pedantic sort of kindness. "The point is, after the last few weeks, Marlo and I have been rather concerned the suggestion was taken the wrong way, and you perhaps got swept up into something you weren't given the chance to see in its fullness."

She shook her head, absolutely understanding where he was headed but unable to figure out what she was supposed to say in response. She'd thought the whispered worries were too much to bear, and she couldn't imagine addressing them head-on, but if she didn't, they'd go on believing the very worst about both Emery's intentions and her own mental capacity.

"Does any of this help make sense of Emery's behavior now?" Marlo asked gently.

"It helps explain the pressure she's under," she admitted, "and why she might not trust herself to be good enough no matter how hard she works."

Her mother snorted. "They aren't concerned about Emery's feelings. They're here to tell you, once and for all, that she's using you."

Her father sat up a little straighter. "I'm not sure getting worked up—"

"There's a money-grubbing social climber looking to entrap our naive and gullible daughter into a marriage of convenience while continuing to bed half the lesbians in Boston, and Arden can't even see it when we paint a picture for her," her mother snapped. "If that's not worth getting worked up over, I don't know what is."

"That's actually not what's happening," Arden said softly.

274

"No, it very much is," her mother shot back. "They just told you. Emery didn't ever look your way until she needed a society marriage for appearances, then suddenly she's interested in you? For what? Your witty banter? Your good-time attitude? Your easy, fun-loving party persona?"

Her father winced. "That's enough."

"No, I'm sorry. None of us wanted to be cruel," her mother said with a sigh, "but I'd rather be brutally honest than politely deceptive. Arden's kind and sweet and quiet, and I know I'm hard on her because I see she can be so much more, but Emery's only playing on a lonely girl's insecurities. She's using her as an easy stepping stone to higher ground."

"That's not true," Arden said more firmly. Then before her mother could beat her down any further, she continued, "I admit I'm not good with people, and I don't have as much practice as you at reading social cues, and maybe your version of the story even had some real truth to it at the beginning."

"Are you just conceding all my points?"

She blew out a flustered breath. "No, because over the last few months, I've gotten to really know Emery, and she got to know me, and now that we have, I can say with all the courage of my convictions that she's a much better person with much purer intentions than anyone's giving her credit for."

Her mother rolled her eyes. "Forgive me for not being convinced by the opinions of someone who falls apart three times a week."

"No, that's exactly why you should trust them. I've never maintained strong beliefs on anything in my life, but I will on this one. Nothing you can say will convince me otherwise."

"That does carry weight with me," her father said seriously, "but hopefully you can see why we have our concerns about your spending a lot of time with someone under the gun to marry, and to do so quickly, with a woman of a certain social standing."

275

Arden laughed. "You can stop worrying. I already told Emery I had no intention of marrying her."

"Oh, thank God." Her mother's forehead nearly sagged all the way to the table.

"Not because of anything Emery's done wrong," she added quickly, "quite the opposite. She's been too perfect. She's so kind and understanding and supportive, and she's shown more faith in me than anyone else in my life has."

"Arden, honey," Marlo said, "I hope you aren't offended. We didn't come here because we don't think highly of you. We're here because we do."

"Then why doesn't anyone trust me to make my own decisions? I'm an adult. I may not be whip-smart, but I'm observant. I may not be good in a crisis, but I'm very thoughtful when given the space to reflect. Just because I'm not exactly the model of what people in our community think a society woman should be doesn't mean I'm incapable of doing good things."

"Of course you are, dear." Mitchell rose. "We merely wanted to make sure you had all the information you need to make your decisions. Now that you have those missing pieces, we'll trust you to do the right things with them."

Arden stood to intercept him before he headed for the door. "Thank you for that at least, but if you really mean it, can you do me one more favor?"

"Of course, anything you need."

"Give Emery the same courtesy."

He came up short of actually stumbling, but it was close. "I'm sorry?"

"You came here because you were concerned Emery had bad intentions with me, and you were prepared to act based on those concerns, yes?"

"I suppose so."

She wrung her hands to the point where the pressure began to cause pain, and the words rushed out. "Then, do the same now that you know it's not true. Act on the knowledge she's better than you thought. She's brighter and more beautiful as a person than anyone's giving her credit for. That's why I won't marry her, and that's why you should make her CEO."

"Well, I'm glad you've had that experience, but a lot of factors go into making a strong leader."

"She has those, too," she blurted out. "She cares about the business, and she cares about the people behind it, which now includes me. She listened to me when no one else did, and she encouraged me to trust in my own ideas. Then she helped make them come to life. I've taken a job with Pembroke and Sun, just a little one, but one that makes me happy. I'm basically going to be a goat herder."

Her mother let out a tiny sound, something like a cross between a gasp and a yell, but her dad laughed. "Now this I have to hear."

"A client needed an environmentally nonintrusive way to keep the grass down around a large solar farm proposed for his property, and I helped Emery land on goats as a solution, but then she came up with an elaborate plan, and the farmer loved it. Only now, we need someone to take care of the goats in the winter. It's just a tiny thing, but since it was my idea and I like them so much, she built me a little cabin. I can work from there for now, or longer if the company expands to, well, more goats."

"That's rather hilarious … and ingenious," her dad said, "a business-based petting zoo full of natural lawn mowers."

"And, Mrs. Clayton." She wheeled almost desperately around to face Marlo. "Remember when I ran into you at the ribbon-cutting last week?"

"Of course. I was so worried about you," Marlo said.

"I got overwhelmed, but not because of anything Emery did, because of all the people and the questions and assumptions." Her vision began to blur just remembering the experience, but she pushed on, needing to say a little more before going under. "Emery and I were discussing a new landscaping and solar light project to make the grounds there, at the office, more appealing, so more people would use them. It could become a chance to show off what solar lights can do for businesses and outdoor environments. I don't know the right words. Emery says it all so much better than me. I'm just babbling."

"No," Mr. Clayton said kindly, "you've said a lot, and you're right. I didn't know any of these things about Emery. She's obviously sparked a lot of new ideas, and she seems to have had a positive impact on you, too. I've known you since you were a child, and I've never heard this much out of you on any subject."

"Really, it's quite wonderful, dear." Marlo reached for her hand." Her company has clearly done wonders for you."

Her face flushed hot. She didn't want them to think Emery had changed her or brought her out of her shell, or whatever other socially prescribed aphorism they thought she needed. This experience was still killing her, which only served as yet another reminder of how ill-suited she was at playing the role of partner long-term. Still, she couldn't close without speaking her truth for the benefit of everyone in the room, including herself.

"Emery didn't change who I am, at least not in any way other than by being herself and loving me for who I already am." Her chest ached as she said the words aloud, but this time it wasn't the sharp, stabbing pain of panic so much as the kind of pressure that came from being full, of expanding, of pressing up against old, outgrown confines. "Emery loves me without wanting to change me," she said again, this time hearing the foreign sound of certainty in her own voice. Then she smiled, a slow, half-quirk, the way she'd seen Emery do when something became clear in her mind.

That's how she'd found the strength to say the things she needed. Not because she'd gotten less panicky or anxiety ridden, but by learning those qualities didn't invalidate all of her good ones. Emery hadn't made her into someone else by loving her. She'd just made her like herself much more for having done so.

Chapter Twenty-One

Emery sat at her desk in a stupor. She didn't know how long she'd been there. Hours? Days? They'd all begun to blur together as she went through the motions, and she wasn't even doing a bad job. She'd held several meetings with staff and clients. The facts and figures came easier now than they ever had. She took solace in that. She also appreciated that her mom had been more present with her, checking in, offering little votes of confidence. Even Theo had been less crass in his comments. A part of her marveled at how long she'd spent trying to convince everyone she could handle everything without breaking down, and then the breaking down ended up getting her the support she'd needed all along.

The whole thing would've felt incredibly gratifying if not for the constant reminder that it had only come about because of Arden, who wasn't there to celebrate or unpack or make sense of anything with her anymore.

She'd picked up the phone to text her at least ten times in the last two days, but she didn't know how. It felt so small to send a few jumbled characters over the airwaves after the enormity of all they'd shared. What would she even say?

"How are you?"

"What's new?"

"My mom said love is more important than everything I've worked for, and I do love you, but not in the way you need, so what's a person supposed to do?"

She let her head fall to the desk and might have stayed like that for a few days if Theo hadn't come in a little while later.

"Perk up, buttercup," he said in a rush. "Mitchell Clayton is here, and he wants to know if he can have a few minutes with you."

"No."

"Come on." Theo gave her shoulder a squeeze. "This morose vibe isn't working for you."

"He's the one who started all this shit-hitting-fans business."

He snorted. "No, I'm pretty sure you started it, which is why you need to end it."

"I don't know how, and after talking to my mom, I'm not even sure I want his approval anymore."

"Fine, then tell him so right now."

She lifted her head enough to look up at him. "Tell him I don't want the company if it involves him all up in my personal life?"

He shrugged. "I'm not sure anyone who matters would blame you if you did, including me."

"Really?"

"I pushed you to play the game because I thought you wanted to win. And I thought you'd be great at this. You seemed to need someone to help you keep your eye on the prize, what with focus not ever having been your strong suit, but if you tell me we focused on the wrong thing, I'll shift along with you. I'm Team Emery, always have been."

Her throat constricted again, but she was getting used to feeling the emotions she'd held at bay for so long. "Okay, send him in."

"You got it, boss."

"And Theo? Thank you … for everything."

He smiled. "Always."

She took a couple of deep breaths, then stood as Mr. Clayton entered. "Good morning, or afternoon."

"Emery." He stuck out his hand. "How are you doing?"

"Hanging in there." They shook hands, and she motioned for him to take a seat opposite her, then braced for impact.

"I'm glad to hear it, and I don't want to take up too much of your time, but I came here to offer both an apology and some increased support."

She blinked a few times, trying to process. "I'm sorry?"

"No, that's my line," he said seriously. "I spoke to Arden yesterday, and I have to admit it's taken me a good twenty-four hours to process because, quite frankly, she caught me off guard."

"Like this conversation has with me," she admitted.

"Fair enough. We're both in uncharted territory. I don't know you well, so I relied on my own limited observations and a whole lot of conjecture when you weren't around much over the last few years, but I think I may've misjudged your character."

She sat back, not sure how to respond. This wasn't what she'd expected out of him or any other member of the board, except for perhaps Brian. "I'm not sure where this is coming from, but I appreciate it."

"All Arden's doing."

Her heart thudded a little harder in her chest.

"Her parents are some of my wife's and my closest friends, so when we heard rumors you'd been leading her along while seeing other women, we found the idea incredibly upsetting, and perhaps we unfairly connected the dots to the board's recommendations that you settle down."

"And you believed I was using her for the sake of appearance with no real intention to work at a relationship? An assumption her mother was all too happy to accommodate, I'm sure."

"I'm not proud to say there was a bandwagon, and we all jumped on. Probably would've ridden it all the way to your undoing as CEO, too, if Arden hadn't defended you rather vehemently."

She swallowed the emotions coalescing into a knot in her throat. "She did?"

"She spoke more forcefully than I've ever heard her speak about how good you've been to her, and the ways you've supported her ideas and blended them with your own for the company. The partnership didn't make a lot of sense to me, and I'm not sure I would've believed it from anyone but her." He shook his head as if he still found the concept a little mystifying. "Anyway, you must've inspired something important, because she found the courage of her convictions where you're concerned."

"I'm honored," she managed to say.

"She also mentioned that you two aren't an item anymore, and I hope my wife and I didn't dissuade you from pursuing—"

"No," Emery said in a rush, letting him off that particular hook. "At least, not directly. There's nothing anyone could've said or done to dissuade me from caring about her. She ended things very much against my wishes, for her own personal reasons. I'm trying to respect her decision rather than push her into something she doesn't feel good about."

"I appreciate that, and really, it's probably a first for her. I just can't help but wonder if she has a lot fewer limitations than everyone previously thought." He grinned a little as if he remembered something. "She told me she's in charge of goats."

She laughed. "They were her idea. She deserves the chance to see the project through for as long as she wants."

"I like the idea of her having something of her own, even if it's a small start, and I'm happy to throw my support behind the project in any way I can. I've always suspected she had more going on between her ears than her nervous constitution allows to shine through."

"There is," Emery affirmed with pride welling up in her. "She's brilliant in so many ways. She knows more than most people can possibly imagine about native plants and sustainable design. She's also got amazing connections in that area. She makes all kinds of connections, honestly. I think it's because she pays attention to people and to things most of us blow right past. And she listens. Really listens. She helped me completely re-envision the way I look at our solar installations."

"She mentioned you have some ideas of your own the board should be paying more attention to, and again, I'm sorry I haven't checked in with you since the funeral. I took a wait-and-see approach with both you and your mother when I should've offered a hand or an ear sooner. Arden asked me to do better on all fronts."

Emery shook her head, finding this all hard to believe, but very much wishing she'd been there. "I'm grateful and a little in awe because the last time we spoke, she told me she didn't want to play that role."

"No, she clearly didn't enjoy the conversation, and it seemed to pain her a bit, but my wife and I left marveling at how well she did, given the circumstances. That's a big part of why I'm heeding her request now. If you can effect that kind of change in Arden over a few months, I owe you the benefit of the doubt here at the office, too."

"I appreciate the opportunity, sir, honestly, but I didn't change Arden. I didn't even want to." She pictured iridescent eyes shining up at her. "I only listened to her, gave her space, and showed a little interest and faith."

"Well, those things seemed to have had quite an effect."

"It's sad she's come to expect such a low bar in how people treat her, or what they expect from her, but she hurdled it on her own. She's so much more than anyone gives her credit for. She just doesn't show it in the way people in our social circle appreciate."

"Funny, she said the same thing about you. Are you sure you two aren't going to give it another try?" He shook his head. "There I go again, meddling the same way I accuse my wife of doing. It's not my place."

"Thank you for realizing that, but you're not asking anything I haven't asked myself a million times in the last week. Arden doesn't believe she can—" She stopped short as a new thought formed.

He arched his eyebrows.

"She doesn't believe she can do the things she's already done." Emery sat back. "She doesn't think she can be strong for me, but she must have been with you, or you wouldn't be here."

"True. She defended you rather fully, if frantically."

"She thinks she can't be an asset to me socially, but she changed your mind, and your wife's too, yes?"

He nodded.

"And she worries she'll let me down in my business pursuits, but it's only her unconventional ideas that have led to my most promising plans."

"Seems like 'unconventionally promising' might be a good way to describe her."

She pushed back from the desk and rose. "I hate to cut our meeting short, but I think I may be having this conversation with the wrong person."

He laughed. "You're excused."

She started for the door, then stopped. "Are you going to talk to the board about the whole marriage thing, or about Arden and the rumors, or I don't know, my actual job performance?"

"I'm not sure any of that's my place, but even if it were, I doubt I could do so as compellingly as you can." He shrugged. "Why don't you call a meeting?"

She furrowed her brow as if trying to make sense of the suggestion. "Can I do that? It hasn't been six months, and I'm not the CEO."

"You're a Pembroke. You have a primary ownership stake in the company, and your father was kind of known for doing things his own way." He stood and clasped her shoulder. "Why don't you uphold your family traditions?"

She grinned broadly. "Thank you."

"I look forward to seeing what comes next."

"For the first time in a long time, I do too."

Then she headed for the door, picking up speed as she went, only skidding to a stop when she reached Brian's office. She didn't even go inside all the way, but peeked in to see him talking to her mother. "I need you to call the board together."

"What?"

"When?"

"Why?"

They shot questions at her in rapid fire, but she only laughed. "A formal meeting of the board, as soon as possible, because if I'm going to be CEO, I better start acting like it."

Then, before they could press her further, she dashed off again. This time she didn't so much as slow her gait until she hopped into the car and fired up the engine. Before speeding off, she googled the number of Luz's shop and dialed.

By the time it had rung three times, she'd gone from zero to sixty and peeled out onto the highway.

"Hello." Luz's voice came through the speakers of her car.

"Luz, it's Emery. I need your help."

"Sorry," Luz said without sounding like she meant it even a little bit. "I'm on Arden's side. I know she trusts you, but the jury's still out on you as far as I'm concerned."

"That's totally fair," Emery said quickly. "And I plan to start working on that immediately, which is why I'm calling to ask for your parents' phone numbers."

Silence met her as she turned off the main road toward the hilly fields.

"Are you still there?"

"Yeah, I just didn't expect the conversation to go there. I'm kind of mad at you, and I had a speech about you not hurting my best friend."

"I would very much like to hear it because I definitely don't want to hurt her."

"But you did, and she doesn't think you meant to, but I'm not sure what to think. You're very good-looking and suave, and while I like that, it also makes me nervous for her, but you want to talk to my parents, which means you probably listen to her on more than a surface level."

"Again, all fair, and the last part's exceedingly true. I hang on her every word, but I'm also happy to listen to you. You've been her protector and her instigator and her safe place since you were kids. I want her to have all those things in abundance, which is why I'd like to bring your parents onto my staff, or Arden's staff, really, if she'd like."

"Well, that's actually really amazing, and I kind of want to know more about that, but things last Friday were really fucked up. Some lady in the bathroom started talking about marriage and infidelity, and that's not okay."

"It most certainly is not." Emery crested the last hill. "I plan to tell people as much, soon, but I need to flesh out some major details and bring everyone on board first."

"Which is why you need to talk to my parents, and not me?"

"I need to talk to Arden first, then your parents, and if all goes well, I might need a new suit in a hurry. Maybe you could address your concerns during my fitting?"

"Ugh." Luz sighed heavily. "Damn you and your temptations. Why am I such a slut for a sexy woman in a suit? It better be lush, and I mean off-the-charts luxurious."

"I'm done playing it conservative to win anyone's approval but Arden's. I promise."

"Fine." Luz caved. "I'll text you my parents' numbers, but just so you know, you're on probation."

Emery pulled to a stop outside the cabin and grinned at the curl of smoke coming from the chimney. "I'll take it."

✳ ✳ ✳

Arden heard the car coming. How could she not? Emery must've been driving like her hair was on fire, and she steeled herself for another emergency, but when she opened the door, her heart soared.

Emery grinned from ear to ear, taking her in, eyes running over her quickly before she swept Arden up in a crushing hug. They rocked together for a few seconds before Emery's arms tightened around her waist and lifted her off the ground to twirl her around. They spun until she grew dizzy enough not to care that she didn't even know what they were celebrating.

She rested her chin on Emery's shoulder, breathing in deeply, wrapping her senses around this woman the same way she encircled her body. It had been only a few days since she'd held her, and yet this felt like a type of homecoming she'd never dared to long for, or maybe she hadn't known how to, because no place had ever felt like home the way Emery did.

The thought jarred her, and she eased back, but not far enough, because as their cheeks brushed together, Emery turned her head and captured her mouth with her own.

She groaned as their lips met, then parted before her brain had any chance to protest. She was deep in a kiss, savoring her favorite taste before she remembered they weren't supposed to do this anymore, and she slid even further down the path to more before she summoned enough coherence to stop. Placing both hands on Emery's chest, she arched back with what little mental and emotional fortitude she had left.

Thankfully or not, Emery got the message and lowered her feet back to the floor but didn't release her completely. "You're amazing."

288

She shook her head.

"You are." Emery kissed her again quickly.

"We're not supposed to do that anymore, remember?"

Emery didn't manage to look even a little chagrined. "Those were the old rules, made in a different world. We've moved past them and everything that inspired them."

Arden couldn't even be frustrated with such a disorienting statement, not with Emery grinning brightly at her. "Did we now?"

"Yes, you were there apparently. I only just found out." Emery took her hands and led her to the bed, where they both sat down on the edge, knees pressed together and angled toward each other as best they could with so little seating area. "Mitchell Clayton came to visit me this morning."

"He did?"

"He told me you got through to him. You changed his mind, not just about us, but about me and my personality and my potential. Arden, you spun him around."

She shook her head. "I didn't know what to say. I barely remember the conversation details, I just, I don't know. I didn't want to cause a scene, but I couldn't let him go on thinking the worst of you when I knew the truth."

"That's right, you knew. You've always known."

"I know you love me and accept me. I didn't know if he'd believe me, but I owed it to both of us to try to get it out."

"I can't imagine the toll that must have taken on you, but you saved me. He's on board, and apparently his wife is, too."

She marveled at the turnaround as warmth spread through her core at the realization she'd helped spark it. "Really?"

"Yes! You broke up with me because you didn't think you could be what I needed, but you were. How did you find it in you to stand up to them without panicking?"

"I did panic. I was a total nervous wreck, but I also knew the truth. I think you helped me see those two things could coexist. For the first time, the anxiety didn't invalidate everything else about me."

"God, that's beautiful." Emery beamed. "And it worked. I've got his full support, and so do you. He's thrilled you're working with the company, and he thinks we should give things another go, and, honestly, none of that matters."

She lifted her hands to her head as if she might somehow stop her brain from spinning. "That's … Wait. It doesn't?"

"No." She laughed, a joyous rumble. "Or, I mean, it matters, but only because it reminded me that other people's opinions don't matter, if that makes any sense."

"Not really."

"They don't really know us. *We* know us," Emery explained, "and when we let them set the narrative, we'll never be good enough, but when we trust in what we know and who we are, they'll come around, or they won't, but it won't matter."

"I don't understand."

"You do. We both do. Arden, you and I have understood what we are and what we need. Every time it's just the two of us, every time we've turned toward each other or relied on ourselves, we've been magic."

She couldn't deny anything there. "But it's not just about us."

"That's where we both went wrong. We let other people make us believe that, but it's not true."

"What about your company, your family, your commitment to the community?"

"Yeah, my company, my family, my community, and my commitment—do you hear the keyword there? *My.* I have to take ownership, or else it doesn't have the same meaning. It has to be me doing what I know to be right, what I know is true. I want my life to have meaning, but it's no use if it's only meaningful for other people."

Arden's smile spread as her heart expanded. "Of course you're right. I wouldn't want any of those noble pursuits to

290

change you to the point where you lose the impulses that made you good and powerful to begin with."

"Which is why you let me go." Emery grimaced slightly as if the thought still hurt. "But losing you would change me, too, and for the worse. I don't want to be the person I was before you came along, and I don't want to live the life I'd have if you left, which is why I need to ask you something very important."

"What?"

Emery slipped off the bed and onto one knee.

She panicked, her heart hammering in her ears as her palms pricked with sweat and her whole body trembled.

Surely Emery had to feel it, but she merely held her hands in her own and stared up at her earnestly. "Arden Gilderson, I have loved every minute with you. The stolen ones, the public ones, the happy ones, and the ones where we freaked out. Every conversation, every kiss, every wild and weird idea, they all made me better, smarter, stronger, and more centered."

"No, no, no," she whined slightly.

"It's true, and I want more of all of it, the dances and long talks, all-night crying jags, and even the anxiety attacks. Will you please do me the honor of not marrying me?"

"Emery, you know I can't." The words were already spilling out before she'd heard the end of the question.

She chuckled. "You can't *not* marry me? Does that mean you *will* marry me?"

Her breath caught. "What did you ask me the first time?"

"I asked if you would *not* marry me."

"What does that even mean?"

"It means we chuck all the pressure, all the outside expectations, all the rules and rumormongering. We don't let anyone else tell us what to do or when to do it. We don't look at dresses or rings or society engagements."

"What about your job?"

291

"I'm going to be good at it, for real, and for as long as it takes, because you helped me see I don't need shortcuts or anyone else's approval. I only need to have faith in myself and someone to confide in when I start to waver."

"But, I can't be that person."

"You already are. Not because we're the same, but because we're different. The last three months have been a nightmare in every way except for you. I lost my dad, I struggled to adapt, I floundered at work, I bottled things up, and I surrendered to my perceived inadequacies. I should've gone under, but I didn't. I clung to you, and you made me a better, smarter, stronger, and more reflective person."

Her eyes brimmed with tears. She wanted to believe her, and on some level, how could she not? Arden wasn't so far gone she couldn't see Emery settling in and growing, thriving in ways she hadn't before, but the old fears didn't just disappear all at once.

"And you already proved you can fight for me when needed, but you won't have to all the time." Emery continued, still on bended knee. "I know you worry about not being able to withstand public scrutiny, but you know what? I don't need you to. That's other people talking, that's the board, that's your mother, it's not us, and even if it were, I don't need you in that area because I'm actually really good in the limelight."

"You are." She agreed quickly. "I'm glad you see it."

"I only saw it because you helped me remember I'm good with people and I find them interesting and compelling, and I'm a decent human myself. I was so scared and grieving when I got home and got kicked out of a job I worried I didn't deserve. I thought I'd have to fake it until I made it, but nothing we ever did was fake. You made me realize I don't have to pretend to be someone else. I'm extra and over-the-top and a little impulsive. That's okay. Just like you're anxious and introverted and pensive, and that's okay too. Neither of us needs to be fixed or made more palatable for public consumption."

Her resolve cracked. Plenty of others had suggested she could be cured or made better over the years, and they'd always seemed to think their faith in her ability to do so constituted a favor, but none of them had ever gone so far as to suggest she had value just as she was. "That's a whole lot of what we don't need. What about what we do need?"

"We're going to figure that out. That's the point of not getting married ... yet. Let's take our time, let's make our own rules and ways of relating. We can date, we can hole up in cabins, we can ease into things, or ease out with friends like Luz and Theo. We can win over our families or tell them to sod off. I don't have the answers, but I want to find them with you."

"I just don't know what I have to offer you beyond what I already have."

"That's enough. You are enough. You're peace to my chaos. You're thoughtfulness to my wild whims. You're a solid foundation to my lofty ideals, and you're the best ideas behind all my execution. You're more than enough. You are everything."

She couldn't argue anymore, not in the face of such perfection or persuasiveness. Instead, she bent down and touched her forehead to Emery's. "You are very good at presentations."

She kissed her quickly. "Thank you, because I still have some big ones to do, and you don't have to be there with me, but it would mean a lot to know you're behind me."

She sighed. "I don't know what I'll feel up to in any given situation, but I can at least promise to always have your back."

Emery beamed up at her. "I think we make a great team, and what's more, I'm hopelessly in love with you. I've recently been told that's reason enough to justify anything and everything else."

She laughed, finally allowing her to feel giddy about that fact instead of overwhelmed. "I love you, too."

Emery arched her eyebrows.

"Don't act surprised." She tugged her up beside her. "I've been a little bit in love with the idea of you since I was a teenager. It just took me a while to accept that reality was even better than my wildest dreams."

Chapter Twenty-Two

"Ladies and gentlemen of the board." Emery stood before the assembly of people charged with deciding her fate, and smiled. She wanted to do well, but she wasn't nervous. "I appreciate your joining us today, and on only a week's notice. I know some of you came a long way to be here, but then again, so have I."

She paused and glanced pointedly at the camera in the corner of the room, hoping Arden understood the word choice as she watched from the privacy of Emery's office. "I am not the same person many of you know, or assumed you knew when we last met. I'm also not the person many have suggested I am over the last few weeks. I have learned and grown a great deal in the short time since my father's passing, but that's not ultimately what I came here today to talk about, nor do I intend to talk about my personal or romantic life."

She glanced around the room, this time letting the gravity of that point sink in. A couple of board members had the sense to shift uncomfortably under what she hoped was a commanding sort of presence.

"What I intend to talk about today, and going forward if you'll let me, is my vision for this company in the coming months and hopefully years. At the end of my short presentation, I will step aside and allow you to vote again, this time on the merits of my plans rather than my reputation."

She nodded to Theo, who dimmed the lights and cued a slide featuring a detailed layout of the Bergman property. "We at Pembroke and Sun have always been the good guys. The ones who care about the community, the environment, the future. Those are the ideas this company was founded on and values I

295

was raised with. After my father died, I didn't know much, but I knew those things, and I knew I wanted to be part of something that mattered as much as I believed this company did. In fact, I knew those things so deeply I absolutely butchered my first client meeting."

Brian chuckled softly in the corner before catching himself. "Sorry."

"It's fine." She smiled at him. "As much as I don't relish reliving that moment, I'm not sorry it happened, because it forced me to reckon with several major issues. But the one most pertinent to this conversation boils down to the realization that even people with the best of intentions can, and should, look for ways to get better. We can't simply rest on the fact that we produce green energy. We need to innovate a new, holistic approach to the ways we do our business so that we showcase a total commitment to conservation, to presentation, to total integration with the landscapes we're professing to protect."

She indicated the image on the screen. "This is our newest land acquisition, purchased as the future home of our biggest solar installation to date, and, as you can see, it's beautiful. But, in order to keep the natural vegetation from shading out our energy production, we would need to use enough gas-powered mowers to nearly negate the reduction in fossil fuels they would provide. I'm not proud to admit it took me entirely too long to come to that realization, but thankfully I've had some help, both to better understand how unacceptable that trade-off would be, and also how we might create a better, more sustainable solution."

Right on cue, Theo changed the slide so the next image popped up, featuring Arden standing in the same field with her three goats, Thoreau, Walden, and Louie.

Several of the board members laughed outright, and others exchanged curious glances while she passed around a few information packets. "I won't go into all the details, but my team and I have drawn up some charts showing the benefits, both financial and ecological, to using grazing livestock to control vegetation growth."

The board members began flipping through the information as she continued. "As many of you know, the woman in the photo is Arden Gilderson, our new Animal Assets Associate. She will also serve as chief liaison to a team of horticulturists and botanists headed by Dr. Eusebio Rivas and Dr. Amada Marcos, both of whom are professors at the university. Together with our installation team, we will enter a multiyear plan to repopulate the solar site with native species of plants designed to facilitate soil protection and natural drainage patterns with an eye toward water filtration and preservation."

She let those parts of the processes sink in for a minute, waiting until she noticed some of the people in the room nod or raise eyebrows to one another.

"The second phase of the larger plan will take place here on our corporate grounds." Theo clicked another slide into place, this one featuring side-by-side photos of their current grounds with an artistic rendering of the vision she and Arden had begun forming the evening they fell apart together. "As you can see, this is a very different style from our rural sites. This one focuses on integrating solar panels into a more elegant, urban setting where clients may not be willing to trade natural beauty for functionality."

Mitchell Clayton lifted his hand. "Emery, can you give us a little more indication of what exactly we're looking at, because I barely recognize the connections between these two photos, but I certainly prefer the second over the first."

"Absolutely." She nodded her thanks for him tossing her a softball of a question. "The drawing is a mock-up of what the photograph on the left could be if we added some stylistic elements to our grounds, blending our panels into the natural habitat and allowing them to shine, if you'll pardon the pun. Notice that each set of solar installations is linked by a walking path, and those paths are covered to varying degrees in trellises that serve as support structures for climbing plants like grapevines or wisteria, so they flower at different times of the year."

Theo clicked again into another sketch. This one showed an evening scene featuring fairy lights, holiday lights, and a lighted fountain. "And in the evenings, it will also become apparent the trellises are intertwined by a variety of solar-powered lighting options, so that by day, we showcase the natural beauty our products protect, and after dark, we use the same space to demonstrate what our products can do for any outdoor setting."

Emery watched as several conservative expressions shifted to smiles, and she couldn't resist glancing over her shoulder to where her mother sat, a look of pride in her eyes. She briefly wondered if Arden was watching her with the same rapt attention, and while she very much wanted to stick the landing of this presentation, she had no desire to drag it out any longer than she absolutely had to with such a compelling alternative waiting just down the hall.

"Again, this project would be executed in conjunction with university faculty and graduate students; we're not winging anything. We're moving toward a totally new era. With research and execution, environmental and technological advancement, our foundations and our futures all work together. This community, this land, this company have the potential to go further down the path my grandfather set us on and my father charged forward with. I don't want to undercut their contributions, nor do I intend to rest on their laurels. If given the chance, I intend to carry their dreams forward in new ways, into new arenas, with a flair that is uniquely my own, because if the last few months have taught me anything, it's that sometimes the biggest changes we can make are not changes at all, but rather having the courage to step more fully into who we've always meant to be."

Theo turned off the slideshow, and Brian rose to take over his place at the head of the table. "Thank you, Emery. I know I have to remain somewhat impartial in the upcoming board decision, but I think it's safe to say that no matter what happens next, we all appreciate the time and initiative you took here."

"Thank you for that, and for your help in making all of this happen after my initial missteps."

He clasped her shoulder briefly. "We all understand there's a learning curve to such a massive shift under trying circumstances."

She blinked back a few tears but didn't try to hide the emotion in her voice as she turned to encompass the entire board. "I'm sure you've heard a myriad of things, and I meant what I said about my personal life not being open to questions by this or any other governing body, but I don't think it's out of turn to give credit where it's due, and Arden Gilderson is due quite a bit."

She glanced back at her mother quickly before adding, "Someone very wise recently pointed out that this company isn't my father's only legacy, and it will not be mine either. I want very much to step into his shoes here at work, but if I am forced to choose between charting my own course at Pembroke and Sun and choosing my own path in how I live and who I love, you should know I will take the latter."

Brian nodded, and she turned to flash a quick smile and wink at the camera before saying, "And now, I will excuse myself to allow you to do what you must. I appreciate your giving me the time to speak my heart, and I promise to respect your right to do the same, no matter what the outcome."

☀ ☀ ☀

Arden was waiting at the door to Emery's office suite, and she jumped up the minute she walked in. Their mouths met first, and they wrapped around each other as much as standing in a semipublic place would allow. They kissed passionately for both too long and not nearly long enough before Arden finally found the wherewithal to step back.

"Wow, you're going to have to cyberstalk all my business meetings if this is what it does to you."

She gave her a little shove. "That was not your average meeting, and you are not going to be any average CEO."

Emery's expression shifted slightly. "I may not be CEO at all."

"I don't believe it. You had them all in the palms of your very skilled hands. I couldn't take my eyes off you, and I sent Luz like three screenshots of you in that suit and vest."

"Well, going in looking like a million bucks helps, so please thank her again for me, but I couldn't rely solely on being the sexiest lesbian in Massachusetts today."

"And you didn't! I knew you could captivate them, but I still don't know how you do it. Weren't you so nervous?"

"Honestly? No." She laughed lightly. "I couldn't have imagined that a few months ago, but I wasn't worried at all. I went in there believing in what I wanted to say, and I've made peace with whatever comes next."

"But you deserve the job, you have a vision, you connected it to the community, you were so magnetic and professional. It has to be enough for them or they're crazy."

"I love your confidence in me." She kissed her sweetly on the cheek. "But on the off chance the board isn't enamored of me in quite the same way you are, we'll figure things out."

Arden wrung her hands as the nerves crept up. "Do you think having my picture in the slideshow was a good idea?"

"You're an essential part of my plans for the future, and I meant what I said in there. You deserve both credit and respect. If they disagree, my mother and I will discuss our next steps, but I won't waver when it comes to anything about you and me."

"I know." She cupped her face. "I believe in you, and more than ever, I believe in me, too. But I would still feel bad if I ruined your big day."

"Not possible. There's no way to ruin any day in which I get to come home to you."

Arden marveled at her, not just at all the qualities she'd always admired, but at the centeredness, the commitment, the calm—all admirable and imminently sexy.

"Plus," Emery continued, "I've been thinking about it, and no matter what happens here today, I really love what you have been working on with Luz's parents, and I want the three of you to redo the grounds at my parents' house, or rather, my house."

"Redo them how?"

"However you think best. We don't have gardens or locally inspired landscaping, and I don't have a greenhouse."

Her heart beat a little faster. "Why would you need a greenhouse?"

"Because there's a woman I really like, and she feels safe and warm and welcome in greenhouses, and I want her to feel all those things wherever I am."

She smiled coyly. "And you think building her a greenhouse will help?"

Emery shrugged. "I don't know. I mean, I know she doesn't want to marry me, but I thought maybe I could entice her to come over a little more often, and if I'm patient and charming enough, we could at least work our way up to living in sin."

Arden laughed, all the tension from seconds ago gone, and she wrapped her arms around Emery's neck. "Living in sin, huh? What would our mothers say?"

Someone cleared their throat and they jumped apart, quickly turning to see Eleanor watching them with an amused expression.

"I can't speak for anyone else's mother, but if my daughter wants to add a greenhouse and another member to our household in any unofficial capacity, I will look forward to more fresh flowers around my home as often as possible."

She blushed profusely. "Thank you."

Emery smiled again, but it didn't quite reach her eyes. "You're here awfully quickly."

Eleanor pressed her lips together. "I'm afraid your presence is requested in the boardroom, and Arden, you are welcome to join us."

"Oh. I don't think I could."

"As you wish, but it's just Brian now. The others have left."

Emery sighed, and she got the sense that must have been a bad sign, but she merely squeezed her hand resolutely. "You can stay here if you'd rather. Entirely up to you."

"I'll come," Arden said without hesitating. "I want to be with you."

Emery intertwined their fingers, and they walked side by side back to the conference room, where they found Brian sitting alone at a large table wiped clean of evidence that a meeting of any magnitude had taken place there moments earlier.

"Welp," Emery said. "I'm getting a real sense of déjà vu here."

Brian smiled weakly. "Have a seat. Good to see you, Arden."

She nodded, wishing she felt the same.

He and Eleanor exchanged a cryptic kind of look as Arden took the seat next to Emery, and wondered how they could do this, again, after all the work and emotional energy they'd put into the last few weeks. Thankfully, Brian didn't let the question go unanswered for long.

"Eleanor, I know that when we sat here last, you stepped in very much against your will, and in doing so, you haven't been given the space to grieve or adjust in the ways you probably need to. The board wants you to know that your sacrifice has not gone unnoticed or unappreciated."

She nodded solemnly. "Thank you."

Brian shifted slightly in his seat. "That just makes what I have to say next so much weightier."

Arden held Emery's hand tighter, aching to take on the brunt of what was to come, wanting to bear it for her, wanting to shield her or shelter her the way Emery had for her.

"Eleanor, at the unanimous request of the board, myself included this time, we would like to ask you to step down as CEO of Pembroke and Sun."

Emery sagged slightly before the words sank in for all of them. In a surprising turn of events, Arden spoke first. "Wait, what?"

Eleanor cracked her smile first. "Thank you, Brian. It would be my pleasure to cede day-to-day control of the company."

Emery looked to each of them, before turning to Arden. "Did they just say what I think they just said?"

Arden shook her head. "I am never coming to another work meeting again."

They all burst out laughing, and Brian hopped up to shake Emery's hand. "You're in. You won. You blew them away."

Emery dropped her hand long enough to hug him tightly, then turned to scoop Arden up once more.

"You did it," she whispered in her ear.

"We did." Emery set her down. "Holy shit, and also what the hell?"

"Language," Eleanor scolded without an ounce of seriousness.

Emery whirled on her. "You were in on this, weren't you?"

"Of course, my love. And you earned it for all the stress you've put me through over the years, but we all figured that if

303

you're going to run this company on your own terms, we'd all better up our game, because every day is going to be an adventure."

She laughed, and the sound kept Arden from dissolving. Only a minute ago, she'd ached to be able to hold Emery up, but now she found the urge to collapse from relief, but she supposed she better get used to those kinds of swings as the non-wife of a newly minted CEO.

"Everyone's waiting for you upstairs. Theo's laid out quite a celebratory spread and several bottles of champagne, as it seems he never doubted you for a minute," Brian said.

"Never," Emery said. "Also, that guy loves to throw a party."

"Well, we've got details to hammer out, but we didn't just do this entirely to mess with you."

"Yes you did," Emery said without a hint of judgment.

"It was the primary motivator, but we also wanted Arden to be here when you got the news, and for you to have a few moments together without a crowd around."

This time Arden reached for his hands as the affection in her chest expanded to include the entire team who'd given her such consideration. "Thank you. It means so much to me."

"Emery was right during the meeting, and on several other occasions," Eleanor said. "You've earned our respect and the right to figure things out your own way. I have faith in both of you to make things work however you need to."

"Thank you, Mom." Emery's eyes watered.

Eleanor's own eyes misted. "I'm proud of you, and your dad would be, too. Now, I'm going to get out of here before I melt into a puddle."

"Come on," Brian encouraged. "Let's go start your retirement party without them."

"I promise I won't keep her too long," Arden called after them.

"Hey now." Emery caught her around the waist. "That's not what I want to hear. I hoped you might keep me indefinitely."

"I will keep you as mine, but I won't keep you from being you or from being present with other people who need you. That's the deal, remember?"

"You're the best."

"No, you are, and now I'm not the only one who sees it, but it's okay. Your light is bright enough to illuminate a lot of different areas."

"What about yours?"

"My flame will still be burning for you when you come home. Besides, if you go glad-hand with everyone else, that will give me the chance to recover and recharge so we can have a little celebration of our own back at the cabin tonight."

"Promise?"

"Yes." She kissed her. "And I keep mine every bit as seriously as you do yours."

"I know." Emery touched her forehead to hers and stared into her eyes. "I love you, Arden."

She hummed a dreamy little sound. "I love you, too."

"I wouldn't have any of this if not for you."

"And neither would I, so we're even." She eased back. "But you're stalling now. Go. Celebrate. Revel in your success so you can tell me all about it after I ravish you tonight."

Emery laughed. "That's a very compelling game plan."

"I mean it. You deserve this moment and all the ones to come. Your work and faith and growth have paid off. You won all the approval you've been seeking for months."

"No," Emery corrected gently, "I got more affirmation than I needed, and I won't lie, it feels good, but yours is the only approval I need."

"You have mine." Arden kissed her soundly once more. "Always."

Acknowledgements

The last year defied expectations, and not always in good ways. It's a long story I won't dive into, but my family ended up living a nomadic life in sometimes precarious positions. The experience did a real number on my sense of self and left me thinking a lot about the experiences that shape our personality and the ways in which we must either work against, or make peace with, all those parts. Emery and Arden are two sides of the same coin in my mind, and in learning to love them, I learned to love myself a little bit along the way. I very much wanted to write broken people who weren't looking for someone to make them whole, but rather for someone to see them in their wholeness. I hope that came across for you in these pages, and perhaps a little bit in your own heart as well.

I'd like to start by thanking my longtime friends and beta readers, Barb and Tony, for their quick reading skills and continued affirmation. Lynda Sandoval is not only my editor and friend, but also a fellow therapy advocate, and all those roles were appreciated during substantive editing. Avery Brooks is my eagle eye and initial copy editor. Carolyn and Susan at Brisk Press continue to wow me with generosity and knowledge. Kevin from Book Covers Online was once again a joy to work with. And my proofreaders, Marcie, Ann, Monna, Diane, Julia, and Jenn are my final defense against the most stubborn of typos. Every one of these people made this book better, and I am so appreciative of them.

I'd also like to offer up my public thanks to Patreon folks for providing me with a safe space to work through the emotional aspects of this work and for the financial support that made it possible to pay my amazing team.

I also appreciate my friends who checked in on me regularly through the events of the last year and kept me going when I struggled to believe I deserved to. Georgia Beers, Melissa Brayden, Nikki Little, Anna Burke, Melissa Leffel, and several others played major roles in my mental health. Susie's and my parents both let us stay with them for long stretches of time, and Will Banks not only let us stay with him, he kept us plied with cheese, wine, and entertainment. Extended family (both by birth and choice) housed us, fed us, transported us, and kept us afloat. I can't possibly name them all here, but I hope they know how much I love them for the ways they stepped up for us.

And as always, both the brunt of the burdens and the gratitude go to Susie and Jackson, who remained steadfast and loving no matter where we were or what else was happening. The last year hasn't really gone to plan, but I can never truly consider any time misspent as long as we spend it together. Jackson, I am so proud of your ability to go with the flow and make friends wherever we land. I hope someday you realize how much your kindness matters in the world. And Susie, my rock, my calm, my confidence, it doesn't matter what's going on around us. I know I will be okay if I get to curl up next to you at night, come what may.

To my creator, redeemer, sanctifier, and giver of all good things, *soli deo gloria.*

ABOUT THE AUTHOR

Rachel Spangler never set out to be a *New York Times* reviewed author. They were just so poor during seven years of college that they had to come up with creative forms of cheap entertainment. Their debut novel, *Learning Curve*, was born out of one such attempt. Since writing is more fun than a real job, they continued to type away, leading to the publication of more than twenty novels. Now a four-time Lambda Literary Award finalist, an IPPY, Goldie, and Rainbow Award winner, and the 2018 Alice B. Reader recipient, Rachel plans to continue writing as long as anyone, anywhere, will keep reading.

In 2018 Spangler joined the ranks of the Bywater Books substantive editing team. They now hold the title of senior romance editor for the company and love having the opportunity to mentor young authors.

Spangler lives in Western New York with wife, Susan and son, Jackson. Their family spends the long winters curling and skiing. In the summer, they love to travel and watch their beloved St. Louis Cardinals. Regardless of the season, Rachel always makes time for a good romance, whether reading it, writing it, or living it.

For more information, visit Rachel on Instagram, Facebook, Twitter, or Patreon.

You can visit Rachel Spangler on the web at www.rachelspangler.com